LEGEND OF THE PAN
- BOOK TWO OF SEVEN -

EDENIC PRAESIDIUM

THE FAMILY BALEY

PETER

CHRISTIAN MICHAEL

PETER

Legend of the Pan :: Book Two
First Edition
By Christian Michael

Legend of the Pan - www.legendofthepan.com
Scroll Media Company - www.scrollmedia.com

Edited by Ellen Sallas, The Author's Mentor LLC
www.TheAuthorsMentor.com

Cover and layout by Christian Michael

ISBN-13: 978-1-7370532-1-7 (Scroll Media)

Printed in the United States of America

Dedication

This series is dedicated to:

Orson Scott Card
Who taught and inspired me with Ender Wiggin.
Who cemented that children can do great things.
Because the world isn't changed by your age,
Only your mind and mettle.

This book is dedicated to:

Garrett and Shannon
You housed and fed me.
Your friendship sustains me.
Your love inspires me.

Acknowledgements

To my pre-readers Hannah and Joshua F., Garrett and Shannon R.,
Sachiko B., Kerry W., Jen and Matt T., Richard D., and Lori DP,
thanks for being my litmus! To Bradley M. and Rachel M.,
who have heard this story more times than any human should
have to. And to Karen B., for your amazing author photos
at The Mill in Greenville, S.C.

Attention Reader

THIS BOOK SERIES IS NOT FOR CHILDREN

The seven-book "Legend of the Pan" series features a variety
of adult situations unsuitable for younger readers.
This is an adult version of J.M. Barrie's Peter Pan.

THIS SERIES IS ONE CONTINUOUS STORY

"Legend of the Pan" is one story broken
into a Prequel (Book 1: Advent), Main Story (Book 2: Peter-
Book 6: Hook) and Sequel (Book 7: Immortal).
A reader could start with either Advent (1) or Peter (2),
but should read Advent (1) prior to Tiger Lily (5).

DO NOT EXPECT REFRESHERS

As an avid long-form fiction reader,
I dislike constant plot refreshers at the beginning of every sequel.
You will get no more than the barest — if any — in mine.

Thank you and enjoy the journey,

CHRISTIAN MICHAEL

Join the Panverse

Stay up-to-date on all books, anthologies and merchandise from the Panverse! Sign up today so you don't miss a thing!

legendofthepan.com/join-the-panverse

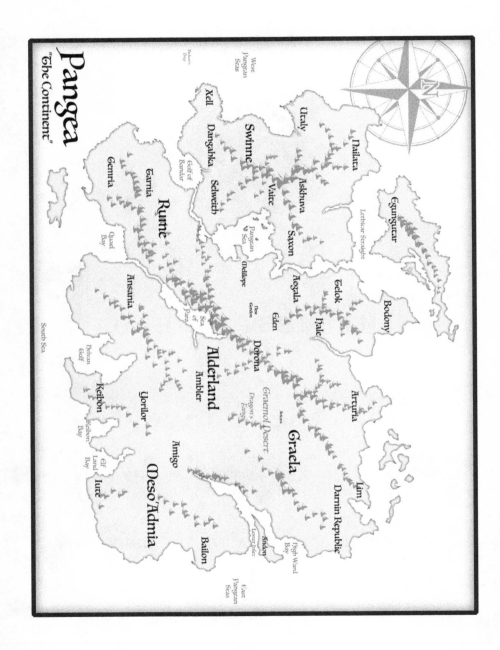

Contents

Dedication 5
Acknowledgements 5
Attention Reader 6
Join the Panverse..7

Commission of the Immortal.....................................13
Prologue..14
1 Neverland 22
2 Eden 36
3 Unionists..44
4 A Plan 52
5 Transfer 60
6 Avicara...66
7 Waking...71
8 The Room...73
9 Costs 81
10 The Fall..84
11 Securing the Baleys 90
12 Interrogation..94
13 Pixie's Fury 102
14 Ex Mortem..110
15 Voices...113

16 Marooner to Mother 116
17 Peter Meet Pan...................................123
18 Waking in the Swamp 131
19 Scouting Party....................................135
20 Adrift 139
21 Poking Around 144
22 Peter and Santi...................................149
23 Aurora..155
24 Time Alone 159
25 Braves Return 162
26 A Mountain Oath 168
27 Gathering Tootles 173
28 Alderland's Support 179
29 Phineas...183
30 Sons of Alder 189
31 A Dangerous Woman 197
32 Waking Tootles...................................205
33 An Idea 212
34 A Third Boy 217
35 Sailing Ashore 229
36 Landing...236
37 The Darkness 243
38 Around Every Corner 247
39 Commission 251
40 Creek Bed 256
41 From the Dance 261
42 Through the Bush 267
43 Shock of Loss....................................271
44 Serpentine Island 276
45 More Boys..282
46 Conference.......................................289
47 Return to the Tree 296
48 River House 302
49 Lady in White 308
50 Devkoron 313
51 Black Tower 317

52 Mindrise...327
53 The Wolf 336
54 Compliments of Roschach 341
55 Dragon's Fangs....................................349
56 Reborn 354
57 Finding the Sixth..................................363
58 Violated 370
59 The Mantle 374
60 Quorum 380
61 Reclamation 387
62 To Split a Tree 392
63 Over the Edge 398
64 To Fly 404
65 Extinguish 409
66 Part of this Island................................411
67 Peter vs Santiago 413
68 Alone 420
Epilogue...425

Mad 439
Commission of the Immortal (Full).........443
Author 447
Legend of the Pan Series 449
More by Christian....................................449

Commission of the Immortal

Eon Four - Qhoraethma
Anderon Era
High Graelan Period
Verses 7-8

The boy who could fly, through eternity's eyes
Dreams of a world in his sight
Rises to challenge, emerges the talent
A mantle forgone from its right

Restoring the balance, that envy unfounded
Righting what once was made broke
Soon so restoring, the Tree to its glory
Origins Immortal awoke

Prologue

L ord Pan of Eden, William Baley, emerged from the captain's quarters to face the Unionist witch who was ripping apart his mages on The Sumter's bloody deck. Casting lightning bolts and flashes of ice, the Unionist shielded herself from alliance counterattacks and used an air blast to knock an Edenon mage overboard.

You silly ass! chimed a golden fairy as she bolted from the dark room behind William around to his blood-smeared face. *You're already exhausted from the last three attacks. We can't lose you! You need to get back-*

"You'll lose me anyway if this ship goes down," William replied and moved past her and the alliance mages shielding the doorway. He glanced at the Swinnen ship bound to his own with a spiked boarding ramp before facing the witch.

I- can't help you, William! Tinker Belle chimed as he stepped out into the cloud-mottled midday sun. Moist, tepid air reeked of the sharp iron of blood and foul scat from dead men. *William!*

"Finally!" The witch smiled at his approach and gathered her power in a flush of smoky blue light before firing three entwined arcs of lightning. William raised his left hand to catch all three arcs and channeled them out of his right hand upward as a web of energy across the enemy ship. In seconds, every sheet of canvas, rope line, and mast burst into flame. Dozens of sailors dropped from electrical burns. Those unharmed rushed to put out the fires spreading across the ship. The witch's face faltered when she realized her lightning had set her own ship ablaze.

William drew up his power and fired a spread of yellow-red balls of fire through his open palms. She twisted out of the way as shock painted her yellow-skinned face, angled eyes, and full lips.

"You son of a bitch!" she countered with a powerful blast of wind.

William braced a magical shield with both arms just in time to divert the gusts, then dove aside as she cast a binding spell. A sailor behind him crumpled to the deck when the spell landed on him instead.

"Back!" William barked at the crew.

Dressed in Unionist red and blue, the midnight-haired witch matched him to prevent him flanking her. Arrows fired by marines slowed and fell lifeless to the deck when they struck her magical shields.

The witch unleashed an attack of ice to drive him back. He diverted it off-ship and countered with broiling gusts of air, which she cooled before the wind struck her. Advancing, she cast quick flashes of light to blind him before unleashing more arcs of lightning.

He allowed the energy to land just above his person upon a robe-like mantle, creating a brilliant shimmer of auroric light over a golden lattice. The witch flinched as William's mantle — the magic that defined the pan — flared with the flush of power, giving him the chance to counterstrike, doubled with his own magic.

She hesitated between shielding herself and rechanneling the energy outward as William had. Her hesitation created a notch in her defense. Energy pierced her body. Her trunk ripped open in a muted explosion that flailed out, her two halves connected only by her spine, before slapping to the deck. Her anchored shields flickered out.

William stumbled to a knee and snatched the starboard rail as his energy bottomed.

You can't keep fighting! Tinker Belle flew across the deck. *You're exhausted. You need to be where it's safe!*

"What do you want me to do, Belle?" William glanced at the enemy ship and motioned to one of his surviving mages who rushed to destroy the ramp in an explosion of fire and wood before helping the sailor bound by the witch's spell. Powerless without lines or sails, the enemy ship drifted away as its crew scrambled to save themselves from fire. "Those selfdamn Swinnens are already ripping us apart. Our mages, no matter how skilled, aren't powerful enough to deal with the sheer number of theirs."

You're to lead from the rear so you remain protected, Tinker Belle growled. *You keep stepping out here and you're gonna get killed. Stay behind and safe! We should fall back to Admiral Liston's ship so he can better protect us!*

Sailors around him policed the dead from the blood-smeared deck. Spelled arrows bristled the corpses of alliance mages and had set sections of wood on fire. William ran his fingers through his thick brown hair and forced himself to his feet. A striking man with broad shoulders, straight nose and full chin, William dominated the deck standing akimbo in his hunter green long coat, open over a voluminous white blouse tucked into forest green trousers, belted and booted in amber brown leather. His high, straight collar framed his shaking head as he took in his decimated crew. "If they all die, I will, too."

"Lord Pan!" Captain Larimund Shelley approached with Leftenant Rupert Dennison on his heels. A stout Alderlander with charcoal skin and broad curly hair, Shelley moved across the deck with the grace of his decades of experience at sea. "Well done, my lord. I think we lost fewer of our own than we feared."

"The fleet?"

"Admiral Liston signals to regroup," Shelley said. "We plan to move on their center now that we've split their right flank. Of all nations to denounce our alliance and throw in with the Unionists, why Swinne!? They do not go down easily."

"Among other reasons, Nailata, Tarnia and Gemria forge the strength of the alliance's maritime forces," William growled. "The opportunity to take out their greatest maritime competition is something Swinne would never pass up."

Shelley grimaced. "They may match our numbers, but I have faith in alliance captains. We are the finest in Pangea. The Unionists can be fervent and dead, for all I care."

"Regrouping is wise," William said. "My family?"

"Rupert, here, checked on them personally." Shelley motioned to Dennison, a tall man with pale brown skin and a broad nose under a mop of sun-brightened curly brown hair.

"They are well, my lord," said Leftenant Rupert Dennison.

"Good," William said. "Bring me a-"

"Captain!" the pilot cried. "Ahead!"

William and Shelley raced to the bridge with Tinker Belle in tow for a better view. A forest of inky smoke columns billowed from a field of burning vessels.

"Report." Shelley scanned the battle.

"There!" The pilot pointed just right of the bow.

A lone ship wove among his own fleet with alarming speed as if carried by the water itself.

"What is it?" Shelley asked as William leaned forward. "We need to retreat, Lord Pan, not fight another ship."

"Wait." With his mantle-powered eyes, William watched magic erupt from the lone vessel toward an alliance craft in its path. An ocean wave carrying the enemy ship flushed forward, grew by a mast's height, and crashed into the ship, which buckled under the immense power and twisted onto its side.

The ohna marina, Tinker Belle gasped.

"What is it?" Shelley extended his spyglass. "Oh … no."

When a second alliance ship in the enemy's path sank in two breaths, a cry rose among the crew.

William gripped the railing.

Shelley paled. "Great Self save us."

"What?" Rupert gaped. "Wh- what's happening?"

"Blasphemers!" Shelley snapped. "A first power! An ohna!" Sailors kissed their knuckles and ducked their heads.

As a third alliance ship attempted to block the on-comer's path, a humpback whale exploded from the surface and crashed upon its side. Sailors on William's ship gasped when a second whale appeared and repeated the attack from another point. More whales breached to batter the alliance corvette. A pale beluga managed to fall on the ship's deck, scattering what sailors it didn't crush.

The ohna makara, Tinker Belle growled. She scanned the field of ships and pointed. *There's a second ohna bearer over there by at least a mile. He's got amazing control to push whales this far across the battlefield.*

"How are they doing that?" Rupert asked.

"There's another ohna," William growled.

"*Another* first power?" Shelley asked.

With its path cleared, the enemy ship darted into view with a fresh wave building from beneath its keel.

"So fast," Rupert said.

"Turn toward them." William's level voice cut the tension. "Now."

Shelley barked orders to get the ship moving again, echoed by his officers. Expert crew darted into action as William raced across the deck and out onto the bowsprit with one hand on a forward line to steady himself.

As the gap closed between the Unionist vessel and The Sumter, William locked onto the ohna bearer on their forecastle — a midnight-haired woman with dark khaki skin and a bold, hooked nose, clad in light, crimson armor. From the woman's right fist danced light visible to the pan and the haraven, alone. She raised the ohna.

"Athyka Bonduquoy." William grit his teeth and reassured himself that while he stood at the fore of The Sumter, her powers would fail. A wave of water climbed from under the hull of her ship but disintegrated two ship spans away from his own.

Athyka scowled when the ohna's power failed on approach. She tried again with a different weave. The ohna's power crossed the waters to open the ocean beneath his ship. Again, the power failed and left a faint ripple across the choppy waves.

The Sumter gained speed, but at William's hand signal, the ship's attentive pilot guided the vessel a bit to lee to avoid hitting them head on.

William held out his hand. "Bow."

One of marines behind him offered their bow and quiver.

William took it, plucked an arrow and used one swift pull to loose an arrow at the enemy ship. Athyka screamed a warning too late. William's arrow took the enemy captain through the eye. As the enemy crew erupted in surprise, their mages threw up tardy shields from their positions at the forecastle.

William loosed two more arrows, knowing they would burn up in the enemy's shields. He then signaled The Sumter's pilot, who angled the ship more to lee as William raced atop the starboard rail and prepared to leap across to the passing enemy ship. Once upon the enemy deck, he could rip them apart.

Before he could leap, the water beneath the vessels welled and drove the enemy's ship away from The Sumter and out of his reach. William snatched a line to keep himself from falling into the water. Several alliance sailors cried a momentary victory while Unionist mages unleashed bolts of fire, lightning and spelled arrows that flared on shields raised by alliance mages.

As Athyka used the ohna to speed her ship away, her ship's exposed aft revealed its name — Unity's Light.

"Is they runnin'?" asked a nearby sailor when Unity's Light avoided the next alliance vessel.

"No." William clenched his jaw and the line in his left fist. Unable to

18

match the enemy's speed or maneuverability, he could do nothing but watch Unity's Light dance around his ships with impunity. He rubbed his face. "Selfdamn it. Richter's Deep, Shelley. I should have seen it. The largest pod spawning waters in Pangea. With the ohnas marina and makara, they can master all water and sea life. We-" He exhaled. "Great Self, we don't stand a chance here."

Shelley stiffened.

"Is it really an ohna? A first power? A holy power of creation?" Rupert breathed. "I didn't want to believe."

"How does it look?" William asked.

Counting ships, Shelley sighed. "What we have now will … we're down by about fifty of our original three hundred, but so are they. Out of their original two hundred and fifty or so, that's a bigger hit on them." Unity's Light avoided ships attempting to block its path as it moved deeper into the alliance fleet. "If they can get out of range of that thing. How far can they wield it?"

"Not far," William growled, "but Athyka can dance out of our reach until she's picked off who she wants. We can't fight all that by ourselves." He grimaced and spat. "It doesn't matter if we have superior numbers and captains if they have the ohnas. It's the same selfdamn tactic they've used since taking those fucking ohnas from their seats. Self damnit."

"What tactic?" Rupert glanced at Shelley.

"The Unionists enticed larger forces into a seemingly easy victory due to the Unionists' small numbers," Shelley offered with a frown. "Then they used the powers of creation to create a bloody rout."

"But … you're the pan," Rupert said. "Can't you do something? We're a fleet of nations! Surely, they cannot hope to stand against our alliance. Not with captains and admirals like Liston, Dubair and Afgunati! Not with you! They say the first powers are as nothing to you! My lord."

"Were I alone…" William looked downward where belowdecks his wife, son, and two guards awaited the battle's end. Fear passed through him at the thought of his family coming to danger before he tamped it to focus on the moment. "But as it stands, even I cannot stop an entire fleet, even a small one. Not when they can do that." He pointed at Unity's Light avoiding alliance efforts to attack and slow it.

"She's going for Admiral Liston," Shelley breathed as Unity's Light turned on the Nailatan flagship. He leaned onto the bannister when Liston's vessel, identifiable by the colors flying above the center mast, sank in moments. Shelley's eyes closed.

"She won't need to take us all out, Shelley," William whispered. "All she needs is to take our finest — the very ones we need most. The rest will crumble."

Moans of alarm died across deck when it became apparent a balance of power had shifted.

"Swinne has made their choice. The Unionists ..." William's breath faded as the situation's gravity settled on him. He flexed his hands and let his eyelids sink. "They have won, Shelley."

"But she's only taken a few more of ours!" cried Rupert. "Surely, if we gang up on her ...!? We can take her!"

Everyone on the bridge blanched in the following silence.

William hesitated once, then twice. "Signal the fleet."

Hatred and despair fought dominance in his chest. Swinne had sided with the Unionists. Eden, his home, was laid bare before the insurgents. He and his family had no place in the civilized world to retreat. Unionist-whipped mobs raged across the continent — there was no safe place to hide from the sway of angry, ignorant masses, incited by quiet political actors. The world burned in a fire fabricated by opportunistic nobles, corporatist merchants and true-believing sheep.

"The message, my lord?" Shelley straightened.

"Disperse," he said. "No rally point. ... Survive."

Shelley relayed orders to the signalman. "How did they know we would be here?" Shelley fisted his thick hands. "Intelligence said they were far to the north. How did they know our route to flank them?"

"Betrayal," Rupert breathed.

"Never!" Shelley snapped.

"No, he's right." William slicked more water from his hair. "We've been betrayed by someone in Eden."

"Eden? Who would betray us in Eden?" Rupert asked.

"Our plans were known only by a few," William said. "I fear my sister has been taken."

"Councilor Baley?" Shelley asked.

William nodded.

"You mean she betrayed us?" Rupert asked.

Shelley stiffened.

Mixed feelings passed over William's face. "She was not part of our planning meetings. We were betrayed in Eden. That is all we need know.

And more importantly, it means Eden-" He didn't want to say it. "Eden has fallen. And my sister, regardless of her role, is likely dead. All Baleys are a target to the Unionists."

"Because we were betrayed?" Rupert asked.

"Because if they knew we escaped," Shelley growled, "Eden would be vulnerable. So much for sneaking you out of the city, Lord Pan. I'm so sorry."

"But what will we do?" asked Rupert.

William scowled. "I don't know."

A silence fell on the bridge. William soaked in the tang of salty air, heat of the sun and the gentle rock of deep open waves rolling beneath their hull while the faint cry of sailors on nearby vessels drifted over the sparkling waters.

"Ere it comes, the days long past, we danced across the waters." Shelley's quiet voice drew every eye but William's. "Fight the fight, fulfill our vows, and go to meet our fathers."

"Aye, away to Eden," said the pilot.

"Aye, away to Eden," echoed the bosun.

"Orders, Lord Pan?" Shelley prompted.

Where do we go, Will? Tinker Belle chimed.

Glancing at the pixie, William used the sun to calculate time and distance in his head. With a final glance toward Unity's Light and his own fleet in flight, he sighed. After escaping Eden under the cover of night, racing for weeks across Pangea to meet up with the alliance fleet, and weeks more asea before finding failure, yet again, he felt void of choices.

"We're in the Far West Pangean Sea? Make for south by southeast." He looked across the waves at a point upon the horizon he could find without sun, map, or compass from anywhere in any weather, a place that ever tugged on his soul. "We make for Algueda." He focused on that distant point. "We make for Neverland."

1

Neverland

Peter stared at the raven's silhouette drifting in the brilliant moon and wished he, too, could fly. With arms out to each side, he mimicked the bird's adjustments to the wind and imagined himself drifting on the same currents of air.

"Great Self," muttered Rupert after the bird's second, grating caw. "Is that a raven?"

"Where the hell'd it come from?" asked a sailor mounting the forecastle behind them.

Peter frowned with uncanny certainty that the raven was watching him.

Pale moonlight painted their path into the starry ocean black as their ship coursed through frigid, rolling waves amidst a forest of icebergs. Frost clung to the ship's railings as the ceaseless arctic wind bathed all exposed surfaces in salty ice. The ten-year-old blinked his emerald eyes against its bite as it ruffled his thick red mane.

The raven cawed a third time.

"Peter!" William's sharp whisper interrupted the moment.

Scowling, Peter turned at his father's call.

"Come, boy, quickly!" William motioned and returned to the main deck.

Peter followed his father down the forecastle stairs and across the slippery deck with Leftenant Dennison right behind. His mother, April, emerged from the captain's quarters where she and Peter spent most of the previous three weeks since Richter's Deep and the month asea prior to that. Her emergence drew their attention, as it always did, for her rich crimson hair bound up behind her head, large green eyes, red lips, pale skin and the stately grace by which she carried herself. Laden with packs, and a heavy coat, she spotted Peter in the dim and motioned him over.

"Peter, quickly." She held out his longcoat for him to slip into. "Before you catch your death! What are you doing out here?"

"What's happening?" he asked as other coat-clad officers and marines gathered amidships.

"We're going ashore," April whispered.

"Really!?" Peter cried.

"Hush!" William snapped and glanced astern. "Sound carries, boy."

"Really?" Peter asked again, now hushed. "Where?"

"Your father says we're almost at Algueda." April lowered the packs.

"Where!?" Peter searched the starry horizon for some distant black speck to indicate land through the field of moonlit icebergs. "Is that why the crow's nest said nothing?"

"Board now." William turned from Captain Shelley and motioned to the Jacob's ladder hanging over the side of the ship as a ladder of heavy ropes. He bent down to grip Peter by the shoulder. "And remember, my boy, we're on mission. Do you understand? This is not the time to play."

Peter nodded, his face grave.

"We're- we're not going to be lowered?" April asked.

"It's too visible." William shook his head. "We lowered the ship's boat during the clouds earlier to keep Unity's Light from seeing."

"How close are they? Why are we getting on the boat if we're not even near Algueda?" Fear threatened April's voice.

"We're almost there," William whispered. "As soon as we get there and reach the reef, the marines will haul you and Peter directly to shore where you will wait for me."

"You're not coming?" April's eyes widened further.

"I have to direct The Sumter through the coral into the lagoon," William said. "Only I can see it in the waters below."

"But- but Algueda…" April gulped.

"I thought it was called Neverland?" Peter asked.

"You'll go no further than the beach. I'll be fine," William said.

"Quickly, now. We're almost there …"

"What's wrong?" April asked.

The bright round moon warped. Peter stepped forward when an angled wall of rippled, auroric light crashed over the ship. Sails, lines and sailors shuddered in its passing. Cries of shock echoed across the deck as a warm, mountainous sunset struck them in fierce orange light beneath a purple-pocked ceiling of low clouds that hadn't been there a moment before.

An island interrupted ten miles of horizon and climbed into low clouds. Ridges of evergreen-carpeted mountains ascended from the shore's edge on their left, shifted into a blanket of deciduous forests through low, rolling hills onward and became heavy jungle flora that stopped at the base of a high conical peak to their right. An arcade of hundreds of narrow rock formations rose from the water along the left shoreline. The lagoon's reef startled the ocean's heavy flow a mile away, a gap The Sumter fast closed.

"Neverland!" muttered one of the marines. "Whe- where'd it come from?"

"Now!" William snapped. "Get them on board and go!" He stripped off his heavy longcoat just as the island's oppressive heat crashed over the long-chilled crew. He took off and handed over his boots, a small, strapped leather tube and his sword to a waiting marine. "Take *very* good care of these things. Do *not* get either in water."

"Aye, Lord Pan," the marine said.

"Grandfather's knife!" Peter cried. "And where's Tink!?"

"She's with us," William snatched a sheathed silver knife from his beltline and added it to the pile. "Go, go, go, go! Head toward Pan's Peak, Dennison! Shelley, prepare to slow!"

Before he finished, Captain Shelley relayed orders to an echoing bosun. Professional sailors rushed from their shock to man battle stations, trim sails and prepare a second ship's boat on the starboard side to tug The Sumter through the coral. As William ran for the bowsprit, sailors helped his family climb down the Jacob's ladder on the port side to a waiting ship's boat laden with marines, weapons and supplies.

"Mages to stern!" bellowed the bosun.

Behind them, Unity's Light pierced Neverland's auroric outer barrier as The Sumter had moments before. A ripple of blue and purple aurora cascaded over the enemy ship a half nautical mile behind The Sumter.

"Cast off!" cried the leftenant at the rudder behind Peter. Marines used oars to push away from The Sumter, moored them and hauled for shore. Algueda's vibrancy beckoned after weeks of ever colder waters, fields of endless icebergs and ceaseless granite skies.

William stood on The Sumter's bowsprit. As The Sumter braked hard to avoid crashing into the reef, he tilted one outstretched arm like a needle to direct the pilot's turns through the vicious coral maze hidden below.

"Hold on," said Leftenant Dennison as their small craft approached the reef. Heavy ocean waves picked up speed and height. The boat lurched over the breaker before the marines could correct. The seat fell out from under April's bottom. She floated up into the air over the outer rail. Dennison snatched the neck of her coat and hauled her back to the seat as he corrected their angle with the rudder. She wailed on their way down into the lagoon and clung to the side of the boat with one hand and Peter's waist with the other. Her seasickness threatened her weak stomach as the ship's boat leveled out over the gentle lagoon waters while the marines hauled for shore.

"Shit," one of the marines muttered. All paused in their strokes as Unity's Light bore down on The Sumter, now at a near stop in tow by the second ship's boat. William raced across The Sumter's stern to stand behind the mages.

"They're going to hit!" Peter leapt to his feet. His mother snatched him as the boat rocked beneath them.

The enemy bowsprit pierced the shields raised aft by the Edenon mages. Feet from its prow crashing into The Sumter's stern, Unity's Light crashed into the coral below. Its bowsprit slapped and broke The Sumter's taffrail as the ship rocked forward in a shudder that rippled from keel to crow's nest. Cast from his perch, the lookout flipped end over end and crashed into the forecastle starboard rail with a muted crunch before slumping into the water below. An enemy mage, too, was cast overboard from his spot on the forecastle. Cries of "beach!" and "man overboard!" filled the air as sailors casted lines to the mage. The flailing man disappeared beneath the waters in a violent froth. Thrown lines now swung frayed at the water's edge.

"HAUL!" Dennison roared. Stunned marines threw themselves into speeding their small boat.

A light show of magic erupted between the opposing mages.

"Sit, Peter!" April yanked Peter back down to his seat. He twisted to watch the small, fizzling battle as The Sumter pulled away. The nestling sunset deepened in brilliance. Sharp hues cast the island and the distant ceiling of striated clouds into polarized shadow while the light danced across the rippling lagoon waters. Warm, salty spray drifted over them in the stiff evening breeze.

A maze of tiny rock towers, islets and twisting shoreline packed the horizon. Marines rowed hard under the direction of the leftenant at the till, who angled the boat toward the narrow, conical mountain on Algueda's northwest corner. At first Peter thought he was aiming for an inlet, but as rowing and waves drew them near, he realized the inlet was actually a gap between the high peak and a smaller spire just offshore northwest of the main island.

Once The Sumter was far enough away from Unity's Light, William returned to the bowsprit to guide them through the coral. As they entered the lagoon, William waved farewell to the captain, took a long dive from The Sumter's bowsprit and swam. The rope line slacked between the second ship's boat and The Sumter as the larger ship caught up with its tug.

"They're free of the coral," Peter said.

Dennison raised a hand in salute to the captain. Captain Shelley raised his own before the bosun shouted orders to get their makeshift tug and its compliment of sailors back on deck.

"Should we wait?" a marine asked about William.

"He said to go as quickly as possible." Dennison leveled his own look at the pan, now speeding across the waters. "He'd catch us up."

The spire to their west blocked the setting sun as they drew near the twisting shoreline. Dusklight reflected off low clouds. Across the panoply of environs washing in warm tropical winds, Peter searched every detail he could find. Thick fronds and palm trees swayed in the breeze. Tiny bays wrapped in snaking arms of rock and flora peeked at them as they passed revealing tiny alcoves and nooks along the shore.

Dennison aimed for coastline just northwest of the peak. He twisted to look back, thinking they had far outdistanced Lord Baley. His eyes widened — the pan followed by no more than a hundred yards. William paused to shout something at them.

"Is he sayin' something?" muttered one of the marines.

"Get us to the beach," Dennison said. "We'll go no further till he gets there."

William yelled something again just as the boat crunched into the white sands.

Two marines in the fore leapt into the shallow water. They gripped the boat's rim and hauled upward when William's cry of alarm grew loud enough to draw their attention.

Dennison leaned to hear him better, when both men standing in the water disappeared in violent splashes.

"What-!?" a marine wiped their spattered blood from his face.

"STAY ON BOARD!" Dennison bellowed, echoed fast by the gunnery sergeant in the bow. "HOLD!"

Panicked marines snatched up their stilettos and crossbows and pointed in all directions as William doubled his efforts to reach them.

"Where- what happen'd to Droni and Tems!?" asked a marine next to Peter, his loaded crossbow weaving back and forth. Others cried in alarm and scrambled to stay out of his line of fire. Dennison stood and rammed his hand around and up under the marine's arm to knock the crossbow upward. The marine snatched the trigger. His bolt fired over the ducking men into the gunny's right arm, who bellowed as it struck bone. Dennison and another marine wrestled the first down into his seat while the others struggled not to leap to shore.

Resisting panic, April mustered herself, reined her queasy stomach and set her hand on the struggling man's arm, drawing his attention. She straightened and locked with his eyes. He slowed as her calm seeped into him. She then gripped his shoulder and, holding her stomach, rose to her feet. The rocking at first panicked the marines, but as they twisted, they slowed at the sight of her outward serenity.

"If you please," she managed. "Compose yourselves."

When their gazes locked upon her, the men pulled themselves together. Awe overcame Peter as his mother took command with such seeming ease. As they fell silent, April resumed her seat. She snatched the rim as the boat tilted under her shifting weight. Two marines attended their gunny's wound above his bicep.

William climbed from the shallows and shook water from his face.

"But Lord Pan-" one of them managed, fearful for William.

William raised his hand to silence the marine and gripped the rail. He eyed the dark jungle, as if seeing something, and waited. Once satisfied, he hauled the entire boat out of the water and up the beach until the rudder canted the boat to port. April stifled a moan at the sudden shift. No one moved as William walked around the boat and lifted his wife out from her portside seat. She clung to him.

"Out," William said. His sure command emptied the boat. A marine grabbed the family packs and proffered William his belongings. William squeezed April's arms to reassure her before he sat on the boat's edge, cleaned off his feet and shook them dry. He pulled on each stocking and boot, then checked inside the leather tube.

"It's so hot," April clutched her stomach and Peter's shoulder. "Why is the rocking worse on the ground? I thought this would end."

"It's always like this, my lady," one of the marines ducked his head. "Pardon, but it is. Once you get off ship, it feels worse'n on."

"Does it stop?"

"It will." William stood and stamped his feet into his boots. He donned his blouse, leather tube over his chest and longcoat, left open down the front. Even he wavered for a moment. "It will."

Parts terror and curiosity gripped Peter as to what creature had taken the two marines. Like his mother, the world rolled beneath his feet.

"Alright, quickly. We have a distance to go." William looked toward Unity's Light struggling to free itself from the reef. "And they will not be far behind us."

"Father?" Peter asked.

"Yes?"

"Where's Tink?"

"I told you, she's close." William took a long look at his son as he pulled on his belt of weapons under his longcoat. He plucked grandfather's sheathed silver knife from his belt and raised it to his son. "Peter."

Peter stepped closer.

"This is now your sword." William set it in Peter's opening hands. "Attach it to your belt and don't hesitate to use it against anyone or anything that may attack you. That is a standing order."

Peter's eyes widened. "Really?"

"Yes," William said.

April's face tightened and her stomach twisted.

"Yes, sir." Peter set about attaching it to his belt.

William turned. "Gunny?"

"I'll be alright, sire." The gunny winced as they bandaged his arm around the protruding bolt.

"This is not the best place, but it must be done." William stepped closer and gripped the bolt and his arm. "Ready the bandage." The gunny grit his teeth and nodded. William snatched it out. The gunny groaned through clenched teeth. Marines wrapped the gushing wound tight to stem the blood. The gunny mustered himself. "Thank you, Lord Pan."

After a long, sad look at the small wound's bloody bandage, William turned to Leftenant Dennison. "Rupert?"

"Lord Pan?"

"I'm sure Captain Shelley needs you back on board. Please, go back."

"My lord, I couldn't leave you. I'm sure Captain Shelley would rather you have every man possible to get you to safety."

"I really would rather you go back to the ship."

"Pardon, Lord Pan, but I cannot." Rupert's voice settled with determination. "I will go with you."

"Alright. Thank you." William faced the men. "You will do as you are told. Don't hesitate to obey. Follow me explicitly. Keep a firm grip on each other, by hand, if you must, and let no one turn aside. Don't touch anything but what I say is safe. Assume everything can and will kill you. We are going to travel around the north base of Pan's Peak to the West Bay. We stand now to the north. There is a path from the West Bay that will give us the greatest chance of reaching the Tree alive. Once we enter the jungle, you will whisper if you must, and only to protect others. No loud cries or warnings. If one of you disappears, we will not pursue you. I can speak, but you may not. This island will do nothing to me. I am the pan."

"Wh- why are we going in there?" a marine swallowed. "Lord Pan."

"The island can serve as our guardian," William said, "if we can first get through it ourselves. Otherwise, we're left at the mercy of the ohna bearer back there." He pointed at Unity's Light.

A pall of despair settled over them.

"We have committed our duty and our lives to protecting the Lord Pan," the gunny's grizzled voice interrupted their moment of fear. "We did not commit so long as we weren't in danger. We committed everything. We will do so until our last dying breath. Aye, away to Eden."

"Aye, away to Eden," echoed the marines.

The moment bolstered them, straightened backs and cleared their eyes. They repeated it in whispers to themselves and to their mates until they all appeared ready to go into hell itself for their duty.

"Good lads," the gunny grunted. "As you will, Lord Pan."

After a brief, sad look across the group, William nodded. "With time, you can learn how to navigate the island. I've seen men do it but only under easier conditions and lots of time. For now, I'll teach you what I can, but do as I tell you. Let's go." William let them surround his family again before they marched into the jungle.

At first brushing hip to hip, the group climbed the hill and veered west through thick jungle flora. William pointed out what he could in the chaotic darkness. Jungle cacophony drowned loud breathing and their footsteps upon an endless mattress of detritus. William's voice alone touched the quiet. They climbed the peak's northern base across twisting terrain, turned west and skirted the mountain's edge. Humongous frond leaves shadowed their path under the fading dusk. Birds screeched and chittered, monkeys screamed and cackled, while other sounds uncountable filled the undercanopy. The greenery smelled sweet of flowers in a greater variety than any of them could count. Shimmering moisture wafted in the air until they disturbed it in passing.

Peter's thoughts meandered between what might attack them and the glory of the greatest adventure of his entire young life.

The group soon emerged onto a beach overlooking a broad, berry shaded lagoon with faint wisps of white, low waves shimmering in pale warmth reflecting from clouds by the nearly set sun.

"Great Self, are we already here?" asked a marine.

From out the forest to the right, a great blur crashed upon the marine and snatched him into the darkness in bare heartbeats. What cries began to rise were interrupted by the gunny's shush from the rear. When they looked to him for more instruction, he was gone.

"I said silence," William growled. "I meant silence. For your sake."

Marines exchanged looks of terror as they backed away from the forest with crossbows raised.

"The path is more open ahead," William said. "Let's go."

"We can't," whispered a marine as loud as he dared. "We can't go back in there!"

Others aimed their weapons at the man to quiet him, but nothing else emerged from the jungle as they backed away.

As terror filled their hearts like small children finding out there was a bogey under their bed, guilt filled William's chest. He had led them all here from Richter's Deep knowing it would kill most if not all of them. He hoped against hope they wouldn't have to die, that he could get them through and teach them the ways of Neverland. The few bodyguards he brought with him on his few short visits in his youth, however, took more than a week of study and experimentation to survive alone in the jungle without him, and then only in daylight.

Only two had died since leaving The Sumter, and yet he felt a thin veneer of hope had popped. He swallowed his guilt — his responsibilities were more important than his feelings about them.

"You can wait here on the beach," William said, "and other beasts will come after you. You can try to swim and you will die. Alguedan night is the most dangerous time to be here. If you can make it alone till day, you have a chance to survive." They blanched. "Until tomorrow night." Eyes glassed. "We carry on, or you all will die within the hour."

Resigned, they reformed their honor guard. William led them south along the West Bay's eastern beach line to a faint break in the trees curving south of Pan's Peak. A two-foot-wide path led into the jungle, shadowed deep by high flora. So long as dying dusklight remained, William paused here and there to point at various bushes to avoid, hidden holes in the ground and for no obvious reason, waited for something only he could see to pass them by. He noted thorners, thrashers, grippers, suckers and sickle vines. Men mouthed to themselves the names of dangers as William ascribed them. Peter attempted to stay focused as they took the path, but soon lagged as he grew tired. April carried Peter first but soon passed the heavy ten-year-old to his father.

Peter woke when the group paused on a small flat six hundred feet up. Free of heavy canopy, his first look at the island's interior enraptured him. The rising moon in the east cast long shadows across the varied terrain. Pale light reflected off a massive snowy peak over a broad desert along the island's southeast and the volcano and broad grasslands to the southwest. A winding river cut the island in half, centered by a whirlpool. To the east, low mountain ranges and ridges wound across the north island to a low jagged point before disappearing against the horizon.

Up the path ahead, just visible around the curve of Pan's Peak, extended the canopy of the largest tree Peter had ever seen.

He gazed in bleary wonder until the bubbling of a broad, shallow creek and trickling falls drew his attention to the obstacle blocking their path.

William held April's hand and stepped first out onto the heavy boulders above the water's frothing surface. She plucked her skirt with her free hand and followed. Sailors picked their own ways across the low rapids. When William reached the far shore and helped April next to him, he glanced as two marines knelt face-first to get a drink.

"No!" he cried.

While others froze in terror, the two bending into the water crumpled and half-rolled, exposing faces eaten away by swarms of tiny creatures.

One marine bolted across the water on foot screaming profanities. He made three splashing strides through the low creek before he collapsed screaming into the wash. He thrashed and fell still as water bugs swarmed over him.

Another marine screamed at his dead comrades from his rocky perch halfway across the rapids when a massive flying creature swooped through the tree gap, drove long talons into his trunk and snatched him into the night.

Standing near the lower edge of the trickling falls overlooking a drop into the jungle below, a marine stepped off the edge and disappeared into the darkness.

As still as stone, two remained — Dennison and a marine clutching his crossbow.

April pressed her face into William's neck, terrified of making a sound when all she wished to do was wail. Her heart raced in her chest most for her son, but lying in William's arm was the safest place Peter could be. Her own safety came next to her fear for William.

William took a slow breath and motioned for the others to continue with care. Both took extra time to stay above the water and reach the shore side by side. One of them reeked of urine.

"Alright," William set Peter down even as the boy clung to him. "I might be strong, but you are still heavy. It's time for you to walk."

April spared a look of alarm at William, but William took a grip on Peter's hand.

"Let's go," he said.

They trudged another hour up the narrow, winding path when Peter could walk no further. "I wanna stop."

"Can't." William snatched him up against his side and blocked the jungle nearest where Peter had stood. April quivered against William's back. William turned to see Leftenant Dennison, alone, remaining. The marine was gone. Dennison gripped his inverted stiletto in one hand and sword in the other. William exchanged slow nods with the young, terrified officer.

The night's long hours wore on William, too. As their final guardian,

Rupert stayed close. William took great care to watch out for him as he did April and Peter, pausing often to nod at dangers.

The Tree grew bigger as they approached round the peak's curve. Terrain leveled off and jungle ended at the edge of a large, grassy clearing on a jut sticking out at the bottom third of Pan's Peak, a thousand feet above the ocean. A slithering nine-foot-high wall of what appeared to be snakes rose fifty feet from clearing's edge. Above them towered the two hundred eighty-foot tree, whose massive boughs radiated two hundred feet outward from the fifty-foot-thick trunk. Low, wild grass filled the outer clearing from jut's southeast cliffside edge visible to their right and around the curve of the clearing to the left.

William paused halfway across the outer clearing and motioned the leftenant to come around. "How're you doing? You can speak."

Rupert's shoulders sank. He savored the momentary relief. "Thank you, Lord Pan."

William's face tightened and tugged April closer.

The young man took in the tree looming over them, awed at its shape and beauty, but seemed surprised. "It's not so big?"

"Certainly not the largest of trees." William inspected it. "Not like the ancient bluewoods or elven al'culars."

"Certainly looks ancient," Rupert breathed. "There's a certain … majesty to it. Is it really …?"

"The La'Du Lira Al'Cular," William said. "The Tree of Life."

"I thought it was lost in the reformation," Dennison said. Starlight bathed the ancient al'cular. The thick trunk bore a gentle twist as it climbed into a thick, broad canopy overhanging a nine-foot-high slithering wall separating them from the root base. "Wasn't it in Eden, prior?"

"Was moved here," William said. "No one's sure how."

"What is that?" Dennison squinted and stepped closer to the wall. "Snakes?"

"Vines, in fact," William said.

"Vines?" Dennison's eyebrows climbed. "All of it?"

April stirred at the exchange.

Dennison approached the wall. "Are they … alive? I mean, like animals?" Several spades popped out of the wall — heads of individual vines — to inspect the newcomers. Dennison paused, then leaned closer to inspect them.

"Sort of." William followed. April narrowed on William as he hefted

Peter more tightly in his arm. "A protective measure created by previous pans. Keeps anyone inside safe from exterior harm."

"How do we get inside?"

William's breath caught. "I'm sorry, leftenant. I wish you had turned back."

April straightened when she realized his intent. Her gasp drew Rupert just as William planted his foot into the leftenant's chest and kicked.

"WILL!" April cried.

Terror and recognition filled Rupert's face. A dozen spades fired at him, skewering him from his head down through his calves.

William spun, sandwiched Peter between himself and April, hugged her against him in an iron grip and ran backwards. Forced to follow, terror gripped April as Dennison's appendages and trunk ripped apart in gory bursts of blood.

"WILLIAM!" her scream stirred Peter from his sleep. Fresh vines appeared at William's approach. Just as he reached the wall, the vines shot outward. She clutched his coat and felt him flinch as a dozen razor-sharp heads stabbed through his coat.

To her shock, the wall shrieked and recoiled from the pan.

"RUN!" William fell backwards in the heart of the writhing, four-foot-thick vine wall and pushed her and Peter to run up and over him.

April snatched Peter and ran for their lives. Once across the wall and several strides beyond, she tripped on her skirts and collapsed to the ground. Peter crashed with an oomph into the thick green grass while April scrambled for William.

"STOP!" William flung out his hand.

April froze a hair's breadth from spades which had fired out from the inner wall and hovered with their points glancing her skin.

"Just- stay," William panted. He rolled over and gripped the vines' thick bases to haul himself across. Past the wall, he used handfuls of grass to drag himself while smearing a trail of blood from his soaked longcoat. Once beyond the vines, April snatched his hand and hauled, then his arm, then the nape of his coat. Halfway across the fifty-foot gap from wall to the massive tree roots firing into the thick mattress of brilliant green grass, she let go and knelt over him.

"Father?" Peter joined his mother.

"Just ... it will heal. Just sleep," William managed. His shoulders slumped and eyelids drooped. "Jus' lay down ..." his voice slurred. April set her hands upon the grass when a warmth and comfort crept up her hand and arm into her chest. A host of tiny glowing specks wafted up from the grass around them, filling the air with the scent of sweet dogwood. Peter, too, caught with it. Both laid down next to William.

Drunk in the warmth flooding his body, Peter noticed his father pull out the small leather tube from his coat, pop the holed top and shake out Tinker Belle's tiny, sweaty figure onto the grass.

"C'mon, Belle," William muttered.

Though tempted to drift into sleep, Peter roused himself. He watched Tinker Belle until he could see her chest rise and fall with breath. Relieved she was here and okay, his focus locked onto the cliffside edge of the inner clearing. Curiosity spurred him to his feet. He ambled past his unconscious parents, along the house-thick Tree roots weaving down into the grass, and out to the cliff overlooking Neverland.

For the first time since their flight from Eden months ago, Peter found a place he wanted to be. Peter hoped to see more in spite of the night's terror. His curiosity faltered as the unnatural warmth from the grass overwhelmed him, again. He sat, laid sideways on the grass near the cliff's edge and soaked in the enchanting island. As peaceful sleep blanketed him, he wondered how fared the staff, citizens and soldiers of his home at the Palace of the Pan in the Garden City of Eden.

2

Eden

The Garden City of Eden burned under a forest of black smoke columns that blotted out the stars. Nine low mountain peaks crowned Eden Valley, tall spires of rock and flora that climbed from the south to the highest peak on the north end. Beneath that highest peak, the Palace of the Pan sat upon a butte filling a quarter of the north side of the lush valley. Inside wealthy vine-draped apartments, shops, arcades, parks, and mansions filling the south side of the valley, Edenons quivered in terror as a foreign army marched its streets for the first time in more than two millennia. Unionist boots marched over dwarf-carved stone bridges and among elven-tended groves, splashed through thousands of creeks amidst hundreds of waterfalls and rapids weaving across the valley and along streets packed with row houses and gated estates. Wellsprings from the northern mountains kept the city verdant year-round with icy virgin water.

Elwin Roschach and his armed guards rode up the East Valley Road, through the palace's Graela Gate, and into the sprawling east courtyard swarming with Unionist troops. Elwin reined in when a horse and rider emerged from the courtyard's inner gate and raised a hand in greeting.

"Lord Roschach." Fenren Thicke reined in before Roschach's taller figure on his large, gray horse.

"Fenren." Roschach eyed Fenren and the crystal torch tucked into his belt — the ohna luminar.

"Welcome back." Fenren led Roschach and his guard through the gate. "Other than the lower sword quarter, the palace is ours throughout."

"Grand." Roschach frowned. "Why did you signal me in?"

"Councilor Baley insisted," said Fenren, whose sun-tipped mop of sandy blonde hair, gray eyes, deep tan, and chiseled face appeared to belong more on a warm beach than a warzone. Clad in a Unionist-issue special forces armor of thick leather panels lined in rectangular metal studs and adorned in strips of red and blue cloth, Fenren appeared out of place to the common soldiers, despite the sword at his left hip and stiletto sheathed on his right.

"Did she?" Roschach smoothed his face. "Lead the way, then."

The three followed the Central Road meandering deeper into the palace grounds. Corpses of Edenon guardsmen littered the road's edges as refuse. Bathing the paving stones, white marble walls, and thick green vinery, blood bubbled as it gathered in collection gates and into central runoffs that emptied in the grand waterfalls pouring out from beneath the palace foundations into the grand lakes and across the valley. The sharp cool of night hid none of the stench. Dying humans unleashed urine and feces as bodies failed. Blood dried out where it did not run.

A tall, slender man with a long face, thick, dark hair, deep eyes, and a thin beard that thickened on his upper lip and lower chin, Roschach scowled against the stench while the horses occasionally slipped the footing of the scum-slicked road. After two miles of a gentle winding among the palace's grand gardens, its ornate complex of buildings, arches and growing grandeur, small courtyards and smaller side streets, the road emptied into the grand Square Al'Cular, a broad, oval-shaped space centered by a large stone dogwood tree signifying the heart of the palace. On the south side of Central Road, the square opened to a series of broad, multi-level landings extending over the plateau cliff overlooking the garden city from five hundred feet high. Smaller ornate palace buildings followed the cliff's edge and the Central Road out to the edges of the palace on either side. On the north side of the Square Al'Cular rose the palace proper, fronted by multiple arcades and arches topping a broad out-bowed marble staircase leading to the gaping sixty-foot-high entrance doors. Cylindrical marble buildings capped in copper domes glowed from a cornucopia of windows, arches and balconies into the hazy evening air.

The group rode across the square and up the stairs before dismounting and handing off their mounts to waiting troops. Inside, they crossed the Hall of Life, a broad colonnaded room a hundred yards in diameter. Troops dragged dead horses and Edenons blocking hallways. Streaks of blood and scat followed in their wake.

Roschach sneered at the dead. "What a waste."

Grand halls and courtyards opened and fell away on each side. Faint cries and clangs of battle drifted on the air where Edenon guards were rooted out and dispatched. Through the largest windows ever made appeared yet more gardens and walks. Manicured grounds extended in all directions. Few windows failed to overlook a garden, the city, or one of the nine towers of Eden anywhere on the grounds.

The hallway emptied into a broad chamber lined with two rows of high, thick columns and flanked by ten sets of double doors. Glass windows stretching long across the curved ceiling bled moonlight across the small fountains and bench-lined pools. All the doors stood open; the central two doors tallest among them admitted pedestrians to the main floor of the Edenic Parliament.

Unionist troops saluted at Roschach's approach; he saluted in kind. The main walk ascended to a broad central flat bottoming a tri-level amphitheater capped with a high dome. Large gaslight chandeliers hung from the ceiling in descending circles from outward in until the broadest chandelier hung lowest. One could stand in the center and have a conversation with anyone sitting anywhere in the vast chamber. At the center of the flat rose a large dais occupied by two dozen councilors and senators arguing under the steady amber light.

At Roschach's approach, the group parted to reveal a serious woman dressed in Unionist red and blue. She marched up to him while all others offered him a bow.

"You lied, Elwin." Her low growl echoed across the chambers. "You assured us bloodshed would be minimal within the palace. Your troops have openly cut down every Edenon they could find. This is unacceptable."

Roschach attempted to loom over Councilor Brianne Baley. Her diminutive stature belied her dominant presence. "I told you there would be costs."

"Costs I've already paid by revealing my brother's move on the

Unionist flank in the West Pangean Seas and enabling you to counter him at Richter's Deep," she snapped. "Justifying the ends by the means doesn't give an unlimited license for slaughter of good people."

"Good people?" laughed a Unionist officer nearby. He cut himself off at a glare from Roschach and stepped back, chastised.

"Councilor Baley, minimizing bloodshed was meant for the city, not the palace," Roschach said.

"Don't split hairs with me, you feckless cur," she snapped. Her large blue eyes, straight nose and full lips tightened under black hair bound above her head in ornate braids. Though in her fifties, she was still a handsome woman. Gasps ripped among the other councilors, many of whom appeared to realize they, too, might end up on the point of a Unionist blade. "You assured me the entire valley would be minimized. We came to use Eden's resources to the good of all Pangea, not get revenge on those you deemed unworthy."

Roschach stiffened. "Eden is guilty of many sins."

"Sins which you yourself committed this day!" Her cry thundered across the chambers. The murmur of conversations off-dais quieted. Her glare burned the air between them. "You will end the indiscriminate killing of palace staff immediately. Is that clear!?"

Taking a controlled breath, Roschach bowed his head. "You're right, councilor." He motioned to the chastised Unionist officer, who left the room to see it done.

"I hold their deaths on your head, whatever the rest of the Quorum says," Baley hissed. "And you will address me as 'fellow.' None of us here stand higher than our Unionist fellows."

"Of course, Fellow Baley, but I'm in the middle of securing Eden as quickly as possible," Roschach said. "I can either secure it slowly and painfully until every Edenon is emboldened enough to cast themselves upon our pikes, or I can take it quickly and scare the rest into submission so we can slay less of them."

Brianne scowled.

"I have ordered more restraint among our men but I will not withhold our speed." He gathered himself. "We will have this palace before the night is through so we can allay the fears of charter members."

"While I laud your hope to speed our victory," she said as her eyes narrowed, "do not sacrifice the innocent more than necessary."

"I do this for the innocent, Fellow Baley." Roschach fisted his glove.

"We all do this for the innocent, so no one across the continent will ever suffer monarchy or abusive tyranny ever again. To end the inequality of the rich and poor. To cease the abuse of the powerful over the powerless! I do not forget why we do this, councilor. It pains me to think you believe I would do otherwise."

Baley appeared to acquiesce. "Recall that as you unleash your dogs on good men and women in this, our new capital. Your mercy will be remembered." *If you show it*, her face clarified.

"Then I will strive to be remembered." He half bowed to her. "Thank you for your wisdom, my lady fellow."

Horns erupted from Unionist trumpeters in the Square Al'Cular, conveying quick battle commands into the air. Other horns echoed the first, ensuring the message was spread across the palace and beyond.

"Fellow Roschach." Baley eyed him. "I was hoping to see you in the Unionist blue and red tonight."

Roschach shrugged his striped yellow and green tunic under his burnished iron plate armor. "I prepared for battle without thinking, fellow. I wanted to ensure I was as prepared as possible, and … was not thinking. This is the crest of my family." He tugged on the white hawk spread at his neck.

"It would do well to represent our cause clearly, fellow." She raised an eyebrow. "Our men and women should know the Unionist cause comes before any single one of us. Certainly more than families or dynasties. I daresay that's the entire point of the cause, Fellow Roschach."

"Of course, fellow." He half-bowed again in acquiescence.

"The Quorum will meet at dawn in the Square Al'Cular," she said to the group. "Fellows Elbert and Kelg are in the city with our foreign dignitaries to ensure every courtesy is extended until this mess is over. Ensure your armbands are visible as you move about the palace. It won't do for you to be mistaken for an Edenon as we finish this business. As Fellow Roschach has assured, you will remain safe. Be here at dawn for the finalization." Her tone dismissed them as she approached Roschach. "I appreciate your zeal, Fellow Roschach. Your thoroughness is valued. Just remember the power of perceived care for the people."

"Of course," Roschach said.

She watched him. "Have you heard from Bonduquoy?"

"Not yet. She expects to reach Algueda in the next few days."

Baley's face tightened but she dismissed the moment of pause.

"Remember our discussion. If possible, bring Peter back to me. I would rather turn him than … than lose him. Losing my brother and his wife are a terrible cost for a brighter future — I had hoped they would come to change their perspectives as I did — but Peter could serve us well by carrying our torch."

"I have ordered April and Peter kept safe," said Roschach. "Once we have the mantle, the Baley family will be returned for an appropriate trial."

"My family line will pay for turning a blind eye when they had power and wealth needed by others," said Baley. "It would be best for the people to see my impartiality and the cause's commitment to justice."

Roschach nodded.

"You have proven your commitment, Fellow Roschach," she said. "Thank you."

"Of course, Fellow Baley." Roschach bowed his head.

"I must see to Matriarch Damian," she said. "She has requested a palace tour before we clean away the Edenons."

"She has never enjoyed the sight of blood," Roschach said.

"No, but she demands it so that no one forgets tonight's cost as we move toward our goals," she said. "Let's go, Alba."

A lean, faded brown woman with a straight nose, clad in leather armor with short-cropped black hair accompanied her out of the arched stairs descending into the eastern side of the amphitheater and out of the chamber. Roschach watched her go as Fenren approached. The two stood alone on the dais with a few Unionist troops left in the chamber as guards.

Roschach scowled once Baley disappeared from view. "Fen?"

"Yeah?"

"If I ever get as pompous as that bitch, you have my permission to slit my throat."

Fenren snorted.

"Seriously. When we're alone?" He poked Fen's chest. "Keep me grounded."

"Will do," Fenren said. "You heard from Bonduquoy?"

"Actually …" Roschach glanced around the chamber and fished out a small clamshell mirror. Opening it, he drew the spellsign into the bottom lid before ringing the mirror on the upper lid with his forefinger. "Athyka Bonduquoy."

The mirror pulsed with faint light. A minute later, Athyka's face appeared, backed by a field of stars. "Lord Roschach."

"Report."

"We have arrived at Algueda. The pan has retreated to shore. We assume he's heading for the Tree."

"I told you to get him before he made it to shore."

"Yes, Lord Roschach. He used the island as I thought he would. We already are dealing with multiple hull breaches, which we will tend to and press forward."

"I want that mantle, Athyka. No mantle, and I think you know what the Edenic Charter will bring down on us. That's our only path to legitimacy with the charter members."

"I understand, Lord Roschach."

"Do you? Because I wanted that mantle at the Deep. You promised it months ago."

Athyka said nothing.

"Get it together," Roschach growled. "I expect you to report the moment you have William in custody. Not a moment later than necessary. Is that clear?"

"Of course, my lord," she said. "I will report as soon as we have him."

"No failures, Athyka," he replied. "Without the mantle, we will face the fury of the Edenic Charter. No number of ohnas will hold off the might of the Graelan high elves or the Alderland legions. They will come down on us like hell itself. Get the mantle and report to me immediately so I can assure charter members that we will maintain it, just like the Baleys before us."

"But the ohnas?"

"We have worked too long to keep our possession of the ohnas from public knowledge," Roschach snapped. "If any of the Baleys escape to reveal what we've done, it won't just be the charter nations coming down on us. Meso'Admia, Rume, Bodony and a thousand other kingdoms will bay for our throats. Hell, even Andon would come after us. Fighting the Edenons and picking off member nations one at a time is fine with ohnas, but with the entire continent hunting us? I think not. Get the mantle and return as quickly as possible. Leave everyone else to that selfdamn island. Is that clear?"

"Yes, my lord," she said.

"Do not fail, or your secret *gift* will be a great deal less secret." Roschach glared for another moment before snapping closed the clamshell. Still scowling, he turned to Fenren. "You go make sure every single one of the pan's personal staff are snuffed. Spare the housekeeping staff, but I want the others dead. Just make sure Baley doesn't see any of it. Let her think we're showing mercy, or that it happened before we sent out those orders. I want them to feel it. And where's the selfdamn entourage from Alderland? I was expecting them already."

"A messenger came through the rimsportal an hour ago," Fenren said. "A delegation is being formed to monitor the … transition … for His Majesty Emperor Benuin's satisfaction to our promises."

"Formed? Now? Where is Ambassador Abydon?"

"I cannot speak to your discussions away from my ears." Fenren shrugged.

"He's waiting for something." Roschach's eyes narrowed. "What is it? … Go finish off the other Baley guards and return to me before the Quorum meets. Bonduquoy's delay is tying our hands. I want her ohnas *here*, and I want them through the rimshift, not by her sailing two months back home. Go quickly before Baley tries to rescue the staff herself."

"My lo-" Fenren cleared his throat. "*Fellow* Roschach."

"Oh, hell, just get going."

Fenren bowed away with a smirk and jogged to gather the men he needed to comply with Roschach's order.

Roschach growled, then headed off to find a messenger to send to Alderland.

3

Unionists

Standing amidships on Unity's Light, Athyka closed her communications device. If the world discovered the Unionists had stolen the ohna khordecs — physical anchors to the eight powers of creation — not even the Great Self would allay their wrath. If the world discovered her secret, none of the rest would matter anyway. Unity's Light tilted as a wave rolled them against coral. Hours struggling to navigate through the reef had punctured their hull twice more. The sun had long set and the moon hovered low in the east.

"Selfdamnit," she growled. Up on the bowsprit, one of their desperate young officers struggled in vain to reproduce the pan's method of weaving through the coral. Exhaustion threatened her knees with every step.

"What'd Roschach say?" Eldnor's voice startled her from behind. She spun, wondering how much he heard, before pocketing her clamshell.

"He's threatening to leave us out here if we can't get the mantle."

Eldnor shrugged as if that was expected, but his attention flicked to the clamshell. With her hand resting on the ohna sheathed in her belt, Athyka touched the side of his face before he could react. Flashing from panic to a dull glaze, his eyes drooped. While touching his face, she sensed his memories and noted what he heard. Before releasing, she wished she had the power to erase them. They disappeared — that had never happened before. She gasped and pulled her hand back.

Eldnor blinked, bewildered.

"My lady," the captain said as he approached. "Pardon, I know you're exhausted, but we can't free ourselves from the coral and we have another hull breach."

Startled herself, Athyka left a bewildered Eldnor to follow the captain up the forecastle behind the gaggle of officers behind the bowsprit.

"Move," she said.

They scattered before her, including the one on the bowsprit.

Standing at the base of the bowsprit, she gripped a line. As she did, so did all the others, their eyes wide. None could see her clutch the ice knife in her long coat or the ripples of energy erupting from the ohna as a light show in her gaze. Energy coursed and filled her exhausted veins. Power reaching out to the ocean below gave her a mental image of the water and the coral within it. She wished she had the ohna makara — the power of creation over marine life — as they did at Richter's Deep, but Roschach sent Winston Runel elsewhere after the battle.

A sailor had been lowered earlier from the bowsprit and dangled a bare foot from the wave crests in order to better see the coral when a goldfish the size of a shark erupted from the ocean and bit him in half. Sailors, soldiers and mages had been on edge ever since.

She needed to conserve her energy but staying on the coral threatened the ship.

"Hold on." Athyka gathered water from aft and drew it up under the ship's hull in a rush. The ship rocked again, but the stern lifted high, followed by the bow. Experienced sailors took the motion in stride while the mages panicked. The vessel lifted a few feet before being carried across the edge of the coral into the crystal lagoon. Athyka took a slow, deep breath at the amount of energy required — the more tired she became, the more energy the ohna drained her.

Clad in black trousers tucked in bloodred boots secured up her calf with multiple belt straps, Athyka tightened her armored leather vest. Once she felt confident she could walk across the deck without collapsing, she descended the forecastle stairs to the deck as the captain approached.

Nighttime Algueda filled the sky as they settled into the lagoon. She motioned to the captain. "Make for the West Bay immediately. Notify me before we enter it."

"As you wish, my lady." He ducked his head.

Eldnor followed her into the captain's quarters tucked beneath the bridge, which she had appropriated when she came on board before Richter's Deep.

"What's the plan? We attacking him tonight?" Eldnor plopped into the chair next to the large table in the center of the room.

Athyka took her seat at the head of the table. Her gaze slid across the large, albeit incomplete, map with "NEVER LAND!" scrawled in red ink in the bottom right corner over the island's name, "Algueda."

"No," she said. "We can't chase him inland like some common dog. This is no mere tropical island."

"An entire island that eats people alive? I still don't believe it," he huffed. "Fairytales designed by the pans to keep people away."

"There are reports."

"All by Edenons." Eldnor crossed his arms.

She scanned estimates of locations and distances penned across the sheaf. "He'll go for the Tree."

"Why? Cuz they think it's the real Tree of Life?"

"You see this?" Athyka fished a coin from her pocket and flicked it. Eldnor snatched it from the air and inspected the imprinted La'Du Lira Al'Cular — Tree of Life — in the center. "Edenic Praesidium" curved over the top and "The Family Baley" curved under the bottom. "That's the Baley family crest. Where else do you think they're going?"

"I still say it's horseshit." Eldnor flicked it back before he fished out a marble ring from a tiny box on her desk — the ohna terra — and rolled it over his fingers.

"I wish you could have practiced with that thing." Athyka frowned, but her mind returned to their encounter on deck. She had only ever been able to press suggestions to someone's mind before. Touching the ohna, she had entered Eldnor's mind with surprising authority.

"There's no soil, stone or heavy metals onboard," Eldnor said. "I'll have to practice when we get ashore. I got a little practice before we went to Richter's. Besides, your ohna didn't work against him. What good are they gonna do?"

"I've been thinking about that." Her finger found the ice knife — the ohna marina — in her belt.

"We have more than the ohnas," Eldnor said. "He can't stop all of our archers and mages."

"He doesn't have to," Athyka said. "If Algueda is truly as dangerous as they say, and the reports are true that the pan will never be intentionally harmed by any of its creatures or its dangerous plant life, then we're fighting him *and* the island." She wondered if she could touch Eldnor's mind without touching his skin, when the door behind him slid open to admit a large, muscled man with midnight skin clad in a thin black leather vest strapped with knives and a sword over a sleeveless gray tunic above gray-green trousers tucked into worn black boots.

"Gregory." Athyka sketched their location on the map in graphite. "You look ready."

"We going ashore?" Gregory asked.

"Where have you been?" Eldnor cocked his head up at the newcomer. "Polishing your knife?"

"I'll do it with your ribs." Gregory leaned closer.

"We have to plan before we go ashore," Athyka said.

"I'm sick of being at sea." Gregory scowled and dropped into a seat. Glancing at the ohna terra lying on the table, he reached for it. Upon touching it, he recoiled and flapped his hand. "Motherfucker."

"We told you not to touch them." Eldnor plucked it from the table and stuffed it into its leather sheath bound under his left arm.

Gregory rubbed his fingers. "The hell you say. That fuckin' hurt! Why does it do that!?"

"It's a first power," Eldnor spat. "The ones that hold the Alterworlds in place. Few mages can wield them."

"But why can't I even touch it?" Gregory flapped his fingers again.

"It's a khordec of one of the eight powers of creation," Eldnor said. "Like trying to grip fire, barehanded."

"Fire doesn't hurt that fuckin' much," Gregory glared. "And what the hell is a khordec?"

Eldnor said, "We told you."

"Well, I wasn't listening," Gregory snapped at Eldnor but softened, glancing sideways at Athyka. "Mum."

"As well you weren't." Athyka twisted her mouth.

"It's the physical anchor of a powerful magic," Eldnor said. "Every ohna has a khordec, as do countless other magics."

"Does all magic have khordecs? A khordec?" Gregory scowled at the word while rubbing his tingling fingers.

"Just magical items that are created," Eldnor said. "The first powers have them. Numerous types of ward and shield spells can have khordecs."

"Even abru'caris can have khordecs." Athyka reclined in her chair.

"Mantles of power? Really?" Eldnor raised an eyebrow. "That, I did not know."

"But you said, 'created...'" Gregory fisted his fingers as the tingling subsided. "I thought the first powers were, you know, like from Temple. Beginning of time and all that."

"No one is completely sure why the ohnas have khordecs, but they do." Athyka inspected the ice knife in her fingers. "That's what these are."

"Those are khordecs?" Gregory asked.

"Ben'khordecs," she said. "*Holy* khordecs."

"I thought you said those were ohnas," Gregory said.

"The knife is the khordec," she said. "The power within it is the ohna."

"Holy, my ass." Eldnor rolled the ohna terra over the tops of his fingers. "The plan?"

"Take The Sumter," she said. "After that, I need to rest. We wouldn't attack now if I didn't think Shelley wouldn't try some brilliant maneuver and sink us before we can finalize our plans. Then we can take more time and plan a proper attack on the pan."

"How will we take The Sumter?" asked Eldnor.

"Head on," she said. "They'll think us impaired. In our right minds, we'd anchor and conduct repairs."

Gregory grinned. "They don't know us."

"Afterward, I want you and Gregory to find a base of operations on the island we can use if we can't retreat to the ship." She turned to Gregory. "Memorize the map-"

"There isn't much on here," Gregory said.

"Memorize what there is." Her gaze leveled. "I'm sure there is much we don't know. Apparently, there's a path leading from the West Bay around the south side of the peak up to the Tree. We'll take that. But the real problem is the wall around the Tree."

"A wall? Like a fortress?" Eldnor fingered the ohna of earth and stone. "Stonework? I can handle that."

"No," she said. "One report was very clear — there's a semi-intelligent vine wall that hugs the base of the Tree. It kills anyone but the pan, and it does so brutally."

"How so?"

"Something about sharp spades," said Athyka. "Essentially cuts anyone apart who comes too close. That's our real problem, because if it's true, we may not be able to get past."

"But the ohnas?"

"They don't work very well in the presence of the Tree. Or, fitfully, rather. The reports weren't clear or either they were incomplete. It seems some of the researchers who actually made it back went mad. If we even make it through the wall, we might be stuck with swords and arrows in a place where the pan is at his most powerful."

"Bugger."

A polite knock interrupted their conversation.

"Come," Athyka said.

The door slipped open to admit one of the young officers.

"Lady Bonduquoy." The officer ducked his head. "The captain sent me to let you know we're almost at the entrance to the West Bay."

"That was fast," Eldnor mused.

"Come." Athyka headed back to the deck. "It's time to cut off the pan's retreat."

Moonlight silhouetted the island as they came around the western end of the bay, in sight of The Sumter anchored at the bay's heart.

"Quietly to stations," she said. Her soft command echoed in whispers across the ship. "Bring me a mage." Moments later a mage hurried onto the forecastle to her summons. Looking him over, she took a hold of the knife. "Eldnor, brace me to the ship."

"Aye." He took hold of one of her arms and gripped the forecastle rail.

The mage flailed when she snatched him by the throat. He clutched her wrist when his back arched and a strangled cry wheezed from him. Through the power of the ohna, she snatched his life force and used it to fuel her energy and control. As it did, whispers of terror filled her thoughts from all those around her. Their minds screamed into her own — endless whispers and questions and opinions that had assaulted her for as long as she could remember. It was happening again — touching the ohna magnified an ability she'd struggled to keep secret since her grandmother caught her commanding squirrels to play. Tamping down the sickness in her stomach, she focused on the water beneath the ship.

"Brace yourselves," she whispered.

The command echoed down the ship before the vessel lurched, carried forward by a welling of ocean beneath the hull. With so much of the ohna's power coursing through her, she could sense The Sumter less than a mile distant. The Edenon ship vibrated with footsteps — its crew had spotted Unity's Light in the moon's ambience and now rushed to stations. A ship's boat was thrown into the water in hopes to turn the motionless ship to bear down on her with their mages.

"We are spotted." A nearby officer watched The Sumter through his spyglass.

"They are dead," she breathed as Unity's Light accelerated.

"They're turning!" cried one of the sailors.

"Fast little bastards," muttered Eldnor from behind Athyka, but her focus cut off her other senses. The bow of Unity's Light ascended as the water behind the ship rushed forward. Sails billowed backwards.

"Those shields won't help," Eldnor said.

Edenon mages mustered on The Sumter's starboard rail to create a shimmering, unified shield that drooped near the water.

The moon disappeared behind Pan's Peak as Unity's Light drew near. Within two spans of The Sumter, Unity's Light tilted forward in a sudden stop. Her bow dropped until the bowsprit slapped and sank into the water. Sailors yelled in terror as the rear of the ship vaulted skyward, then see-sawed, casting the bow skyward with Athyka and Eldnor upon it.

Athyka bellowed as her wave raced onward for the Edenon vessel.

Edenon mages unleashed a flurry of desperate magical actions to stop the wave, which struck and vaulted the ship sideways. When its keel struck the shallowing seabed, it rolled onto its side with a crash. The Sumter's masts, yards and sprits snapped. Men and supplies flew across the beach, followed and carried by the wash from the wave climbing the sand into the tree line.

Athyka released the mage. He crumpled to deck gasping for life with veins blacked and visible even in the faint starlight.

"Prepare the boats, captain." She glanced at Eldnor and Gregory. "We finish them off now."

Ten minutes later, the three agents, five mages and twenty sailors climbed from ship's boats onto the crystal white sand of the West Bay. The mages and sailors advanced on the broken Edenon vessel with crossbows, swords, empowered hands and magical shields raised. Athyka waited from a distance as they searched the boat. Sailors, mages and cargo littered the broad beach.

Once safe, a mage waved her and Eldnor to the ship. Corpses lay piled onto the inside of the starboard rail where they had crashed and were trapped in the deluge. Tangled in lines and boxes, they had drowned in the water rushing back down the beach from the attack.

"Is that …?" Eldnor inspected a figure lying on the railing near the bridge now hovering eight feet above the beach.

"Who is it?" Gregory asked.

"This is Captain Desmond Shelley," Eldnor said. "Greatest since Roulain … What a shame."

"Didn't seem that difficult to beat," Gregory said.

"Hardly seems comparable when facing an ohna." Eldnor glared a moment before reaching up to tug at Shelley's coat, as if to make his corpse more presentable.

Gregory crossed his arms and glanced at the ship. Unionist soldiers searched the lower decks and other cabins.

"Only two sailors survived the strike." An officer approached Athyka. "We've dispatched them."

"You didn't bring them to me?" asked Athyka.

The officer stiffened. "Pardon, my lady, bu-" He cut off and snatched his right arm before collapsing to his knees. A guttural scream ripped from his mouth as his arm quivered. He arched and slumped, panting.

Athyka gripped the ice knife in her hand as she loomed over him. "Unless I order you to kill someone, leftenant, you will do nothing, is that clear?" She had hoped to use her powers on an enemy combatant and felt amped for having no one to kill. She struggled not to end his life.

The leftenant sobbed while his left hand hovered over his excruciated right arm. Blood dripped down the inside of his coat sleeve and onto the sand. Before he could rise, the sand swarmed. Everyone backed away as it rushed the drooling blood and overwhelmed the screaming young officer. Hundreds of tiny creatures shredded his skin as he shrieked. The swarm rushed down his open throat. Dying in moments, the smell of blood and fluids filled the air.

"Shiiit," Eldnor growled. As the figure crumpled and shrank into the beach, Athyka skirted him on her return to the ship's boat.

"Get me back on that selfdamn ship," she growled. "I need rest before I deal with this fucking island because as soon as we can head inland, we're going after Baley, that bitch, and his boy."

4

A Plan

Peter bolted upright from his thick mattress of grass. His crimson hair stuck out at angles as he cleared his muddled vision. Sitting near the edge of the cliffside, Peter's green eyes locked onto last night's vista with fresh awe as the midday sun revealed it anew.

"Neverland," he breathed. As if on command, thousands of flying creatures erupted from the endless forest canopies. His heart fluttered with wonder at the sight, wishing he, too, could fly. He climbed to his feet and stretched before taking a careful look over the cliff's edge — no nearer than he dared — to note how high they were. Backing away, he faced the vine wall, which rose nine feet high, about thirty feet from the nearest of the larger roots. Several spade heads paused as he drew nearer. They stopped as he did, then backed away, mirroring him until they returned to slithering within the thick wall.

Toward the Tree, flowers bloomed, butterflies drifted by and clouds of tiny motes swarmed throughout the Tree's great canopy. The sweet smell of flowering dogwood filled the crisp morning air cool with breeze. Roots taller than men flew outward from the base of the tree and narrowed as they wove downward into the clearing's thick mattress of short-cropped grass. Large, narrow vertical walls of man-thick-sized roots wove a web of arboreal flesh. Peter wiggled through the tangle into the void beyond.

Beneath the Tree, bare light bled from outside, but squinting, he made out a faint ring of light indicating the breadth of the Tree's base. Despite the Tree's mass above, its main trunk rested on the tangle of massive roots round about its edge. A broad concave chamber nestled beneath.

"Hello?" Peter followed the gentle descent towards the center of the chamber. "Hello?"

The ground leveled off at the bottom. At the rear of the chamber, the root system formed a flat wall where they dipped down over the cliffside. A pocket formed by the roots felt like a room to Peter as he walked in. The faint pale light bleeding through allowed him to navigate, though he could make out no detail. A bare breeze from the back of the room drew him into the roots. Among them, roots shaped like steps led to a narrow opening. Wiggling through, he gripped the roots, stuck his head out and found himself staring down the cliff face five hundred feet to the jungle below.

"Wow."

Faint chimes tickled the air.

"Tink!" Peter returned to the chamber and spotted a narrow, vertical silhouette against the faint backlight. Reaching out, he felt a rough texture under his fingers. "A tree?" Peter rubbed his hands up and down the gentle bark and wondered if more light made it down here later in the day. "Weird."

Peter's next step met open air and he fell into a hole. He barked a few sobs and wiped his nose before exploring the hole with his hands. Three feet deep and wide, the hole climbed from its deepest point at the base of the tree and shallowed. He caught his breath and rubbed his banged knee before climbing out and continuing with greater care.

Tinker Belle's distinct chimes pierced the thick root wall. As he drew nearer, he made out his father's baritone and his mother's tenor voices when their words became clear.

"You sacrificed that boy!" April cried. "You didn't even try to find a way through! How could you do such a thing?"

"I tried to send him back!"

"Did you know you were going to kick someone in, all the way back at the beach!?" April demanded. Her eyes widened when he hesitated.

"I'm out of options, April!" he cried. "This is the *only* place I know where you can be safe!"

"For all those men!?"

"I had to get you and Peter up here," William said. "No matter the cost."

"But you just kicked him in!" her voice quivered. "How could you do such a thing!?"

William said nothing. Tinker Belle floated nearby.

"And- and those marines," April managed. "You knew they would die. You knew it!"

"Of course, I knew it. This is Algueda! They call it 'Neverland' for a reason!"

"Was their entire role to die just so we could trap ourselves up here!?" she asked.

"I needed to get you two safe! That's all I've been able to think about."

"We can't give up here!"

"We're not giving up," William said.

"What do you call this!?"

"Algueda will keep them at bay," William said.

"For what? Just us?"

"We can't let them have the mantle! If the Unionists get the mantle, they will have much more than Eden!"

"The mantle be damned, William! We just sacrificed all those men for ourselves!"

"It's my duty to protect the mantle, even above their lives—"

"It was also your duty to keep the ohnas out of the hands of the Unionists!"

"I'm not getting into that discussion again," William growled. "Belle's plan can move us forward. We're not going to wallow over what never happened."

"You cannot sacrifice yourself for us, William! You cannot!" April glared between him and Tinker Belle. "And Peter! Peter is not ready for that kind of responsibility! We need you to fulfill your duties, not pass them onto your son in some kind of wild bet! I will *not* gamble with your lives!"

"There is no choice," William said. "I... we've come to the end of our road! There's nothing else I can see!"

Peter wiggled through enough to peek over a root to spy on the conversation.

"You can fight," she growled. "Keep the mantle and use the island to your advantage and get us back to Eden."

"And if they take me while you two are stuck in here?"

"Why are you staring at the worst-case scenario!?"

"They just chased us here! There's nowhere else for us to go they can't follow."

"Use the mantle the way it was intended! The way the histories claim!"

"I barely know anything about this self-forsaken mantle. Those lessons amount for nothing. No one knows more than platitudes and histories. We barely remember how to pass the damn thing."

"Don't be such a coward, William!" April countered. "There is nothing so ignoble as a man who gives up before he tries."

"I'm not in your father's sitting room," William said. "This isn't after-dinner philosophy. I'm trying to think of you and Peter. I can't protect you from the men and this island. I have to do *something*—"

"Something, William! Not nothing! Not giving up and running away on a gamble to save time when—"

"Tinker Belle has thought this through!"

"I don't want to hear what she has thought through."

"She's more than two hundred years old!"

"Think for yourself, William! For once! Think for yourself!"

"I have! From the moment I married you—"

"You've been thinking of her bosom!" April cornered him. "You've been thinking of her in the dark of night when you're with me!"

"I have not!" William stammered.

"When you're lying in my arms and put your face on me, you're thinking of her body! I know you are because I know what you two have done!"

"I'm not!" William yelled. "Whatever, however I've failed, you have always been who I married, not her!"

"Then listen to me, William! Stop listening to her!"

"I can't!"

"Why not!?"

"She's my guide! She's been with me a lot longer than you!"

April paled and her eyes glassed. She recoiled like a slap in the face.

"April—"

"Go, William," she turned away. "Go with your lady and sacrifice yourself for me. Your *second*."

"Selfdamnit, April!"

"GO, William!" she pointed.

William approached when Tinker Belle flew into his path in a flurry of fading sparks.

Peter retreated into the roots so his mother would not see him as she stormed by. As William and Tinker Belle conferred, lines on his face betrayed his mantle-gentled aging. At sixty years old, William appeared in his late 30's, but today appeared to carry the weight of his half-century.

"But, April—" William started.

Tinker Belle cut him off with clear points in her chimal voice only the pan could understand.

William grimaced under a brilliant midday sun painting the inner clearing. "So, Peter might live?"

Tinker Belle chimed and pointed into her palm in emphasis.

"Great Self be damned," William coughed. "Alright." He walked out through the vine wall as Tinker Belle landed on his shoulder.

Peter crossed the soft grass to where his mother stood near the cliff. "Mom?"

April wiped her tears. "Hey, my little bird." She pulled him in for a hug. "Where you been?"

"Why were you two fighting again?"

April grimaced. "Tinker Belle has a plan. Your father likes it."

"But you don't."

April frowned.

"And what's a bosom?"

Hesitating, she drew a long, slow inhale. "Well … it's …"

"Is it like a hug?" Peter asked.

"Not exactly, son," April said. "It's like … here." She pressed her breastbone. "It's where we hug."

"Oh …" Peter said. "Why would dad think of Tink's bosom?"

April exhaled slowly.

"And a plan? What kind?" Peter piqued.

"A risky one," April said.

Peter shrank. "Mom, why're you two always fighting?"

"Well, your father …" April inhaled. "With the Unionists and the fighting and … it's just a difficult time to find the right way ahead. Your father and I disagree on what that is."

"Why are the Unionists chasing us? Why are we fighting? Why can't we just go home?" Peter asked.

April sank to the grass, drew Peter into her lap and wrapped her arms around him. "Do you remember what I told you about the Unionists?"

"They want to take control of everyone?"

"Yes," she said. "And they think they're doing it for the right reasons."

"How can you control people for the right reasons?"

"Unionists believe their way is the right way," she said, "and that because they have great intentions, all the things they do to achieve them are justified."

"Like how?"

"There's an old belief that 'ends justify means,'" she said, "which means that if you were about to say, eat too much candy and get sick, they could take your money away so you couldn't spend it on candy."

"That's not fair! That's my money! And my choice!"

"But they believe that if they force you to do what they believe is moral, then they are justified in taking away your natural rights."

"So, they want to control everyone for good?"

"In a way," she said. "You see, of all the thousands of tiny city states and huge empires like the Swinnen Hegemony that rule hundreds of millions of sentients, not all governments are moral or right or fair. In some, the people suffer. Some get rich by taking advantage of others, some get rich by helping others. We live in a big, complex world full of countless intelligent beings who make lots of decisions every day. Some decisions are wise and some are not, but those decisions belong to the beings who make them. So, when a people allow their kings to rule, or their parliaments, or their presidents or emperors ... they allow their government to exist by not fighting back."

"What does that have to do with the Unionists?"

"The Unionists believe that there should be only one government, one rule over all sentient beings. They believe this government can be smarter than the people on the people's behalf. That the people can be better if the government makes them better."

"But how would they make them better?"

"They can't, Peter," April said. "A government is only as good as its people, because from the people comes their government. If you can't trust the people, you can't trust the government that comes from it. We have to let each group figure out what's best for themselves, even if it hurts."

"But what if the Unionist government is bad?"

"They don't believe their way is bad. They think it's okay to disregard the decisions of sentients if it doesn't align with Unionist doctrine. They decided that their way of living is better than everyone else's, so they want to force their version of 'right' on others. Through a single nation, they can make everyone happy."

"Can it?" Peter asked.

"Would you want someone else to show you how to play or would you want to figure it out yourself?"

"No," Peter said, "I choose how I want to play."

"Nations all over Pangea have figured out their own way to live. Some leaders are evil, but those leaders belong to their people. Hundreds of thousands of years of history have proven that when people can't stand their government anymore, they fight back and change the leader. It's their nation and their responsibility. It's their way to play. Do you know why?"

Peter thought about it a long moment. "Because ... it's really about if they want to listen to their king or not. If they don't like their ruler, it's their responsibility to ... take that leader out."

"Yes!" she hugged him. "You're so bright, my beautiful boy."

"*M-o-m-m-m.*"

April chuckled. "My very *handsome* boy."

"Why do they want the mantle?"

"If they can take your father's mantle, they gain his ability to communicate with all sentient life forms. It's why the pan has served as such a central arbiter of continental trade and conflict for millennia and why Eden has become such a fulcrum of power and wealth among empires who could so easily crush us. The ability to communicate accurately between two conflicting parties is among the most powerful abilities in magic, and unique to the pan. It's why Eden enjoys the most diversity of culture and thought than any other nation in Pangea. So many variant cultures and ideas have created lots of conflict in our little valley, but it also has produced amazing innovations and businesses that produced great wealth. Unionists would steal what they could not earn in order to control those who would not enlist in their idea of perfection."

Peter scowled.

April played with his hair, "Also, by possessing the pan's mantle, the Unionists can control Eden's role in the Edenic Charter."

"But they're wrong! They can't just steal it and that be okay."

"Actually, no, they're right," April said. "When the Edenic Charter was first penned between Eden, Graela and Alderland, it specified that whoever had the mantle would speak for Eden, but did not limit how that mantle could be acquired. If they can take the mantle from your father, they will have the full legal authority it implies. If they don't, Graela and Alderland will send armies to stop them."

"They can just take it?"

"It's our own fault for not writing in protections. We thought the spirit of a law would live on, but we have learned that the letter of a law can be as easily turned against its intent when some re-interpret it to serve their own ends."

Peter sank. "Why can't they just go away?"

"I wish they would, too," April sighed. The wall parted as William returned with two groundhogs and the scattered pack of supplies lost during last night's attacks on the marines. "Me, too."

5

Transfer

Bats and nightbirds swooped along the vine wall to peer at the curious newcomers living inside. Their small bodies darted by firelight like shooting stars in the chaotic darkness of Neverland night, snapping up the swarms of bugs hovering just above the edge of the vine wall, drawn close by the crackling light of their fire.

Legions of insects hovered outside the edge of the wall. Animals called, chittered, and screamed. Echoes of birds and great battles thundered through the jungle forests. Cricket chirps and cicada stutters filled the cool wind sharp with the new and exotic smells of Neverland night.

After William and Tinker Belle ironed out her plan, she kept away from the group. Peter searched in vain for her in the Tree's canopy throughout the evening.

"What are we going to do, William?" Fire sparkled in April's gaze. "They will come sooner or later."

William focused on her, then drooped. "Have you thought of any alternatives?"

"We could stay here, couldn't we?" she eyed the ever-writhing wall of vines and the bugs refusing to cross it. "Can they get in here?"

William's mouth twisted. "I don't know how much that will do to stop them, long-term. It's … marginally intelligent, but … I don't think it's effective enough. Besides, if they surrounded the clearing, they could starve us out."

April's face tightened. "And if you attacked them? As you are?"

"Baleys are powerful mages," William said. "It's one reason we were selected to receive the mantle and how we've kept it for so long … But I fear our tenure as pan has weakened us. I'm powerful but I did not train well enough with just my magic. I am not confident of victory."

"But you're the pan," Peter said. "You can do anything."

William's face tightened. "I wish it were so, son."

April gazed again into her worries.

"You know," William took a slow breath to calm his stomach and leaned close with a twinkle in his eye. "There are *boys* on this island."

Peter's brow sank. "Boys? What do you mean?"

"I mean there are boys across the island," William's focus slid to a point along the vine wall that drew his attention then returned to Peter. "Hidden within the nests of great beasts. Silverback apes ten feet high! A crocodile that's forty- fifty feet long! A spider as big as a village hut! Boys of all colors, shapes and sizes."

Peter's eyes grew as saucers. "But … where do they come from?"

"No one knows," William shrugged. "Why they're here, or why they hold boys in their nests, is a mystery."

Peter peered into the darkness as if he could see them now.

"Can I tell you a secret?"

Peter nodded.

"Neverland has an alterworld."

"But I thought you said it didn't! You told lots of people!"

"I know, I know," William said. "But it was a secret to protect it. It's called Earth."

April hugged her knees and set her chin upon them.

"Earth? But … who lives there? Like the elfmen of Aklia or the halflings of Doon?"

"Human vacants," said William.

Peter frowned. "What's a vacant?"

"They were an ancient anomaly — humans who had no magic at all."

"But lots of people don't have magic," said Peter.

"Everyone in Pangea has a little bit of magic in them. Some have just a little, some are simple laymen, and some are mighty mages who become wizards and witches and other great practitioners. Those who have just a little bit of magic can participate with magic. If a mage or wizard were to cast a spell or other energy upon a person, that little bit of magic inside them is what interacts with spells and stuff. Without that spark, the magic has no effect."

Peter shrugged.

"That means if I were to try to bind you like the guards at the palace would do to an intruder, it would do nothing."

"Really?"

"Vacants were killed everywhere they were found across Pangea," William said.

"Did they send the vacants to Earth?"

"Scholars believe they migrated during the great exodus at the start of the reformation," William said. "Just like all the other nations and species that moved on to the Alterworlds once they were discovered."

"But why would anyone want to kill people who have no magic?" Peter asked.

"Our world depends on magic, Peter," William said. "If magic doesn't affect you, then all our abilities to enforce laws come under threat. The powers at the time decided killing vacants was the best option."

"Even Eden?"

"That was prior to the Great Reformation," William said. "Back then, Eden was little more than a garden for snakes."

"The dragons," Peter recalled his lessons.

"Right, the dragons."

"Have you been there? To Earth?"

"Once. I was very young, and was very different," said William. "Life was different." He locked eyes with April.

"What was it like there?"

A smile tugged at William's mouth. "It wasn't what I expected. I thought I'd find a lot of ignorant farmers. Since they didn't have magic, I thought, what could they do? I was very surprised."

Peter crossed his legs. "What did you find?"

"They had come so very far," said William. "Time is different there — no one even remembered coming from Pangea. All talk of vampires and dragons and witches and bogeymen and pixies? It was just ancient myth and tall tales to them. The Great Reformation happened eight thousand years ago for us. For them, I think … well, the best previous pans could guess and calculate, by now, humans have been on Earth about twenty thousand years. Time is a bit different there. They had covered the entire surface of their world, a world shaped round like a ball. They had built great structures – tall pyramids, like the towers of Curgu'a; great schools of learning on massive marble pillars; high towers like the Graelans; carved living sculptures and painted such beautiful art! They are a people of great wonder, great knowledge. They have such passions, cultures full of life and love. They have embraced so much of who they are."

"And they have no magic?"

"No magic." A smirk tugged William's beard.

"Then what made you different? After you came back?"

"Earth was … difficult for me, in a variety of ways," William said as April hooked a strand of hair behind her ear. Her faint freckles and emerald eyes danced in the firelight. "When I visited, I thought I knew it all. I came home a different man. Among other things, the people of Earth taught me that possibilities are not defined by magic or our limitations with it, but rather by our imagination." His voice softened. "I owe much to them. Without them, I would never have caught your mother."

"You met mom on Earth?"

William smiled. "No, I met your mother in Eden. She was the prettiest girl I'd ever seen, and she didn't want anything to do with me."

"Why not?" Peter asked.

"I … I wasn't a very nice person," William said. "I only thought of myself and about what I wanted. I thought I knew all about the world. It turned out I was wrong. Really wrong."

William and April watched each other across the fire.

"So … where do you think the boys come from? Earth?" Peter asked.

William mused. "Bridges, like Algueda, are entangled with their worlds, Peter. I suppose it's … well, very possible, actually. Every alterbridge is connected in very special ways to its world, in ways still mysterious to some of us."

"Even you?"

"Yes, even me. Every pan has things to learn when they become the pan," William said. "We never learn it all. We just pray what we do is right. We pray that our loved ones survive." William's gaze glassed. "We pray our loved ones forgive us, most of all."

April's face tightened.

63

"Peter…" William eyed the darkness at something only he could see, then sat up. "I want you to take very special care of grandfather's knife. It's yours now."

Peter gripped the silver knife in his belt line and nodded.

"I have another gift for you, though, truth be told, you may hate me for it."

Peter straightened. "What is it?"

Chimes filled the night as Tinker Belle approached. Her tiny bolt grew in the black. She entered the clearing from the cliffside and veered for Peter before setting onto the boy's shoulder.

April sat upright.

Peter frowned at Tinker Belle, who had never done that before.

"I love you son," William said. "But … I—"

"No!" April sobbed. "No-no-no-no-no! NO!" She scrambled to her knees.

William gripped Peter's arms. "I love you, son. Please forgive me."

"NO!" April struggled to stand over her skirts, ripping them as she forced herself up. "NOT YET!"

William pressed his palm to the boy's sternum. Golden light swirled down his arm, over his hand and across Peter's chest.

"Let him go! Let him go! Let him go!" April cried as she latched onto the two and struggled in vain to push them apart. Light flowed over Peter and into his eyes, nose and mouth. She ripped at Peter's coat to free him when the La'Du Lira Al'Cular blinked into a midnight sun. She looked upon it, then twisted and fell to the ground while shielding her face in the crook of her elbow.

William, Peter and Tinker Belle remained oblivious to the Tree as the liquid power flowed between them. Peter arched while the light overwhelmed him. As the last flowed from William into Peter, the boy ascended into the air. Tinker Belle hovered, likewise, above Peter. The ground beneath them trembled.

In the sky above, brilliant blue-green auroras danced across the sky before a shimmering strand, like lightning, fired downward through Tinker Belle and Peter into the ground below. The air filled with the smell of life.

A false, heatless sunrise broke across Pangea that startled those still awake. Peter's eyes, nose and mouth became beacons of that light as he rotated into the air. The earth quaked when all fell to a sudden, quiet stillness. The boy's head fell back and from out his mouth came a cry that echoed across the nights of a thousand worlds.

Peter crowed.

The sound carried across waters and shores, plains and mountains. The people of the continent woke and trembled. A wind rushed into the clearing and swirled upward around him and Tinker Belle into a violent torrent, killing their small fire.

As quickly as William began the transfer of the ben'cari, Peter collapsed to the ground and as the dying winds carried Tinker Belle away into the darkness. The Tree's light died.

William collapsed, flopping with the side of his face into the outer coals of their dead fire, unconscious as it melted his skin.

Terrified and furious, April sobbed. Her breaths stuttered as she clung to the grass. Gaining her bearings, she opened her eyes but cried out when the air struck them. She closed them again and dragged herself in search of her son.

"Peter! Peter! PETER!! PETER! PETER, come here! PETER!" she begged. She choked off her sobs and crawled onward. When she felt him, she checked him over with her hands and groped for his face. When she heard him breathing, sobs erupted from her mouth as she clutched him to her breast. "Peter."

6

Avicara

Elder Againa pressed Horticul Ylnia into the cushion of his bed as he moved his mouth from her moaning lips to the curve of her neck. Her right arm tightened around his neck while her left slid up under his arm to grip the muscles of his back as he rocked into her. Her knees climbed his hips and her heels encouraged him deeper before his large right hand slid up her spine to grip the base of her lower left wing.

Ylnia moaned as he took a firm grip, and then tightened around him as he used it as leverage. Chimal moans filled the space and soon became barks as Againa grew insistent. Their lights mingled until neither was distinguishable from the other, a tiny rolling flame of passion as she begged him to drive deeper and felt the fingers of his left hand tangle and grip her hair.

A rooster's crow ripped the air. Both froze as a new energy washed away their building climaxes, one so powerful as to make their passion seem cold. Againa scrambled from her to the opening to his branch and yanked open the curtain.

A noonday sun blazed on the midnight horizon, obscured by the canopy around his branch. He leapt out and fired upward through the tree's canopy just before a yellow column of light — a bare spider's thread at this distance — blinked out. The daytime sky returned to starry midnight as the crow's echo faded away.

What is it!? Ylnia ascended with him, as did thousands of other startled pixies from their burrows, nests and nooks. *What was that!?*

Elder Againa locked onto where the light had interrupted the horizon, then focused on a faint wave of green auroric light rippling across the sky, a whisper of what it once must have been to come so far so fast. *Return to your feather, Ylnia. I have duties.*

Elder Againa, she curtsied and rushed to gather her dress.

Againa returned to his branch, yanked on his long shorts, bound his white hair into a ponytail and raced through the high bluewood trees foresting the rolling hills. Passing other startled pixies hovering above the wood, he veered for the six decamillenial Al'cular rising five hundred feet at the forest's heart. Pixies called questions as he passed.

Alongside the other elders, resplendent in their youthful beauty as common to aging pixies, he passed through a gaping hole forty feet wide into the hollow Tree and descended. At the bottom, the broad stump of a smaller tree rose from the Tree floor as a dais.

The silver-toned elders gathered in a circle. Their pale glow warmed the dais and offered deference to the middle-aged queen who stood at the center, a figure who appeared older by her youth than them in their near millennia.

It has passed, declared the stocky Elder Baath. *The la'du lira ben'cari has changed owners.*

Queen Mabsadora's thick black hair appeared combed in haste down the side of her face and her teal gaze gathered the elders and eldresses in one look. *There was no word from Tinker Belle such a thing was coming.* She shivered. *This is very unexpected.*

There hasn't been an unannounced passing in two thousand years, growled Elder Broug.

Might a pan have died? gasped Eldress Iol, a slender pixie with flowing silver hair.

Tinker Belle has failed, barked Eldress Egoura. She glared from a round, youthful face beneath a trim haircut close to her scalp. *I said it from the beginning that sending a tinker was a mistake.*

Do you now decide the wisdom of the aurora's word? Eldress Xemnair raised an eyebrow and her square jaw.

She is not our queen! Egoura snapped. *Mabsadora is! The aurora's role is not to lead governmental affairs.*

The aurora's role is to advise, chimed Elder Alban, the oldest and most handsome of the males with his broad shoulders, curly hair and beautiful face. *No aurora has the presence of mind to manage affairs of state.*

However well respected and honored, Baath insisted.

My queen, might something have happened to Tinker Belle? Againa's deep chime silenced the rest. *Could she be injured or somehow incapacitated? She alerted us to the passing between Kellogg and William. We have no reason to believe she would have failed to contact us should another passing have been necessary.*

It's only been twenty years! cried Egoura. *The la'du lira ben'cari hasn't been passed in so short a span since the minder wars!*

It doesn't mean anything has gone wrong. Elder Ugan scratched his crazy mop of hair. *Humans are rather hasty with things.*

It's not the humans we must blame but the bloody tinker! chimed Alban.

I was a tinker! Letheria rounded on Alban, spurring a litany of arguments among the rest.

Mabsadora silenced them with a raised hand as she gazed into thought, then regarded Againa. *What do you know, Againa?*

Nothing, at present, my queen, Againa chimed. *Tinker Belle hasn't sent me a messenger in some time, and the last missive was a warning about some human collective calling themselves 'Unionists.'*

Unionists? Bah! Humans and their politics! Broug growled. *Always bouncing between groups and individuals, groups and individuals. There is no balance in their collections.*

There is no balance in their hearts, chimed Eldress Anra Deia, a short, diminutive pixie with a strong nose. *You expect their governance to do for them as a whole what they cannot do for themselves, individually?*

This is just more evidence for ending our relationship with the pan, chimed Iol, which drew moans of sufferance from others. *I've said it before, we ought to be connected to the humans as little as possible! None at all, I should say!*

You'd say the same if the breeze startled you, Ugan chimed.

The histories are clear on how the pans saved us, chimed Eldress Auia, a pixie with full curves and the thinnest dress.

That was eight thousand years ago, snapped Iol.

Might the Unionists have taken the ben'cari? asked Mabsadora.

I think we would have known if the ben'cari had been taken by force, chimed Againa. *It has been tried in the past and the haraven at that time clearly knew what was happening, and she was with us when it happened!*

But would we? asked Anra Deia. *We do not share the haraven's connection with the pan. Only Tinker Belle would know for sure, and how can we know what has happened without speaking to her directly?*

We should consult the aurora, chimed Baath. *Only she might know without a missive from the haraven.*

Mabsadora pursed her lips. *I will consider our options. I will send for you when I have a response. Until then, please calm your wings and feathers and let them know all is well. Elder Againa, if you would remain behind?*

Sharing glances, the elders and eldresses bowed and curtsied away. Mabsadora approached Againa with a faint glance at his frame before she met his face. *Is there anything you aren't sharing with me, Againa?*

Againa stiffened. *Why would I do such a thing, my queen?*

I know you favor the tinker, chimed Mab. *I worry that favor could color your handling of her.*

I have no need to handle the haraven, queen, he chimed. *She is a mature pixie.*

Far younger than any haraven prior, chimed Mab. *And a tinker to boot. Tinkers aren't known for their constancy.*

You did not approve of the aurora overruling you, he chimed.

I approved of sending an experienced pixie, she chimed. *Not one barely out of her feather. The aurora has never interfered before.*

And you did not approve of her—

You use that word as if you could be a judge, elder.

If I am going to discuss the situation, I will discuss the facts of the matter, he chimed. *Which includes what might color your opinion, as well as mine.*

You overstep yourself.

I fulfill my duty as an elder advising a first among equals.

She cooled. *I would have you deal with the aurora. You have before.*

I would not entreat on the aurora without a summons, chimed Againa.

You have before.

And I was spared.

You might be again. She seemed to favor you. Her attention flickered to his frame again. *You smell like you were recently favored.*

His countenance darkened. *Are we done, your majesty?*

Mabsadora mulled something while returning his gaze, then waved him off. *Consider our blindness, Elder Againa. With Belle's last missive and now the mantle passing, it's fair to say chaos comes. Without foreknowledge, we may be bare to something against which we cannot prepare. It is my responsibility to prepare the flock for all such possibilities. While I cannot force you, I can ask you. Please, entreat the aurora.*

Elder Againa hesitated. *I will consider it.*

As he flew away, Mab took a slow breath. She could not explain why she felt as she did, but the passing of the ben'cari felt ominous in ways other interactions with the humans never had. Though queen for three hundred years now, she was new to the role by many standards, and yet in all her education from the previous queen and the histories, something felt off. Their connection with the pan went back to the Great Reformation, when the Alterworlds were planted and the ohnas first appeared, though even among the pixies in their long lives and memories, the exact history was murky of how the pan-haraven relationship formed. The aurora seemed to know and yet aurorae were never known for being clear with anyone, even pixie monarchs.

Mab shook her head. She never understood the humans — their short lives and constant changes in political positions baffled her. Pixies took centuries — sometimes generations — to debate ideas, and, more often than not, movements failed when the years disproved the need to change. Humans seemed to ache for it, even when they reached a pinnacle of prosperity. Their inability to remain still in even the best of conditions wove distrust among the pixies.

Protocol demanded an envoy of Avicarans travel to Eden for passing of the ben'cari. Mabsadora, herself, visited Eden when Tinker Belle assumed the role of haraven. Though the world seemed at peace then, she knew such things changed in instants among humans. With the unannounced passing, Mab suspected that not only had the mantle been passed in some form of desperation, but that Eden, herself, likely strained under the presence of violent struggle.

As Broug pointed out, the human obsession with groups always trumped the value of individual life, for humans obsessed more over outcomes than over the value of the present. For her, any violence wrought by such obsession with power produced appropriate outcomes.

As she took off, she scowled. *It's no more than they deserve.*

7

Waking

"What the hell was that?" Athyka made it onto the deck. Sailors ducked out of her way with quick, knuckled salutes. Tethered to the starboard rail opposite them, a startled white goat with a red blaze down its head bleated and raised its ears at her arrival.

Eldnor rubbed his face standing at the port rail. "The sun."

"What'd you see?" she inspected the verdant panoply of stars.

"Right now, not much." Eldnor held his face.

"Were you out here?"

"Yup," he said. "Suddenly the selfdamn sun rises at midnight. Then a rooster the size of Lubar's Peak crows."

Athyka turned from Pan's Peak to Eldnor. "Are you blind? Someone bring me a lantern!"

"I can see, sort of." He tried to focus on the brilliant white moon. "It's just fuzzy at the moment."

Athyka grit her jaw. "He passed the mantle."

"What?"

"He passed the mantle."

"*That's* what that was!?"

"Send a force to shore, immediately."

"Sure," Eldnor said. "Master Ithmus!"

"Agent Duluth." The head mage approached wearing standard-issue Unionist robes embroidered throughout in silver to indicate his role and position.

"Gather a landing party with another mage and a few sailors."

Hesitant, Ithmus obeyed.

"He passed the mantle?" Eldnor asked. "To who? The bitch?"

"Who else do you think?" Athyka growled. Men argued with Ithmus. "There a problem?"

"Lady Bonduquoy…" Ithmus hesitated. "The men are afraid to go ashore. I don't think we should go until we have a better plan than last night."

Athyka's gaze slid over the men. "They should be more afraid to stay here." She rested her hand on the knife in its sheath on her belt.

Ithmus winced. "What are you doing?" He raised a magical shield and then attempted to cut off her magic. His own flared in bouts of green light as he tried to counter her. Athyka raised an eyebrow. He exploded in a flash of blood and pureed flesh that bathed men and a shield Athyka raised just in time. Seconds passed before the sailors and mages realized their master was now liquid spray across their faces and down their throats. They stared, unsure what they saw, when the first man screamed.

Unable to see well, Eldnor almost vomited from the stench of flash-burned human.

"Now…" Athyka lifted her hand from her knife to pull a strand of black hair from her face.

Men rushed to prepare a ship's boat for launch while the mages retreated from the vomit-painted deck.

Athyka turned from the smell to Eldnor. "Go ashore and scout the beach and the inner tree line."

"Why?"

Athyka scowled.

"Fine." He raised his hands. "Be right back. What do you expect me to find?"

Athyka paused. "If you come back alive, or at least with all those you left with, that will be the confirmation we need."

"Of what?"

"A path to the pan."

8

The Room

"**O**pen in the name of the People's Union of Pangea!" The soldier pounded on the heavy wooden door with the bottom of his gauntlet. "Open or be burned out!"

"This is a holy place!" came the return cry of an old man. "We seek no quarrel with you! Leave us in peace!"

"This is your last chance!" the soldier barked. "Open now or suffer the consequences!"

"Please!" the voice begged. "Leave us in peace!"

"Open now or we will open it, ourselves!" the soldier roared and kicked the door.

Torchlight flickered over dozens of soldiers waiting outside the ancient stone building built along the base of one of the nine peaks overlooking the valley of Eden. Surrounded on both sides by tall row houses along the winding narrow street, opposite a small courtyard and an open view of the valley, the monastery stood out for its swirling multi-colored vines accentuating the intricate, blue-veined marble and tall, arched windows.

An interior crossbar slid away before the door cracked open. The soldier reared and kicked it open just as light pierced its edge. Inside, a monk splayed across the stone, knocked away by the door. Soldiers poured into the warm-lit chamber.

Fenren sat atop his horse behind the troops forcing their way in. "Why the Andonese?"

Sitting next to him clad in snug, metal-accented leather armor, Amra Alba frowned. Her short-cropped black hair rocked against the dim Eden night. "Everyone, Fenren."

"But the Andonese? They don't care about Edenic politics. They're ambassadors, not allies."

"They should. Politics affects us all."

"Right," Fenren said. Screams erupted from the monastery's upper floors. "Found the nuns."

Amra eyed the building as her horse's ears flicked in a cool breeze laced with smells of mineral water from thousands of garden pools throughout the valley.

"What're you going to do with them?"

"Fellow Baley has offered them protection," she said.

"You call dragging them out of their home, protection?"

"They won't let us in to search for Edenons." Her eyes narrowed. "All buildings will be searched."

Fenren shook his head. "Those men are going to search more than the buildings."

"Why would you care?" Amra eyed him askance.

"Why wouldn't you? I thought you wanted equal protection for everyone."

"Enemies of the state don't deserve protection," she said.

"They weren't enemies of the state two days ago. Suddenly the state changes and you get to own people because they didn't fight alongside you?"

"That's seditious, Fenren. If you aren't for us, you're against us. Are you for us, Fenren?"

"I'm here with the Unionists," Fenren said as more screams erupted. "But this seems a bit heavy handed."

"Sometimes being heavy handed is necessary."

"I don't disagree, but you get more flies with honey."

"Aren't you supposed to be at the palace?" she asked.

Fenren's horse danced. "I'm supposed to be on a warm beach in Utaly right now, not assisting your rape of helpless women."

"There will be no rape." She frowned.

"So, all those beautiful, soft-skinned, blue-haired beauties are being gathered to the palace just for their protection? Not the huge Edenon harem the parliament president is so fond of? I don't see anyone else banging down their door for *their protection.*"

She glared. "You don't sound so fond of our new Union."

"I'm fine with the Union," he shrugged. "I'd still rather be elsewhere."

"Not happy as Roschach's errand boy?"

Fenren scowled. "At least I don't serve a Baley."

She clucked her tongue.

"Agent Alba!" One of the soldiers approached from the monastery. "The search is underway. We're securing the nuns. What shall we do with the abbot?"

"Leave him." Amra glanced up the building. "Once the women are in the carts, perform a thorough search for any hiding places. I want any potential prisoners before we set fire to the place."

"Yes, agent." He saluted and returned to the building.

"You're not going to have anyone left to rule if you keep burning their buildings down," Fenren said.

"When the locals know their place and allow us to search their homes, there will be no trouble." Her horse danced at the edge in her voice. "They have nothing to fear if they have nothing to hide."

"Right." Fenren searched the ornate monastery covered in stone faces and historic events. The scene twisted darkly as a chorus of screaming mouths in the torchlight from the mob below. "I'm sure that's why everyone in town locks their doors at night."

Amra opened her mouth to speak when the midnight sky lit up as if by a noonday sun, turning from black to purple to gold to blue to a near white in seconds. Everyone froze when a crow thundered across the sky. Horses danced in terror, soldiers snatched out their weapons and the city, those already asleep, woke in horrific silence.

Fenren struggled to keep his yellow bay under control. Aurorae thrashed across the sky, warbling blue-green light across the brilliant gold bathing the world. As his horse bucked and spun, Fenren glanced through the small empty courtyard toward the Palace of the Pan sitting above the city. From the heart of the palace rose a faint, narrow column of fading yellow light.

The crow died and the midnight sunrise disappeared, leaving the same cloudy panoply of stars behind.

Countless horses' screams replaced the thunderous crow. Fenren tightened his grip on the reins and leaned close to the bay's ears. "WHOA, GIRL! WHOA!" He raised his voice to draw her attention and focus on him. He encouraged her to trot her nervousness down the nearest street before bringing her back. He stroked her neck and forced himself to project a calm he could not feel himself.

Amra struggled with her bucking mare while the soldiers scrambled out of the way. Fenren drew closer and snatched her horse by the bit and pulled it in a broad circle, using his horse to calm hers. Once they could slow, she took the reins back. "Thank you."

Fenren nodded. "Let's get back to the palace."

The two let their horses burn off energy by sprinting down streets bristling with people leaning out of doors and windows. They coursed down the stone-laid roads through the heart of the city and up the western road to the palace's Swinnen Gate. Once inside and halfway down the Central Road, a soldier on a horse blocked their path.

"Fenren Thicke?"

"Yes?" Fenren reined in.

"I've been sent to find you, sir." The soldier saluted. "Please come with me."

"What is it?"

"I was not told, sir," the guard said.

"Is it in the library?"

The guard nodded.

Amra followed them to the Square Al'Cular, then south to the main library complex on the south side of the road. At the grand entrance to the library, a single-room building built high above the complex that sank toward the waterfalls in varied steppes, the two passed through the broad archway and turned down a wide spiral staircase past windows overlooking the panoply of more dome-capped structures. They wandered down long hallways, across library chambers, small bridges and down into the main library building, a dome-topped room two hundred paces across filled by a maze of curved two-story bookshelves lined in walkways around about a large circular librarian's command post staffed by a small army of bookkeepers. The library was empty of patrons and a ring of guards sequestered the librarians to their station.

"What is it?" Fenren reached the captain in the center of the large chamber.

"Agent Thicke?"

"Yes?"

"Please, this way." The captain led them across the chamber, past high shelves and fields of low-lit tables to a large archway leading to the next library chamber. Once outside, he turned left on a small ramp leading around the rear of the main library's circular building, then turned inward among high rock walls of the plateau, emptying out into a tiny gorge set into the rockface under an angled wall admitting faint city light reflecting off low clouds.

Trees and bushes lined the walls of an alcove garden centered by a small pool of water hugged by bushes and benches. The bare warmth of gaslights and handheld torches interrupted an aroma of fresh-cut grass and roses filling the cool evening air. A thin stream of water slid down the rock wall at the back, sourced by a man-made cut in the stone, down gentle falls that pooled near the far side and then wove in a stream to a pool in the center of the garden pressed against a small, pentagonal sitting area with four benches. Soldiers stood across the grass and among the floral bushes while an old man stood off to the side under the grip of a guard.

"What is it?" Thicke picked out the officer in charge.

"This whole place just, lit up." The major spiraled his finger round about the space.

Thicke searched the garden. "Where? Did someone see?"

The major pointed his thumb at the old man and led him to the gardener garbed in simple black trousers, a white blouse and green vest. In the torchlight, the old man's eyes were almost white — frosted, blind and wet with running tears.

"Did the light do that to him?" Thicke asked.

"No, sir," said the old man. His bushy mustache ruffled from his heavy breath full of emotion.

"Been stone blind since birth," said the major.

"Then how could he know?"

"Cuz I saw it, sir, I did." The man choked a sob. "Ain't never seen nothing before now, but I saw it." He breathed. "A- a tower. A … line, a broad line, like a- like the trunk of a tree, shot straight up out of the garden pool." Tears welled as he clutched at his hat. "It was … beautiful."

"You *saw* it?"

"Yessir," the man wept. "Magic, it must be. Great magic."

Thicke shared a look with Amra before turning to the pool. "What can you show me? Did you just see the light? Could you see more?"

"I've never seen it before." The man motioned at the bubbling pool at the heart of the garden butted against a small pentagonal stone patio with four benches. "But it came upward from the stone and the water, lit up the benches and…" He choked down another sob. "I never seen a bench before!"

"Got it." Thicke crossed the plush grass to the smooth stonework and fished out his crystal torch. A rotating yellow light appeared inside a moment before the entire courtyard lit up as if under a brilliant, sourceless noonday sun. Soldiers gasped in shock as mutters of "ohna" echoed within the tiny alcove. Kneeling over the pool, he shed his coat and hiked his sleeve before sliding his arm into the cold water to inspect the smooth stone base and walls. He paused, returned his hand to a smaller, triangular rock fit at the top of two other stones, just under the lip above the surface. He pressed; it clicked. The water sank and swirled downward. When it disappeared, the stones descended in a staggered spiral staircase.

"After you," Amra said and raised an eyebrow.

Fenren descended the dripping stairs a full rotation before reaching the archway of a small, dry room. Numerous carved golden panels lined the round chamber's one curving wall beneath a dome marked in latitudinal and longitudinal lines. Fenren, Amra and two officers gazed in wonder as the crystal torch's unnatural lighting brought the cool, musty room and intricate goldwork to life.

Against the far wall stretched a broad golden plate, a topographic map of the whole of Pangea. Though yellow in its golden plating, the texture of the intricate map indicated frost along its northern and southernmost edges, heavy forests and grasslands inward along an endless stretch of desert crossing the heart of the continent but for heavy jungle at each east and westernmost end. To the left of the continent, hung a plate of an island ripped in two, dotted by tiny islets and marshes. On Pangea's right hung a plate that looked like a ball cut apart and laid flat. Other plates covered the remaining walls, gilded in various languages stacked atop each other. A grin grew across Fenren's face as he reached up to brush the map of the continent with his gloved fingers, then widened as he touched the map of the island.

"That's Algueda."

"What's that?" Amra touched the other map.

Fenren raised an eyebrow. "You don't know what that is?"

"No," Amra said. "Should I?"

"That is Earth."

Amra hesitated. "Bullshit."

"No, it's true." Fenren took the room. "It's behind here, somewhere."

"What? Earth?"

"Sort of. Major, alert Fellow Roschach that the room has been found. Immediately."

The major saluted and disappeared up the spiral stairs.

"Earth is … behind these walls?" Amra asked.

"Close enough." Fenren walked along the panels and scanned for catches. "It's to Algueda."

"Seriously?" Amra's eyes flared.

"Yeah," said Fenren. "If we can get it open? Algueda to Eden in ten seconds."

"I apologize, Agent Thicke." The captain ducked his head. "But … what will get us to Algueda from here?"

"A rimshift, captain." Fenren tilted his head up at the room's high seams. "A rimshift hides behind these walls. If we can get it open, we can get Athyka, her crew, and that self-forsaken mantle here within the week."

"And if we can't?" the captain asked.

"Then we will ignite the largest land war in Pangea since the Minder Conflicts. A war we will not win."

The captain gulped. "Well."

"We just have to trust Athyka to do what she does best — hunt people down," Fenren said.

"What are her chances?" Alba asked. "I've only met her in passing."

"William is a politician, not a military strategist," Fenren said. "But Algueda gives him the advantage. If he can keep Athyka at bay with that island, there's a chance he'll win. For now. If he tries to fight her on any kind of even footing? I know Athyka. He will lose, but only if he fails to use Neverland."

"What is it about that island that scares people so much?" Alba asked.

"Somewhere in the history of the pan, some practitioner helped shape this island into the ultimate defense against pan's enemies," said Fenren. "The pan can retreat to this island that kills anyone but him. Honestly, if

William can just keep that island between him and Athyka? We may never get it from him. There's a reason we tried so hard to get him before he reached that island. All the pan really has to do on Neverland to survive is just keep his wits."

9

Costs

April clutched Peter's limp form as the distant sunrise warmed the moist morning air. Tears dried up hours ago as she rocked her unconscious child. She sang into his ear, desperate for him to wake. She needed his voice, his life, his love and his eyes.

April could not see.

William woke to indescribable pain. Pushing from the cold coals of last night's fire revealed the horror of what happened after he passed the mantle. He gasped in agony and hacked as he sucked in ashes from the pit. Every attempt to pull pieces of brittle wood and coal from his melted face drew flashes of pain so sharp that he dry sobbed and moaned.

While April waited for Peter to wake, she recalled William telling her in the dark of their early nights together, after passions had subsided, how he became the pan. Every new pan fell into a deep sleep that lasted most of the next day. How would Peter, a boy, react? Would he wake sooner? Later?

Most of all, Neverland's newfound silence scared her most. Even the breeze slept. Had Will's promises been for naught if the island slumbered as surely as the new pan?

William managed to open his good right eye and searched the early morning blue. To his surprise, his gaze did not penetrate the deep shadows around him as they once did. Without the mantle of the pan, he was just another mage — not even a wizard class.

"April?" William attempted to speak. Hacking erupted before blood and puss spattered from his throat scorched by the fire-heated air. His lungs shuddered and he collapsed to the grass.

"I love you, William," April's voice died.

William managed to catch his breath and crawl to April. He touched her arm but scanned the clearing for Tinker Belle.

"I haven't heard her," April answered his unspoken query.

"I'm-" William whispered, afraid to use his throat. "Sorry! I'm sorry!"

April rocked Peter while tears slipped down her cheeks.

William set the good side of his forehead on the grass.

"It's been quiet," April breathed.

William sat up and inspected the impotent wall. He tugged on unresponsive roots, then looked up in sudden horror. Not a call, bark or howl echoed throughout the jungle. William realized his worst nightmare had come true.

Neverland slept, as did its protection of his family.

His face paled and good eye drooped closed. He whispered as loud as he could with cracked lips. "It was … my best option." He crawled to her to caress her cheek. "You know I would give anything to save you. I will do anything to save you both."

As tears drooled down her face, she opened her eyes.

William gasped. "Oh- oh self, April."

Her emerald eyes were ghosted white. "I loved you, William."

"A- April," he stuttered. "I'm so sorry. Great Self, I'm so, so sorry. I- had no idea! I love you, April! I would never have done such a thing if I'd known! I'm so sorry! I'll do anything I can, everything to protect you and Peter."

"I forgive you," April whispered.

William leaned forward and kissed her.

Using all the weight she could, she slapped his face off hers and spat onto the ground. Her voice broke. "Then do it."

William quivered in agony from where she struck the melted side of his face. Stretched across the ground, he fought to maintain consciousness. Minutes passed before he stumbled to his feet and swooned. He faced Peter and April, took a slow breath and flexed his weak, personal magic.

He exhaled with relief, having feared it would fail as all the others had. Gazing upon his family one last time, he crawled through the wilted vine wall and disappeared.

Quivering in rage, April heard his footsteps fade away. Terror replaced her anger as he left. Clutching Peter, she cleared her throat. "William?" Her voice grew. "William? William!"

Clutching Peter, April shrieked William's name. She buried her face into Peter's crimson mane as sobs wracked her.

Struggling to see through his tears, William never turned back.

10

The Fall

D appled sunlight painted the jungle in glowing spots as the group of ten mages and thirty sailors cut their way eastward across the northern base of Pan's Peak. Athyka stopped in the middle of the forming path to catch her breath. Though the island slept, she still felt exhausted from broiling humidity. The sailors and mages had been silent since losing Ithmus. Eldnor winced at each bright light and Gregory struggled to stay quiet.

"Athyka?" Eldnor paused when he realized she had stopped moving.

Athyka loosened her blouse at the neck, tugged it open and flapped it to air her top. "This selfdamn heat."

"Are you alright?"

She pulled her canteen and took a controlled sip when she wanted to gulp it down. "I'm fine." She looked to Eldnor. "How do you feel?"

"Fine," Eldnor said.

"Good." She scanned the jungle and tapped the hilt of the ice knife sheathed in her belt. "William passed the mantle, which means if he's playing guard, he'll only have his magic to protect him. Gregory, you grew up in the jungle, correct?"

"South Alderland," Gregory said.

"Deploy out and strafe." She searched the canopy. "If he comes at us, I don't want him expecting you."

"What about Neverland?"

"It's asleep." She pointed. "If there's only one time you can go out there, this might be it."

A grin crawled across his face and he approached the flora.

"And Gregory?"

He paused.

"Don't kill him."

A shadow of disappointment passed over his face. "Of course, not, mum." He disappeared.

Eldnor looked after Gregory. "Sure he won't die in there? Everyone else seems to."

"Gregory was not sent because he's big and scary, but because he was a southland shadow."

Eldnor's eyebrows climbed. "Seriously?"

Athyka nodded. "One of Alderland's elite."

"What brought him over?"

"Same as Fen," Athyka said. "Money."

Eldnor harrumphed.

"But Fen also came for Roschach."

"You'd think he could be loyal to a cause, too," said Eldnor.

Athyka scanned the jungle.

"Don't we need more strategy than this?" asked Eldnor.

"He's cornered," Athyka said. "And he's down to his mage powers, alone. No mantle, no great strength or speed or healing. He's just like us, only he doesn't have an ohna, either."

"Baleys are supposed to be powerful mages."

"No one who relies solely on external forces can truly grow strong, themselves," Athyka led them onward. "The Baley family leaned so long on that mantle, I'd wager he can throw fireballs and arcs, and I doubt he's even accurate. Besides…" She gestured at the mages at the fore and aft of their small party. "The moment he tries to form an attack, they'll descend upon him like hungry dogs."

As the morning heat built, mages drenched in sweat opened their formal long coats. Soldiers clad in leather and metal plating tugged open their necklines as deep as they dared. Their unwashed bodies reeked in the powerful heat after sailing for weeks across icy waters.

"To hell this heat," Eldnor gasped. "Weeks of freezing weather from Richter's Deep and we walk into a selfdamn oven."

Athyka wiped sweat from her brow as she eyed the silent, motionless jungle. "I worry what will happen if all this wakes up around us."

"I thought the silence was good, too," said Eldnor. "Now it's freaking me out."

"C'mon." Athyka marched onward as the mountain curved slowly to the south. "This is taking long enough. I thought this would be two miles. It's been two hours."

"This place is crazy," Eldnor muttered. "I've been staring at the same landmark, but we've turned. We did turn, right?"

"Yes." Athyka panted and fished open her neckline enough to draw in the air. "Selfdamnit. Where's that breeze?"

They pressed when the mages ahead paused to gaze upward. Everyone joined them.

The canopy of a massive tree stuck out around the far bend in the terrain. Though still a distance away, they made it out through the jungle flora.

"Great Self," Eldnor breathed. "Is that? No, that's not *the* Tree. But ..."

"It's definitely an Al'Cular," Athyka said. "But it's rather young."

"That's young?" Eldnor turned.

"The Graelan Al'Culars are millions of years old," she said. "The La'Du Graela Al'Cular once reached two miles into the sky before the draco wars."

"What happened?"

"Set the thing on fire," Athyka said. "The Graelans saved it, but it's nothing like it once was. It's an open face hollow now. Only reached half its original height, which is still incredibly tall."

"Never heard that," said Eldnor. "Hard to imagine such a thing. Have you seen it?"

"No," said Athyka. "Few humans have, and they're all long dead. C'mon, let's move."

The group pressed onward when they came across a low, bubbling creek.

"Don't drink anything here," she said. The men turned outward, watching the thick jungle despite poor visibility. Athyka scanned the tree line when a faint thought drifted to her — the faint image of her face.

She turned, attempting to narrow in on the source of that thought, when something punched her in the chest. She gasped.

Eldnor spun — an arrowhead quivered from the top of Athyka's left breast.

"DOWN!" he roared. Athyka slumped to the ground as the mages raised their hands in search of an attacker. Eldnor made a guess and unleashed a wave of earth through the jungle that vaulted trees and bushes in a rush of dust and scree. One knee gave out under him as his strength faltered.

Mages unleashed a wave of fireballs, shards of ice and arcs of lightning into the jungle around them in a blitzkrieg.

"Cease fire!" Eldnor croaked. Dust, steam and smoke billowed from the piles of scree. He crawled to Athyka, who lay on her side and struggled to breathe.

She snatched him by the vest and hauled him close while gasping for air. "Get him!"

"Yes, ma'am." He pulled the ice knife from her hand. Though less experienced, he focused on the trees parallel to their path standing beyond his initial blast zone. In a flash freeze, tree bark exploded in a successive rip, though few trees collapsed. Athyka had done better, but every sailor and mage ducked at the concussive blasts. Tree splinters whizzed past them, bounced off magical shields and buried into other bushes and trees nearby. Tops of the smaller trees bent and snapped in a long, echoing crash. Sunlight filled the jungle floor long devoid of sunlight. "Do you see him!?"

"No," answered one crouching mage before his left shoulder twisted and his body slammed to the ground. The rock that struck him bounced off into the jungle.

"He's getting through our shields!" a frantic mage scanned the forest.

"He's not using his magic!" Eldnor barked. "Look for his magic signature!"

Four soldiers burst into flame on the opposite side from the injured mage. Eldnor returned to Athyka's wound. The fletching was higher than the arrowhead, indicating a high shot. He scanned the jungle around and above. A faint shadow caught his eye up high to his left. He raised his ohna terra forward of himself, away from the shadow but focused with the ice knife while squatting behind one of the soldiers. Already exhausted from brief use of the ohnas, he flashed the group of trees nearer the shadow.

The explosion caught the soldier next to him and drove both over Athyka, who screamed as the arrow twisted inside of her. The mages snatched them off Athyka. Eldnor pointed. "There!"

The mages turned when a fireball caught one in the head at the jaw.

"Shit!" The mage behind him wiped off liquified human for the second time in a day.

The remaining two mages converged to bring shields to protect the group when a man's scream ripped through the air, followed by a bellowing laugh.

The group waited with shields and weapons raised when Gregory appeared through the trees hauling William by wrists wrenched behind his back.

William stumbled into view. Reaching the circle, William tripped and fell despite Gregory's grip. Two pops echoed from William's shoulders before he screamed and hacked blood.

"That's right, ya fucker!" Gregory raised his boot and stamped down on William's head, drove it into the ground and knocked him unconscious.

"Hold!" Eldnor staggered through the circle as Gregory raised his boot again. "WAIT, selfdamnit!"

"What?" Gregory's eyes narrowed. "Why?" He let his foot rest on William's back to keep him pinned to the ground.

"We got him." Eldnor bent over the quivering lord of Eden. "Don't kill him."

"What fun is that?" Gregory spat.

"We need to find out about his mantle, retard!" Eldnor spat. "And Athyka's been hurt."

Gregory looked to Athyka.

"What'd you do to his face?" Eldnor leaned closer. "You barely kicked him."

"I didn't do that," Gregory said.

"Bag him up and prepare him to move." Eldnor straightened. "We gotta get her back to the ship."

"How bad is she?" Gregory asked.

"Just get the selfdamn pan ready, Gregory!" Eldnor returned to Athyka as Gregory fished out cord from one of his pockets to bind William's elbows.

Eldnor knelt next to Athyka, who focused on breathing. "Make a litter and prepare to take her back to the ship. Gregory? Deal with the pan. I will go deal with his family."

"Why do you get to go get his bitch?" Gregory protested.

"Because Lady Baley has to be unspoiled so we have something we can threaten her with."

Gregory hauled William over his shoulder and spat at Eldnor. "C'mon, boys." The remaining mage and five sailors followed him into the jungle. "Let's move."

Eldnor wiped the spit from his tunic with his glove, flicked it into the forest, directed four sailors to return Athyka to the ship and signaled to those remaining to follow him deeper into the jungle. "Let's go, before this island wakes up."

1 1

Securing the Baleys

Hours passed while Peter lay unconscious in April's arms. She had left him once to empty her bladder and gather food from the supplies William retrieved. Fear built as Peter failed to wake. Midday sunlight burned her skin when she caught wind of distant explosions. She hugged Peter all the tighter.

Neverland breeze cooled as the sun climbed above the Tree's canopy and drowned her in its wind-washed shadow. Peter's body broiled with unnatural heat, and though she sweat from holding him, she would not let him go. In her heart, she feared William was gone.

A year past, William spun her across the ballroom at her beloved annual Dogwood Gala. As always for her parties, he played a delightful trophy husband throughout the evening. She pulled him through an endless train of high-ranking couples, heads of state and politicos she knew or wanted to meet. Though he encountered many in his role as pan, she could lead that night in formal dress and proper fun. Like a young stag wooing his besotted doe, they danced and drank and laughed away the night. Even now she recalled with fondness for her charmed life and beloved husband.

Hours of post-gala intimacy she often so relished ended long before sunrise when William froze. A vision overwhelmed him of a figure stealing the ohna marina, the first power over water, from its anchorage in the alterworld Kregge. Scouts and emissaries sent forth did not return.

The annual gala had served as an opportune kickoff for trade conferences a decade in the making. Pressure to stay and arbitrate discouraged William's pan-driven duty to seek out and return the ohna. His ability to speak to any person of any language — lingual or magical — set him at the center of peace and trade negotiations. Leaving would unsettle planning by countless trade officiators and could cascade stock changes, shift monetary stability, fracture long-desired peace accords and more.

William delayed his departure with confidence that he could follow the ohna once the conferences ended, but parties delayed and extended conference proceedings. His presence was demanded at meetings he never before had been requested to attend. Problems arose at every lull.

He woke one night knowing a second ohna had been stolen. Unable to further delay, William headed for the ohna marina, but en route felt the loss of more. As theft continued, their distribution obscured his ability to hone upon any single one. Meanwhile uprisings erupted in stable territories and dismissive border disputes broiled in open war. Dissonant voices blamed him in parliament for the instability while they stirred populations to revolt.

April's role shifted from trophy wife to peacemaker between cross-continental dignitaries. When William left at his mantle's insistence, relationships crumbled under tides of finger pointing. Pan-arbitrated peace accords devolved into votes of no-confidence. Unionists flooded the parliament to blame William's failure to protect the powers, then vilified his absence when he left to recover them.

It wasn't until they headed for Richter's Deep that William came to understand how orchestrated everything had been — the Unionists had arranged the meetings to keep him in state when he needed to leave, created strife in secret, blamed it upon him in public and destroyed his forces with powers they had no right to wield; whose theft from their holy sites threatened the continued existence of the continent and alterworlds beyond.

Her fairytale life evaporated. Now faced with starvation, an unconscious boy, dead husband and complete blindness, she struggled in vain to fight off the terror welling in her breast.

April sang a hymn from temple, hoping to entreat the Great Self to their plight and soothe her soul. Pressing the side of her mouth to Peter's forehead as she rocked him, she sang, hoping for him to wake, and inhaled the smell of her little boy — the wild nature of his youth and indomitability of his spirit.

"I used to love that song." The voice of an unfamiliar man ruptured her peace.

Her mouth kept moving, but her voice gave out.

That wasn't William's voice.

"Don't stop," the voice growled. "It's beautiful."

April's heels tore the hem of her dress as she dragged herself and Peter away from the voice.

"Just like the rest of you," the voice continued.

Gentle bootfalls on plush grass encircled her.

"Your fire, your tenacity," the man continued. "Your red hair." The voice approached. "I love redheads. Especially ones like you, with the pale skin and freckles."

April gripped Peter.

"I bet you're just one sweet lay," the voice leered. "I never wondered why William married you. Though, I can't imagine how he put up that mouth of yours."

April dragged Peter toward the Tree roots.

Men laughed.

"You're just making it easier for my men," the man said. "They like it when the women squirm."

Abject terror filled her breast. She stopped moving, confident the men would never allow her to reach the Tree. Fingers snatched her hair and drew a cry from her mouth as the voice pressed his lips to her ear.

"You know, I can't figure it out. Why did he give it to you, a worthless bitch, before coming off to fight us, hm?"

"Wh- what?" she breathed.

He took another firm grip on her hair.

"Why did he give you the mantle?" he growled.

"He did-" she stopped herself. "I- I'll never tell you."

"It doesn't matter," the voice growled. "I'll have it soon enough. The mantle will be ours, you will belong to my men, and I'll give your boy, here, to Matriarch Damian, herself, as a gift. The boy will never remember his filthy parents. He'll not remember you or anything you stand for. People like you … make me want to bring back crucifixion."

Lips smiled against her ear.

"Then again, why not?"

Peter was yanked from her hands.

"Wrap 'em up," Eldnor snapped. "Let's get back to the ship."

Rough, groping hands wandered her body as she struggled in vain to rage against them. After the initial molestation, they bound her in ropes and threw her over a shoulder.

"You can go to hell!" she managed.

"Oh, my dear…" The fingers found her hair and wrenched her face upward as his breath washed over her mouth. "You're truly about to find out what that actually means."

12

Interrogation

With the bitch and boy in hand, Eldnor's hackles rose the longer it took to return to the West Bay. Every step of his boot, crunch of a leaf or snap of a twig thundered in his ears against the island's absolute silence. Brilliant sunset amber cast long, jagged shadows through the jungle as they pressed westward along the narrow path south of Pan's Peak. Coughs of the sailors and mages startled the quiet. When the sun set and the West Bay came into view through distant hills, Eldnor leaned toward the mage behind him. "When did the Tree flash last night?"

"About an hour past sunset?" the mage shrugged.

Eldnor's face tightened. "Pick up the pace. Let's go."

Shadows deepened and the West Bay appeared no closer as time wore on. Men grew nervous enough to draw their knives as they moved through the jungle. Silence screamed at them.

"Wait, wait, wait," Eldnor panted and drew the group to a stop. He raised his hand for everyone to listen as he scanned the darkness. Rushing heartbeats stuffed his ears, drowning out the silence. He pinched his nose and popped his ears to clear the building pressure of heat rising through his body. For a moment, he could hear the silence.

Something buzzed.

Eldnor spotted a large bug just visible over the shoulder of one of the sailors in the rear who seemed unaware of it. Unsure if he could wield the ohna well enough, he nodded at another sailor, who also spotted the bug. Now aware everyone watched at him, the sailor struggled not to move. The others slowly raised the flats of their swords and moved into a position to try and swipe off the bug without injuring the man. He squeezed his eyes and stood still as they rushed the bug. It bolted into the air and flew away. A mage found no visible damage on his armor and shared a nod.

Relieved, Eldnor prepared to lead them onward when the rising buzz of a swarm filled the air. A great host rushed in from the trees over the mage and three sailors. "RUN!"

The group bolted forward, leaving the three soldiers to be stabbed again and again with long needle stingers. Their screams carried through the air that exploded with sound as Neverland woke in a rush outward. The group raced along the path and Eldnor killed several beasts that attacked them at the front.

A frenzy of magic erupted between Eldnor, the mages and the men, who dropped April and Peter to fight off beasts rushing in. Moments later, the fight ended as the predators raced away from the group.

"What the hell?" panted one of the men.

"Get the boy and the woman," barked Eldnor. "Move!"

They rushed down the path with swords and powers raised. Minutes later they broke from the jungle out onto the beach and paused to catch their breath. The Sumter lay north along the sand where they lost the leftenant the previous night. Waiting sailors waved from where they had landed a ship's boat from Unity's Light. The group boarded and hauled for Unity's Light sitting in the middle of the bay.

The night watch officer met them at the portside rail and directed sailors to receive the prisoners.

"Put the woman in the brig and the boy in the empty cabin next to Athyka's and post a guard," Eldnor said. "Where is Athyka?"

"The lady is in her cabin. She said for you to report immediately."

Eldnor glanced at the bay. "Pull away from the island, officer. Just outside the lagoon."

"Why?" the officer asked.

"This bay is a death trap."

The officer glanced at the overturned ship. "As you command."

Minutes later, Eldnor stepped into Athyka's quarters. "Athyka?"

Lying upon her side, Athyka half turned from the far wall. A sheen of heavy sweat painted her pale skin. "Report."

"Bitch is in the brig." Eldnor stuck his thumb out. "Boy is next door."

"Finally," Athyka said. "I need– I need you to do something." Her labored words gurgled. Exposed with her dress untied and peeled back, her wound had thawed and swelled. Puss oozed and blood congealed along the wound's edges.

Eldnor inspected it.

"Why didn't you have the mages do it?" he asked.

"After what I did to Ithmus?"

"Fair point." Eldnor sat on the bed behind her. "Is this in your lung?"

"No," she said. "Barely, I think. A graze?"

"I have a few ideas," he said. "What do you want me to do?"

"I want you to pull it out, then freeze the injury through."

"Seriously?"

"Yes," she said. "It works in colder climates — slows the injury. Seal it with ice, then you can heal it as best you can. Here." She held up the ice knife as best she could without twisting her arm.

"Hold still, I might be able to do a bit more than freeze it through." He plucked the knife and pressed his hand to the side of the wound near her neck and shoulder. His thumb curled under the arrow and he leaned over her to eye the crude arrowhead sticking out the front. "Where the hell did he get these? They look ancient."

"I don't care," Athyka growled, then cried out as he snapped the arrowhead off the front. "FUCK, Eldnor!"

"Not done yet." He gripped the arrow.

"Just gimme a selfdamn- YOU SUNUV-!" she cried out.

Having yanked out the bloody arrow, Eldnor tossed it aside and reached around to press his palms on the entry and exit wounds like a vise. She screamed and thrashed as magic scored the wound and healed it. For her, the cold burned like hell. Then, she sank panting against the bed. Sweat poured from her skin and her remnant energy faded. Eldnor spared a glance into the loose front of her garment and popped an eyebrow with appreciation, then inspected the rear wound. A small mound of scar flesh indicated the entry point, as would the front. Skin encircling the tiny bumps was discolored and would likely remain that way.

"Gimme," she managed. "Give me the ohna."

"But, Athyka, you can barely-"

"Give me the selfdamn ohna, Eldnor," she managed.

"Fine." He handed it to her. His eyes fluttered before a look of concern fell over him. "Are you alright?"

Half-rolling to her back and holding the ohna in her left hand, she grabbed his forearm.

"What- are you-?" Eldnor dropped to his knees and his back arched.

When she took the ohna back, something in her tapped Eldnor without her prompting and sucked energy through their gentle touch. Delicious and addictive, she wanted to take it all, but Eldnor's skin purpled and veins bulged. In a panic, she yanked her hand away and he collapsed to the deck. She scrambled from the bunk and leaned down. "Eldnor! Eldnor!?"

Ragged breaths slid across the wood next to his gaping mouth. She had never done that without specific intent. She rolled, gripped his arm and returned some of that precious energy. He blinked, bewildered, and clutched his head.

"Selfdamnit, what just happened?"

Athyka kept her contact and reached out for his mind. His face slackened and hand hovered as she erased the last few moments, replacing it with a simple trip in a crowded cabin. "Are you alright?"

"Huh?" Eldnor pushed up from the floor. "Yeah, sorry. Just- lost my balance I guess. Are you alright?"

"Yes, of course," she said. "You healed me. You don't remember?"

Eldnor shrugged as Athyka cursed to herself.

"April is in the brig?"

"Yes," he said.

"And the boy is in the other room?"

"Yup, and out like a light."

Athyka paused. "What do you mean, out?"

"He's unconscious," Eldnor said.

"William was awake," Athyka said. "Did you find April awake?"

"Yeah," Eldnor said. "She was singing to the boy."

"But the boy's been out? This entire time?"

"Yeah ... why?"

Athyka's eyes narrowed. "What if he gave the mantle to the boy?"

"To the kid? Why in hell would he give the boy the power? Especially when he decided to attack us with a bow and arrow?"

Athyka sat down on her bunk. "How do we verify?"

"We wait for him to wake," Eldnor said.

"We can't wait, if it's a magical sleep," Athyka said. "We need to know now."

"How do you expect me to find out how he gave the mantle to the boy? I never learned the mantle resonance test. That's out of my league, even with the ohnas. I thought you might know."

"Devkoron would know," said Athyka. "Did you try waking him? We could interrogate him."

"Didn't care about the kid, really."

Athyka grimaced. "Eldnor, wait outside for me. I'm going to change, then we're going to go talk with the woman."

Minutes later, Eldnor led the way into the hold. A lone lantern warmed one of a pair of iron-barred cells circled by dozens of lecherous gazes gleaming from the black. The air reeked of unwashed sailors packed tightly to leer upon the redheaded beauty curled up near the rear of the cell against the wooden bulkhead, unmoving and exhausted.

Bullnecked and with arms as thick as most men's thighs, the sergeant at arms stood watch over the cell's only door to keep the others at bay. He turned at Athyka's approach, unlocked and opened the door to admit them.

Under the light of the lone lantern, Eldnor entered the cell and knelt to the right of April. Athyka stood over her. The three of them filled the tiny space.

"Is she hurt?" Athyka asked.

Eldnor shook his head. "She passed out from exhaustion, but I think she's fine."

Athyka touched April's feet and flushed her with a burst of energy to wake her. April flailed, disoriented, before she retreated against the bulkhead. Panic gripped her. Her breasts pulsed upward with breath, drawing grunts of interest.

"Sleep well?" Athyka sneered.

April drew her knees up against her breasts to hide them and hold onto something.

"Come now, it's impolite not to speak to your hosts," said Eldnor.

"I can promise you a few things in return for some information I want," Athyka's voice found its edge. "Like security, for one. I can make sure you aren't touched. I just want to know a few things."

April struggled not to quiver before them.

"Or, I could leave you to the crew," Athyka said. A chorus of hoops and vile catcalls erupted from the audience.

April's face tightened.

"I could make sure you're fed." Athyka cut off the men by raising her hand. "You wouldn't worry about hunger. You'd almost ride in comfort. Even get some bedding in here, away from all the men."

April kept her eyes to the floor.

"We might drag you behind the ship as we wind through the coral." Athyka flicked her nails. "I hear sharks are pretty heavy along the reefs. Lots of things to eat out there."

April did not respond.

"I could even offer you protection when we return to Pangea," Athyka continued. "You're likely to be considered a political prisoner – after all, your husband was the tyrant, not *you*. He's older and obviously in command of the injustices he's committed. We wouldn't have to pin his crimes on you. You'd be mandated to some nice prison or a mild form of house arrest or something of the like."

As Athyka continued, April's breath evened out. Eldnor raised an eyebrow at the disdain that crawled across her face.

"Or we might tie you to the mast and use you for dart practice." Athyka's voice hardened. "There's all—"

"Where…" April's eyes cracked open, looking downward. "Where is my son? Where is Peter?"

"The boy? Peter? He's sleeping like a rock." Athyka crossed her arms. "Why?"

"He's my son!" April snapped. "I want him back!"

"Now…" Athyka gripped April's chin. "I want to know why he gave it to the boy."

April froze. "What do you mean?"

"I mean…" Athyka leaned in. "I want to know what that sunuva bitch hoped to accomplish by giving the mantle to his son? What was his purpose?"

"What're you talking about?" April stammered. "He didn't give Peter the mantle. A child pan—!"

Eldnor slammed his fist into her face and sent her across the cell floor. Her head smacked the bars of the next cell with a dull ring. Two of her teeth rolled across the hay matting. Blood drooled through her gaping lips. A moan ripped from her throat.

Athyka's fluttering gaze darted to Eldnor — he had hit April by Athyka's mere wish. She hadn't even tried to command him or come close to touching him. Was it coincidence?

"I'm talking about the sleeping boy, a boy who refuses to wake up, a boy who has been given the pan's ben'cari."

April sat up, but cradled her head lest they should try to hit her again.

"I know all about it," Athyka continued. "I want you to tell me how to take it from him before I try killing him to get it."

April took a long, slow breath. Fear drained from her. In her heart, April knew she would never leave this ship, alive.

Athyka raised an eyebrow in surprise at April's moment of courage.

Still fighting terror, April turned her bleeding face upon Athyka, revealed ghosted white eyes and spewed a mouthful of blood upon her.

Athyka recoiled in fury. "FUCK!"

April closed her eyes before Eldnor could rear his fist and waylay her again. Snatching the front of her dress, he laid into her. April wailed, raising her delicate hands in a desperate attempt to soften his vicious blows. She snatched at him and caught a necklace when the touch of a small stone ring sent fire through her. April screamed as her hand clenched around the ohna.

"Gimme that!" Athyka stepped over Eldnor and grabbed April's fist.

April threw a punch at Eldnor when Athyka snatched out the ice knife and nailed April's left wrist to the wall, forcing her fingers to pop open and release the ohna from the magical burn marks steaming from her palm.

April wailed, thrashing as her hand boiled in pain, growing colder until all sensation died.

Eldnor took a firm grip on her chin and punched her again, sending her against the bars of the next cell.

Somehow free from the knife, April hugged her hand against her and paused. Her blind eyes widened.

Her hand was gone.

All she felt now was a jagged icy blunt where her hand had broken off at the wrist.

Madness wormed through the widening cracks of her mind. Horror descended as reality slipped away. April didn't hear the two of them leave screaming at each other, barely noticed the sound of a fight erupting outside the cell or the sergeant at arms go down fighting. Bare feet rushed into the cell before a dozen hands tore her clothes and explored her intimate places, places only William had ever lovingly been. She didn't notice the fight among her rapists as they fought over how to violate her.

April was gone.

13

Pixie's Fury

Tinker Belle's mind, body and heart resisted waking. The first thought to pierce the murk was her new connection to Peter. Peter was now pan.

Her heart crashed against her chest. Tinker Belle sucked air.

Where was he? Where was William? Where was- where was she?

Alarm forced her mind to the surface, and she opened her eyes. The world was dark. Was she blind? Blinking eyelashes revealed something wrapped against her face. She pulled her arms and tried bending her legs to find her entire body bound. When her wing shifted, she flinched — it was broken.

A hiss cut the air and her bindings vibrated.

She thrashed and cringed when she twisted her wing, again. *Self!*

As vibrations descended upon her, she panicked. Her eyes lit up in bright yellow. Fisting her fingers, she blew apart the strands in a burst of sparks and fire. A spider's web burned outward from the shredded cocoon. As she fell, a hairy green spider first charged across a dew-sparkling web, then fled as it disintegrated from beneath its legs.

Belle snatched at a leaf and swung into a bending branch as the spider fell into foggy mists below. The upper third of her right upper wing dangled limp from the stem. She clenched her teeth, swung herself to the tree bark, worked her way down to the nearest branch and sank into its crook. She wanted to sob. She needed to get to Peter. The tree around her was too small to be the La'Du Lira Al'Cular. She somehow had been blown from the Tree all the way down the cliff and had been caught by the spider without suffering more than a broken wing.

Thank you, Great Self. Tinker Belle pressed her hand to her face.

Fear and shame welled inside her — this wasn't how her plan was supposed to go. She should have woken with Peter and April, safe inside the Tree's inner clearing. William would slow the enemy enough for Neverland to finish them off while the mantle stayed secure, away from their hands. Per her connection, she knew Peter was not in the clearing, but further to the west, and still unconscious. The Unionists must have somehow gotten him.

Belle knew they would try to save Peter for their retraining programs. She recalled that young blonde boy brought in by the Unionists to speak before the parliament of the evils of the Edenic Charter and its policies of 'appeasing evil' through nonintervention. He sobbed and begged them to cut his chains, to enforce morality across the continent as they were responsible to do, and by doing nothing while evil existed, Eden deserved to fall. Unionists paraded the young parrot as an example of ascendant thinking — for if a child could see and espouse their ideals, it must be moral.

What a farce, Tinker Belle spat.

The entire plan hinged on Peter staying out of trouble alongside his mother. If the Unionists discovered Peter had the mantle, his life would be forfeit. To men and women who believed moral ends justified all means, there was no cost too high in pursuit of their ideal society or state.

Tinker Belle gritted her teeth and bent her wing down before her. Gripping each side of the break, pain raced down her stem. Tears welled and she hesitated.

A hiss signaled the return of the spider racing up the trunk. Another one appeared behind it.

Shit, Belle hissed. Taking deep breaths, she gripped her wing with all her strength and bent the break as much as she could. A wild chimal scream erupted from her throat. She twisted in pain. The bone was now fully broken but ligaments clung between them. Even as she sobbed, the advancing spiders gave her no time. Unable to use her own magic against herself, she resorted to bending the wing and turning her mouth to set the remaining break between her teeth. As the chitter of the spiders drew ever nearer, she clenched her abs and bit as hard as she could, even as another scream ripped from her throat. She stopped as the pain grew too great, spit blood and, with strength from her desperation to reach Peter, ripped the remaining ligaments. She collapsed against the tree and quivered in the excruciation pulsing through her.

Tinker Belle clung to consciousness by a narrow thread just as the spiders reached her branch and scurried around to approach from both sides.

Hell no, you don't, she rolled onto her side, up onto her knees and twisted to fire rippling golden bolts of energy at the creatures. In her panic, her shots flew wide but scared one spider into retreat. The other raised its fangs to pounce but missed her as she twisted out of the way and off the branch.

Tinker Belle snatched the bark and screamed as her weight yanked the nerves extending up to the stem of her upper right wing. The spider appeared over the edge of the branch and made for her. Gripping a loose piece of bark from the trunk, she hauled it out, raised it into the air and drove it into the spider's multiple eyes when it came within reach. It screamed and scrambled away as the second gathered its courage and advanced.

She threw the piece of bark at it, gripped the tree, raised her left, empowered fist and fired a bolt of energy into it. The exploding spider bathed her and the trunk in its goo.

Great Self, she gasped as her ears rang. She could no longer hear the other spider. With adrenaline rushing through her golden veins, she flapped her wings. Despite the agony, she had to get to Peter.

Belle bent her knees, fluttered her wings to ensure they would carry her, and bolted into the air. She wove through gaps in the upper canopy to stay out of reach of the treetop grabbers while remaining low and difficult to see for high flying predators. Birds, bugs, monkeys and lizards howled and snatched at her passing. Her missing wingtip almost got her killed more than once, but she destroyed more than a few predators. She circumvented Pan's Peak and reached the West Bay.

She came to a dead stop just outside the tree line and found the corpse of The Sumter. *Oh no. NO!* Her fists quivered before she spotted Unity's Light just beyond the bay. *NO!*

Belle skirted the bay, followed the rocks and fired low across the water, hoping to disappear in the moon's shimmer. She came in at top speed and slowed near the hull. She hit hard, but clung to the planks, her legs drooping for a moment. Her missing wingtip almost cost her ability to slow. Golden blood oozed down its stem. Her head pounded from the brilliant pain climbing up the nerves in her wing. Dizziness overwhelmed her. Once it slowed, she fluttered along the outer hull up to the bowsprit and peeked over the rim lining the deck.

Rum's heavy stench struck her so that she had to hide a cough behind a hand. To avoid shadows, she crawled for the fore gangway and froze when two humans stormed onto deck from the aft gangway. She dropped down next to the lip above the gangway, unable to go down without being seen, and recognized Athyka from the battle at Richter's Deep.

"What the hell were you doing!?" the man erupted. "You just froze her hand off!"

"The bitch is being cagy!" Athyka cried. "We don't have time, Eldnor! We don't have time for her games!"

"We were just getting started!"

"She grabbed the ohna terra!"

"I'd have handled that!" He rubbed his hand. "I- why was I hitting her?"

"So she'd loosen up!"

"I didn't want to hit her. Why did I hit her?" Eldnor clutched his ohna. "I don't hit women!"

Athyka reached out to touch him and he backed away.

"Why, Athyka? This isn't the first time I've been doing things I didn't want to do. What's going on? Is it the ohna?"

"Of course, it is," she said. "You should hand it to me."

Eldnor retreated again. "I want to know what's going on. Something is really messed up right now. What's going on!?"

"You're stressed." Athyka tried soothing him.

"No! You! You're in my head! I couldn't see it. I keep having these blanks when I'm around you. I can't remember. I can't- I can't!" Eldnor fisted the side of his head as he backed away from her. "You're in my head! How're you in my … You're a selfdamn daleen. You- you have to be!"

"Now you're just talking crazy." Desperation crept into her voice. "You don't know what you're talking about."

"You are!"

"Wait..." She touched her belt. "Where's the knife? Where's my ohna!?"

"What have you been doing to me, Athyka!?" Eldnor yelled.

Tinker Belle rolled over the lip and dropped below the highest edge of the staircase — out of sight from the rear entry — before snapping her wings out and gliding down. She tilted dangerously toward her injured wing. She dropped and rolled against the corner setting and flattened herself into the crook just as a coughing sailor stumbled past her on his way up to the main deck.

Now below deck, the odor of rum was physical, a buffer that thickened as she descended. Grunting echoed from somewhere deeper in the ship. The smell of sex and blood brought her up short. Panicked, she refocused on her bond to the pan. A third, floral smell reached her, one that brought her up cold — a perfume of roses.

Peter wasn't down here, but April was.

Tinker Belle pressed herself against the wall and tamped down her tears. She turned at the middle deck and descended into the hold.

A single lantern rocked over one of two brig cells nestled against the starboard hull halfway down the hold and flanked by stacks of boxes. She flutter-hopped across storage containers, over netted stacks of barrels and up to the top of the steel cage. Below, Tinker Belle found hell.

April lay catatonic beneath a fat, grunting sailor. Men lay about the room in various states of dress — some lay asleep after winning and taking their turn, others dead for losing. Even the sight of the ice knife nailing a severed hand to the hull next to them seemed unimportant in comparison.

Tinker Belle almost screamed. Light patters of blood smeared April's body and the stench of sex filled the hot, thick air. Bits of her crimson hair dotted the cell where men had grabbed and ripped it off in a frenzy to take her; April stared half-lidded and empty as she struggled to breathe beneath the heavy sailor taking his time. Two dead sailors lay slumped and bled out alongside them on the tiny cell floor, losers in the quick and deadly fight to be first.

Tinker Belle gasped at April's tourniquetted left stump of a wrist, ignored by the sailors for their amusement. The fairy held her hand over her mouth as her tears dripped onto the cage beneath her. Struggling not to sob or draw attention, she wanted to scream like she did when she ripped off her wing.

Those selfdamn animals! Those self ... damn ... animals!

Fury billowed in her heart. Her power multiplied with her rage and an aura of golden light expanded from her to near the size of a human. She gathered power into her hands as light filled her teary eyes and she floated next to April's catatonic face. At her appearance, the chubby-faced sailor's dull eyes turned and widened in a sudden horror.

Fuck the charter, she fired a pair of bolts through his face, splashing his head across the hull backing the small cell.

April did not change, still unaware the warmth bathing her neck was now the blood flowing from his open neck. The fairy choked off a sob, heeled her sorrow and raised her hands before she blew a billow of sparks into April's nose. While the magic wormed its way into April's brain, Tinker Belle turned away from the vile picture and struggled not to vomit.

Ragged inhales preceded April's eyes fluttering open to reveal heavy yellowing from strain.

"Uuhhh ... " April's ghosted eyes struggled to focus on Belle's golden shimmer. Warmth fled from Belle when she realized April was blind.

"Hello?" April whispered.

Tinker Belle chimed.

April managed to focus. "Tinker Belle?" As the heavy weight of understanding settled on her, tears flooded her blank gaze.

Tinker Belle chimed again. April's heart raced. Belle knew the rising panic would drag her back into madness and barked a chime to get April's attention.

"Belle! Belle," April moaned. "Please, don't ... Peter! Save Peter!"

Tinker Belle sobbed as April's mind ebbed.

Freeing her right hand, April groped for Tinker Belle. Her fingers bent one of her wings in her grip and drew her close to her panting, bloody mouth.

"Save Peter, Tinker Belle." April's voice broke. "And ... " April paused in half sobs, unable to gasp from the weight of the man atop her. "Save Peter, Belle ... " Her voice failed, except for a final, quivering charge. "And ... see these bastards to hell." April's cries fractured. Her grip faltered.

Belle fell into the pool of thick blood flowing across the deck. She knelt and sobbed. Forced again to cut herself off, she rose into the air near the top of the cell and paused as Lady Baley struggled to breathe.

I'm sorry, April, Tinker Belle managed. She drew on her power and multiplied her aura until its brightness filled the entire hold. *I'm- so sorry.*

The pixie unleashed a torrent of broiling heat that burned through both men and April in seconds — it was the quickest mercy she could muster. The blood boiled and the smell of its iron pierced the room. She released her power to watch a brittle breeze, caused by the sudden heat, swirl April's ashes into the air.

Tinker Belle screamed with a fury that startled every waking sailor on board and drew the rest from their slumber. Her chimal cry echoed and rebounded throughout the ship before she flew up the fore gangway to the middle deck where most of the alarmed sailors stirred in their hammocks. Men twisted in horror at her emergence from the lower deck, a brilliant interruption of their stuppored gloom.

"A PIXIE!" screamed one before the dark room erupted with a mad, drunken stampede to flee. Tinker Belle unleashed rage upon them, setting dozens of hammocks ablaze in her first strike of power. Men's screams echoed through the low-ceilinged room as she blew holes through chests and stomachs, exploded heads and disintegrated limbs. Quiet hedonism burned with a new hell.

When she struggled to find anyone else to make suffer, she flew up the aft gangway to the main deck where the fire had climbed and now set cargo aflame. The pixie entered the rear hallway and found the cabin where Peter lay. She bored a hole through the thick wood before heavy black smoke billowed from within. *Oh no.*

Inside, the room drowned in charcoal air.

Peter? Tinker Belle crawled through the hole. *Peter!!*

After dropping to the floor and walking its length, she found the bunk and Peter passed out atop it. She tried to wake him when the door to the room swung open behind her.

Coughing, Athyka stumbled inside and groped for Peter's bunk.

Tinker Belle lifted into the air, regained her powers and raised both glowing hands. Her golden appearance and the ghostly aura blazed the midnight smoke like an arriving demon.

A terrified Athyka dove aside as the bolts brushed her shoulder and blew apart the door across the hallway. She fled the room.

Tinker Belle found Peter's limp body. *Wake up, Peter! Wake up! Wake up right now! Please! Please wake up!*

Though Peter breathed, he did not respond.

PLEASE! PETER! WAKE UP!! Tinker Belle flushed him with various magics as she had April, but the boy's strained breathing revealed he lacked the clean air needed to wake. *PETER!*

Drained and exhausted, Tinker Belle struggled to summon violent power she had rarely used, only for it to hesitate. Furious, she summoned as much as she could and fired bolts to blow a small hole in the side of the ship on Peter's far side to create an immediate exit. The blowback sent her through the open doorway into the opposite room. After her head stopped spinning, she staggered back to the hallway. A cry drew her eyes to the main deck where an enraged Athyka cut down her dark-haired companion.

Turning back toward Peter's room as the thick smoke cleared to reveal Peter's bed and a large portion of the wall completely gone. Tinker Belle raced to the edge just as Peter's limp body disappeared into the midnight ocean below. *PETER!!*

She dove into the black water. Vision was dim and wings did little to propel her. Desperation arose in her breast. She spotted him sinking into the depths and stroked hard. Latching upon his green coat, she turned upward at a moon-rippled surface and despaired how she might drag a boy thirty two times her own weight. As her hope drained, sure they would both die, Peter was yanked from her grip and disappeared into the black below.

Her screaming lungs forced her to the surface while the ship burned and sank as a mountain of wood and canvas. Searching the darkness once more in vain, she latched upon a piece of loose wood bobbing in the heavy waves.

Peter.

14

Ex Mortem

The gilded white door frame defied the eternal black within. Heartbeats pulsed stronger as the muffled moans faded away. Echoing pants screamed from the black. Bootfalls on carpet preceded a boy with black hair bursting from the doorway. Fear painted his face as he sprinted down the rolling corridor. Paintings fell from walls, console tables tipped inward toward the ornate hallway carpet and windows along the right wall shattered in sparkling, violent moonlight.

Dressed in his simple woolen shirt and trousers, the boy raised his arms against the glass that cut at his skin and face. Violent wind sucked him through the distant door and out onto the tumbling deck of a ship rocking through great rolling valleys of hurricane-driven waves. Their rogue, widening jaws loomed high in the storm, crashed across the deck, ripped off the mast and cracked the ship across its belly.

Lightning revealed the silhouette of a monstrous beast within an approaching wall of water. Great widening orbs bathed him and the deck in eerie yellow light. The beast's yawning jaws drowned all hope from his soul before the extensive upper snout snapped over the boy, mast and deck with an earth-shattering roar.

Now far below, the raging surface ascended from his extended hands as the midnight depths sucked him downward. Lightning above revealed the two halves of the sinking vessel bleeding out dead sailors. His eyes followed the trail of dead men to the beast, now below him, its jaws expanding as the ocean sucked him down in a vicious swirl. He screamed what little air remained in his lungs. The silhouette of great jagged teeth closed around him on both sides, drowning him in the void.

Enclosing darkness balled him up, tucked his arms against his chest, his knees up over his elbows, and twisted his head downward in a fetal position. Frigid seawater soon boiled with heat. He lost all sense of time, up or down, breathing or eating.

Wakefulness flooded him. He resisted the suffocating cocoon and fought firmament, kicked down and wrenched back with his head. He heard a small crack. Pushing again, the crack snapped louder, followed by others. The roof of his confinement broke open. His desperate flail speared his arm outward to grab scree-covered soil outside. From there, his shoulder emerged, followed by a head and a desperate suck of air through a gaping mouth.

Green goo erupted from his throat. Vomit followed, along with more fluids from his sinuses and hacking lungs. He wiped his eyes, crawled up from his prison and stumbled weak-kneed to the ground. Blinded, he crawled across sharp, skin-gouging scree until his hand found water. He splashed along until it deepened enough for him to plunge his face in to clear his clouded vision. The echoes of his heavy breaths and splashing feet rebounded upon him and loudened as he moved away from the nest.

Dim light bled through long, razor teeth dangling before him. Though first terrified, he discovered vines and roots that in silhouette made the gaps appear as glowing teeth. He peered outside through those teeth and realized he was in a cave.

Beyond the vines, fresher air and faint moonlight bled through the heavy canopy above. Shock and terror welled as he found a scummy swamp echoing with cries and songs in a midnight chorus. He ventured down into waist-high water. Dozens of splashes rushing away from him gave him pause, but he pressed onward over soggy mounds and across water deep enough to swim. A shoreline appeared ahead, rising from the water before steepening upward as high cliffs. Thunder from a nearby waterfall rumbled off to his right. He marched onward with the current, sure it was heading downhill, when it flowed into a cave. Unsure if he had followed it correctly, he grabbed wet leaves from a nearby mound and dropped it onto the water, which flowed into the cave. Hesitant, he stepped inside. Fresh thunder filled the darkness and clean moisture wafted past him. He kept his arm to the wall to the right until he spotted a waterfall curtain ahead. Wiggling past, he took in his first fresh gulps of air.

Here, a broad pool of water met the gulley between two spurs, from which wound a narrow creek that emptied into the side of a broad river leading in either direction. Across the river stretched miles of desert flanked by a snow-capped mountain. To the distant right rose a volcano whose peak glowed with faint lava, anchored by a grassland as expansive as the desert. The boy spotted the freshwater of the river. He stumbled down the shoreline and fell to his knees, plunged his body beneath the surface and gulped while scrubbing gunk from his body. What once had been a blouse now netted across him as filthy strings; his trousers frayed below the knee with holes throughout, as if eaten away by some powerful acid.

Once sated and sufficiently free of the sticky goo from which he'd come, he stumbled onto the beach and fell again to his hands and knees as he sucked in the clean evening air.

Now free of the swamp's murk, Santi turned about, soaking in the amazing view, when he spotted the largest tree he'd ever seen rising from the base of a peak a few miles distant. His whole being warmed at the sight of it and he knew that was where he should go. But even as its safety called, deep within cried a madness, one framed by a bright doorway of eternal darkness. He quivered, inside, but as he always did, he gathered his courage and stepped forward to climb to the ridge and follow the mountains toward the Tree.

15

Voices

"**O**h, mother," Wendy Moira Angela Darling tugged her skirts as the breeze tickled her large brunette curls. She sat erect on a stone bench overlooking the south end of Serpentine Lake in London's Hyde Park. "I wish father would spend less time at the bank."

"Your father works very hard to provide for us," said her mother, Mary. "And finely, too."

"I know," Wendy sighed. "But it would be grand to see him more often."

Mary's prim face softened as she touched Wendy's hand. "It would."

Trees growing from Serpentine Island a dozen paces away pirouetted in the breeze. Sitting on the edge of the water, behind a small stone lake wall, opposite the island, Wendy and Mary soaked in the quiet of the pond from the south side of Hyde Park. Trees behind them joined the chorus as gusts meandered through and ruffled grass and lake alike. Young mothers in their finery walked in pairs pushing prams along the broad brown gravel path behind them.

"He did promise to come, didn't he, mother?"

"Of course, dear," Mary smiled. Sitting upright in her striped Victorian dress with her curled brown hair flattened in a sheet down the side of her face from the center part, common in Victorian fashion, Mary's bright blue eyes, petite nose and full red lips were softened with fewer powders than most women her age. As often commented, she appeared more as her daughter's elder sister than mother. "George recited this morning the time and location for our picnic."

In miniature to her beautiful mother, Wendy's curt nod hid her worry father would, yet again, be caught up in work. She frowned at the ravens strutting throughout the small island's flora. "John feels so much like him, now. Now that he's in the Navy."

Mary's pretty mouth tightened and she squeezed Wendy's hand. "We must be brave, my dear. We are Britons. We do what must be done, and your brother serves proudly."

"He does that," Wendy agreed.

"Did I tell you Elizabeth's daughter, Arabella, is with child?" Mary cleared her throat.

"Is that so?" Wendy asked with a bare tilt of her head. "Already another?"

"She has that fetching young husband of hers," Mary said. "Two children in two years and still they take no time."

"You and father didn't wait between John and me," Wendy said.

"But we took a break between you and Michael," said Mary. "Give ourselves a breath, I should say."

"Yes, a breath," Wendy said. "Such a lovely thing."

"Especially for the cause, you know," Mary said. "Wasting time rearing more children simply will not do."

"Quite right, mother," Wendy said.

"Oh, Mary Darling!" a woman's voice echoed behind them.

Mary waved at a passing woman she recognized.

Wendy pressed a hand against her belly to imagine bearing a child and feeling none the happier for it. "I should like to imagine such freedom as having none at all."

"I fear your father might wish for grandchildren," Mary said. "He does dote on Michael too much, I think."

"Mm," Wendy murmured when a rather large raven paused near the water's edge of the narrow stream of water separating the lake wall from the island. The raven appeared to cock its eye. She scowled, as if able to hear from its thoughts a specific interest in seeking out her face.

"The ladies are gathering for another march next week. Your father protests my involvement beyond more than organizing and supporting."

"You said his banking fellows are unkeen on the idea of women voting."

"Of course, they are, the silly old men."

The thought, *all men are silly,* interrupted Wendy's mind.

"Silly," Wendy blinked as if the thought came from the raven, by a reply so aptly spoken. "Yes, all men are."

As Mary chuckled, Wendy sensed the raven's displeasure at her misinterpretation of its statement; as if corrected, the raven seemed to imply that it meant all humans, not merely males. She felt aghast such a thought might come from the raven rather than her own imagination, yet doubt cracked her certainty.

BALL! BALL! Echoes of other thoughts drifted from barking dogs nearby.

"Wendy? Did you hear what I asked you?"

Wendy started. Her nervous giggle covered her alarm. "I apologize, mother. I fear I'm suffering flights of fancy."

"What flights?"

"Well … as if I heard the dogs over on the lawn barking about their balls."

Mary covered her laugh with her hand. "Oh, Wendy, what an imagination. Certainly, those dogs are men!"

"Mother!" Wendy covered her own bright laugh, grateful for her mother's validation, and pushed concern from her mind. "What was it you asked, mother?"

"About Cynthia's party next week." Mary calmed. "Have you thought what you'd like to wear?"

"Ah, yes," Wendy said. "I was thinking my lavender dress from Christmas."

"That's a lovely one," Mary smiled. She prattled on the event as Wendy's mind returned to the island. The eyeful raven had disappeared, leaving behind a strange fear it would not be the last time she would see it, nor the last time she would hear such strange thoughts.

16

Marooner to Mother

Water lapped at Peter's crown and ankles. Opening, his emerald eyes met the round, golden eyes of a woman with silver hair. She appeared to be sticking out of a ceiling of water. They watched each other before she drew nearer. Peter twisted and found that he lay on a rock rising a few inches from low waves in the midst of a great plain of ocean. Water rushed from his thick crimson hair down his face. His eyes followed a trickle of rock formations leading up to a spire piercing the sky from the edge of the lagoon while his tongue noted a sweet, lingering taste on his lips.

"Strawberry ..." he said.

A heavy ceiling of clouds hung low and the sun's coming rise offered a bare warmth to the distant sky. More than a mile distant, Neverland appeared out of reach when he spotted the woman, again, now hovering beneath the surface of the dark morning waters. Peter knelt as she drew nearer the surface. As she emerged, her flowing hair hung limp down her head, and framed her big-eyed doll's face.

"Who are you?" he asked and then licked at the lingering hint of strawberry as his eyes latched upon her rosy pink lips.

"I am Estelle." She cocked her head to the side.

He looked around. "Do you- live here?"

"Of course," she giggled.

"Where?" he asked.

Her gaze painted the length of him. "I could show if you were still the pan."

"Still the what?" asked Peter. "Do you know my father?"

"Is he the pan?"

"Of course," Peter said.

She gazed at the island. "No … the pan is no one's father. He is new."

"New? The pan's my father!" Peter stood up.

Estelle prepared to speak when she was yanked beneath the surface in a torrent. The water boiled with activity below. When it stilled, a woman with green eyes, yellow spiky hair and midnight skin emerged from the water to her neck. Her hair mussed, Estelle returned with glares at the newcomer.

"Who is this?" asked the second, a woman with a large jaw and broad shoulders.

"I'm Peter."

"He was the pan when I found him," said Estelle. "But he died before I could get him to the rock. Gave him the breath of life and pumped his heart. He came back rather quickly."

"What?" Peter asked.

"Why'd you do that?" the second glared at her. "He's not the pan!"

Estelle glared at the newcomer. "Because. He's a little boy. Little boys don't deserve to die."

The second huffed. "He's not the pan." Her eyes wavered between disappointment and hate.

"My father's the pan!" Peter stammered.

The larger one leaned in. "No. The pan is new. Just emerged this morning from the swamp."

Peter frowned.

"You can still smell the mantle all over this one," said Estelle.

"Yeah, I smell it," said the second. "But it ain't him."

"What do you mean, emerged? My father just brought us here. How-how did I get here?"

"Your big ship sank," Estelle said.

"Everyone can smell it, too," said the second. "It reeks of men and fire from here to the shoals."

"What ship sank?" Peter struggled to scan the bay against the dim. "Where?"

"Not far," Estelle motioned just south of the rock.

Peter's face tightened as he made out small chunks of wood bobbing in the low waves. He sat down and struggled not to cry as his eyes glossed over. Fear threatened the shock of waking alone on a rock a mile from shore.

"Don't cry," growled the large one.

"Oh, he's sad." Estelle set her hand upon his foot.

"He can die," the large one said.

"Qunis!" Estelle scolded her and faced Peter. "He's just a lost little boy. And besides, he already did. For a moment, at least."

"Have- have you seen my mom- or my father?" Peter cried.

"No, sweetie," Estelle said. "A woman survived the sinking, though."

"My mom?" Peter's eyes widened. "Wait, how did we get on the ship? Why am I out here?"

"We don't know," Estelle said.

"They bring war and dead men," Qunis growled. "Leave the boy. Let's go home."

"But he'll die out here!" Estelle said. "He's not the pan!"

"That's the point," Qunis snapped again. "He's not. And you should have left him dead when you found him."

"I can take you to shore, young man," Estelle held out her hands and offered a smile.

Peter wiped his tears. "Do I just- climb in?"

"Yes," Estelle smiled.

Peter dropped into the cold water fully clothed and allowed her to scoop him back against her. Estelle's slender arms hugged him close before casting off. Peter held up his feet so her knees wouldn't kick him and was surprised by their speed. Minutes later, she slowed and rotated him into the shallows of the beach.

"Set your feet down and get out of the water before the shallowsharks get you," she pushed him. He stumbled from the water up onto a rocky beach — the northern arm of the West Bay. He turned and gasped.

Estelle sat hip down in shallow water, bare breasted as she grinned. "You're such a cutie. A shame you aren't still the pan. We like the pans when they grow up." She eyed him in a way that made him uncomfortable. "You do look like William."

"You- you knew my father?"

"C'mon, Estelle," Qunis called from deeper water.

Estelle ran her tongue along her upper lip. "Oh yes. We knew him very well, but there's a new one now. Hopefully he grows up soon, too." She grinned, then focused again on Peter. "Try not to die, cutie." In a twist and splash, she disappeared into the shallow surf.

Peter's mouth drooped — she had a tail like a fish!

"A mermaid," he breathed as the two disappeared under the lagoon's low surf. Fear replaced wonder when a ragged caw drew his attention. A raven fluttered in the distance along the convex curve of the northbound shoreline, away from the West Bay. It flapped upon a rock above the low surf and fluttered its wings before cawing again.

Curious, Peter picked his way over the rocky shoreline, over pebbled beach sand and across bulky rock formations jutting out from the steep, jagged soil climbing into a northeast-bound ridge. The raven hopped back and forth as it followed the shore. It fluttered to the water to peck at something, then circled trees above the beach. The boy had never seen a bird behave so and, with no clear plan, followed. For his moments of panic, the raven was a welcome distraction. It meandered, flew into the tree line and returned a moment later. Peter frowned when it dropped fruit near him and withdrew up the beach. Peter picked up and inspected it before venturing a bite. Sweet juice ran down the side of his face as he chewed. He couldn't remember the last time he'd eaten, or anything clearly since exploring the lawn under the Tree and sitting with his mom.

He fought fear at the idea his ship had sank. He couldn't remember much since sitting with his father by the fire. Times had been so tense lately that just sitting with both of his parents by a fire — even with them fighting — seemed wonderful to the endless chaos since fleeing Eden. Even the weeks aboard their ship were spent apart — his mother couldn't think straight from seasickness, his father avoided the cabin except to sleep. While alone, Peter watched his mother cry from loneliness but then nag his father when he did try to relax inside. William avoided any meaningful questions which only heightened his mother's need to question him. Peter couldn't understand why they didn't just act the way they used to before the trade conferences last year — everyone said they were a perfect couple, in love and an amazing team. Peter wasn't sure what that meant anymore, and now he was alone on Neverland and unsure where his parents went or why he woke up on the ocean.

Though the raven's caws drew him onward, Peter questioned whether he could trust it. Since the bird fed him, that would have to be enough for now. He followed its meandering path along the shore for an hour, pausing as the raven paused. The midnight bird never let him approach.

"Hey … I-" Peter felt stupid for wanting to ask the bird a question. "I gotta get back to the Tree. Can you show me? The big tree up there?" Peter pointed up through the peak separating him from it.

The raven cocked his head to the side as if watching him, then thrust into the air and swooped into the jungle tree line.

"Hey. HEY!" Peter chased it to the trees where it disappeared and found a small bubbling stream trickling from uphill. A faint bleat drew Peter's gaze onward through the jungle where, in the distance, a white goat with a red blaze chewed on a distant bush. The raven's caw drew his eyes upstream where the bird sat upon a rock, waiting for Peter. With no other option, he followed it to the peak's base over boulders and past frothing pools as the ground steepened. The raven's caw drew him to the top of a small waterfall, which led upward into the mouth of an a-frame cave.

When Peter glanced back, he paused. The winding stream fell away below him, as did much of the jungle canopy, to reveal a small bay tucked east along the northern shore. The tri-horn spire rose just off to his left, cutting a stream of clouds in two.

The raven's caw echoed now from within the cave. Mustering his courage, he followed into damp, chilly air hovering just inside. He leapt back and forth across the narrow rushing stream as he climbed into the mountain, pausing here and there as the light dimmed. Cracks of light first revealed a path but soon fell away into darkness. A mix of fresh spring and sour standing water wafted through the narrow stone pathways. As Peter's eyes adjusted, he noticed stars painted along the cave ceiling. He squinted — they weren't stars, but tiny glowing dots. Though faint, he could see just well enough to press onward.

The stars faded before he reached an expansive room underlit only by the faint glow from the cave behind him.

"Hello?"

A faint caw drew him to his left.

Gentle, guttural moans of the island breathed around him. Even as light faded, he walked with his hand to the wall until he reached another crossway, stepping out into a small open chamber void of all light.

"Hello! Raven?"

There came no response.

"Raven!!"

When silence, alone, responded, fear pitted in his stomach. Unable to see and afraid to turn back, he considered his options. Time passed. Peter searched again for the cave but could see only darkness. Terror welled within him and he struggled against the tears building in his eyes. At first overcome with fear, the wet streams down his cheeks flared with cooler air.

Air moved.

Peter turned his face until he found the source of the breeze and walked with arms outstretched until his fingers brushed rock and the sides of another cave. He followed the winding path through the misshapen veins. As he continued, the smell of fragrant life filled his nostrils, drawing him to move faster until he was sprinting into the growing light.

Peter slid to a stop after emerging from the side a tall a-frame cavern lit by sunlight reflected from unseen skylights. The long chamber extended to each side. Gentle steppes climbed to each angled wall which ended ten feet above the bottom in a line of angled blocky columns. Light bounced downward from the apex until it warmed the entire space.

Gaping, the boy turned about beneath the well-lit end of the chamber. The high inward leaning walls bore dozens of intricate lines carved into the stone forming ancient symbols. At the end of the chamber, lit in warm amber sunlight, rose a *bas-relief* carving on the far wall of a woman with her legs tucked under her bottom and weaving hair covering her breasts. Her arms lovingly cradled a pregnant belly. Heavy vinery carpeted the walls and hung to the chamber floor. Warm, dusty air thick with moisture gave the view a holy feel, wreathing the lower side of the carving and bearing it up with a spiritual grace. He never liked Temple when living at the palace, but standing here, he understood why mom always wanted to go.

His stomach's gurgle interrupted the moment. Opposite the Mother, darkness painted the end of the high chamber. Peter approached the shadow to find great stones blocking what appeared to be a tall doorway and a possible exit. He climbed up a few, but verified that he had no capacity to get out that way and turned back.

Peter approached the vine-wreathed Mother and discovered that she was carved upon a lone, narrow wall separate from the actual end of the chamber. Light bled from either side, drawing him around the corner to find a low, broad opening draped in vines and glowing from warmth beyond. Small doors into empty stone rooms hugged a high-ceilinged, sunlit hallway, at the end of which stood an intricate stone arch into another dark cave system. With caves behind and before, he had little option but to continue. Soon after pressing into the darkness, the trickle of water reached his ears.

"The creek," Peter said. "Thank the Self."

The cave twisted as the gurgle of water echoed louder. Darkness thickened and the descending ceiling forced him to crawl while the floor steepened in descent. Unable to stop himself, he slid the last few feet and rolled into an open, lightless chamber echoing with rushing water. He walked with care and stooped until his fingers found the edge of the icy rushing creek. A faint thunder rumbled to his left. As he looked toward it, he made out a faint light under the water — an exit.

Afraid to retreat or advance, Peter had to try something. He turned downriver and followed the shore by touch when the cave wall on his left closed against the water's edge until there was no way to continue ashore. He tried walking in the shallow only to find it, too, cut off by the narrowing walls. With the thunder of the falls closer than ever, he ventured deeper into the river when the power of the current took his feet out from under him. He sputtered to the surface, terrified by insufficient light in the swirling chaos, when his head brushed the ceiling — it was coming down! He raised his hands, desperate to grab a hold and pull his way out, but the plunging rockface forced him below the surface.

Peter tumbled in the frigid midnight when he crashed into one boulder, then another. He cradled his head before his body whipped into a squeeze on the side of the underwater river. Opening his eyes, he spotted a faint soft blue light shimmering only a few seconds away. Kicking at the rock in panic, his lungs burned and vision dimmed. A lucky kick dislodged him before being consumed by the rolling torrent and growing light.

17

Peter Meet Pan

Tinker Belle woke to a world she didn't want to see. Aches filled her body and heavy heartbeats rocked her chest. Lying on her side, she gazed at an outer world as tilted as her inner; she wanted nothing more than to return to the depths of dreamless sleep.

Instead, the approach of water drew her attention. She blinked gritty eyes and pulled her head out of sucking damp sand to discover herself half buried on a marshy beach. How she wasn't dead escaped her, but she knew that might not last much longer. Even so, she wasn't sure she cared.

Peter was dead. She felt the link to his mantle sever after losing him in the black water last night when Unity's Light sank. The boy drowned without a fight. That made her angry.

Belle winced as she moved. Clinging to that lone board in choppy seas drained what little she had left after attacking the ship. Only the faint image of a raven circling between her and the brilliant moon came to mind from last night. Ravens loved eating pixies, so that had to have been nothing more than one of her worst fears joining the rest.

She wiggled her arms from the marshy sand just as the tide moved in. She sat up and used the incoming saltwater to wash off the mud clinging to her skin. Waves came in faster than her attempts to extricate herself.

Her heart picked up as the water rose. Small roots entangled her feet. Her frantic kicks jostled her upper right wing.

C'mon, she chimed, gripped the roots under her bottom and stamped hard to free her left ankle. A wave drove her into the sand. She gasped as it ebbed just before another crashed and spun her about while she remained tethered to the scree below. Her lungs burned until the wave subsided and she found her left ankle caught up even worse than before. *No you- NO!* Wrenching it out sprained it just as a wave crashed into and dragged her through the marsh. Hugged on all sides by reeds, she lost up from down.

Tiny snapping mouths glanced her skin, the passive predators all around waiting for their meals in the coming tide. Amber dawnlight warmed the water in several directions while waves pounded. At last, she found a thicker root to grasp and kicked up from the bottom. She gasped with air and spotted a huge, stick-legged bird plodding through the reeds. When she appeared, it bolted for her.

Belle spread her wings just in time to catch a wave and ride it out of reach of the bird's long, broad bill snapping at her. She snatched a reed, put feet down again and sank just enough to see above the frothing surface. The bird hadn't spotted her new location as more waves came in while Belle caught her breath. She tucked her wings and braced against each low wave until something else caught the bird's attention and drew it away.

Belle turned and, with an eye for the bird, waded her way through the forest of reeds until she found a small turtle. It chewed sideways on a fallen reed and raised its slow, doleful eyes.

She waited for it to try and kill her. To her surprise, it opened its snapper mouth to reveal long, jagged teeth. Her eyes widened. In the slowest attack she'd ever seen, it put one foot forward, then another and turned with its shell, then placed another. She cocked her head, almost amused. *This place is selfdamn nuts.*

Belle rounded the attacking turtle and climbed upon its back. It paused and cocked its head, then turned in vain to get at her. She searched for the large birds and fluttered her wings dry. Her small golden vest and long shorts, embroidered throughout in lacy gold thread, had held up better than she expected. She tugged on it to a better position and reached inside to adjust her breasts. She fished it out of the crevice of her bottom before stretching her arms, legs and neck.

The turtle turned about in vain. Clearing her head, despite her heavy heart, Tinker Belle fired into the air southward along the ridges of the north island.

While free of the dangers of the marsh, her heart felt ever heavier. The pan was dead. Her unwanted mission was an utter failure. William had to be dead. April …

Memory of April drew Tinker Belle up short for a moment. While fluttering her broken wing was painful, she forced herself onward. Ahead, the Tree's upper canopy peeked above a distant ridge line. She thought she could feel the pan's heartbeat even now, but it had to be a ghost of a memory. William had given Peter the mantle, and Peter was dead. What happened if a pan died without passing it?

Her first pan, Kellogg, told her the mantle had been passed for so long that no one knew what would happen if a pan died before passing it. Pans had survived every attempt on their life — at least long enough to pass the mantle — for millennia, though history grew fuzzy during the Minder Conflicts two thousand years prior. Who knew what would happen?

Prior to leaving for Eden, Queen Mabsadora told her nothing about the haraven's history. The aurora's meeting involved few words and brought a faint blush to Tinker Belle's cheeks. She knew Mab was furious the aurora had intervened in her selection, but still didn't know why.

Failure burrowed deeper in Belle's heart as a mountain of shame weighed her down. Her absence from her flock had only worsened her hunger for affection, making her weak to the lustful eyes of her pans. She felt worse than a whore for having let them watch and touch her, and was never certain if her power had overcome them or they had acquiesced on their own. She knew what she was – she only wanted to do better to rectify her mistakes. Peter, in the brief moment he was pan, could have been that chance. She could redeem herself by serving him in the dignity her office demanded. But now Peter was gone like any other shipwreck from her life — at the bottom of the ocean.

Tinker Belle cried and pressed her hand to her tears. Sobs erupted from her as she struggled to fly and avoid predators. Inadequacy and failure filled her mind with curses and screams. She remembered being chosen by the aurora, the virulent debate among the elders, the worries of her best friends and lovers, and the fear of her own heart.

She never wanted to be the haraven, or a guide to anyone or anything,

125

and this just proved herself right about all.

THIS IS BULLSHIT! she screamed amidst her sobs. Tears clouded her vision so that she was forced to land on a tiny swinging branch in the top of a random tree. She sank to her ankles and sobbed. Her greatest fears had come to fruition. Not only was the pan dead, but now Tinker Belle was stuck on Algueda. How would she get home? She could not fly across countless miles of ocean from here to the continent. She was stuck, possibly forever. She paled at the idea of dying here of old age, or by being snapped up by some aerial predator, or some unseen grub that latched onto her foot while she slept or—

Belle froze — the pan just cut his foot on something.

What in hell?

She bolted into the air and turned westward along the ridge. Teary eyes settled on a point far beyond what the jungle allowed her to see. Though she could not see him, she knew the pan was somewhere in that direction. The pan. *A* pan was alive somehow. Belle soaked in the sky now blazing with morning sunlight. There was a crazy hope, a chance Peter still lived, a chance at redemption, a chance to do it right.

Closing her eyes, she said a prayer. She swore on purpose and promise a blood oath to the Great Self that if Peter were truly alive and still boasted the ben'cari, she would serve with honor and live up to the expectations of her flock, her ancestry and her creator.

Please, she whispered. *I swear on all I have and all I could ever do ... I will serve you.*

With that, she opened her eyes, accepted the chance the boy could be alive, and extended her senses. The bond pulled her eyes again toward the central island area. But if Peter were alive, why would he be there instead of the Tree? She tried to shake off the disbelief. If Peter survived, where would he head?

She then smacked her forehead. *Just follow the bond, stupid.*

Tinker Belle flew low over the tree canopies to discourage high-flying predators from dive bombing while avoiding the foliage and any tree-bound predators' reach. She picked up speed, sure Peter must have somehow survived. She crested the top of the low mountain ridge and veered just west of a broad swamp hugged by low mountain offshoots and spurs. Magnolias, oaks, and cedars raced below as her certainty grew. She crossed a rushing river and halted only paces from the pan, hidden in the flora.

PETER! she chimed, looking around. *Peter! Where are you? Peter?*

A boy with midnight hair, clad in tattered longshorts, stepped out of the trees raising a stick in defense in his right hand and a half-eaten purple fruit in his left. "Name thyself, demon, so I may cast thee down!"

Tinker Belle frowned. *You're not Peter! Where is Peter?*

"I don't know of any Peter!" the boy cried. "And for sure, I would cut him down should I see him, as well!" He raised his stick as if a sword with an erect posture and his feet outward in a deliberate stance. He flicked his thick black hair from his eyes with a twist of his head.

To Belle's eyes, the mantle shimmered around him. Tears dripped down her cheeks. *Then it's true. He's dead.*

"Speak your purpose, demon!" he cried.

I am no more a demon than you are.

"Lies."

Have you seen a demon before?

"No, but I know you are one!"

How do you know?

"Well ... you are a spirit! And a dangerous one!"

Dangerous? More like hazardous, she appraised him. *Lower your stick. I have no intention of hurting you. I couldn't even if I tried.*

"What? Why not?" the boy asked.

Because you're the pan, she chimed.

"I'm the ... what? I'm the 'all?'"

The PAN, boy. I suppose it translates awkwardly.

"What are you talking about? What's a pan?"

The pan, boy, is the herald of the Great Self. You are now ... it. Belle's face contorted with disbelief. *But how in hell are you the pan?*

The boy's outstretched "weapon" quivered with effort to hold it up.

Getting tired?

He redoubled his effort to steady himself.

Just drop it, child. I'm not going to hurt you.

"How can I trust the word of a demon?"

I'm not a demon, I'm a fairy!

"A- a fairy?" his eyes widened further.

Great Self in a handbasket, YES! A fairy!

"You have leapt from bad to worse!"

GREAT SELF! she turned, gathered power in her glowing fists and fired at a nearby tree, obliterating it in an explosion of splinters and flying branches. Flinching, the boy dropped the fruit to grip the stick with both hands, crouched and retreated from her. Belle gathered more power into her hands and unleashed it upon the boy.

Time slowed as the rippling power crossed the distance between them. Though the air sizzled with its destructive energy, it ignored the stick and passed over him like a breeze, even as the ground inches away from him shredded in a warbling explosion that covered him in dirt. He gasped and coughed the burnt air while his hands groped at nonexistent injuries.

I CAN'T BLOODY HURT YOU, YOU SILLY ASS, NOW DROP THE SELFDAMN STICK! she erupted.

The boy flinched and dropped the stick.

I thought it was hard enough with a man. Great Self, help me.

"Of whom do you speak, de- fairy?" he worked to slow his breathing.

The Great Self?

"Is that a ... god?"

The Great Self? He is the creator.

"Is he the God of the pope?"

The pope? I don't know anyone called the pope.

"You- you do not know of the pope!? How can you not know of the pope!? He is the ruler from god! His representative upon our fair Earth!"

Wait, Earth? You come from Earth?

"Of course! Where else could I come from!?" his eyes widened and alarm grew. "Do you come from one of the under realms?"

For Self sake, calm down! she spat. *This is why I hate children. And men. Just- humans. Self, I hate humans.*

He frowned.

Now, she balked at the memory of Peter's loss. If this boy had the mantle, she still had failed in protecting Peter. *There is much we must talk about.* About to ask where he came from, instead she asked, *Where are you headed?*

The boy wondered if he should tell her, then pointed. "I am headed toward that massive tree up there upon that ridge."

Really? her eyebrows popped. *What fortune. That's where we need to go.*

"With you?" he asked.

Her brow drew down.

"Oh ... alright, then," he said.

She motioned for him to join her as she neared the river. *Do you have a name?*

"I am Don Santiago Carrillo de Valencia the third," he swelled his chest.

That's quite the name, she chimed. *Is there something shorter I can call you?*

"You may call me Santi," he said. "And you? What shall I call you?"

I am Tinker Belle, your haraven.

"Haraven ... I can't quite figure out what that means. Several meanings are in my mind, but I do not know from where they come!"

You are the Pan, young man, she chimed. *Yo-*

"Help!" a boy's voice echoed through the trees. "Hel- ll- help!"

Santi and Tinker Belle raced up the gentle ascension to the top of the ridge before emerging on the bank of the frothing river rushing eastward. Heavy trees looming over the narrow river darkened the water but for the narrow strip in the center warmed by bright sunlight.

"There," Santi pointed at a figure tumbling in the tumultuous brown water. "It's a boy."

Another boy? How many of you are there!? she gasped when the boy drew close enough for her to recognize his unmistakable crimson hair. *PETER! That's him! Rescue him, boy! Quickly!*

"What?" Santi stammered.

RESCUE HIM!

Santi took off alongside Peter tumbling in the stream. He searched the rocky bank for any sticks he could extend. He snatched a long branch still wet with the morning frost and ran up to a gentle spur near the water's edge with the stick outstretched. "Grab it!"

Peter's wet fingers groped at it in vain as the water dragged him onward. Santi dropped the stick, sprinted again and snatched a vine from the ground. He reached another outcrop and tossed out the line. Peter screamed and ducked beneath the waves.

That's a snake, boy! Tinker Belle screamed.

Santi dropped the snake in shock. The snake disappeared into the river's tumult. Santi raced again along the shore in search of another tool when the thunder of a waterfall ahead reached his ears.

Quick! Before he goes over! Tinker Belle chimed.

Santi spotted a small flattish rock splitting the crest of the falls. He sprinted with surprising speed to pass Peter, swing out, veer in and take a flying leap to the rock. He underestimated his leap and slid off the end. His hand snatched its lip as the water pouring over him doused him. He hauled himself up onto the rock while panting with the shock of cold and heart-pounding excitement.

As the boy tumbled closer, Santi braced himself, slicked back his midnight hair and extended his arm as Peter reached the edge of the falls. He snatched Peter's forearm and leaned to counterbalance the boy's light weight. Peter swung free from the water over a hundred-foot drop into the blackness below. As he reached the apex of the swing, Santi was tempted to let him go.

Just to watch.

Peter swung back, brushed the rush of the fall and hung still beneath Santi.

"Can you get a grip on the rock!?" Santi yelled over the roaring water.

"I can try!" Peter gasped.

Time froze, the world fell still and a silence blanketed the boys. Unfamiliar energy twisted within and ripped from Santi. Golden light snaked from his chest, wreathed in blue-green auroric light, down his arm and stabbed Peter in the heart. In moments, the bridge connected, power passed and, with a brilliant explosion of light, both children returned to real time.

To Tinker Belle, there was only a powerful explosion that knocked Santi back into the river and Peter over the empty chasm, followed by both boys flying over the edge into empty air.

Tinker Belle screamed before she followed over the edge and into the murky swamp, below.

18

Waking in the Swamp

Wake up, you silly ass!!

Waking with a start, Peter sat up in the shallow water at the edge of a large, frothing pool thundering with a waterfall crashing a hundred feet from its apex above. A swampy shoreline rung the rocky pool and encroached noonlit water hugged in deep shadow. The sour smell of decay struck his nose. The boy with midnight hair lay unconscious a few paces away, half out of the water on the same mucky shoreline.

Peter! Tinker Belle flitted into view.

"TINK!" Peter lit up. "Where have you been!? Where's father? Wait, did you just say my name!?"

Self in heaven, Belle chimed. *Yes, I did.*

"Cuz I've been really thinking about-" Peter lit up. "TINK! I can understand you!"

What the hell?

"Tink!" Peter gasped.

You have the mantle now!? She pressed her palms to her forehead. *What just happened?*

"How can I understand you!?" Peter asked.

She hesitated. *I- I don't know why, Peter, but you're the pan. Again.*

"I'm- what? No. I can't be. Father's the pan."

Tinker Belle mustered herself. *You are the pan, Peter. How else can you understand me?*

"I don't know … but it can't be because I'm pan. Father is the pan!"

Peter … Tinker Belle chimed. *You are pan.* She glanced at the other boy. *Again … What the hell just happened?*

"I'm *not* the pan," Peter stood in protest as grimy swamp water drooled from his clothes. He walked to the boy and rolled him over moments before a snake could strike the boy's face.

PETER! Tinker Belle cried. Peter shooed it away before checking the boy.

"Who is this?" Peter asked.

Tinker Belle clutched her thundering breast. *His name is Santi.*

"Santi? Where's he from? The Unionist ship?"

I'm- I'm not sure, Peter. He appeared this morning. He was wearing the ben'cari before … you somehow got it from him.

"The mantle? That's impossible."

It's not impossible, boy. Trust me, he was the pan just a minute ago.

Peter scowled. "Father is the pan."

Listen, you silly ass! Tinker Belle drew close. *You're the pan! Period! You think I don't know who the pan is!?*

Tears welled in Peter's eyes. "I- I can't be."

Tinker Belle winced and fluttered close enough to set her hand on his cheek. *I'm sorry, Peter, but your father gave you the mantle the night before last.*

"Wait, he gave it to me?" Peter linked through his tears.

Of course. Don't you remember?

"Last thing I remember, I was at the Tree with mom. Where's mom!?"

This time Tinker Belle's throat tightened more than she could overcome. She closed her eyes. *She's …*

A faint thunder echoed through the swamp behind them counter to the nearby waterfall.

Peter spun. A darkness lumbered through the swirling green gases drifting over an archipelago of moss-carpeted mounds rising from the dank water. Trees climbing from soil or scrum bowed outward at the approach of a monolith, a beast of such size as to send all others scurrying away.

Peter, get out of here! Tinker Belle panicked.

Peter planted his feet.

Peter! GO!

"Hush, Tink," Peter said.

Great reflective yellow eyes shimmered in the dappled swamp light as the beast approached in slow earth-shuddering steps. Out of the murk slid leathery skin and rows of bumpy ridges lining an amphibious snout larger than a horse cart. Lying flat, the beast's head rose as high as the ceiling of a small house. Peter faced the monster with his fists on his hips in his peculiar way. Its snout preceded the rest of its head by paces, which meant its tail stretched further into the murk than even Peter could make out.

"A crocodile!" Peter cried.

Peter, what are you doing, you silly ass!? GO!

Peter hesitated to say he was the pan — he couldn't be the pan — but if he was the pan, the croc wouldn't hurt him. Instead, he just tamped down his fear while pretending he was brave. "Come, Lord Crocodile!!"

Lord WHAT??

The beast veered askance of Peter and paused within two paces of Santi lying unconscious on the shore. It waited, as if for Peter to move aside.

"You want the boy?" Peter asked.

Clicks erupted from the beast's throat.

Peter hopped back and forth over the boy. The beast did not move. "He wants Santi."

Why the hell would he want a boy?? Food?

"I don't know," Peter said. "WAIT!" He spun so fast Tinker Belle flinched and raised her empowered hands and glowing eyes. Peter pointed at the boy. "He's one of the boys! The boys lost on the island that father told me about!"

What?

"He's one of those boys father talked about!" Peter lit up at Santi, who lay face down upon the muck, half out of the pool of water. "I didn't know they came out on their own."

Tinker Belle frowned.

Glancing at the croc, Peter made up his mind. "He'll be one of my men."

One of your what?

"I have to assume father is captured and mother is, too. Perhaps I escaped from the brigands and fell unconscious before the mermaids rescued me."

Whuh- Tinker Belle paused.

"We'll take him with us."

What in hell are you talking about!? We have to get you off this island and home as- I don't know. Somehow!

Peter faced her. "We can't leave. We must find father. He will know what to do."

Peter, Tinker Belle chimed, *I hate to tell you this, but your father ... he's ...*

"Let's get back to the Tree, Tink." Peter waved her off.

Peter, I don't think you fully understand our situation... Tinker Belle hovered as Peter knelt to pick up Santi and toss him over his shoulder.

A deep guttural rumble from the croc's throat vibrated the scummy water in protest.

"I am the pa-" Peter faced the crocodile and cut himself off. "I am Peter!" He bopped the croc on the smooth skin between his massive nostrils, almost afraid the croc would snap him up for doing so, then giggled when the croc did nothing. "So there!"

He marched off through the shallow river leading away from the frothing pool beneath the waterfall and noticed the beast lumber in pursuit. Peter waded to the far shore and paused at the foot of the steep ridge.

We could just go that way. Tinker Belle motioned to their left. *There's probably a way out if we- but no, you're going to climb it, aren't you?*

Peter had snatched a hold with one hand and started climbing with Santi over his shoulder. He had never felt better or stronger. He dug his toes into the rocky soil and scaled the rock with an iron grip.

Hovering close, Tinker Belle scanned the canopy as they ascended into the foliage. She landed on the back of Peter's green longcoat and gripped his crimson hair at the nape of his neck.

I'm coming along for the ride, boy. He smiled at that before she muttered to herself, *In more ways than one, it seems.*

19

Scouting Party

Tiger Lily stood alone on an endless floor of water frozen to such stillness as to reflect the encircling wall of blue smoke. Holding her staff vertical before her and both eyes closed, she listened to the rhythms of the universe breathing. Out of the fog cried men in pain and death. Magic crashed and metal clanged. Ocean vessels creaked and great white sheets of cloth flapped. The cacophony vibrated the water with each rise and pulse before fading under the laughter of boys.

Her eyes opened. A small white bird fluttered from the blue smoke into the open space. She snapped her bow from a vertical hold out before her in a straight, horizontal line just in time for the little white bird to perch upon its end.

A smaller yellow bird fired from the fog and encircled the little white bird in tiny loops and circles before perching upon its shoulder. Within the fog darted about a shadow, whose passing ripped and rushed the blue mist. She knew the shadow belonged to the little white bird, but did not understand how they had separated. The shadow circled the circumference of the fog before it looped and crashed into the watery floor. From that point, heavy ripples growled low in the throat, like a mighty amphibian whose glowing yellow eyes peered from the base of the fog. It sank into the smooth floor and the birds returned to the blue mist.

In an explosion of auroric light, a mighty island thrust upward from the mirrored floor, filling the horizon and shattering the drift. Waves crashing outward ignored her. Gasps of real men echoed. She withdrew her staff.

"Tiger Lily." A hand upon her shoulder drew her from the trance.

Opening her eyes, Tiger Lily found the same island in the same place before her in a panoply of vibrant colors under the bright, cresting sun. The canoe rocked with ocean waves just beyond the island's lagoon. The braves around her and in the other three canoes gasped at their sudden arrival to the island.

"We are here," said Tiger Lily, clad in an over-the shoulder thick cotton dress cinched at the waist with a colorful belt of beaded leather. While the braves wore their braids down their backs, her thick black braid circled her head. Like the other braves, she wore breechcloths and leggings from the knee to her moccasins. She, alone, wore a single-shoulder vest that wrapped around her trunk in beaded patterns taught by her grandmother and the tribe's eldest and most honored squaw, Rain Singer.

"The land of the Tree." Her father motioned from his seat behind her. "Onward."

Sharing glances and looking to her father for reassurance, the men resumed their slow, steady strokes through the ocean waves.

"Another trance?" her father asked in his low rumble. His deep-set brown eyes scanned the island beneath a full, straight brow and long nose. A tall man for their tribe, his long muscles still paddled in the swift, short strokes to match the shorter brave at the bow of the canoe.

"Yes," she said, "but now a smaller yellow bird circles the little white one. And a shadow."

"A shadow?"

"I will tell you more, tomorrow."

As one, they paddled forward, crested the reef's break, and entered the lagoon.

"We are north, turn east." She pointed to their left.

The men looked from her to her father for a nod. They paddled onward with tired but steady strokes past an ancient alpine forest to their right. Her eyes locked onto the highest point of the low ridges lining the eastern side of the island, sure she would stand there one day.

The canoes moved southward along a forested shore and a narrow inlet between the main island on their right and ridged islet to their left. As they rounded the curve southward, they found themselves at the mouth of a river. To their surprise, the water flowed inland.

"We will follow." Her father directed them down the river.

Mountainous terrain and gentle inlets rolled by to their right and a broad desert on their left. High ridges dove into the water from both sides as terrain climbed upward. Water quickened between the narrowing walls and twisting turns, rushing with froth and roil over unseen boulders hiding below the shadowed waters. The narrow canyons opened again to reveal a broad desert waste to their left and steep, rippling forested hills to the right.

"Here." Cougar eyed a distortion in the water a mile distant as the two canoes approached the pebbled shore.

"Don't touch the water," said Tiger Lily as they drew near. "Beach high."

Braves moved into the back of the canoe with practiced grace enough to lift the bow out of the water. After landing high, they stepped onto the beach and hauled the canoes above the waterline.

A stocky man with narrow eyes, bold chin and full lips, Red Badger hesitated. "I am sorry, Great Cougar. I doubted your mother."

Great Cougar squeezed his arm before both scanned the north island and across the river to the great desert of the south island, but found a barren waste stretched dozens of miles below the same distant snowcap they spotted on their way in.

"How can this be there?" A brave motioned at the waste. "Was it not a sea of sand before?"

"It was," breathed another. "There is more land than there was, and so many kinds so close together. What is this?"

Great Cougar held up his hand to calm them, even as his own heart thundered in his chest. He looked to Tiger Lily.

"This is your place, father," said Tiger Lily. "You must become one with it."

Great Cougar glanced at Badger and faced the rest. "We will split. Red Badger, take your canoe to the south island and explore to the far coast. Return at sunset. Wolf Brother, stay with Tiger Lily here on the beach." He scanned left and right. "Remain very alert."

Wolf Brother nodded. Red Badger took his braves in two canoes across the river to the far shore.

Facing the trees washing in the wind, Cougar closed his eyes and inhaled. "Breathe, brothers."

The others did the same to slow their hearts and calm their nerves.

"Eyes up," Cougar said before leading them into the forest. "Let's go."

As the braves melted into the terrain on either side of the river, Tiger Lily's stomach tightened. Her people had traveled generations since forming in the far west so they might find a place for themselves and their unique ways. To stand upon the sand foretold in a vision when her grandmother was a little girl, and to draw in the deep rich smell of its earth and vibrancy of its breath thrilled her. Her heart pounded as her eyes traced the flora hanging out over the high back of the beach as it swayed in the heavy breeze.

Like her grandmother, Tiger Lily began having visions at a young age. Now eight years old, she was beginning to see the flow of spirit as her grandmother taught her and would one day carry her mantle as the tribe's seer. Though heavy, it was a burden she was eager to own. As she and the brave scouted the beach for a freshwater source, she paused.

"Ah ... they found the lady of ice."

20

Adrift

"CAPTAIN!" bellowed the lookout from the crow's nest. "OFF TO STARBOARD!"

Rocky Dorsman, captain of the Hover, moved to the bridge's starboard rail and squinted against the harsh sun shining over the icy waters. Several hundred yards off floated a figure clinging to something large and half-submerged.

"Hard to starboard!" he barked. The pilot spun the wheel and the ship tilted to port as it turned.

The Hover groaned as loose objects tumbled across the tilting deck. Sailors snatched lines, some even precariously swinging off the deck as the ship canted. The captain clung to the starboard rail as it vaulted skyward beneath his feet. His knuckles whited while he kept his eyes on the distant, bobbing figure.

"Furl sail!" His every command was echoed by a terse first officer or roaring bosun. As the ship righted, sailors scrambled to raise the sails. "Prepare a ship's boat."

Harry Bristol emerged from his quarters next to the captain's and climbed to the high starboard rail with the gathering mages. Across the waters, the ship's boat approached the figure, inspected it, tied a rope around it and began its return. Drawing nearer, Harry recognized a woman clinging to a heavy block of ship's hull, her hair splayed across it and the bottom of her left fist locked against it just before her face.

A leftenant behind the mages shooed all aside but Bristol, a slender, narrow-faced man with close-cropped dark hair and coarse stubble over sunken cheeks, as he directed sailors to reposition the mast-braced pulley and lower a line.

"With care, Dobney!" the young officer in the ship's boat yelled upward at the officer directing the pulley. A line of men pulled the rope with care until block and woman rose dripping from the water and steaming with frost. Clearing the starboard rail, the pulley swung inward so the men could gather her with care and set her on deck before backing away.

Harry knelt, tugged hair from her face and leaned in. "Great Self, it's Athyka."

"Aside," barked the bosun as Rocky knelt next to Harry.

Reeking of rum, the ship's doctor knelt on the opposite side behind Athyka's back.

"She's alive," he slurred for his drink and his accent. "But ..." He delved her hand bound to the board and recoiled in a shock. "What the hell is that?"

Harry touched her frozen fist and flinched. "Shit. She's got an ohna."

"An ohna?" Rocky's eyebrow rose.

"Her face is frozen to something on the wood," the doctor loomed over her. "And there's a faint tear here." Hauling her from the water had ripped a small tear in her cheek. "When this thaws, it will bleed badly. I need warm water. Now!"

Men ran to the galley to instruct the ship's cook.

The captain inspected the semi-frozen fist. "Is she dead?"

Athyka's sudden moan startled the men. Dorsman leaned in.

"Can you hear me?"

Her eyes cracked open to reveal heavy redness throughout and black-rimmed irises. They latched upon Rocky half-lidded, then flared a bit on Harry standing behind him.

"We can try to melt the freeze," said the doctor, "but it might get messy. Rular, go get my bandages." He pointed a sailor away on his errand.

"She was on Unity's Light," Harry said. "She was the first sent after the pan."

Athyka's breath deepened.

140

"Can you understand me?" Harry leaned over Athyka. Her eyes struggled to focus.

"Drop sail, return to course," the captain directed a leftenant who passed the word to the first officer. Sailors scrambled to their duties under a frigid mid-afternoon sky. A few minutes later, the cook emerged holding a steaming pot of water by its thin handle in one hand and a ladle in his other.

"We can't use boiling," the doctor directed the pot to the deck and stirred the water with the ladle. He pointed at the cook. "Prepare more." The cook saluted and returned to the galley as Rular appeared with bandages from the doctor's supply.

"I fear taking too much time or she'll lose the entire cheek," said Harry.

"Aye," the doctor lifted the ladle of water steaming against the cold and waited until he could dip his finger in without burning.

Harry leaned over Athyka and stirred her again. "Athyka."

She managed to lock her eyes upon his face.

"We're going to try and free you from the block," he said. "This may hurt."

The disoriented woman groaned.

Dorsman directed one sailor to brace the wood and the leftenant and another sailor to brace Athyka. "Hold her down so she can't twist away."

"Ready?" the doctor asked.

"Go," Harry said.

Despite his drunkenness, the doctor slid a steady hand under Athyka's chin from behind and drooled the warm water down the side of the board over her face.

"It's too cool," said the doctor. "We have to use warmer."

They waited until the steam was faint in the second ladle before trying it. They poured several before her skin gentled with a pinky white against the icy blue gluing it to the wood.

Consciousness and pain wormed its way into Athyka's sluggish brain.

"I think feeling's beginning to return," said Harry. Pain filled her eyes. "Use the hotter water. We have to get her off the board quickly."

"Are you sure?" the doctor paused.

"It's cooled off enough. Use it."

The doctor waited for the captain to nod before ladling it direct from the pot.

Her eyes winced and her free hand fisted, then started slapping the deck.

"Is it working?" Dorsman inspected her face.

"It's not happening quickly," the doctor said. "There's something else stuck to her face other than the wood."

Blood seeped down the side of the wood. She tightened. "Sshhtp."

"We have to get you off this board," Harry inspected the ohna. The doctor ladled the water faster, pressed his fingers on her cheek from across her mouth and tried to work it free without ripping it.

"SHtahp," she jerked with her frozen fist sticking to the board.

"I'm sorry, Agent Bonduquoy, but we have to get you off." The doctor ladled more water. Gushes now seeped through the gash in her cheek and flushed trickling blood through her teeth.

"Fffck, shtap!" she moaned as tears formed in her eyes.

"Hold her down or she'll rip herself," said the doctor. The leftenant and sailor pinned her as the doctor worked her cheek. "This is too slow. She'll bleed out before we can get her off.

The cook appeared with a fresh pot.

"Then use as hot as you think you dare," Harry said.

The doctor ladled from the fresh pot, waited till he was satisfied, then raised it over her face. "Pin her."

Athyka moaned in expectation.

The doctor reached around her neck, cupped her chin and braced her head. He dribbled hot water down the board onto her face. She screamed through her teeth and thrashed. After a heaved breath, she screamed again and flailed.

"Hold her!" the doctor snapped.

The sailor pinning her snatched him by the throat and hauled him off of her.

"Sailor!" Dorsman shot to his feet when the leftenant drew his sword to stand over her. Dorsman darted into the leftenant's swing arc and, snatching out his knife from his belt, struck at the young man's throat in a fist-strike, leaving a hole in his carotid. Even as a stream of blood pumped from his neck, the leftenant raised his sword while his pupils fluttered.

Sailors ripped the first sailor from the doctor when the leftenant struck at Dorsman. The captain parried with his knife and then cut the man's throat wide open. Blood showered him and Athyka as the man staggered in a failing attempt to stay upright before slapping to the deck, dead.

In the chaos, Harry grabbed the pot itself and poured it down the board. Athyka screamed before two sailors knocked Harry across the deck and sent the pot tumbling in a spray of burning water. The doctor stumbled from the fight, grabbed Athyka's face and ripped it free of the board. While she bellowed in agony, a sword appeared from out the doctor's stomach as a sailor ran him through. His back arched and he dropped to his knees before another sailor stabbed the soft of his right side, coming out from under his left rib cage. The doctor said nothing as he collapsed spasming to the deck.

As sailors freed Harry from his two attackers, he pointed. "She's a daleen!"

Cries of "minder" and "daleen" echoed across deck as Athyka clutched the bloody gashes down her face. Though she tried to stand, her left fist remained frozen to the object sticking out from the block of hull. A terrified sailor charged with his sword.

She threw out her free hand at the man, who staggered and slapped face-first into the deck before his skin frosted blue. Another attacked from behind. At a look from her, he turned against other sailors. A melee broke out as Athyka raised her open bloody hand at anyone she thought might approach her, revealing skin missing from her right rear molars and bare cheekbone, exposing most of the inside of her mouth, and thinning up to the right side of her scalp. Blood drooled down from the rip of her exposed skin and cheek. In all her movement, the crimson drips snaked over her wild eyes. She opened her bloody mouth and screamed. Her head snapped downward when Dorsman slapped her head with an oar from a few feet away.

Athyka dropped limp to the deck and the final sailor attacking the others staggered to his knees.

"HOLD!" Dorsman roared as the other sailors had prepared to run him through. Panicky sailors retreated from each other, all afraid of their minds being enslaved.

Harry loomed over Athyka. "More hot water, immediately!"

"Aye!" the cook ducked his head and took off running.

Dorsman wiped his face with his thick forearm and knelt next to her hand still frozen to the board and found the pommel of a small ice knife in her fist.

Harry shared a look with him before turning to a sailor. "Bring me the dwarf."

21

Poking Around

Fenren crossed his arms and leaned against the column behind the highest seat in the parliamentary amphitheater. Commoners and Unionist-approved wealthy nobles and merchants alike warmed the room with their presence and their murmuring. He frowned at their backs and the great act all played. The commoners pretended to understand power, the wealthy lapdogs pretended to love the poor, and the Unionist leaders on the main floor pretended to actually care about anyone but themselves. Fenren thumbed the shape of fire carved into the top of the crystal torch tucked in his belt.

"My dear fellows!" Roschach's raised hands and smiling cry drew thunderous applause. "Welcome to our new home!" The cheering deepened. "Our long journey to victory here in Eden is complete!"

Fenren sighed.

The sight of the Baley family crest — a circular symbol of the tree of life with trunks and foliage at the top and roots at the bottom — still hung in the glass window high on the rear wall of the chamber's dome. He leaned his head to the side to get a better view as Roschach roused the crowd.

"You seem enthralled," a woman said behind him.

Fenren turned his head. "Amra."

Agent Amra Alba joined him while Roschach gestured in his bright white general's coat fronted in heavy golden horizontal bars down his chest. His thick black hair swept from a square-jawed caramel face and bright eyes. "He's so pretty."

Fenren snorted a chuckle.

"Why aren't you down there holding his cape out and billow it like wind and stuff?"

Fenren's face tightened.

"Give him a reach around ..." Amra mused.

"Oh, c'mon," Fenren snapped. She smirked. "That's not an image I wanted in my head. Or ... anywhere, really."

"I think you two are cute."

"I think you have problems. What do you want?"

Amra crossed her arms.

"We will press our advantage across the continent." Roschach's voice filled the acoustic space. "Now as a member of the Edenic Charter, we will join our brothers in Alderland to create the bonds of brotherhood of men across the continent. Together, we can forge an empire of equality for all, to share the wealth of this world so that no one is greater or lesser, more or less powerful ... in this world, we are all the same!"

Fenren squeezed his eyes and sniffed. He caught Amra watching him and raised an eyebrow.

She shrugged and turned back to Roschach.

Fenren rolled his eyes.

"Baley's worried," said Amra.

"Baley's always worried."

"Roschach has been anything but forthcoming about our progress on Algueda."

"Did you ask Roschach?" asked Fenren.

"I'd rather ask his girlfriend," said Amra.

"Are you normally this charming?"

"I'm always this charming."

"Then you can go charm yourself," Fenren said.

"Oh, cute. Cursing me without using big people words."

"Bitch said what?" he raised an eyebrow.

"You're an entire year old, I think."

"What do you want, Amra?"

"Baley wants to know Bonduquoy's progress," Amra said.

"Then ask Roschach."

"Roschach's above my paygrade." Amra shrugged.

"I'm not in a paygrade."

"Don't secretaries have paygrades?"

Fenren leaned off the column and walked away. Her bootfalls echoed in his wake. He stopped and faced her. She picked her fingernails with a stiletto as she sauntered up to him.

"Can't handle a little needling, Fenren?"

Roschach's rising voice preempted his response as he welcomed a man standing beside the quorum. A stocky man of midnight skin approached and mounted the dais in a robe of white and green bound by a thick leather belt and an intricate metal buckle. His thin layer of black hair bore intricate symbols cut to indicate his rank and status. He walked sandaled feet across the smooth marble to stand beside Roschach.

"My dear fellows, our brother from Alderland." Roschach bowed to the newcomer. "Lord Humrail Abydon."

Abydon stepped forward to address the applauding congregation.

"My friends of the People's Union of Pangea!" He mimicked Roschach's raised hands and drew a similar roar of applause. "I come bearing the support of the Holy Empire of the Alderlands. Emperor Benuin himself is pleased to see the people of the continent finally drawing together to seek an accord of purpose! The king assures me that he now feels free to pursue his own long-awaited campaign to bring the nobles to heel and gather all the peoples of his holy empire under a banner of brotherhood with you!"

The crowd cheered and Fenren raised an eyebrow.

"He promises armies and resources to help spread the faith of this great fellowship." Abydon's words carried across the masses. "All he asks is your beloved patience as he works to change his people's hearts and minds from the dirty traditions to which they have clung. Our people are good but misguided and need time. I have seen the movement among my people, dear fellows. I assure you, a passion for liberty from the struggles of this world and ancient responsibilities wells within Alderlanders across our vast empire. Thank you for leading the way! Thank you, Fellow Roschach!" He motioned to Roschach, who offered a humble smile and slight bow that drew the applause to a roar.

Fenren returned to Amra. "We're doing everything we can to secure the mantle and protect Peter. What else do you want to know?"

"Specifics."

"Specifically, we're doing everything we can to secure the mantle and protect Peter."

"That's cute."

"Also, specifically, go fuck yourself. If Baley feels dissatisfied with Roschach's iron tongue, then she can go ride some other motherfucker for her intel. Roschach's in charge of securing the mantle. If Baley wanted to get the ben'cari, she should have cut off her brother's dick herself before he snuck out of the palace right under her nose. So, if you want other people to do your dirty work and then ride them to death with juvenile questions, go back to the pussy swamp on the bitch from which you sprung. Are we clear, *Fellow* Alba?"

Amra's jaw tightened and her eyes narrowed just as the crowd roared again.

Fenren smirked, turned around and walked away tapping the crystal torch in his belt. He wondered why they hadn't received communiques from Athyka as planned, but he wasn't about to tell that snarky bitch a selfdamn thing. He reached the end of the walk and paused to lean again on a column.

Roschach took command of the crowd once more, before presenting Abydon a small statue of silver and gold as a token of the new Union's appreciation for his support, smelted from Edenon coins straight from the pockets of the filthy rich, so he said. Fenren remembered them smelting a random bronze statue of a rabbit from the garden and coating it in fool's gold to produce the damned thing.

Roschach and Abydon were all smiles during the exchange, but it was obvious to Abydon the thing wasn't gold as much as it was obvious to Roschach that Abydon's speech was complete bullshit. But then, neither had even tried to lie to the other, just to the attendees here for the show.

"When you do hear something…" Amra's stiletto tapped the side of his ear with her lips inches away. "Baley expects an update. On the boy, *and* the room."

Fenren half turned his head until the stiletto pressed into his cheek. She waited. He waited. She then tapped his cheek and withdrew the knife.

"She wants the same updates Roschach gets on your translations."

"Roschach is the only one offering permission to see inside." Fenren faced her as the crowd roared at the end of Roschach's speech. "I'm not playing your go-between."

"I'm not returning to Baley withou-" Amra trailed off.

With his thumb resting on the tip of the ohna luminar, her eyes fell dark. In his mind, he directed light to fill her corneas so that she could not see. He prepared to threaten her when a tear welled her eye.

"Uncle Harold?" she whispered.

Fenren hesitated.

"Great Self, Uncle Harold ..." Tears drooled down her face.

"What do you see, exactly?"

"My uncle..." Fear filled her face. "I- I'm sorry. Oh, please. Don't make me see him. Don't make me see him!" She snatched at Fenren while her eyes locked upon a face that was not there.

Fenren started. She was seeing a face? Fenren hadn't intended her to see anything but light—that wasn't true. He wanted to instill fear through light ... but what had the torch done? He almost released it, wondering what it might do to him in turn. A power of creation was like no magic he had ever used. Was it intelligent? What was it doing? Looking again to the terror in Alba's face, he leaned in. "If you don't want to see your uncle, then you will steer clear of making demands of me. Is that clear?"

"Y-y-yes," she quivered.

Fenren leaned back. Stone-faced Amra Alba was the stoic among them, the one who made jokes but never rose to a prod. She stood here now as a little girl with eyes of fear caused by a face that did not exist. Fenren pulled his finger from the torch. Her fluttering lashes washed away what she had seen. When her eyes focused on his, she retreated, shoved quivering hands down to her sides and marched away. Fenren tapped the crystal torch again. He felt shaken. Using an ohna never felt like using magic to him. Magic was a force that affected reality. Using a power of creation felt like using reality, itself.

Alarmed, Fenren marched down the nearest stairwell, away from the roaring crowd and the memory of Alba's strange terror.

22

Peter and Santi

Peter climbed the southern road gapping three paces per step. He stopped to catch his breath at the Tree's outer clearing. "Wow. That was so cool."

Exhausted, Tinker Belle caught her breath on his shoulder. *How the hell did you just run like that? I've never seen your father do that.*

Peter approached the vine wall. Spades snaked out from the wall and narrowed in on Santi, as if to threaten him away from Peter.

Peter ... Tinker Belle warned.

The spades drew close enough to prick Santi.

"HEY!" Peter cried. The spades recoiled back. "Leave him alone!"

They rattled in protest and drew away.

Tinker Belle gaped. *You just ... you just- what did you just do?*

"Move," Peter growled at the wall, which split to create the path of thick, woven green roots. He stepped down on the other side and turned back. "Don't attack him again."

The spades withdrew into the wall as Peter set Santi down next to the fire. The familiar scent of dogwood filled the inner clearing, warm with early afternoon sun.

You just SPOKE to them!? Tinker Belle cried. *Oh self, Rupert.*

"What're you talking about?" asked Peter.

Tinker Belle opened her mouth to speak when Santi moaned, raised his hand to his forehead and cracked open his eyes.

"Mother of God." Santi sat up and cleared his muddled vision. "What just happened?"

"Welcome to Neverland." Peter planted his hands on his hips. "My island."

Your island? asked Tinker Belle.

"Your island?" Santi rubbed his eyes. "Never-what?"

"This is Neverland." Peter offered his hand. "And you are one of my men."

Santi ignored the hand. "Where is this?"

"I told you," Peter said. "Neverland."

"What- augh!" Santi caught whiff of the dried filth covering him. "What happened?"

"We fell off a waterfall," said Peter.

Santi looked from him to the fairy. "What happened?"

He just told you, Tinker Belle chimed.

"Are you going to answer me?" Santi asked Tinker Belle.

I just did. "She just did."

Santi eyed Peter. "No, surely. I could understand her just a while ago. Can she still understand me?"

"Yes," Peter said. "Tink understands everyone because the pan does."

"But I cannot understand her any longer?"

"No," Peter said.

"But I could before? Why?"

"That's because you were-," Peter cut himself off from saying Santi had been the pan.

He was the pan, Peter, Tinker Belle chimed.

Peter spared her a low glare.

"She said before that I was the one? The- whole?" Santi tried to translate the word in his head. "All? I could understand her before."

"Pan," Peter coughed. "She said you were the pan."

"Yes." Santi cleared his eyes. "Who are you?"

"I'm the pa- I'm Peter," Peter said.

Santi scowled before he clutched his head. "Ay. My head is splitting. I heard her speak before. When was that?"

This morning.

Santi narrowed on her again.

"This morning," Peter half chuckled. "Time flies when you're having fun, you know!"

Santi rolled his eyes before squeezing them. "I feel like I got kicked by a horse … everywhere."

"You hit the water pretty hard," Peter said.

Santi's eyes opened again. "Something … happened. One moment, I was saving you, the next … some kind of thing happened. An explosion, like gunpowder, but I didn't see any smoke."

Peter just nodded.

The mantle transferred to you, Peter.

"It was the mantle," Peter said.

"Mantle?" Santi lifted his shirt to reveal heavy bruising up and down his side. He touched his ribs and hissed; several appeared purple and swollen, as did the side of his face along the right jaw and neck. "Ay … What is going on?"

He's from Earth, Peter. He won't understand any of this.

Peter hunched before plopping down next to the firepit. "Alright. So … how far back do I go?"

Start with the reformation. The alterbridges and the pan.

"Ah."

Do you know the story?

"Of course, I do!" Peter stammered. He recited his lessons from his tutor. "Okay. Thousands of years ago, the Great Self created the alterworlds. He used the First Powers, also called ohnas, to connect each of them to Pangea. Shortly after, he created the mantle of the pan and gave it to then-Lord of Eden Astekar to protect the powers."

"Wait, who is this Great Self?" asked Santi.

"He's the creator," Peter shrugged.

Santi shook his head.

"So, he gives Astekar the mantle, which gives him long life, great strength, protects him from the ohnas and makes his own magic stronger. Astekar was already a mage."

"You said lord of Eden. I know of Eden from the Bible. Is this the same? With the Tree of Life?"

"Yeah!" Peter smiled. "At least, it used to be! That's my family symbol. But now it's here."

"What is?"

"The Tree of Life."

"Where?"

Peter looked at something behind Santi.

Santi turned and for the first time noticed the massive tree rising over him. His eyes widened in wonder before he could remember his question. "This is the symbol of your family?"

"Yeah. Father is pan."

"And your father is now lord of Eden?"

"Yup," Peter said.

"So, he is a king?"

"Kind of?" Peter asked Tinker Belle.

Yes, he's a parliamentary monarch.

"Oh, yes. A parliamentary monarch."

Tinker Belle's brow drew down.

"And if you are king, then you must live in a palace?" Santi's brow climbed.

"Well, we did, but," Peter said, "I'm not sure where we're going to live now."

"What? Why not?" Santi straightened.

"Because Unionists." Peter shrugged and fingered the dead fire. Shifting ash revealed a glinting object, beneath. "The war. I'm not sure we can go back. We left in secret. I think …" Peter's fingers latched onto something. "Besides, I like it here." He scanned the island. "It's a lot more interesting here than it has been at the palace for a long time."

Endless war councils, fiery parliamentary sessions lasting days, Edenon soldiers crowding hallways where Peter often played, and countless other changes brought him up short. He shook it off.

"There's no going home." Peter fished a sheathed silver knife from the ashes, his eyes widening. "At least, not for now."

"I would go home if I could," said Santi. "I miss my father. Ay, I live in a lovely country, upon which run many horses — stallions — and great sailing ships upon her coast. I had a beautiful family. I …" Santi frowned. Something haunted his eyes. "I missed them before I got here."

Kellogg's dagger, Tinker Belle spotted the knife.

"What is that?" Santi asked.

"It's my grandfather's knife." Peter pulled the knife out of the sheath. Silver gleamed in the late afternoon light.

Your father gave it to you, Belle chimed.

"Oh yeah." Peter smiled, then glanced at Santi. "You weren't with them before? Your family?"

"No," said Santi. "We traveled to a place very far from home. My grandfather became a Jesuit late in life and followed the pope's commission to the New World to save the savages."

His eyes slid to Peter and Tinker Belle, blinking, then looked away. Peter noticed a few tiny gleaming specks in them.

"What happened?" Peter asked.

"I …" Santi lost his words. "I, uh … I did something terrible. I made a mistake. Something I can never change."

"I'm sorry," Peter said.

"So, where are we? Are w e in the Bahamas?" Santi ran his fingers through his thick black hair.

"Bahamas?"

"The Azores? Mediterranean? Or are we beyond the horn of Africa? Indian Ocean?"

"We're somewhere between Pangea and Earth," said Peter.

"We … we are not on Earth?"

"No," Peter said.

Sort of, Tinker Belle chimed.

Peter turned. "What do you mean?"

Tinker Belle overlapped fingers from one hand over the other. *Do you know how a button connects two overlapping pieces of cloth?*

"Yeah," Peter raised his head.

Algueda, like all alterbridges, exists both on Earth and in Pangea.

"What did she say?"

Peter translated.

"Ah," Santi said. "So … how shall I get home?"

Peter shrugged. "I don't even know how you got here. Or why. But since you're here now, you're gonna be one of my men."

"Your men?" asked Santi. "Why your man?"

"Of course!" Peter stood. "This is the pan's island, which means it's mine until we find my father! Which means we're gonna have lots of adventures! We're gonna hunt sailors and beasts and explore the volcanoes and the mountains and the forests!" He spun around and thrust out an invisible sword, riling himself up.

"So …" Santi climbed to his feet. "What now?"

"Well, I suppose I'm gonna have to send you out to get more boys. We can't have an army with only one."

"You want to create an army? Where?"

"You'll recruit more boys from all over the island!" Peter grinned. "And then we'll be a force to be reckoned with! And then we can get my father and he'll get us back home." Peter planted his fists on his hips, spread his feet and puffed his chest.

"And … how, exactly, am I to do that?"

"You don't know!? Come now, man! You must use your keen senses!" Peter rounded on Santi. "To gather boys from the island will take all the cunning and know-how a smart boy can muster! Are you smart? Are you clever? Can you muster!?" Peter loomed.

"Y- yes," Santi said.

"Good," Peter said.

"What happened earlier?" Santi asked. "At the waterfall? Something … happened, between us."

"Well …" Peter scanned the clearing and cliffside and latched upon something. "Look at that!" He pointed at a thin stream of smoke rising from a forest on the opposite end of the north island. "That must be my father!"

Tinker Belle drew near. *Great Self, someone did survive.*

"It must be," Peter said. "We'll find him, immediately."

No, Tinker Belle chimed. *I'll head out around evening. Let's get you both set up for a while, then I'll go scout the fires.*

"But why not now?"

Peter, the mantle helps you, but you still need to eat and rest. You can't keep going indefinitely.

"I'm not the pan," he insisted.

"I thought she said I was the pan?" Santi asked from behind them. Peter waved dismissively.

And besides, Neverland at night is even more dangerous than the day, as you already know. She poked his chest. His face tightened. *So, gather firewood and some food Santi can eat without killing him.*

"Fine, but in the morning, we're going." Peter returned to Santi.

After a controlled breath, Tinker Belle followed.

23

Aurora

Aurora Vara floated in the nether — a quantum fabric between the low realm of the physical world and the high realm of ascendant heaven. She kept her distance from great creatures of untold age and size who lived here — the magnalarks — as they drifted by in the distance, if distance could be measured in the nothingness. To encounter their minds could burn her own to cinders. Her 700 years as a pixilark — even as an aurora straddling the realms — were as nothing to their hundreds of millions of years of life. And yet, knowing she could not approach them, worry riddled her as it grew more difficult even to sense their presence. Change was coming to the lark race. Soon, the last magna would transition to become a pixie and herald the end of the two-phase lifecycle of the lark. On that day, she knew, the pixies would pay a difficult cost for love to continue without them.

An inverted stream of voices, images and memories of things yet to be and already done flowed by. Flashes of moments wove themselves together in a pattern that made sense only to the mind of an aurora.

"Draco in the selerie!" cried a woman.

"Proud and insolent youth," growled a deep voice, "prepare to meet thy doom."

"I love you, Haephan! I love you!" screamed a girl.

"I need your help, old woman," said a man. "I need to find someone. I need to find Haraven."

"Dark and sinister man," answered a boy, "have at thee."

"The next haraven will be a tinker," said a teenage girl.

"PETER!" the girl's voice echoed in the swirl.

Aurora Vara twisted about in the closed rose blossom where she slept. Visions crashed through her mind. Dragons wreathed in shadow, violent humans of varying breeds, dwarves at war, high elves and a thousand species at risk from unseated ohnas.

Hovering along the nether, Vara graced the edge of the real and unreal. Swirls tightened and singed her, drawing cries of pain and moans of fear from her bloodred lips.

Swirling chaos lifted from her into a tornado of memories yet to happen, at the center of which floated a ten-year-old redheaded boy with emerald eyes. Glowing in golden ambience, the child turned his face skyward and crowed. The piercing roar filled the space and drowned all other noise. As the aurora's eyes climbed the column of light rising from his eyes and mouth, she saw another figure staring back.

The immortal, she gasped. In a blink, the vision collapsed and Aurora Vara leapt from the heart of her rose bloom to the stone floor, anchored against an angled wall of soil at the far end of a long, arched chamber. A long pool of glowing water stretched most of the length of the chamber, a room shaped like a half cylinder laid on its side with her rose blossom at one end and double doors at the other.

Aurora! her attendants gathered around her. *Are you alright!?*

Vara raised her hand to silence them and sat up. She clutched her head as the pounding subsided.

Aurora Vara, pardon, but we've tried to wake you.

Why?

Elder Againa has come, the attendant gulped. *Unsummoned.*

Great Self, has it come so soon? Aurora Vara raised her elbows so her attendants could pull her onto unsteady feet. *Admit him.*

Yes, aurora. She rushed out through doors opening under the hands of large paladin fairies.

Elder Againa stepped through doors at the chamber's far end. The tall, stately pixie wore a long vest embroidered in shimmering thread over his powerful elder frame under a mane of white hair. His nose wrinkled at the pungent smell of rose oil that filled the chamber.

Aurora Vara quivered inside. Events moved faster than she had prepared. *Againa.*

Aurora Vara, he bowed his head. *I apologize for coming without a summons.*

She raised her hand to forestall him, then twisted it.

Againa's body wrenched upward into the air, wreathed in violent light. He tried closing his fingers as his body twisted from the tips of his wings to his toes. A scream erupted from his mouth.

And yet you came, she whispered and clenched her fist.

Againa twisted again. Another bloodcurdling scream ripped from his mouth before he collapsed to the floor and tumbled down the steps into the glowing pool.

At Vara's gesture, her attendants rushed into the water to right him so he might breathe. Vara held out her arms for nearby attendants to undo and pull away her filmy floral robe. Nude, she walked down steps into the water from her end of the long, luminescent pool. Hair clung to Againa's panting, open-mouthed face. Held up just enough to breathe by her attendants, the tall pixie locked onto Vara's approach.

What brings you, Againa? she cupped his face.

Againa tried in vain to stand. His head fell again before Vara reached under to lift his chin and press her bloodred lips to his. He responded, an addict at the first taste of his drug after a long sobriety. When she broke, he panted with exhaustion and the rising lust of her touch, a touch he had fought for years to forget from their first experience, an experience that had stuck with him like a narcotic.

I apologize, aurora. His muffled chimes vibrated the water. *I came about the haraven.*

About the passing ben'cari, yes, she chimed.

He eyed her through the wet, white hair clinging to his face. It was no surprise she would know. *Queen Mab wishes to withdraw the haraven and leave the humans to their fate.*

Mab does not like bowing to others. Vara's eyes narrowed. *But even she did not send you. You came of your own accord.*

Yes, aurora. Againa managed to swallow. He forced himself to his feet. His chest met the height of Aurora Vara's face, drawing her eyes.

What does she hope from you coming? Aurora Vara asked.

These events startle the flock; elders and eldresses first among them. They would have your counsel.

Without me offering? That is unwise, even for the elderate. And then you come on your own, despite their threat to make you, and despite you telling them off. Here I thought you wanted to stay away from me.

Againa quivered under her lusty inspection. Her firm breasts floated just beneath the surface. *I would not have them sacrifice another from ignorance.*

But you know. Her pouty red lips smiled as she ran her finger over his chest. *You know very well.*

Againa clenched his jaw as desire filled him. *I come as an arbiter and beg your mercy on those who would call on your unoffered counsel.*

You will have it. She kissed his chest, sending a fluttering wave of desire through him. At a gesture from her delicate fingers, her attendants began removing his clothes. Her magic emanated by her intimate touch. He sprang to life at her belly. *But mercy is all I will offer.*

Lust overwhelmed him now. Her mere touch filled his mind — her foreplay washed his mind away. When she licked his nipple, an orgasm ripped through him as the attendants continued disrobing and holding him up.

Tell them I said nothing to you. She smiled. *Or I will end you in such pain as to terrorize any other who might come unbidden, to the end of our race.* She hesitated.

A moan erupted from his mouth as he quivered to take her.

And you can tell them to take their questions about Tinker Belle along with them to hell. The aurora's eyes darkened. *She was chosen by powers greater even than me. While I know not the council's specific criteria for their distaste, what I know of the tinker speaks well of her selection.*

She pressed her breasts to his abs and clutched his ass, encouraging him to grind on her belly. Caught in her power, he succumbed. The attendants left the pool. He lifted the petite fairy to press his mouth to hers. Desire filled him with lust and strength. She climbed his body, spread her legs and sank down onto him, drawing another moan as he gripped her hair and bit into her neck. Arched backward by his overpowering lust, she wept at the horrific vision of the coming future.

She is the spark we need for the fire to come.

She closed her eyes and lost herself into his machinations before both sank beneath the chaotic surface of the luminescent water.

24

Time Alone

Why me, why me, why me? Tinker Belle followed the crest east along low mountain ridges. In the growing dim, the column of fire smoke faded into the background. In the murk, nocturnal predators hadn't yet gone hunting while diurnal predators bedded down.

Peter didn't want to believe his parents were dead. She was stuck on this goose chase, but if she could prove his dad wasn't out here, she might keep Peter near the clearing and away from danger until she could figure out a better plan.

Tinker Belle faltered and veered to a nearby branch so she could stop and tamp down her panic. Her previous plan was an unmitigated disaster. She might be able to talk Peter through his feelings, but alone, she felt helpless.

Great Self, what I am doing!? she muttered. How could she convince Peter his parents were dead? He didn't want to hear it; she struggled to say it. Every time she came near to telling him, the memory of April's face locked her up. Could she reveal that she, Tinker Belle, killed his mother? Would he understand it as a mercy or would he hate her? Could she ever tell him?

What were you thinking, aurora? Tinker Belle pressed her forehead to the branch. *Why me? I don't wanna do this. I was happy back at home, wandering the forest with the rest of the tinkers.* She exhaled. *Anything but this self-forsaken place.*

She closed her eyes.

What do you want, Great Self? How am I supposed to do this? Why am I even here trying to help children do what men can't handle?

Tinker Belle knuckled her tears.

Chin up, Belle, she returned to the air. *And get your ass in gear. No use crying over plucked flowers.*

Racing through ravines of crowded tree canopies, she aimed for where she had seen the smoke, but darkening sky swallowed its outline in the same dusky color. She stopped, again. *Self damnit, Belle. You and your stupid emotions!*

Tinker Belle scanned the trees, ever aware of the coming night, and turned to the Tree when a monstrous, snaking shadow rushed the canopy beneath her.

Her eyes slid downward. *Shit.*

She bolted westward as near the canopy as she could. The shadow snaked in pursuit and sent legions of flyers into the air.

Belle's wings buzzed and heart raced as she struggled to flee from her only one, unescapable nightmare, one suffered from her youngest days as the tiniest pixie in her small tinker feather.

A dragon.

Her sparking trail lit up a thousand startled eyes from under millions of heavy leaves. The hidden monster worked to cut her off by racing ahead and veering into her path, creating a shuddering wave of treetops in its wake. Panic filled her breast.

Forget this. She forewent her fear of flying too high and bolted above the canopy. In an explosion of flora, the dragon fired up before her with wings outspread and a mouth snapping down. *SHHHIT!*

Belle twisted aside just as the mouth snapped closed where she was about to be. She darted eastward and the dragon flapped its monstrous wings in pursuit. Every beat of its mighty wings sounded like countless smaller sets raking the air.

Great Self, they're back. They're back! I knew. Holy hell, I knew it!

The dragon snapped at her ankles with the crack of a hundred clapping beaks as it twisted in pursuit. Tinker Belle sucked air in gasps as she fled from before it. With her dwindling energy, she gathered power into her hands, stopped in mid-air, and fired at the beast with all she could muster.

The dragon exploded as a hundred ravens. Each veered to avoid her two powerful bolts in a cloud of violent cawing. A lone raven looped and gathered the others. For a brief moment, it watched her, before leading them away into the night.

HA! Tinker Belle barked. *What the hell was that!?* Nervous laughter ripped from her throat. *What the actual- I am in the wrong damn-* Her chimal scream sent nearby birds to flight. She gained her bearings, spotted the north shore a quarter mile away along low hills, and paused at the sight of a faint blue glow. After scanning for ravens, she flew north over the rolling grassy hills down into a shallow leading to the ocean. At the base of the ridge where it flattened out, a massive tree stump, the width of a small house, rose from a broad field of tall grass. Round about its outer, top edge, small symbols reflected moonlight with a magic-born resonance. She landed on the stump's glass-smooth surface to touch them. They lit her face in their ethereal glow, but she sensed nothing more to them. The ancient, semi-petrified tree betrayed any estimation of its age. She tarried for a while when something caught her eye. She rose and walked to the far end of the stump, underlit by the symbols there.

Something else glowed in the night. It passed by the top of the hill just west of the stump. Taking to the air, she flew low to the hilltop and peeked over its crest through wind-tickled grass. A shimmering figure entered the trees at the far end of the small field. Tinker Belle crossed the distance. The figure moved among the sparse trees of a broad copse of cypress, still further. She drew nearer for a bare glimpse of a tall, stately woman in flowing robes. Could it be a specter? She tried following it, but as she rounded a bend in the terrain, the trees ended in another gap overlooking the westbound beach — the figure was gone.

Tinker Belle was sure she had seen … no. She shook her head. *You're losing it, Belle. You're … losing it. Go home. You need the rest. Yeah … you need the rest.*

Taking one last look around, she flew westward along the shore while her fury rebounded about the dragon.

Self damn ravens!

25

Braves Return

"How many such places can there be?" asked Wind Sprint. "We passed ten such cities on our way here. Is it real? In a place the size of a house, we find a stone village larger than any I have ever even heard of! What kind of place is this, Great Cougar? If all of these people are gone, is there only death here?"

Great Cougar stood within the archway at the far end of what had once been a massive stone chamber now open to the golden evening sky. Broken walls remained, their ancient ruins a testament to the intricate mastery of its builders. The path ended two steps beyond the archway in frayed bricks drooping into an open-air drop. The path that once crossed a gap in the terrain to cliff-perched buildings now disappeared to the stone-littered, waved-crashed bluffs below. He turned back.

"We stand here today. So long as we stand, this is a place of life."

Wind Sprint took a long look at Cougar's solidness. "But … the- the things we have seen? The thrashing tree that killed the stag! The bush that enticed Runner on Waves and sang him to danger? The little bugs that followed He Who Speaks with Low Voice when he scratched and bled upon the ground?"

Great Cougar set his hand on the young man's shoulder. "We are strong people. We have survived the tribes who chased us across the purple mountains, the great plains, through the heavy forests to the winding, warm ocean. We survived their arrows and spears. We survived crossing the frothing waters, the water twisters, and the week-long storm. We reached the crystal blue waters and sailed into the sunrise. My mother's vision of this island has come true."

Wind Sprint straightened and offered a reluctant nod.

"Come," Great Cougar called to the others. "Let us return."

Once beyond the complex, they loped through the forest while dodging known dangers. As the sun set far to the west, the warm sky glowed tangerine before shifting to an ocean-cooled mauve. Cries of daytime fauna faded and the waking nocturnals created a new chorus among the trees.

All scanned for dangers, but when Cougar whistled, everyone stooped and drew close.

Wind Sprint drew near to look over his shoulder in the growing murk.

In the distance, a small white rabbit chewed on flora near the edge of a dark thicket.

"What is-" Wind Sprint began to ask when Cougar raised his hand.

A herd of deer emerged through the growing murk. Cougar lowered his flattened hand and the group sank close to the ground.

Wind Sprint looked between the herd and the rabbit, who now stood motionless. Deer sniffed at the air and raised their ears, first toward the braves, then outward. Plodding across the terrain, the herd burst from some unseen event. All looped into the murk from which they came.

"What do you see?" Wind Sprint whispered as he searched for an unseen predator.

Cougar raised his hand again, then pointed at the rabbit — now in a different location.

Wind Sprint thought the rabbit might be an indicator for some invisible predator. The rabbit had changed location and had resumed eating. "I don't-"

Cougar snapped his hand up again. Wind Sprint cut off, but so had the rabbit, who stood motionless with both ears raised. Cougar half turned his head and tapped his mouth, then pointed at the rabbit.

Wind Sprint focused on the rabbit's mouth.

Blood dripped from its small snout and whiskers. Wind Sprint's eyes widened, now able to identify a large doe lying dead beneath it. Cougar motioned for them to step away.

Stunned, the braves melted through the trees with their gazes locked on the tiny predator until it was well out of sight. They exchanged worried glances before Cougar led them onward, this time with greater speed.

Great Cougar led them to the river shore. They jogged west across beaches that changed with each turn, over small streams and up rocky ridges. Their landing appeared a half mile up the beach when they reached the base of a high, narrow waterfall crashing into a broad pool hugged by walls of rock and high beach sand. A creek snaked from the pool through rippled terrain to the river. While open and sandy on their side, a wall of thorny bushes lined the opposite bank at the base of a steep spur.

Before they descended the hill, Hawk Singer whistled a warning. The men melted into the boulders moments before something large entered the base of the waterfall from the backside. The dark-eyed head of a large, leathery animal emerged, followed by a long neck. At second glance, they realized that wasn't the head, but the snout of a much greater beast. Four paces later appeared large mounds on either side of the top that, once past the thundering water, cracked open to reveal massive yellow orbs.

"A crocodile," breathed Wind Sprint.

The beast emerged like a walking longhouse with huge clawed feet that sank into the wet, rocky sand as it slid outward from a cave hidden behind the falls. Halfway from the waterfall to the river, its yellow eye turned up to the rocks where the braves hid. The men waited in terror, for fate to draw the mighty predator upon them. Instead, a low guttural clicking vibrated the pool of water around it and outward to the river. The braves clutched their ears as the vibrations made them feel sick. A minute later, the crocodile's eye turned forward and blinked before it continued out into the river.

Great Cougar rose, forced himself to calm, and led them to the winding stream. Despite the crocodile's broad, heavy weight dragging over the terrain, the stream remained dark and deep. The braves searched for a shallow way across but found none.

"I will go first," said Great Cougar. He took his spear, held it above his head, and took a step into the water. The braves held their breath, having seen calm creeks boil at the crossing of prey. He sank to his knees, then waist and up to his neck before he was forced to kick off the bottom and stroke with his free arm and legs. The braves hugged the edge of the creek as he kept his motions smooth and used his long limbs to his advantage. He climbed the far bank into a crouch under the wall of thorny bushes leaning out over the creek. He motioned for them to follow.

One by one, they entered the water and swam as he did. Finally, Hawk Singer slid into the water. The others waited. Two reached their arms out and pulled him up. Rising, his black hair brushed the thorn bush. The vibration rippled through the bush above them before a looped strand sank around his head and snatched tight around his neck, its long thorns digging into his throat.

Knives flashed and cut him free from the bush while other loops sank in search of prey. Hawk Singer's strangled gurgles drew their eyes back. Though cut free from the bush, the remnant vine continued tightening around his neck by its thorny grip.

The braves dug the tips of their stone blades with great care into the top skin of his neck to dig out the vine. Wind Sprint managed to sever the loop enough to prevent it from choking him, but each length maintained its grip by embedded thorns. They snatched writhing ends and wrenched them free as his ankles sank into the water. All the while, they retreated from the dangling ends of the bush.

Hawk Singer gasped and clutched at his bloody throat. The two held the ends of the writhing snare and, with care, tossed them to the water. "Wait, NO!" Great Cougar cried. When it struck the water, the braves, now hovering knee deep in the creek, flinched. "Onto the beach! Now!"

The men scrambled onto their faces and dragged Hawk Singer along with them as he hacked for air. He screamed with his ankle still in the creek until they could wrench it out to reveal a long razor-toothed eel latched upon it.

"Crawl," Cougar growled. "Quickly."

The four men low crawled down the beach as the thorn loops draped lower. Hawk Singer screamed into the sand as the eel thrashed with its long, narrow body to dig out his flesh.

"MOVE!" Cougar bellowed. As two emerged, the loops reached Wind Sprint and Hawk Singer, who kept their arms and heads tucked. "Keep moving, just stay slow."

Hawk Singer made it to the edge of the curtain of thorns. The others gripped him under the shoulders and hauled him the rest of the way out, leaving a bright trail of his blood. Wind Sprint drew his knife and stabbed the eel to death. It thrashed, releasing Hawk Singer, and the men retreated while it bled out on the beach. Using their supplies, they bound up Hawk Singer's ankle wound as he quivered.

"Carry him, let's get back to the canoes." Great Cougar checked Hawk Singer's pale face as they crossed the sand to the canoes. Tiger Lily, Wolf Brother, Red Badger and the final two appeared from shallow hides in the beach. Badger had a bandaged arm, the others bore more than two bandages apiece.

"What happened to HawkSinger?" asked Red Badger.

"Thorn looper and an eel," Great Cougar said. "Dawn Catcher and Hunts Like Racoon?"

"Close calls with ... surprising predators." Red Badger's face tightened.

"Yes," Great Cougar said. "Surprising predators, indeed."

"Wolf Brother drew too near a bush that cast many thorns." Tiger Lily crossed her arms. Wolf Brother scowled, then flinched at the sting of a dozen small bleeding pocks in his face. "I had to dig them out before they got too deep." She scowled. "They burrowed as I attempted to remove them."

"Can we survive this place?" Red Badger asked.

"This place comes with dangers," Cougar faced the others. "We have seen the spear frog and the wolves, the needle swarm and the thickets which are bigger on the inside than the out. But we have also seen such ... abundance and beauty." He paused. "The people here farmed and left flat land for us to till. Game is abundant. The safe water is sweetest of any my tongue has tasted. There is plenty here if we rise to manage its dangers. This is a nature for stronger men." He leaned in. "*We* are stronger men."

All of them straightened.

"We found a good landing," Red Badger admitted. "South side of the island. It is protected to the sea and sits between the two mountains."

"That is good," Great Cougar said. "This is our home, now. It was foretold. We must rise to fate, for fate has already offered her hand to us. Will you rise?"

The men exchanged slow looks and nodded. Clinging to his brothers on either side, Hawk Singer attempted to straighten. "I am with you, Great Cougar."

The others took heart at his courage amidst his pain.

Great Cougar set his hand on Red Badger's shoulder and motioned at the island. "Then let us return to tell the people. We are home."

The men mounted the canoes, cast off, and began their arduous journey to return to their people still floating beyond the great auroric barrier.

26

A Mountain Oath

*M*INDER! - DALEEN! - *She's in my thoughts, she knows my thoughts. - It's like she always knows what I'm thinking, always! - You think you're so smart, you little bitch!? I guess you don't need dinner a second night in a row, do you? - She's gonna come out and take us all, I just know it. Daleens are real!*

Though her mind had roiled for hours, waking came slow to Athyka. Other peoples' thoughts, mixed with decades of painful memories, tortured her as they often did, but the fresh thoughts cutting her mind were in real time. Her eyes cracked open, surprised to be alive. The pain welling on the right side of her face clarified that wasn't the best of outcomes.

Dwarf will tend her until proper report… Harry's faint thoughts startled her. She could tell he was near, if not in the room. *Will inform Roschach tonight.*

Like most people, his thoughts came less in words and more in bottled concepts fueled with various emotions. She squeezed her eyes and opened them again. Movement caused pain on the right side of her face. She winced, which hurt even more. Something thick padded the right side of her face. Braving her tongue, she shuddered at the feeling of gauze where her cheek should have been. She vaguely remembered calling others to her aid and seeing men die through their own eyes. Her gut twisted in shame that she had lost control. Exercising it with care was one thing, but flagrantly snatching men's minds was a sign that her grandmother was right about her.

A cool cloth on the left side of her face startled her. She found the thigh-thick forearm of a dwarf leaning over her, dabbing her face. Her eyes flared. He noticed but ignored her as he checked her bandage and cleaned any exposed bleeding. Once finished, he withdrew to sit on the other side of the small cabin. Though she could not see him well, she heard the faint digging of metal on wood.

A dwarf. Of course.

Algueda any moment... Harry's faint thoughts reached her again. He was too far for her to try to reach and her head hurt too much to try. The thought of returning to the island flared terror in her for a moment before she squashed it with her grandmother's cruel instruction fueling her effort.

Athyka took deep breaths and tried lifting her right hand. Her entire body was bound to the mattress under her. She fished out her arm and worked to free herself from the sheets.

"Whoa der, lass." The dwarf rushed over. "You won't be goin' nowhere, I tink."

She scowled. "Let me up."

He set his hand on her breastbone and held it there. She flailed against his steely arm, then punched it in protest. He didn't seem to notice.

"You're in no condition ta go anywhere." He shook his gray mutton chops over chubby dwarven cheeks. His bulbous nose seemed almost comical between his tiny round spectacles. "Sides', Agent Bristol ordered you ta stay in bed."

"Of coursh he did," she growled through her head bandage. "He sic'd his halfling to keep me here."

His eyes darkened. "Still a better position dan bein' a selfdamn minder on a ship full o'sailors ready to fill you wit arrows."

Athyka exhaled.

"Specially since you killed der doctor weeks from shore." He let her go.

She closed her eyes. "Shit."

"Aye." He crossed his arms. "It's hard enough to survive ou' here *wit* a doctor."

"Won't matter soon," she said.

"Why's dat?" he asked.

"Because Algueda," she said.

His eyes narrowed.

"You want to go there."

His eyebrow flickered. "Don't much matter what I want. If I ain't here, I'm in da brig."

"For whose shafety, exactly?" she asked.

He did not respond.

"Can I at leasht shit up?" she said.

Hesitating, he stepped back.

She winced and jerked on the sheets to free herself but paused as her face burned.

"If you tear off dat bandage, I'll have hell ta pay," he growled.

"M'already paying it." She squeezed her eyes as she rolled to her left, trying to brace her head so it didn't twist about. She kicked free the sheets and rolled out with care to sit upright. The weight of the bandage tugging her injury inspired a scream she wouldn't let out. Nerves fired down the side of her face and right arm. She opened her left eye to see the dwarf standing there in a horizontal striped shirt over his thick frame and heavy belly. Short black pants hugged his legs and a red cap reclined atop a balding head. "Got a name?"

"Arlagosmy," he scowled.

"Common to Gurlenka, yesh?" she asked.

The dwarf hesitated. "You know dwarves?"

"Met a few."

He appraised her.

Can leverage this ohna... Harry's thoughts drifted again. Her left eye climbed to where Harry sat in the captain's quarters with the captain nearby, his own fears bubbling like soft waves washing on a beach. Harry's magic amplified his thoughts — as did all mages.

"Hear 'im, do ya?" Arlagosmy asked.

She looked to the dwarf. "They're going to get you killed. The island isn't for the unwary."

The dwarf harrumphed again. "I ain't leadin' dis expedition."

"Don't have to, to get killed."

"You tink I'm gonna help you? Don't even try, lass."

"Get me back the ohna," she said. Her heart fluttered with desire to touch it again. "I- I need it."

He said nothing.

170

Suppressing desperation welling in her to touch the ice knife again, she inspected her bandaged hand. The curled fingers were numb and balled up in gauze. Her right fingers caressed the bandage — the gauze was cold. Faint wisps of moisture smoked away. "How long have I been in here?"

He eyed her hand and for a moment, flared with surprise. "Hours."

Athyka's mind raced. Her hand was still ice *hours* after being bandaged and tucked into a warm bed. Her eyes narrowed as her heart picked up.

"I tink it's time you laid back down." He approached her.

Her eyes darted to him as he raised his thick hands, knowing she could never resist the muscular power of a dwarf. Her right hand darted up between his arms and gripped his throat. Ice raced up his throat and lanced up the sides of his chin while billowing outward down his biceps and into his belly.

Arlagosmy locked up when a flood of vile images rushed from his mind into her own.

"You- fucking-!" she coughed. Ice that had once crystallized a few top layers now thickened inward toward his heart. She stemmed the flow of his gut-wrenching memories, sure she would kill him should she see more of the hundreds of human children he had used and disposed of. Locking her power in place as best she could, she emptied her stomach on the floor. Her stomach heaved while she used his neck to keep herself upright.

"How- how did-?" he squeaked in horror as she rummaged his mind. "You can't do dis! You can't- Ahm a dwarf!"

Spitting, she wiped her mouth with the bedsheet and tried to do more than just see into his mind. She wanted him to feel pain, to burn his mind out on the spot, but whatever allowed her into his mind didn't allow her to do more. She didn't want to see into such evil.

Turning, she suppressed the desire to freeze him to death, sure that without his presence on board she would already be dead. She withdrew the ice from his racing five-chambered heart.

"Lishun to me you worthlish fuck..." She drew near. The fumes of her bile wafted up his nose. "I know exactly what you are. I don't care if the shailors just dishlike you for being a dwarf. If they find out what you do to children, they will rip your shkin off and drag you in shark watersh just to lishun to you shcream." She quivered in fury. "I will plant in every mind what I just shaw. You will never reach Algueda or further than the next league before they cut off your ballsh with shomething dull. I will enshure they do nothing elsh for hoursh and hoursh. Are you with me?"

Tears rolled down his face and he nodded.

Had she the strength and courage, she would kill him. Instead, she spit on him. "You will get me the ohna. You will asshure Brishtol I am not a daleen. Tell him the men who attacked him were … my previoush ashociates. Trying to protect me." She panted. "If you don't, I'll ensure they shtab your worthlessh dick with shomthing shmall and dull until it can't be found!"

Arlagosmy quivered.

"I want your oath," she growled. "A dwarven oath."

His eyes fluttered.

"Yeah, a mountain oath."

Terror struck him. His new place in the world settled deep. He would be forever locked by whatever he promised her, to pain of death. The woman knew. He was desperate to be anywhere else, but she had him. When he hesitated, he felt her inch the ice closer to his heart.

"How'r you doin' this?" he strained.

"It doesn't matter, you shelfdamn shit." She prepared herself to survive without him. "I want an oath to obey as I direct in the shpirit I direct and to protect me and my intereshts at all timesh."

He shut his soaked eyes. When they opened, they glowed a deep red with magic smoking away at the outer ends. "I, Arlagosmy Goraschborad, swear by da Mother Earthen," a distortion appeared around him, "swear ta you-"

"Athyka Bonduquoy," she gritted.

"Athyka Bonduquoy, co- … complete obedience. I will obey all c'mmands in tha' spirit you direct and … and …"

"To protect me and my intereshts at all timesh." Athyka's glare bored into his.

"Ta protect you n'yor interests at'all times."

"So be it!" she pressed her thumb into his throat.

"So be it!" he managed as she pinched his airway.

The distortion snapped inward. His frame twisted against the ice. He couldn't scream by the painful oath or the frost ripping at his muscles. Instead he quivered until the magic settled throughout his body and mind before he fell over and slapped the floor. She withdrew the ice from his vital organs. As hope drained from his face, she collapsed onto the bed.

27

Gathering Tootles

Grandfather lay still beneath the simple woolen sheets. A thin bar of moonlight split the wafting curtains and reflected upward from the plain tile floor. White adobe walls glowed a thin blue from the underlight. The old man lay in shadow, hidden from the light by the bed beneath him. Unblinking eyes gleamed in frozen horror at the boy now backing away. Echoes of distant laughs and screams filled the space. The bar of moonlight intensified, casting the room with polar shadows and a rising dread.

Santi retreated, aware the desperate panting filling the room was his own. Unable to take his eyes from his grandfather, he backed into the door. As the walls closed in, he yanked it open and dashed into the hallway beyond. The gilded white door frame behind him yawned wide with an eternal moaning black. His heart pounded as memories of muffled protests grew faint. Mud carpeting the stone floor muted his racing bootfalls. A portrait of Jesus Christ fell from the left wall. On the right, beneath bars of moonlight from vertical windows, a simple wall table and stone wash bin tipped over and shattered across the floor in a chorus of ear-piercing screams.

Racing through the chaos, he staggered onto the deck of a sailing ship rolling in hurricane seas. Frigid wind snatched at his coarse blouse and thick hair. Mountains of midnight waves loomed and crashed against the ship. The mast cracked and the deck shuddered amidships as the vessel broke in two.

As it sank beneath the boy's feet, his eyes climbed to a sky drowned in murky torrents of rain and wind. Flashes of lightning illuminated a single wave growing above the others; within it loomed a monstrous shadow whose glowing eyes flooded the water. Its long jaws widened and snapped down upon the ship, finishing it off and casting the boy and all within its bowels into the depths of the Atlantic. As he sank, he screamed as the same long jaws, now from below, closed in around him, cutting him off from the lightning-flashed chaos of the surface.

Santi sat upright with a cry. After the initial startle, he found a massive dancing tree looming above him and a wall of writhing vines a few paces away, several of which paused to glance his direction before continuing onward.

"Hey, you okay?"

Flinching, Santi found the red-haired child kneeling over him in a white blouse tucked loose into belted green trousers over bare feet. A green longcoat and soft brown boots lay folded by a nearby fire pit.

"Whoa, just ..." Peter paused. "You were crying in your sleep."

Santi wiped his face with his wrist as he rolled away onto his hands and knees. "I'm fine."

"Are you sure?" Peter asked.

"Yes, I said I'm fine!" Santi snapped.

"Alright, alright." Peter pushed up. "Ain't gotta be angry about it."

Santi glowered at the grass.

"You, uh ... wanna talk about it?"

Rolling onto his bottom, Santi searched the words. "I lost my grandfather."

"Was that what the dream was about?"

Santi nodded. "We were, uh ... in Brasil. A beautiful Spanish mission in the south country. My grandfather was a, uh ... priest. Jesuit, specifically. He- he died there."

"Sorry," Peter said.

Santi's face tightened. "At least, I think so."

"Think? You're not sure?"

"It's a little fuzzy, really," Santi said. "I get … flashes. Moments of memory."

"Were you there?"

"Yes," Santi said. "For a brief time. After he died, we returned for Spain. I do not remember what happened after we left."

Peter said nothing.

"I see him in my dreams staring at me." Santi's voice faltered. "It is not something I wish to see."

"Yeah," said Peter. His stomach tightened with his own familiar fears. "Um … Well, are you hungry?"

Santi blinked away his tears. "Yes, I am."

"Be right back." Peter bobbed on the balls of his feet and approached the vine wall.

Santi paused when he realized Peter hadn't walked through. Peter looked along the wall to a point a few paces away. "What is it?"

"I'm not … sure …" Peter walked along the wall, which split at his passing until he reached one particular point.

Santi straightened.

"There's … someone here," said Peter.

"What?" Santi stood.

"There's a boy, right here." Peter's gaze narrowed.

"Another boy?"

"Yeah," Peter said. "Right here." He leaned in toward the wall as the spades paused to watch him.

"What are you talking about?" Santi stammered.

"Here he is." Peter dove both hands into the wall. "I got him!" Peter gripped something and sank shoulder-deep into the vines.

"What are you doing!?" Santi cried.

Peter vanished into the plant.

Santi crossed himself with his hand, tapping his forehead to his breastbone and his left to right shoulder as he muttered a curse. "Mother of God."

Peter's muffled voice emerged and the plant calmed. Like a babe from a womb, Peter's goo-painted crimson mane broke through two thick vines. He wiggled out an arm and leg to brace himself before he reached to pull out a child covered thick with transparent green gunk. Peter pulled and worked him out until both fell to the grass.

"Where did he come from!?" Santi's eyes flared as he retreated.

"The plant." Peter bent over to catch his breath. He stepped over the new boy and, hesitating, rolled him onto his belly. Goo poured out across the grass, ejected by his stomach and lungs. The boy hacked and coughed.

Santi neared the cliffside as his breath quickened. He searched Neverland for a sense of reality when a distant pterodactyl took to air from the jungle far below. "Ay, Mary!"

Peter gripped the boy under his arms and rolled him over before he and Santi bent over to get a look at the child who bore a large, long nose, wavy black hair and angled eyes.

"What the hell is going on?" Santi clutched his hair. "Hail Mary, full of grace. The Lord is with thee. Blessed art thou among women, and blessed is the fruit of thy womb, Jesus. Holy Mary, Mother of God, pray for us sinners, now and at the hour of our death."

"What are you saying?" Peter asked. "Who is Jesus?"

"Why are my words in Spanish!?" Santi rocked himself. "Ay, help me."

"What's wrong?" Peter approached. He tilted to the side to get a better view of Santi's face.

"What's going on!?" Santi cried.

"Are you okay?"

Santi snatched Peter by the shirt and hauled him close. "What is going on!?"

"Calm down, Santi!" Peter snapped.

"Tell me what is going on! Where am I!?" In a panic, Santi spun with his grip on Peter's shirt in his right hand and dangled him over the cliff's edge and bellowed, "TELL ME WHERE I AM!"

Peter pushed from mid-air and drove Santi back several steps before both fell to the grass. Santi scrambled over him.

"Tell me where I am!" Santi snatched his shirt, again.

"Hey!" Peter kicked him up and over. Santi leapt to his feet and rounded on Peter who blocked his first punch but missed the second and folded over with a fist to his gut.

"You brought me here! I am in purgatory!" Santi panted. "You must finish me! I cannot wait here!"

Peter punched Santi and sent him across the grass. As his father taught him, Peter snatched the silver dagger out from the sheath in his belt and crouched. Santi held the side of his face Peter hit and climbed to his feet.

"Finish it, Peter!" Santi glared at Peter's silver dagger. "Do what must be done!"

"What is wrong with you!?" Peter stammered.

"FINISH IT!" Santi screamed.

Faint bells signaled Tinker Belle's approach. Santi spun to the approaching fairy, but soon found himself flipping over the grass after Peter shorted the distance and slammed him in the side of the face from behind.

Peter flailed his hand. "Ow!"

Lying on his side, the stunned Santi clutched his face while taking breaths to slow his panicked heart.

"Calm down!" Peter sheathed his knife.

Santi tried to collect himself.

Hey! I just found ... Tinker Belle flew in and paused over both of them. *What happened?*

Peter flung his crimson hair out of his eyes. "Nothing. You okay, Santi?"

Santi pushed himself up from the ground. "Yes."

"Good," Peter breathed.

Right ... She looked between the two before spotting the new boy unconscious by the wall. Her eyes widened. *Who in Self's name is that!?*

Peter turned. "Oh. Yeah."

Oh yeah? Yeah!? Where did he COME FROM!? Tinker Belle stammered.

"Where'd *he* come from?" Peter motioned at Santi and shrugged.

That's not an answer! This child didn't just pop out of nowhere! Where'd he come from, Peter?

"I found him in the wall." Peter pointed.

Calming, Santi rubbed his face while his eyes fell upon the new boy. "How did he get into the plant?"

"It took him from Earth, I think," Peter said.

"Why?" Santi asked.

Peter shrugged. "I dunno. I just know he's here now. Just like you."

"Wait, is that why I'm here? A plant took me?"

"Did you wake up in a plant?"

"No, it was ..." said Santi, "the swamp."

The crocodile ... Tinker Belle chimed.

"Now..." Peter inspected the boy clad in coarse woolen trousers. "I think we need to go for a swim." He picked up the boy and threw him over his shoulder. "This boy is really light! What is it you found, Tink?"

There's a ship on approach, she chimed. *I don't think they've pierced the veil yet, but they're close.*

"Veil?"

The thing we passed through when we reached Neverland.

"Oh yeah." Peter faced the wall.

"Hey, wait!" Santi said. "What am I supposed to do!?"

"You're coming!" Peter called over his shoulder. "He's your responsibility!"

"Wait, why is he my responsibility!?" Santi stood and followed Peter through the wall.

"It's your job to get him ready. Him and others."

What do you hope for him to accomplish, exactly? Tinker Belle chimed.

"Santi, I need a steward to care for Neverland while I take care of pan business and find my father."

Santi followed Peter across the outer clearing and the tree line. He wondered what pan business entailed, but a job might mean purpose, food, and a place to figure out where he was and how he could get home. "Does this job pay?"

"Sure," said Peter. "We'll start with my help in you not dying."

"From what?" Santi asked.

"From the island." Peter motioned at the flora on their way into the dappled morning sunlight.

28

Alderland's Support

In the northern gardens of the newly renamed Grand House of the Union, formerly the Palace of the Pan, Roschach led Lord Abydon up stone walks and ornate, shallow-stepped staircases winding through gentle plateaus resplendent with colorful and exotic flora transplanted from across Pangea. Two of Abydon's attendants followed at a distance.

"You promised you'd have the mantle," Abydon said.

"Our people are on Algueda right now securing it."

"Securing." Abydon paused halfway across a circular landing hugged by heavy tree foliage. Sunlight bathed them through the narrow space between abundant flora. "*Fellow* Roschach, when we began speaking last year about our … negotiations with Emperor Benuin, you assured me you would have the mantle while William was still here in the palace. Now he's ten thousand miles away and your people are still securing it?"

Roschach's face tightened. "William is no longer the pan."

Abydon's eyes narrowed. "The crow? In the sky?"

"Yes." Roschach restrained himself from cursing. "We believe he gave it to his wife."

"Why in Self's name would he do such a thing?" asked Abydon.

"We think it's some kind of ploy."

"Some kind of ploy? You say that with as much dismissal as the idea he could escape from this very palace! With his entire family. And two hundred of his closest supporters."

Roschach opened his mouth to protest but Abydon's raised hand cut him off.

"Let us make clear what happens to us both if you fail to get the mantle, Elwin." Abydon's face darkened. "Graela will descend upon us with the full might of every citizen old enough to wield a blade or bow. We need not worry about torture or interrogation or imprisonment — there will be none. They will wipe out both Unionists and anyone from Alderland known to be colluding with them. I can allay Benuin with promises and bureaucratic quicksand and you, well … You perform your little magic on these true believers all you like, but there's no dissuading the high elf king from cutting our throats himself. And if he doesn't get me first, Benuin, in all his angry senility, will re-emerge long enough to make me suffer before Uron can get here. Before either of them can get to me, I will get to you, and you know what I do for Benuin so he can keep his pretty hands clean."

Roschach said nothing.

"This little game you're playing will end immediately or you might find how quickly I can turn Benuin's slave armies from the Admians in the southeast against our allies here in this …" Abydon glanced at the gardens round about him. "…This lovely valley you feel so safe inside."

Roschach swallowed. "I assure you we will have the mantle in a fortnight."

Abydon sucked on his own tongue, then flicked his hand. A faint barrier of air formed around them, muting sound and obscuring them from view. "If you do not, Roschach, then I will tell Baley what you had planned. While William was the kind one, his sister is not. She sacrificed her brother for this cause. She believes — really *believes* — in Unionism and was willing to let her own brother and his entire family die for it. You? She won't hesitate to grind you to dust and consider every moment for the greater good."

Roschach hesitated. "Shall we?" He motioned along the path. After a nod from Abydon, they both continued. The shield fizzled as they passed through.

"Remind the quorum that I assure our support according to our pre-arranged trading and labor rights for Alderland workers with Eden's continental contracts. Once you secure the mantle so the charter remains solvent, I can secure Benuin's signature on the alteration to very long-standing agreements between our peoples. But my ability to delay is coming to an end."

Both mounted the top of the steps and walked through an arch into a high rock wall. Tall, ornate wooden doors stood open guarded by a compliment of Unionist soldiers. The hall twisted before ending in a large domed chamber centered by a high dais topped by three inlaid concentric rings and a platformed walk on both sides — the Eden Rimsportal.

"Secure the mantle or I won't be able to convince Benuin not to respond, as he's legally bound by the charter," said Abydon. "He will wonder what took me so long to alert him unless I can convince him you had the mantle this entire time. Get it, or all our heads will roll."

Roschach spotted Fenren standing behind Abydon's silent attendants and tightened his jaw. "I assure you, Abydon, we will get the mantle and the heir ready directly."

Abydon faced the portal as it popped to life. The three spinning rings created a ball of glowing, swirling blue light that filled the amberlit chamber. "I hate using your rimsportal."

"Really?" Roschach asked.

"It leaves a ringing in your ears. Like there's not enough power in it to deliver you properly."

"You always make it."

"Gives me a headache," Abydon said. "Make this profitable for us both, Elwin. I'd rather raise a glass with you than a sword against you."

Roschach nodded. Abydon marched to the end of the right long walk, mounted the steps and strolled into the ball of light. His two attendants rushed after him, disappearing in their own faint flashes before the travel master deactivated the portal with a gentle pop.

"He's not wrong about the portal," Roschach growled and led Fenren away. "I'd rather Eden just rebuild it. Or build another."

"Terrible idea."

"Why's that?"

"Two rimsportals in the same city? The entire city would be destroyed."

"You're kidding."

"You don't know?" Fenren asked. "It's something to do with how they work. Activate two rimsportals in the same city and boom."

"Since when?"

"Earliest days of rimsportals."

"I didn't know that." Roschach frowned as they reached the top of the stairs overlooking the palace and the city. "Report."

"Other than my brief respite for your lovely speech and putting Baley's cunt in her place, the elf and I have been recording everything in the room. Once we find out how to access the rimshift, we can get Athyka and the others home in the blink of an eye."

"I wonder if that selfdamn rimshift is even there. Why wouldn't William have used it to go directly to Algueda?"

"Maybe he thought he could win?" Fenren shrugged. "The fool believed many things I doubt were remotely true about his chances."

"I'm not worried about his chances," Roschach said as they followed the stairs. "I'm focused on ours."

"The elf's worried about the powers."

"Why?"

"Says the ohnas have been unseated too long. He's worried what that will mean for the alterworlds."

"What does he suggest?"

"Putting them back immediately."

Roschach barked a laugh. "Not till we finish this transition. We will keep them as long as necessary."

"What if it destroys continental highways to the alterworlds? Or continental stability, itself?"

"The continent existed long before the alterworlds. We don't need them. They fled. They left. This is our continent now. The less of them, the better."

"And Abydon?"

"I have an arrangement to ensure Benuin is in no place to block our support there, with or without Abydon," Roschach said.

"You mean the witch?"

"Yes, the witch. That's a long-term strategy, but we need the mantle now. If Athyka is out of commission, I can't spare another ship. I need the room. Get it done or we're finished."

"I'm on it, Elwin."

"Good, because if I'm not stressing about the mantle and the rest of the quorum breathing down my neck," Roschach growled and pointed after Abydon, "I've got that fucker to worry about."

"We'll get it, Elwin. One way or the other, we'll get it."

29

Phineas

Margia Wells rode the saber-toothed tiger over the narrow winding path rising from the milk-white mist carpeting the swamp's hidden, reeking waters. Cloaked in crimson and black, Margia kept a grip at the nape of the cat's narrow dorsal mane while her hips swayed in the custom blue leather saddle. Her hood draped over midnight curls, thick black brows, full pale lips and pristine tan skin interrupted by her rich brown eyes lined in black.

Soldiers followed afoot two miles from their bivouac through a swamp that grew darker with each step and fouler with each breath. They held their steel-backed leather gloves over their faces in futility to stifle the stench.

Margia's darting eyes classified plants and animals by genus and subgenus as far as their limited visibility allowed. She tensed when a low mound appeared through the mist, signaling the end of the winding path of crumbling soil. A thin carpet of moss upon which they trampled kept the path from crumbling into the milky white mist. She halted twenty paces short of the mound, ten short of the broad web of counter-rotating magical barriers only her practiced eyes could see. Even the mages following her could not see the intricate shields protecting the wide plot of barren soil before the stairwell leading down to the mound's small, inset door.

Thumbing the ohna faunora draped from the silver necklace hanging at the front of her breasts, she glanced to the line captain and nodded.

He motioned at a soldier to approach the hut. The soldier marched within ten paces and barked, "Duchess Namotha Hivere of Utaly! Come out!"

The saber-toothed tiger sniffed at the air, then sneezed loud enough to startle the soldier.

He spared a nervous glance at the large cat before looking again to the hut. "Namotha of Utaly! By order of Fellow Roschach of the Quorum of Faith of the People's Union, come out!" He advanced to the top of a stairwell of a low-set door. Only the top of the small, inset door was visible from where she sat.

The soldier made two steps into the well to knock on the door, but scrambled in retreat before stumbling to his knees. He clutched at his throat, wheezing with a growing gurgle. Black bile spewed from his mouth across the wet muck before he drowned and died on the spot. No one moved to help him; all struggled not to flee.

"NAMOTHA HIVERE!" the captain bellowed.

"Tried knocking, did you?" a faint voice called from the rear. They spun to face a hunched older woman in a ragged charcoal robe. Her graying hair bound in a haphazard bun and her strong nose dominated her haggard coffee-colored face. Her round eyes might once have been beautiful but hate darkened her half-lidded gaze. A smile interrupted her disdain like a morning sunset.

"Namotha of Utaly?" asked the captain.

"You see any other beauties round here?" she spat. With a glare for the soldiers, she hobbled with a knobby cane down the center of the moss-carpeted path, forcing them against the crumbling edges. She grinned yellowing teeth at their fear. Drawing near the corpse on the ground, her smile widened. "Tried to knock, did he?"

Margia's eyes narrowed.

Namotha faced Margia and locked onto the object hanging at her breasts. "I could feel that the moment you entered my swamp, zoologist."

"I didn't think you'd remember me."

"Oh yes, the eager little Admian zoologist in Curstal," Namotha said. "Hard to miss such a pretty girl all the men spoke of."

Margia gripped the necklace.

"Do you not remember me?" Namotha tilted her head.

"Everyone remembers you, Namotha," Margia said.

"Of course, they do," Namotha snapped with a disgusted look up Well's figure. She raised a hand toward the pool of tarrish bile still leaking from the dead soldier's gaping mouth. Flame caught and raced into his throat and belly. In moments it consumed him in a small cloud of moldy black smoke that burst upward in a mushroom cloud and left behind a burn mark in the shape of his body upon the ground. Metal pieces and faint leather scraps remained. She stepped at the fore of her hut.

"We brought the boy." The captain motioned. Two soldiers marched forward and dropped a hooded and bound figure before her, adorned in a green outfit trimmed in gold with silver-lined boots and several signet rings on each hand.

Namotha's smile twitched. "And the price?"

The captain opened his mouth to speak when Margia raised her hand to cut him off. He fished into his saddle bags, hefted a large coin purse and tossed it at Namotha. She ignored it as it clinked to the ground at her feet.

"Fine, fine," said Namotha. "Does he have any magic I should know? Any mage training? He's not a wizard class, is he?"

"None that we're aware of," Margia said. "He's the seventh of a seventh of a seventh. Chances are he's inbred somewhere along the line."

"Of course he is," said Namotha. "He's a noble. Put him inside."

"Wait," Margia said as the cat shifted beneath her. "Strip him."

The men unchained the figure and stripped him naked before stuffing his things into a sack. His warm black skin contrasted with the pall of gray soil beneath him. One brought the sack to Margia before both returned to the figure. They lifted him and waited.

"It's alright, now." Namotha waved at the hut. "Your men won't die." When she smiled again, the two men tensed. Margia saw the shields change in quality. Even with the ohna's amplification of her own natural magic, Namotha's skill paled her own.

"Go," the captain ordered after a reassuring look from Margia. The two passed the burn mark of their former compatriot and down into the well. The door opened of its own accord and the fireplace sprang to life. Both men stopped halfway down the short stairs before ducking under the low hanging thatch. They set the figure onto the bed and quick-stepped out. Neither looked at Namotha as they returned to the line.

"I wonder." Namotha raised an eyebrow while eyeing the ohna. "What is it like to wield the power of the Self? An original power of creation?"

"I don't believe in superstition." Margia straightened. "I serve nature."

"Oh? It's superstition to believe the ohnas come from the Self? Powers designed to connect dimensions like Pangea and the Alterworlds? You think that's natural?"

"Nature gave us life," Margia said. "I will serve it, always."

"You control the god you claim gives you life?" Namotha smiled. "You don't see the irony?"

"I don't believe in gods," Margia snapped.

"And yet you worship it with every breath," Namotha spat. "Don't set out a salt lick, girl, and say you have no horses. Call nature what you will, but when you claim it bears the intelligent complexity to spawn humanity and worthy of your adoration but then deny it as your religion, I see only your blindness to conflicts of reason."

"I didn't come to debate religion with you, witch," Margia hissed. The cat beneath mewled with aggression.

"Your ohna won't protect you from my spells." Namotha ignored the cat. "Nor will it protect your precious kitty."

The men tensed in fear of a fight between the two.

Margia's heart climbed, amping the tiger, before she calmed herself and forced the same into the beast through her control by the ohna. "Do your work. I am leaving a small contingent. For your protection."

Namotha said nothing as she set both hands on the end of her cane.

"Per the original agreement, you have one week to make this one pliable," Margia said. "Roschach wants to ensure he's pliable and enthusiastic to our cause, but not a mindless drone. There can be no evidence of what was done here."

Sufferance painted Namotha's face as she sneered at Margia.

Margia waited for her to move, but when Namotha did nothing, Margia motioned for the line to return the way they had come.

Namotha waited for her and the men to disappear into the mist before she restored the shields of magic around her mound and pursued the caravan. She sensed them through the swamp and kept her distance.

At the end of the path where the greater force had camped, Margia wasted no time to gather her main force and head out of the swamp. As ten men bedded down for the night, Namotha used prebuilt spells lodged across the terrain to hide her approach.

The witch hobbled into camp, unseen, and fished out a small pouch. Untying it, she sprinkled fine green powder into the steaming cooking pot. She returned to the head of the walk and waited. Over the next hour, all ten men ate and died as their stomachs melted from within, opening their guts and burning out their intestines through their abdomen walls onto the soil, outside. She walked through camp to ensure all were dead before burning up them and their belongings before returning to her hut.

Though exhausted, she barred the door and motioned to the chains binding the bagged figure. They loosened and fell. Handsome and young, the striking young man with black skin and braids adorned in silver beads was a sight of muscle and youth. His thin goatee framed a powerful chin beneath a broad nose. His high cheekbones, small ears and clean lines created a face of beauty, though he reeked of urine and a foul drug used to keep him unconscious. The smells wafting from him competed with the heavy incense tinging the air. Semi-conscious, he moaned as the chains fell away to reveal bruising and blisters where his manacles had been.

She ran her fingers over a powerful chest and arms and down over his body. "Hello, handsome." She pulled a thick chain and large manacle resting near the head of the tiny bed and fished it around his neck before snapping it shut. The manacle sealed at the join with magic. She whirled her finger in a small motion at the cauldron bubbling above the crackling fire. A thin stream of steaming green liquid snaked into the air. She looped it several times to cool it before reaching over to pinch open his lips. The liquid pooled above his mouth and dripped through the gap. Once he swallowed it all, she motioned to a small bowl of incense in the corner. A thin stream of smoke danced upward and soon filled the tiny room with its pungent odor.

The man thrashed as the concoction bubbled in his belly.

Against the wall to her left, a small table held a knife and several groups of powders. She motioned to the steam rising above the cauldron and drew it, condensing it into a snake of clean water. She dripped it onto the three powders before using small wooden spoons to stir and mash each one into a paste. Once satisfied, she burst the remaining water into mist, took the wicked knife and slid the flat of each side over each paste in successive layers. She eyed it in the firelight and returned to the young man, whose eyes cracked open.

"Where am I!?" he moaned. He raised muscled arms as if dead weight.

Despite her frailty, she batted his hands away and drew close while holding her knife behind her hip.

"Oh, good evening, Phineas." She grinned and cupped the side of his face. "I'm glad you could join me."

"Wh- where am I?" he moaned in a thick stupor.

She thumbed his thick lips while she licked her own. "You're in my home, young man."

"Why?" he breathed.

"Because you're the seventh," she hissed. "Another seventh. Always a *seventh*."

His eyes widened in terror at the darkness drowning her face.

She gripped his chin. "But don't worry … you'll still be the seventh. You'll just be MY seventh."

His eyes widened. She kissed and sucked on lips moaning in fear. Though panting with excitement, she glared upon him with such hatred that he froze.

In a flash, she knocked his arms down, raised both hands to grip her inverted knife and drove it into his gut. He stared at it sticking from his belly before his back arched and a gurgled cry ripped from his throat.

His arms and legs tightened, his spine creaked with stress and foam bubbled from his mouth. She set one hand upon his forehead and ran her other hand over his abs to delve him. As he collapsed to the bed, twitching and writhing with half-lidded eyes, she smiled and rubbed his chest again while the knife in his gut grew white-hot with heat.

"I will return to my rightful place," she ground her teeth. "I'm coming, Benuin. You and all your sons will suffer for your sins. When I am finished…" Her grin widened. "You and the sons of Alder will die."

30

Sons of Alder

"**M**AKE WAY FOR ALDERLAND!**"** bellowed the lead cavalryman as the formation thundered into the riverside village. Soldiers going about chores scattered from the path. Clad in thick metal-plated leather armor lined in green and white, battered from regular use and glimmering from polish, the senior officer led them through camp and reined in before the town's two-story inn.

Prince General Edmon of Alderland, first son of Benuin, dismounted an ash-gray stallion and handed the reins to a quick attendant. The stocky figure with dark coffee skin and a thick, close-cropped beard scanned the village square boiling with activity. His large brown eyes checked rooftops, corners and dark windows in one smooth glance. His short hair carpeted the crown of his head from his hairline to his occipital bun at the back, leaving the sides of his head where ornate shapes of hair were cut to indicate his rank and position. The intricate golden symbol of the Prince General of Alderland inlaid a right pauldron covered in scratched hunter green. Dust covered him from head to foot but for his reddened eyes and tongue-cleaned lips.

"Prince general…" A man sauntered out of the front of the inn at the top of the broad stone steps clad in green armor. Bearing a similar hairstyle to the prince general but for different shapes along the side of his head, the narrow-jawed brigadier general frowned down at his older brother.

"Lyphic." Edmon climbed the stairs.

"Questioning our security?" asked Lyphic.

"Always." Edmon knocked the bottom of his fist on Lyphic's pauldron.

"You look like shit," Lyphic muttered for Edmon's ears.

"You ride a hundred klicks with barely a break to piss and look as good as me."

Lyphic snorted. "You expect me to sink to your level?"

Edmon chuckled. "Debrief me."

"Come." Lyphic led Edmon into the inn's main room twittering with officers and messengers. Maps blanketed the rear wall while a fire roared from the side. Lanterns illuminated what the fire and open windows could not.

"ROOM!" barked the sergeant at the door. Everyone came to attention as Edmon entered but returned to activity at a dismissive wave of his hand.

"Prince general, welcome to Lower River." A colonel straightened from leaning over a map-covered table in the center of the room.

Edmon motioned to a nearby slave who rushed to bring a cup of coffee with a deep bow before backing away. Edmon sipped on the steaming brew and inspected the table. "Report."

"Of course, prince general," the colonel said with a nod. "Meso'Admia has brought her legions." At a wave of her hand, four junior officers rushed to clear the table of unnecessary papers to reveal a larger map beneath, scrawled in graphite and peppered with small notes and erasure fudges. The map revealed a deep river canyon inlaid with a shallow shoreline stretching outward a half mile on either side of the river winding northward to the base of high cliffs. The width of the terrain varied as the map travelled north but narrowed as it climbed into heavy mountain ranges. The village stood at the center of a narrowing decline from the Ardruman Mountain Range that cut a gap between the high cliffs on the southeast and ended at the river. Marks indicating battles painted the shallow valley bottom except for where terrain spurs pincered movement. Further north of the battles, a winding road indicated the primary path for the Alderlander legions to reach the canyon bottom and forded the river a few miles south across a broad sand bar.

"We're hunkered in here and here." The colonel pointed. "They've been attempting to send small forces downriver to come up behind us, but the canyons are unkind a few miles south of here and the cliffs are too high to easily rappel. We've spaced troops of archers along the wall and keep it well-lit at night.

"No chance of boating upriver?" Edmon asked.

"The canyon's narrow and the water turns into rapids," the colonel said. "No one's coming up that way. Hell, no one should go down that way, either."

Edmon scanned the main battlefields. "Losses?"

"Light, so far. They were here first, but we dug in better."

"Father demands progress." Edmon fingered the map.

"Father will get it." Lyphic reached across the table and circled a small force with his finger. "We're equipping the light cavalry to ride north into the high canyons with belladonna."

"Poison?" Edmon straightened.

"Everyone gets their water from the river," said Lyphic. "Since we're downriver, it's unlikely they'd expect us to poison *them*. And we'll prepare ahead of time to avoid it."

Edmon mulled. "A good idea. If it doesn't work?"

"We also plan on moving on three fronts the day after, regardless of whether the poison works." Lyphic motioned up the river valley. "They've been able to stall our advances with dug pikes to force us to narrow into their funnel."

"Turning this into a trench war," the colonel said with a frown.

"We're already fighting in one," breathed a lieutenant next to her, then blanched when he realized he'd spoken unbidden.

"True enough." Edmon barked a laugh. Lyphic smirked. "If unconventional. Which classes are we sending?"

"We have the slave regulars for the meat grinder," said the colonel, "but only after a regular echelon can pierce the eastern bank, otherwise they're just fodder."

"I have two volunteer battalions on the west bank preparing for the offensive with fresh supplies and weapons just brought in from Rithica," said Lyphic.

"You know those are the last supplies for a while?" Edmon asked.

"Yes, my lord," said the colonel. "We received reports before you arrived about the southern front."

"Good," Edmon said. "The regulars?"

"We use regulars to keep the line while we shift the other forces for special actions," said the colonel. "When the regulars tire out, we may temporarily shift slaves to support."

"Not the volunteers?" asked Edmon.

"We're working on keeping them well fed and rested between advances, per Prince Negrin's advice."

Edmon shook his head. "Negrin, Negrin, Negrin."

"With respect, prince general, his furca has been a surprising innovation that has greatly helped."

"That so?"

"You'd be amazed how fast we've moved without needing the typical supply trains," said Lyphic. "I thought it was folly, but I've changed my mind."

"You?" Edmon's brow flickered.

"I change my mind," Lyphic said. "Sometimes."

"You are not my brother," said Edmon.

"Negrin can't find his way out of a bathroom," Lyphic said, "but he finds surprising things in those books he beds. We're already seeing a surprising return on investment by treating the volunteers better. They fight harder and longer when they get better rest periods. Makes me wish we could replace the entire force with their likes."

"That would be awfully expensive," Edmon said.

"Prince Negrin told me himself that he would wager the time costs would pay out faster," the colonel offered. "For every fighter who volunteers, the prince estimated he would be worth more than three of our conscripts and ten of our slaves. If that were true, the cost of keeping one volunteer well fed would be far cheaper than all the regulars and slaves we employ, not to mention accrual of training and equipment costs."

Edmon pondered that. "That's difficult to imagine. I can't think of a day when slaves weren't central to Alderland's armies throughout history."

Lyphic inspected the map. "Nor I, but I'm all for finding better ways to victory."

"Can't disagree," Edmon said. "Anything else to report besides numbers?"

"The Unionists have sieged Eden," said Lyphic.

Edmon paused. "What?"

"We got word yesterday." Lyphic set his hands on his hips.

"Any word about whether they possess the pan's mantle?" asked Edmon.

The colonel frowned. "Does that matter, my lord?"

"Father will not be happy," Edmon growled. "Actually … it does."

"Invading Eden requires our immediate response," said Lyphic.

"Funny thing that," Edmon said. "Abydon revealed to me that if an invading force were to retain the mantle, we don't. The charter is attached to the mantle bearer, not the state."

"But aren't the two intrinsic, my lord?" asked the colonel.

"Not per the charter." Edmon paused as something tickled the back of his mind, but he dismissed it. "I looked it up, myself. He's right. The charter follows the pan."

"So, if the Unionists can conquer Eden *and* get Baley's mantle, we do nothing?" Lyphic uncrossed his arms.

"That's right," Edmon said. "Have we heard from Ambassador Abydon?"

"No," Lyphic said. "This news came through the long scouts. I haven't verified if father knows."

Though Edmon appeared as stone, anxiety built. Inside, he knew shifts in Eden meant more than Alderland's persistent border disputes with Meso'Admia. Among the longest ruling human dynasties in recent Pangean history, the Baley family had overseen Eden since the Minder Conflicts. Negrin always said they survived for two reasons: the prolonged life of each pan and the figurehead nature of their rule — which reduced the power struggles inherent to most other monarchies. The parliament ruled the Edenic Praesidium proper, managed disputes in the surrounding territories and served as a forum for Pangean states to discuss solutions to international issues.

Edmon met William ten years ago during Emperor Benuin's visit to the parliament, and doubted the pan had the steel to deal with insurgents like the Unionists. Diplomats were not warlords, but that was not Edmon's problem. "Anything else?"

"Nothing of substance, my lord," the colonel said.

"Prepare a report for his majesty. I will carry it with me through the rimsportal at Ostansia," Edmon said. "I need a bath."

"Aye," Lyphic said. A sergeant called the room to attention as Edmon exited the rear of the building. Soldiers led him to a tent erected for him within the officers' cordon. Once inside, he paused for a breath.

"My prince general." His slave, Sunta, moved to free him of his armor. "Your bath is almost ready and food has already been prepared."

Sunta removed Edmon's armor with swift efficiency. Once free of the armor and boots, the prince general stripped off his own clothes and passed a veil to the far side of the tent where a thick mattress had been set in the center and a copper tub steamed at its foot. A slave girl stood next to the tub wearing little. A thin gold chain looped a narrow waist above wide hips and a transparent skirt hung low from her navel to her calves.

He sank below the surface, scrubbed his thick beard and hair and surfaced to wipe his face. The slave bathed him as his head lolled upon the tub's curved copper lip and exhaled stress from his lungs. His thick muscles relaxed in the heat and the slave's ministrations drew his eyes up her body. He fondled her as she worked, then motioned for her to climb in. Once in, he pulled her to slide on him and rock. Soon gripping her body to drive her down harder on him, he climaxed. Finishing, he reclined and motioned for her to continue bathing him. She climbed out and obeyed.

He dismissed her and plucked fruit from a nearby tray while dozing. The tent danced in afternoon breeze rushing down the descending terrain westward into the village. Spotted sunlight from herds of high clouds rippled across the wind-dancing canvas. He picked up his head from sleep. Sunta stood next to his tub.

"Yes?"

"Prince general…" Sunta ducked his head. "Two High Guards request an audience."

Edmon had fallen asleep. When he climbed from the tepid water, the slave moved forward to towel him off. The High Guard? He motioned at Sunta who unfolded Edmon's hunter green robe and dressed the general before tying it off and tugging it smooth of wrinkles. Edmon stepped into proffered slippers. Through the veil, Edmon motioned at Sunta, who poked his head through the tent entrance to speak to the guards outside. They pulled aside the flaps to permit two haggard men wearing special light armor and covered in more dust than Edmon had worn on his arrival.

The two men knelt. "Prince general."

"Rhuys." Edmon's heart beat faster. "Why are you here and I don't see my brother?"

Rhuys gulped. "We bear … difficult news, my lord. We have failed.

The heir is missing."

Edmon's brow sank. "Tell me how this is different than the last time."

"I apologize, sire, but he's been gone two weeks," Rhuys said. "He's never evaded us this long."

Edmon motioned to Sunta. "Summon Lyphic."

"As you command." Sunta bowed and left.

"Where were you?"

"He evaded us in Wysteria a week's ride from here. We followed his trail south and discovered his necklace at an inn in Hypstrom. It was being traded but we could not figure out how they came by it."

"Where's the other half of your team?"

"I sent them to Suwannee, my lord."

Edmon crossed his arms. The heir had eluded his guard several times, always trying to flee from his responsibilities and the weight that came with them. For all Edmon was responsible for the armies of Alder and their constant fighting over the southern borders with northwest Meso'Admia, his first responsibility was to protect the Seventh, Heir to the Throne — he had no greater duty. Every time the boy eluded his guard, Edmon appeared as a fool before their father, the emperor, and had to spend time away from commanding the nation's armies to find and bring the heir to heel. This was getting out of hand and though calm outside, inside Edmon boiled.

Lyphic entered the tent seconds after Sunta stepped in and pulled the flap open.

"General?" Lyphic frowned at Rhuys, then stiffened. "What happened?"

"The heir is playing games with the high guard again," Edmon said.

Lyphic focused on the kneeling men.

"That boy has got to be brought to heel," said Edmon. "He can't keep evading his own guard."

"Thoughts?" asked Lyphic.

"Unhappy ones," Edmon said. "Go clean yourself up and prepare fresh mounts. Dismissed."

"Yes, prince general," relief washed over Rhuys's face as he and the other rose, saluted and left.

"Not going to kill them?" Lyphic asked.

"No," Edmon said. "Men who face their mistakes, or mistakes fate thrusts upon them, deserve a chance to fix their problems."

Lyphic mused. "Not sure I'd have been so kind. They can't keep up with the boy."

"Gael taught him how to evade them," Edmon barked. "That bastard is going to send our nation into yet another selfdamn civil war so the heir 'can play.'"

"It's time we shook up the high guard," Lyphic said. "This happens too often-"

"The only person who's failed, here, is me," Edmon said. "He's my responsibility."

Lyphic waited.

"Tomorrow I leave for the rimsportal," Edmon paused, "but I'll go the long route. He said Hypstrom. That's near the River House in Suwannee. Rhuys was right to send two of his men there. I'll go there, first. If he's there, I'll drag him with me back home. If nothing else, perhaps I'll intercept him if he's already on his way out."

"Small chance," Lyphic grunted. "Gael was always best at hide and seek. He taught Phineas well."

"Oh, one way or the other, we're going to go after him, too."

"Bringing him to heel?"

"No," Edmon growled. "I'm beating him with it."

31

A Dangerous Woman

Bristol and Dorsman waited amidships as Smee escorted Athyka onto deck. A bloody bandage wrapped under her chin and over the crown of her head, yet she followed him as if he were her herald. She stopped a few paces shy of the two and waited. Fifteen sailors circled her with crossbows drawn and ready.

Her eyes flickered to the sheathed ice knife tucked into Bristol's belt, this thumb rubbing its pommel. To her surprise, a faint blue light snaked from the ohna to her chest. The nearer she came, the thicker it grew. No one else seemed to see it and she struggled not to race for the knife. The need to touch and hold it grew in her breast. Her left frozen hand quivered with anticipation until she pressed it against her hip to hide it.

Dorsman crossed his thick arms.

"I apologize for my behavior yesterday, captain," Athyka tilted her head. "I'm afraid I was under a great deal of stress."

"I had to kill my own men," Dorsman growled. "My own men turned on me."

Athyka's heart fluttered at his tone.

"The dwarf is under specific instructions to pull apart your appendages, starting with each finger, if you attempt anything on any of us," Dorsman glared.

"That won't be necessary, captain," Athyka drew on her link to the knife, desperate to pull on its power without having to touch it. The presence of the ohna amplified her daleen abilities. "You see, I'm afraid you have the wrong of it. I'm no minder, at all."

Harry barked a laugh. The circle of armed sailors tightened butt stocks to shoulders.

"Some kinda balls on you," Dorsman rolled his chin. "You think we don't know minders when we see them?"

"You've met minders before?"

Dorsman's glare deepened.

"You don't have to have seen a dragon to recognize it," Harry raised an eyebrow. "Dorsman has a trustworthy crew."

Athyka struggled to listen to them while she drew in the ohna's power. She had never been able to take control of a man before, only influence his thinking and then hide her presence later. There on the deck in the panic of her agonizing stupor and the deep link she'd achieved with the ohna, she had taken control of several men, forcing them to fight to protect her. She didn't even know which men had helped her- no, that wasn't true.

Laurel had been a seasoned sailor on Dorsman's ship for ten years and pulled his weight. He had grown up with a loving mother and absent, alcoholic carpenter father before landing a rare opportunity to learn sail when most positions were reserved for the children of sailors.

Ansley was a womanizer more often than the women were willing. He had never met his father and his mother treated him with disdain for as long as he could remember. He had crewed for Dorsman for six years this past summer and had hidden contraband in the powder magazine.

Lieutenant Hawkins loved men and had hid it for years. He began sailing when he was caught with a Temple minister's son and was forced to take a commission offered by his grandfather. He kept his habits to the brothels in Tangerine and Two Moons but had begun flirting with one of the sailors soon after Richter's Deep. He kept it a secret until Dorsman began mounting him regularly in the captain's cabin.

The last man was the crew's outcast. Horb hated the sea but couldn't start over so late in life, so he worked hard and kept away from everyone else. He detested his life and lot and his father for selling him in the slave markets in the southern Alder.

Memories appeared before her of these men with rich detail as she had never before experienced. She knew them well from her brief touch on their minds and, in the moments she realized she hadn't answered a question, found her answer.

"What the hell are you doing, minder!?" Dorsman advanced.

"Yes, you asked about the four members of your crew who helped me," she winced. "I apologize, my head … I'm struggling to concentrate. I was unaware they were on board, but I have a history with these men. They were only trying to protect me because I saved each of their lives in the past."

"Tryin- what absolute horseshit-" Dorsman's eyes widened at her audacity.

"Lieutenant Hawkins was a fine young man," Athyka said. "I admit, we only met recently when he was in Oltheda. I was conducting business when I ran into him at the Tailor's Second."

Dorsman coughed. Harry's eyebrow climbed.

"Intelligent young man but got himself into a real pickle," Athyka said. "It seems someone called him a low frog," — a homosexual — "and he drew swords against men he wasn't capable of defeating. I admired his bravery and saved his life. He owed me his own. I fear he was only trying to protect me."

Dorsman struggled to speak. "There are dead men on this ship, some of which turned on the others. You're telling me they were willing to risk their lives for you? Even if what you say is true about- the lieutenant," his eye fluttered, "there's no selfdamn way you randomly knew four members of my crew."

"I'm afraid I have." Athyka ignored the men still aiming heavy steel-tipped bolts. "You see, Laurel and Ansley both crewed a ship I was taking to Meso'Admia some years back when we were attacked by pirates. Naturally, I don't take kindly to boarders and I fought with the crew. I can't say I realized they held so much regard for my life as to threaten yours. I apologize for those they killed."

"And Horb?"

"Similar situation."

Dorsman sucked on his tongue. "Go get Horb."

"He's not dead?" Athyka's brow flickered.

"Ol' Horb?" Dorsman's eyes narrowed. "Oh, no. Got him down in the brig."

Athyka's stomach sank to her feet, but she blinked slowly and met his eyes. "Please, bring Horb up. I'd like to thank him."

Dorsman snapped his fingers and two sailors jogged for the fore gangway. He eyed Smee. "I wanna know what this bitch told you."

"Tol' me nuffin," said Smee.

"Know what Horb told us?" Dorsman growled.

Athyka shook her head as frigid wind tugged her hair.

"Said he never heard of you his entire life."

Athyka scoffed. "You think I've made a career like some spy from a story using her own name everywhere she goes?" While she joked, fear rose in her. Could she plant an idea for more than the time it took for Horb to make a decision? Permanent changes to men's memories had never been possible — she created decision points by pressing "intention" against their minds and once her influence activated their choices, they carried on her instructions believing they set their own courses. But planting a memory? Grandmother had spoken of the ancient daleens who reached full ascendancy — the psylocks — who could erase whole men from their bodies and replace them with mindless slaves. Dubious of the idea's validity and with no desire to destroy men completely, interacting with the ohna enhanced her influence. Could she get to Horb in the few seconds it took for him to cross the deck from the gangway? She could hear thoughts, but she always needed a line of sight and close proximity to do more than listen.

Now, desperation drove her. When Dorsman said nothing else, she pretended to inspect her fingernails to hide her fifty-yard gaze. Panic drove her to reach out with her mind, against even her grandmother's training, and ran naked into a terrifying forest of men's thoughts from the sailors around her. Most of the thoughts crashed against her as fear, some lust, one with simple disdain and a few laced with familial longing — she reminded them of a mother or sister unseen for most of their lives while asea. She lunged, attempting to identify Horb-

Fear. If I go near her, again, she'll take my mind... Horb's thoughts crashed into her as if he screamed into her face. *She already done it. She could do it again. Destroy me. Remold me. Know the stories like everyone else. Daleens master thousands and take over the world. Chains will allow guards to kill me easily. Can't go see her again.*

Athyka struggled not to gasp. She sat within his mind like it was her own. As he mounted the aft gangway behind her, she plunged through his memories in search of a ship she might have taken at some point, some common figure she could claim she had taken, some- THERE.

The sailors walked Horb onto deck like escorting a feral, hungry tiger. Horb stared at the ground, sure that if they locked eyes, she would take his mind. But- … how could she do that? She's no minder.

"Horb." Dorsman's eyes snapped to the hunched sailor.

"Cap'n." Horb saluted as he and his guards came to a stop a few paces behind Athyka.

"Care to share your story with the daleen?"

"Daleen, cap'n?"

Dorsman's eyes narrowed and pointed at the woman. "Athyka?"

Athyka turned with as much grace as she could muster despite the throb numbing the right side of her face.

Horb blushed. "I- Cap'n, it's my fault."

"Your what?"

"This is Lady Turnstone." Horb motioned to Athyka. "Saved my life, she did. We was in the northeast near Egun when Univeans tried boarding us on The Atlanta, they did. Part o'the wars back'n."

Dorsman's eyes widened. "You told me last night you'd never seen her before in your life!"

Horb quivered. "I'm- I'm sorry, cap'n. I was afraid."

"You're doing something to him!" Dorsman pointed.

Having planted the sliver of a memory, Athyka had returned to drawing more of the ohna, if she could. The connection had grown stronger once Horb had begun speaking. She turned that drawn power to Harry.

When Eldnor held the ohna terra on Unity's Light, its presence muted her ability to affect his mind — all ohnas had a similar effect.

She fought in vain to use her connection with the ohna to influence Harry while he held it in his hand — his contact with the ohna made him immune. Trying to influence Dorsman might create a stumble on his tongue that would draw the attention of the frightened sailors pointing their crossbows. When Dorsman yelled, she faced him. "How could I do such a thing?"

"You're a minder!"

"Can you prove it?"

"My men just turn-"

"And this gentleman here, recognizes me from a ship he sailed … ten years ago?"

"You planted that thought."

"Then find a sailor here who sailed with him."

Without turning his head, Dorsman shouted, "Who here sailed with Horb!?"

"I did, cap'n," said the bosun.

Dorsman turned, his eyes widening.

"It's true, Univeans struck us near Egungutar several times. Can't say I remember her, specifically, though. We ferried often through those waters before it sank."

"You're influencing them!" Dorsman rounded on her.

"How could I possibly do such a thing?"

"It's your magic!"

"I'm just a mage, not a witch." Athyka's brow drew down. "I'd have to cast powerful spells. Being a mage, I can't cast spells. Do you see me using magic?"

Though they stood ready to strike her down, Harry shook his head. "She's not using magic, captain."

"Minders have their own magic," Dorsman growled.

"How would you know such a thing, captain?" Athyka asked.

"I've done my studies."

"Then how close must a daleen be to influence men?"

Dorsman's mouth opened and shut.

"I'm no expert on minders, but last I read, common ones had to be within a few feet. Weak daleens have to touch others. Their abilities are not permanent and they can't plant false memories."

Dorsman's jaw tightened.

"While I am many things, Captain Dorsman, a daleen is not among them. First of all, I am an agent to Fellow Elwin Roschach, leader of our beloved Quorum of Faith, and you will give me the due respect my position demands," she said, an edge to her voice, intolerant of her treatment. "Second of all, I am an ohna bearer, and you will return the ohna marina, immediately."

"You failed-"

"What I did was save an ohna from a violent pixilark who ripped apart my ship," she snapped. Members holding crossbows faltered.

"A pixie?" muttered several.

"The fairy attacked you?" Harry's eyes widened in surprise. "The haraven?"

"Yes, the thing attacked me and destroyed my entire ship," Athyka growled. "You should be amazed I'm alive at all, Captain Dorsman." Her voice climbed. "I still have a mission on Algueda and I intend to finish it. Now, you will return the ohna to me and we can plan to secure the mantle."

"Harry's got the ohna now," Dorsman grimaced.

"Harry will return it." Athyka kept her attention on Dorsman.

"That's not how this works." Harry straightened now that she had set the decision in Dorsman's hands.

"I'm no daleen, but what I am should still give you pause, Rocky Dorsman," she growled. "I am the active authority from Roschach himself, to secure the mantle and I don't care what setbacks we have, I am still in charge of this mission. Now give me the selfdamn ohna."

"I'm in charge here!" Harry protested.

"Bristol is Roschach's backup to Unity's Light." Athyka kept her focus on Dorsman. "I am senior agent until I am dead or removed by Roschach himself, neither of which has occurred. Until it does occur, we will go where I say and how I say."

"You lost your whole bloody ship!" Harry exclaimed.

"And survived a fucking pixilark." Athyka finally looked at him, then to Dorsman. "This is your ship, but this is my mission. Are we clear?"

Dorsman ground his teeth but appeared far less certain than he did minutes ago.

"You can't be listening to this!" Harry stammered.

"She's right."

"What?"

"Selfdamnit, she's right," Dorsman admitted. "Give her the ohna."

"No fuckin way-"

"Give her the ohna!" Dorsman barked.

When the armed sailors and mages faced Harry instead of Athyka, he hesitated. Dorsman waited until Harry tossed it. Smee caught it for her, drawing eyes of surprise. He held it out for her to pluck it from his hand. Dorsman's eyes fluttered between the two while Athyka's heart pounded with desire at touching the ohna again. Once more in her hand, it flooded her with power and ecstasy. She fought against revealing it while struggling to cope with a hundred confused voices crashing into her mind. The ohna doubled down her abilities.

"Now, captain, bring The Hover about. We've passed Algueda by four leagues to starboard."

"What?" Dorsman asked.

"Now, captain."

Dorsman thought another moment, then motioned to his first mate who relayed orders to bring the ship about.

"Also, I need you to prepare your best divers. The ohna terra was lost during the sinking and we will need to retrieve it from the lagoon as soon as we arrive."

"Aye," said Dorsman.

Athyka almost smiled. The ohna not only pulled their minds to hers, but now broadcast her to them without effort. Even Harry nodded quickly. She took a breath as full control of every human on board slipped into her fingers.

"You're … dangerous." Smee watched her askance. She wasn't unduly influencing the dwarf — fear did its work.

A smile tugged at the side of her mouth. "I will finish my mission." She gripped the ohna. "Then we'll see."

32

Waking Tootles

Peter dropped the small, scummy child into the shallows of the rift river south of the Tree. "Wash him, will you?"

"What?" Santi asked.

"This is gonna be your role now, Santi," Peter said. "You will gather me an army of boys from across the island."

"I'll do nothing of the sort!" Santi protested.

"Hey, I just saved your life!" Peter snapped.

Peter. He saved you!

"You didn't save my life!" Santi stormed past Peter to flip the other boy over in the water to ensure he could breathe. Seeing his failure, Peter winced.

"Yeah, I did, with the croc," said Peter.

"What croc?"

"You did-" Peter realized Santi had been unconscious the entire time. "I saved you from this massive crocodile! It was hyuge and was coming right for you!"

That's true.

"What'd she say?" Santi asked.

"That I'm right!" Peter puffed his chest.

"She said nothing of the sort!" Santi pointed with his free hand.

"She did, too!"

BOYS! Tinker Belle's bark caused both to flinch. *Calm yourselves.*

Though Santi could not understand her words, he understood the gist.

You both saved each-

"If this is true, about the crocodile, then we are even, no?" Santi suggested.

Wiggling his pinky in his ear, Peter shrugged.

"So … you need to find your father but must defend this island. I would return home, but have no one to help me craft a boat. If I help you defend the island, then you can help me build a boat, yes?"

Peter exchanged looks with Tinker Belle. "Yes."

"Then I agree to build your army," Santi said. "But. How do I find these bo-"

"Yes! Now we can get started on finding father!" Peter smiled and planted his fists on his hips.

We need to begin scouting the island, chimed Tinker Belle. *This was only the first wave of Unionists. I'm confident more will come.*

"What? Why?" Peter turned.

The mantle is the most powerful of its kind. The Unionists have already stolen the ohnas from the alterworlds. That doesn't include the mantle's political power. He who possesses it also possesses the loyalty of many of the more mystical factions in Pangea.

"You mean folks follow the mantle, just because?"

Well, sort of, Tinker Belle chimed. *Many Pangeic religions hold the pan as either a deity or elemental. If the Unionists can hold the mantle, they can hold strange allegiances. We must deal with the Unionists, immediately. While Santi finds more boys and you look for your father, I can begin scouting the island for any other Unionists who may have survived. Or any others who may be coming.*

Though Santi couldn't understand her chimes, he clung to Peter's replies to gather what he could. Meanwhile, he plunged the boy into the water and pulled him up, then did it again. The boy's arms were big enough to give him difficulty in holding them. With a quick glance for Peter and the pixie, he slipped his hand around the boy's neck and used it to plunge him in and out of the water.

As he did, his heart quickened.

Suddenly he was back to a few weeks ago, another neck between his hands with another face, one staring up at him in terror, one that clung to his wrists. His heart raced as he plunged the boy. To have easy and absolute control over life-

"Santi!" Peter called. Santi snatched up the boy, realizing he had more than imagined holding him under. To his relief, gasps erupted from his mouth.

Guilted that he had left him face down in the water, Peter walked over to help pull the child onto his feet. Tinker Belle, however, watched Santi.

"Hey, hey! Cough it up!" Peter slapped the flailing boy on the back. Viscous green drooled from his throat in coughs and hacks. "There you go! C'mon, help me get him onto the beach."

Santi helped them up the beach where the boy sank to his knees and rubbed his eyes.

"You okay? Can you breathe?" Peter asked.

The red-faced boy grunted. "Where am I?"

Peter smiled. "You're on Neverland!"

The boy fought panic. "Where?"

"Neverland!" Peter smiled.

"Where is that?"

"It's … complicated," Peter smirked at a frowning Santi.

"How did I get here?" the boy coughed.

Peter squatted next to him. "Neverland has brought you here, of course."

Santi frowned.

"The- the place brought me here?" the boy asked.

"Yes. Neverland brought you here."

"But- why?"

"What language is he speaking?" Santi asked.

"You … don't understand him?" Peter faced Santi.

"No! How could I!? He's speaking a language I've never heard!"

Looking from Santi to the new boy, a grin crawled across his face. "This is so cool!"

Peter.

"What's so cool?" Santi asked.

"Ha! I can talk to both of you, but you can't talk to each other!" Peter said.

This isn't "cool."

"Why not?" Peter asked.

"How am I supposed to communicate with him!?" Santi stammered.

"How am I supposed to know?" Peter shrugged.

You're going to have to help him.

"What? I have things to do," Peter protested.

Like what?

"You just said we have to go fight off the Unionists!" Peter said.

"How can I understand you and you can understand him, but he isn't speaking our language?" Santi asked.

Oh, buddy.

"I'm speaking High Gruen," Peter shrugged. "I don't know what you're speaking."

"That- what?" Santi asked. "You are speaking Castilian. I understand you perfectly!"

"It's the mantle," Peter cringed. "The- The mantle translates." Peter kicked sand.

The new boy stared at the pixie.

I told you, Peter. You have the mantle.

"FINE!" Peter rounded on her, pointing with his finger. "I have the mantle. But I'm NOT the pan!"

That's what being the pan means- Tinker Belle closed her eyes. *Great Self, help me not murder children that deserve it.*

Peter fumed.

"How am I supposed to be responsible for him if I can't talk with him?" Santi asked. "If he doesn't speak Castilian, what does he speak?"

Peter looked to the boy. "What's your name?"

The boy tried to say something, but instead achieved only a series of vowels, still unable to pull his eyes from the fairy.

"Hey. Hey!" Peter waved. "Look at me."

The boy moaned.

"What's your name?"

"He sounds like a trumpet with all that hooting." Santi's brow drew down.

"My name is Vernogenos," the boy breathed.

"Verna- Veren-" Peter scrunched his face. "How about we just call you Hoot?"

"Tootles," Santi said at the same time.

Exchanging glances with Santi, Peter nodded. "Sure. We'll call you Tootles."

The boy gulped up at them. "Tootles?"

"Yes." Peter motioned to Santi. "This is your … captain. You are now one of my men."

"*My* men," Santi corrected.

"For *me*," Peter emphasized at Santi, then looked again at Tootles. "I'm in charge, but when I'm not around you do what he says, okay?"

Tootles locked again on the pixie. "What is that?"

"That's my fairy," Peter smiled.

"A FAIRY!" Tootles scrambled backwards.

"Why is everyone terrified of her?" Peter asked.

"She is a fairy! She will take my soul!" Tootles cried.

"Tink?" Peter stood. "She's harmless."

Tinker Belle's brow drew down.

"When you leave, how am I supposed to understand him?" Santi asked.

"I don't know!" Peter said. "But you got more of them to find and you'll have to figure out something."

"More? I don't even know how you found this one!" Santi stammered. "How am I supposed to find more?"

"I can't do everything for you! Are you a man or not!?"

Santi stiffened. "I am a man."

"Good then! Figure it out!"

Santi glowered at the sound of his father's words echoing in his ears. He swallowed the tightness in his throat as he turned to Tootles. "What am I going to do with you?"

The boy started. "Aragon?"

Santi's eyes widened. "What? You know of Aragon!?"

Tootles rattled off in his own language before Santi threw up his hands. "Wait, wait, slower, please. But … I think some of your words sound … kinda familiar. But not really. I think he's French."

"Are you French?" Peter asked Tootles.

"No," Tootles said. Santi looked to Peter for a translation. "I'm from Gaul! Is he from Andorra?"

"He said Andorra." Santi pointed at the boy. "He knows of the Pirineos!!"

"See," said Peter, "I knew you two would figure it out."

"Where am I?" Tootles sputtered.

"You're home," Peter said.

"Home?" Tootles asked.

Peter smirked. "Yeah. There are no parents here. No rules. Just adventure. Like the one we had an hour ago."

"Adventure?" asked Santi and Tootles.

Peter smiled. "You know, when I rescued you."

"Rescued me?" Tootles asked.

"Ah!" Peter raised his finger. "From the spade plant."

Tootles shook his head.

Peter threw up his hands. "The dangerous spade wall that protects my home! We walked in, and then, wham! We had you! It was a vicious struggle! The plant wouldn't let you go, but I refused! I said to the plant, 'Let go of this boy! He's mine!'"

"You did?" Tootles breathed.

Santi's brow drooped.

"I did!" Peter clenched his fist in front of him for emphasis. "We fought for what seemed like hours! I finally managed to fight my way in and beat it up from the inside! Then I dragged you out and into the ocean!" Peter's hands motioned the fight. He pointed to the sky as if it, too, had been part of his story.

Seriously? Tinker Belle chimed.

"Yes, seriously," Peter shrugged.

"What did she say?" Tootles asked.

"She said the plant was strong and was going to eat you!" Peter's face lit up.

Tinker Belle frowned.

"I offer an invitation." Peter leaned in and offered his hand to Tootles. "Join me in having the grandest adventures a boy could ever have and go look for more boys lost in Neverland! We will make our own rules, our own bedtimes and our own destinies!"

"B– but…" the boy hugged himself. "I want my mother."

Peter hesitated. "Why would you want that?"

"What'd he say?" Santi asked.

"He wants his mother," Peter said.

His answer surprised Tinker Belle. Like all boys, Peter should hunger for his parents.

"Cuz … " Tootles trailed off.

Peter smiled. "You have no reason better than mine. Therefore, by the laws of Neverland, you and Santi must build me an army!"

The boys waited.

"We have enemies upon our doorstep!" Peter exclaimed. "We have no time to lose! You two must gather as many as possible. War is upon us.

This is your charge! But first, we're gonna go get my father. I'll bet you he's at that fire we saw earlier."

Tinker Belle clenched her teeth — she never found the campfire.

Tootles spared a glance at the pixie again. "Please, don't let her eat me."

Peter laughed.

Realizing Tootles was afraid, Santi motioned at Tinker Belle and shook his head, as if to convey no danger.

Cocking her head to the side with a glare, Tinker Belle gathered power into her hands and fired into the tree line, causing a tree to explode and rain down wood chips upon them.

Santi's eyes became saucers and Tootles stuttered in horror.

You aren't the pan now, you silly ass, Tinker Belle pointed at Santi. *I will mess you up.*

"Tink," Peter glared, then faced them. "She's fine. You're fine. She's not going to kill you. Calm down."

The boys gulped.

33

An Idea

Dozens of quiet minds linked to Athyka like tiny strings held in the fingers of her will. The hunger in their bellies, the cool of cold air across their skin, the pressure in their bladders, the aches in their loins from long months asea and even itches across their body fed into her mind. She feared no one, for all were now hers. Absolute control aroused her. She used it to terminate all lust, fear and doubt within the agents, mages and crew. Touch, alone, permitted her to listen to the dwarf's thoughts, but she had his mountain oath.

Standing in the captain's quarters, she smoothed her dress, tucked her hair and approached the mirror. She paused. Her eyes had changed. She raised a hand and produced a small flame to get a better look at her irises.

Throughout her youth living and training with her grandmother, a daleen hiding in plain sight, Athyka had feared purple appearing in her eyes. Her grandmother bore a few faint reflective amethyst specks in her irises and was lucky enough the ignorant local villagers either failed to notice or thought they were pretty. When Athyka found her own first specks, she didn't leave the house for weeks. By the time she matured, she had the same handful as her grandmother, and, like her grandmother, she proved to be weak in her psylism — the power of the mind.

Standing before the mirror, Athyka found a dozen new amethyst specks in her irises reflecting in the tiny bulb of light. Only the most powerful of daleens had full purple irises — the psylocks — who could challenge even the high elves at their psylism. They awakened in powerful shocks that broadcast their maturation across the continent, an event known as a mindrise. Even low sentients like animals seemed to sense and obey a psylock.

Could the ohnas be amplifying her psylism? Could she ascend to the full power of a psylock?

Athyka struggled against the terror and desire fighting for her focus. Hope grew within her breast to be more than she always had been, to reach that ultimate moment. Her breath quickened at the idea of experiencing her own mindrise.

Eyeing her face, she tugged on her bandage and unwrapped it from her head to examine her injury when her eyes latched upon the scarring on her face and widened.

The shape of the gash that ripped open her face, revealed her molars and took pieces of her ear was in the shape of a handprint.

April's severed hand.

Athyka quivered in a moment of uncertainty before the captain's thoughts returned her attention to a more immediate goal — reclaiming Eldnor's lost ohna. Eyeing the gap in her face, she focused. Frost formed from the scabbed edges of the rip and grew inward to fill the space. Pondering how permanent the injury might be, she shuddered.

Gathering herself, she left the cabin and climbed onto the deck drenched in tropical heat and humidity inside Neverland's lagoon. She mounted the forecastle to lean over the base of the bowsprit. Unity's Light lay broken on the lagoon bed eighty feet down, visible through the crystal blue waters. The Hover anchored just above the wreck and a team of sailors assembled to dive to the depths in search of the ohna terra, lost with Eldnor.

The fool died when he attacked her. Clutching the ohna of soil and metal, his disrespect of its power cost him his life. He limited his understanding to soil, alone. When she flashed out a common steel knife and cut open his throat, he sank to the deck and drowned in his own blood. He could have stopped her blade, but he died a fool with the same unidimensional view of power as his politics.

If Eldnor's body sank straight down, the ohna terra should be alongside the ship. She probed the depths, thinking the water might serve as a conduit of the ohna's magic, but nothing stood out.

Athyka made her way to the portside Jacob's ladder and descended to the waiting ship's boat. As the men rowed for the wreck, Athyka unwrapped her loose left fist. Curled blue fingers steamed in the tropical heat. Her nerves twinged at the freedom of movement and exposure to brilliant noonlight. Regret over the costs of the mission disappeared under the rising pain in her nerves and import of her current task.

She leaned out over the port side of the ship's boat and lowered her hand near the water. The bloody froth of dying sailors gave her pause. How would she help a diver get safely to the bottom without dying? She didn't have the ohna makara — the clear coral that controlled all sea life. Winston Runel took that with him to Helvan Gulf from Richter's Deep.

Athyka withdrew her hand while the men around her waited. The crew waited. The dwarf waited. Not a word had been spoken in hours as men moved at the prompt of her will. Her eyes climbed to The Hover's bowsprit sticking out over the water, then looked to the water itself.

At her prompt, sailors on deck rushed to the bowsprit, tied a pulley, slid through a rope and tied a loop on the far end. A sailor hooked his foot in and gripped the rope as others lowered him to the water's surface. The men in her ship's boat rotated so she faced the wreck. She fished out the ice knife, stuck the blade into the water and closed her eyes. To her surprise, information flooded her mind about the water. Though she could not see fish or wood or sand, she saw these objects as silhouetted gaps in the water, itself.

The smile growing on her face faltered as she focused her power. A swirl appeared beneath the sailor dangling below the bowsprit that grew. Air snaked through the vacuum down to the sunken vessel and widened with the whirlpool. Sailors worked to keep her ship's boat stable as the hole widened to twenty, thirty and fifty feet across. The sailor on the line descended, but the water grew too heavy and her energy waned. Suddenly she lost control and the whirlpool rushed inward and collapsed around the man. Her ship's boat spun through the water and rocked in the violence.

She kept a bare grip on the knife and yanked it with her as she leaned to remain inside. The sailor below was long gone, she knew. While opening the whirlpool, she sensed thousands of creatures waiting to kill whatever drew too near. Water bathed her and the sailors in the chaos and she hissed as it splashed her icy fingers with warm water.

Athyka sat up and held her frosty hand. Eyeing the water on her fingers, she grit her teeth until the moisture seemed to disappear. Her hand felt better. She had taken life from the water in the men on deck when she took it, first, from a mage and, second, from Eldnor by accident. Might the ocean, itself, carry its own energy?

She sheathed the ohna marina and dangled her blue fingers near the ocean. Gentle splashes washed over it. She almost screamed as her nerves came to life, but she sucked in the water through her pores and gasped as power and energy wormed up her arm. She clutched the ice knife with her right hand and focused on the water. A snake of water swirled from the surface to her curled blue fingers. Too small to permit fish, it allowed her to touch the surface without baring herself to predators. As the water engulfed her fist and the initial pain passed, she searched the water for a tap. Minutes passed when something shifted and power flooded her. It rushed up her arm and into her body. Her heart exploded with movement. Colors grew vibrant, sounds panoplic, smells rich and varied ... life grew abundant.

With new energy, she prompted another line and another sailor to be lowered from the bowsprit. With her power renewed, the whirlpool opened in seconds and exposed in diameter an eighty-foot stretch of ship and seabed. Touching the water with her fingers gave her finer control, even so far as keeping her ship's boat motionless while leaning over the edge of the whirlpool to give her a better view.

The sailor moved about the dry lagoon bed to pull scree aside and search for the stone ring. Crabs rushed away from him back into the water. Bottom feeders flapped in the sand, dying in the heat. Looking into the chasm, her eyes latched upon something near the edge of the whirlpool. She moved it and the sailor until they fell within the vessel's shadow. He brushed sand aside when a beached eel struck and latched upon his palm. He held his hand aside while the creature dangled and thrashed, drawing blood, and continued with his left.

"There!" Her eyes gleamed when he exposed the stone ring. Despite the thrashing eel, he plucked the leather thong, pulled the stone ring from the sand and returned to the looped line for the men on board to haul him upwards just to the surface. Athyka closed the whirlpool and moved her ship's boat beneath the man. He lowered it into her hand while another sailor stabbed the eel to death and pulled it from his bleeding palm.

Athyka gripped the ohna while still drawing in power from the lagoon. She faced Pan's Peak and, glancing at the small snake of water in her hand, got an idea.

34

A Third Boy

"I don't see him," Peter whispered as the three boys squatted behind a bush.

"What does he look like, again?" Tootles whispered.

"Tall, brown hair, beard, blue eyes, wears a big green coat like the one I left in the clearing," Peter said.

"Do they kinda look like him?" Tootles shrugged. "I've never seen such pale men."

"Really?"

Tootles shrank. "N- no."

"I'm not angry with you," said Peter.

"Oh. I mean, other than you and Santi."

"I am Valencian!" Santi declared.

"Hush," Peter said.

Fifty paces away, six men lounged around a small campfire in a clearing near the island's steep western shore, south of the West Bay, hugged by jungle flora.

Santi glared before looking again at the small campfire. "These are your father's men?"

Peter's face tightened. "No. They were not on the ship."

"Is this the same campfire you saw earlier?"

"No," Peter said.

"Then where did they come from?"

"They must come from the enemy ship."

"If that is so, then we have the element of surprise," Santi said. "We ought to attack immediately."

Tootles doubletook. "What?"

"We attack." Santi straightened. "We can take three before the others even know we're there. We have the advantage and know the island better than them. Peter and I are strong. Tootles you are … quiet. You can sneak up on them."

Tootles shrank.

"This is true." Peter's hand tightened around the hilt of his silver knife. "We could. I could get the big one and you two could go after the others."

"Peter," Tootles stammered. "I- I have never attacked a man before. I am not so very strong, I think."

Peter scrunched his mouth.

"But we can take them now," Santi leaned in. "Surprise is a great advantage."

"I want to find my father, not attack random men," Peter admitted.

"But this is your chance to drive away your enemies," Santi insisted.

"We- we need more boys than us," Tootles muttered.

"Fortune favors the bold," Santi said.

"You're right," Peter said. "But I'm with Tootles."

Tootles smiled.

"We're outmatched and other than my knife, we're unarmed," Peter said. "They have swords and crossbows. That doesn't include any mages among them."

"Mages?" Santi stiffened. "Witches?"

"No, mages," Peter said. "Witches are rare. Maybe that woman was one?"

"What woman?" Santi asked.

"She was chasing us on that ship."

"What's the difference?" Tootles asked. "Are not all shamans powerful?"

"Common mages can't weave spells," Peter said. "They can use magic, but if they stop focusing, the magic goes away. Wizards and witches can create magical constructs that work without them being there, called spells. Plus, they're way more powerful."

"Oh," Tootles said as if he understood.

"We are facing those who wield magic!?" Santi paled. "Why didn't you tell us that?"

"It's not a huge deal." Peter flicked his thumb. Fire appeared over the tip. "My family are mages."

"You wield it!" Santi leaned back.

"Yeah, not like father, though." Peter dropped his hand, extinguishing the flame. "But you're right." He nudged Tootles's shoulder with his elbow. "We need more men."

A small smile tugged at Tootles's nervous face.

"If they have no mages," Santi insisted, "we can take them now."

"I'm not going to rush in and get killed before we find father," Peter said. He turned when Tinker Belle, sitting on his right shoulder, tapped his neck. She motioned that they retreat. He nodded. "C'mon. Let's get started before these guys come looking for the Tree. Maybe the other fire is where father is."

Peter and Tootles retreated through the bush. Reluctant, Santi joined them. Once around the bend in the steep terrain, Peter led them along the north island's southern, winding shore before following the ridgelines north to avoid the swamp.

We need to plan well, Tinker Belle chimed once they were far enough away. *If we do attack the Unionists, they will not be easy. Many are trained soldiers-turned-mercenaries. The Unionists did not send fools.*

Peter nodded.

"What did she say?" Santi asked.

"She said those men are probably well trained," Peter said. "We can't just expect to kill them all just because we surprise them."

Well said, Tinker Belle hovered next to them. Faint sparks drifted down from her body before fading a few inches behind, drawing Tootles's attention.

"You said we had to get more boys to build an army," Santi huffed as they grabbed small trees to haul themselves up the steep terrain.

Peter! Tinker Belle shouted. He paused. When she pointed at a large, coiled snake that ignored Peter but readied itself for the other two, Peter stood in its path so the boys could pass unharmed. *Show them what to look for so you don't get your new army killed.*

Peter blushed. "Right."

"How are we supposed to find them?" Santi asked once they passed the snake.

"They're everywhere," Peter said with a shrug. "Watch out for that." He pointed at a small plated beetle nibbling on bark. Green amber drooled from gashes in the bark left by long fangs hidden beneath its head. Peter pointed out dozens of other dangers without thinking.

"More boys?" Tootles asked. "Where?"

"They're in the forest, like you two." Peter pointed at a thorner. "That explodes if you brush it, and it smells like sour milk, if you pay attention."

Tootles eyed the woods as he followed, as if afraid boys would appear from nothing.

"How can you say they're everywhere?" Santi asked.

"Can't you feel them?" Peter stopped, then marched off into denser brush. "C'mon. Just step on the roots."

Exchanging glances, Santi and Tootles took care to stay on tree roots rising from dry sandy soil as they followed him into a thicket. Inside, the thicket appeared much larger than the outside. A thick layer of icy mist filled a quarter-mile-wide gorge lipped by heavy trees looming over the tops of its white, chalky walls. They turned along its outer edge, below which hovered thick white mist filling the gorge.

How can you sense them, Peter? Tinker Belle asked. *William never mentioned being able to sense these children like you do. Or even recognizing half as many dangers as you have. I was just hoping you remembered something he shared with you, but he never shared this much with you, I know that much.*

Peter shrugged. "I dunno. I just can. Don't you?"

"No," Santi said.

Tootles gazed down into the hole. "Yes."

Peter, Santi and Tinker Belle stopped.

"I- I can," Tootles stuttered. "He's ... he's down there. I don't know why, but- yes. There's someone down there."

"See!" Peter smiled and marched to the right as the gorge widened.

"What is this?" Santi stammered. "Stairs! In a jungle like this!?"

"Yeah." Peter headed down. "Father said Algueda is as old as the continent. Maybe older."

"How old is that?" Santi asked.

Peter tried to recall as the stairs curved around the inside wall of the gorge. "Millions? Tens of millions?"

"Years?" Santi asked.

"Yeah."

"Impossible!" Santi said. "The Bible says the earth is only six thousand years old!"

"Bible? We're not on earth, Santi," Peter said.

Descending into the mist, the three soon struggled to see even each other.

Santi fell quiet as the milky air thickened so that he struggled to breathe. Tootles, likewise, coughed and covered his mouth with the crook of his elbow.

"When my father takes command, we'll beat the Unionists." Peter cleared his throat. "He's very powerful. I'll give him the mantle back and we'll take care of all this."

Santi's eyes narrowed. "The pixie said I had the mantle."

"Yeah, well, I have it now."

"How did you get it?" Santi's face tightened.

"I've been thinking on that. I think when you touched me, it came back to me."

"It was mine."

"It was my father's, so it was his. Tink says he gave it to me."

"Then how did I get it!?" Santi snapped. "If it was mine, then it belongs to me!"

The three descended beneath the fog to meet a vast, open gorge two miles wide bathed in pale, even light. A small waterfall fell from a cut in the rock on the far end down into a great pool that narrowed into a creek that wound into a low jungle.

"Mother of God," Santi said. "This hole is not this big!"

"Wow," Peter said.

Standing at the back, Tootles peeked from around Santi's broad shoulders. He focused on a point on a hill just left of the gorge's center.

"Let's get down there," Peter said. They reached the bottom of the stairs and followed a path paved in flat, joined stones out into the forest.

"Dangers are different here," Peter said. "Keep your eyes open."

Falling quiet, the three navigated the twisting path and made several turns. Piles of stone bore straight-cut corners and lines of foundations that peeked from overgrown flora and hills of broken soil.

"This was once a city," Santi breathed.

Peter spotted figures in the greenery. "Keep it low, Santi. We're being followed."

Santi reached for a sword at his hip that wasn't there, then fisted his fingers as they continued.

Great birds drifted across the sky beneath the pale fog — hawks, sparrows, bats and a score of buzzing insects and fliers crossed the space.

Cries, howls and fluttering filled an active symphony of trees and other flora dancing in a breeze that circled the gorge in a gentle rush. Unlike direct sunlight, paleness filled the space and gentled its shadows. Compared to the heavy jungle behind them, predators were easy to see wandering among bushes. With few shadows, they circled the group from a distance, wary of the newcomers.

"If one approaches, don't look at it," Peter said. "They'll spit at you and blind you."

"What?" Tootles asked.

"How do you know that?"

Peter pointed at nearby trees where the bark had been melted.

Santi scowled at Peter. "Why are you so careless?"

"I have the mantle," Peter shrugged.

"What does that mean?"

"It means nothing here will harm me."

"Why?" he asked.

"Because Neverland is for the pan," Peter said. "Who ... is my father."

Tinker Belle said nothing.

They marched in silence as the predators circled closer.

"If they will not attack you, then give me a weapon," Santi hissed.

Peter clutched his dagger and paused.

"If what you say is true, then we are defenseless and you, who cannot be touched, hold the only weapon!"

Tootles nodded.

Peter grimaced. "Alright, but I want this back." He pulled out the sheathed knife and held it hilt-first to Santi, who took and drew it from the sheath.

"This is ... silver? This is weak."

"It's a blue blade."

"Blue? It's silver."

"No, I mean it's magicked."

Santi flinched and held the knife away from himself. "What do you mean?"

"I mean it was made with magic," Peter said. "What is it with you and magic?"

222

"What does that mean?" Santi asked.

Peter plucked the blade, stabbed down at a nearby rock several times with all his strength. To his surprise, the stone block cracked under the sparking blade. For a moment, Peter remembered playing with the dagger when he was younger. His father always pulled it out when he told stories of his own father, Kellogg, and growing up around the palace, traveling across Pangea and all the adventures he had had. The knife had been Kellogg's gift to William when he took on the mantle, a small poignant heirloom of his family's history. Peter didn't care for it, opting, instead, for wanting to play with the great big swords hanging on walls around the palace.

One day in the palace stables, a horse tied near a busy doorway got spooked and managed to injure several people. Bound by a small chain that locked up by the horse's violent yanking, his father leapt into danger, used the dagger to cut it free of its metal bonds. A few minutes later, the horse calmed enough to be managed, again.

Awed at his father's bravery and the power of the tiny dagger, his father told him the dagger represented the power of their family, but also more importantly, the power of a single person. Though small and unimposing, the magic of a sharp mind pointed in a single direction could cut old ties and free others from bondage. From that day onward, Peter wanted to wear it as his father so often did. Now, he suddenly would trade a thousand such daggers to see his father again.

He held up the blade for Santi to see the edge suffered no damage.

Santi took it with reverence.

"It's blue, which means it was made with magic and only another blue weapon can damage it. But it doesn't do anything magical, it's just really strong and sharp."

Santi held it with awe and graced the edge with his thumb. "This is amazing."

"It's like the Roman weapons," Tootles said.

"Roma?" Santi asked. "Did he just say Roman weapons?"

"You still can't understand him?" Peter asked.

"I heard Roma!" Santi said. "Does he mean Rome? The city of Rome and its empire?"

Peter relayed the question.

"The Romans, yes!" Tootles scowled. "They attack our homes! They invade our lands. We were driven from them."

Peter relayed the answer.

"But … Rome hasn't been an empire for a thousand years!"

After Peter relayed, again, Tootles shook his head.

"They invaded our lands generations ago," said Tootles, "and continue to press us further north into the dark forests."

Santi marveled. "You must be from central Europe. I knew I recognized your accent. Rough, though. Perhaps France or Burgundy. But … that is impossible to say Rome is still invading your lands!"

Tootles shrank and said nothing after Peter's translation.

"You're from earth, right?" Peter asked Santi.

"Of course!"

"Then maybe he's not from the same time as you."

"Same- time? You jest! It is the year of our lord, 1429!"

"In Eden, it's 8,574 advent exodus," Peter said. "Lots of countries across the world use different years."

"But he's saying it's … four hundred A-D!" Santi said.

"So?"

"So, that means he's a Celtic savage Rome conquered under the Gallic Wars!"

"I don't know what any of that means," Peter said. "Do you think he's lying to you?"

"He must be!"

"Why?" Peter suddenly felt like his mother. "What would he gain?"

Santi opened his mouth and shut it.

"I don't know how you two got here or why." Peter shrugged. "But you're both from earth. At least you have that in common." He pressed onward.

Santi fisted his hands as Tootles followed Peter. When he realized he was being left behind, Santi caught them up and scanned the jungle. "If you have this mantle and can sense the boys, does Tootles, also?"

Peter shrugged at Tootles. "No. Don't see it on him."

"You can see it?" Santi asked.

"Yeah." Peter climbed halfway up the mound and squatted. He motioned the others to follow. "Get behind me."

As they slid behind him and peeked over his shoulders, shock painted their faces.

A gorilla twenty feet high appeared over the top of the mound and sniffed at the air. Deep set black eyes spotted Peter through the trees. It sniffed at the air, looked again at Peter, and lumbered off into the forest.

"It can smell you," Peter said, "but it couldn't see you."

"The boy is in the mound," Tootles said.

Santi understood what Tootles meant by tone and face. He fisted soil with his fingers. "Why can you two sense these things and I cannot!?"

"Hush," Peter scowled, "before you draw him back."

"What was that?" Tootles whispered.

"It's a gorilla," said Santi.

"What is essoongoriya?" asked Tootles.

"See, you two are chatting, already," Peter said. "Tink, would you provide a distraction?"

Is this the best way to get the boys?

"Know of another way?"

I do not approve of this.

Peter shrugged. "Then you get the boy out."

She scowled. *You owe me.* She zipped up around the gorilla's head. It huffed and swiped its massive paws, then followed her as she drew it into the forest. *Don't get killed!!*

Peter continued toward the mound's apex, where a smaller mound rose, covered in stones, scree and animal bones.

"He doesn't understand what I mean!" Santi said. "He's just repeating words!"

"Here he is," said Peter.

The boys joined him on the mound. At the mound's center glistened a thick, green wet bubble.

"Go ahead," Peter motioned.

"What?" Santi stammered.

"Pull him out," Peter said. "You said you wanted to know. Well, here's one."

"That's disgusting!"

"Did I come from something like this?" Tootles asked.

"Sort of," Peter said. "If you want to be my steward, then you have to be willing to get the boys! This is how I rescued both of you!"

"You didn't rescue me!" Santi retorted.

"Well- not you, but Tootles!" Peter pointed at Tootles. "Or are you just afraid?"

Santi straightened with a murderous glare. "Fine." He approached the glistening bulb poking out of the top of the nest. He cringed at its wet, gooey texture. Sparing a glance at the other two, he gathered his courage and pushed his fingers down into its thick green viscous matting. He twisted and gagged. Tootles covered his mouth when a stench arose. "This is insane!"

"He's down there," Peter said. "Get him out."

The initial nausea passed and Santi returned to the mound. Steeling himself, he dug and pulled away thick green goo linked with long yellow-green strands. Moss-infused muck soon littered the mound as Santi tossed it aside. He paused to avoid retching. Scum painted his forearms when he flinched after touching something solid.

"What is it?" Peter leaned over the hole.

"I touched something," Santi gulped.

"It's probably him."

Santi spat and glared at Peter. "Help me."

Peter motioned to Tootles, who reluctantly moved to help. The three boys exposed the hairy head of a boy buried upright. Together they dug as deep as their arms could reach. They gripped the boy under his shoulders and hauled. Though Tootles tugged in vain, Peter and Santi planted their feet and forced the child upward. Initially resistant, the boy began to move. They pulled him back and forth and soon a deep fluttering suck wormed its way up as the vacuum behind him drew air downward. With a pop, the boy heaved upward before falling onto the side of the nest. They dragged him to the side.

"What's wrong with him?" Tootles asked.

"Did we just dig up a corpse?" Santi glared at Peter.

"No." Peter slapped the limp child on the back.

Goo spewed from his mouth as his stomach and lungs heaved.

Somewhere in the distance, the gorilla's mountainous roar sent thousands of creatures to flight.

Santi's face tightened.

"Quick." Peter slapped the boy on the back again. Green mucous poured from his nose and mouth in fits before the first breaths of air sucked down.

Tinker Belle's chimes preceded her from the forest before she halted above them. *I don't know what you did, but it's coming fast!*

"Crap, c'mon!" Peter snatched up the boy as the three raced down the hill through the jungle. A second roar of fury announced the gorilla at the mound they left.

"Why does it even have the boy!?" Santi cried.

"Who cares!?" Peter made for the stairs. The boys wheezed and panted when they reached the base of the stairs but kept walking as the massive gorilla thundered closer.

"UP! UP! UP!" Peter cried while the others wheezed for breath. "Here!" He flopped the unconscious boy onto Santi's shoulder. "Get him up! I'll hold off the gorilla!"

"You!? What can you do to *that!?*" Santi asked.

"I'll stop him. Go!"

Though exhausted, Santi and Tootles stomped up the narrow staircase. They paused just at the ceiling of mist just as the giant gorilla exploded from the trees and veered for the base of the cliff walls beneath their stairs. They pressed themselves against the wall behind them as the beast struggled in vain to climb up rock walls smoothed by time and water. Faint cracks gave no hold for the gorilla's thick gray fingers. It barked and roared in protest at their thieving. Spotting the bottom of the stairs, it lumbered over. Peter stood a dozen steps up with his hands planted on his hips to bar the way.

"Are you sure he won't hurt me?" Peter asked his shoulder-bound fairy.

Sure, she gulped.

The gorilla huffed, roared, beat its chest and rushed within a few paces of them and stopped. It repeated its show of aggression, but it would not attack Peter. A grin crawled across Peter's face.

"He won't do it."

C'mon, she chimed. *Let's get moving.*

"Sure," Peter climbed the stairwell. The gorilla tried to follow, but the stairs were too narrow for its wide bulk. Its furious roar hurt Peter's ears until he drew nearer the others. Together they climbed into the thick mist in their return to the thicket.

Outside in the heavy tropical heat, the sun above appeared not to have moved. Santi shook his head. "This is not possible."

Peter, I'm going to go scout the ship, chimed Tinker Belle. *I want to see where they are, now.*

"See you soon!" said Peter.

She darted off as Peter led them to a small creek where they washed off the new boy, whose midnight skin emerged from the dissolving gunk. His thick lips and broad nose sucked in air as they washed him clean. He wore a red robe thinned in places, as if eaten by acid, with one loop over his right shoulder and patterned in black and white. Once clean, they tightened his robe to keep it on and carried him onward until they found the main path leading to the Tree from the West Bay.

Exhausted from so much walking, no one spoke as they reached the outer clearing.

"What is that sound?" Santi asked.

Peter walked northward with the wall on his right and Pan's Peak curving upwards on his left. At the northernmost point in the outer clearing, he pulled fronds apart and peered through gaps in the jungle. He gasped.

A rogue wave snaked between the towering islets peppering the lagoon north of the Island and turned. It crashed up the steep terrain and wove its way up the eastern base of Pan's Peak as it drew closer to the Tree. At the head of the wave rode an entire enemy sailing vessel.

"To the Tree!" Peter shouted. "Now!"

35

Sailing Ashore

S mee emerged deck to the noise of a ruckus. Sailors raced to batten down all loose items, furl sails and arm themselves. Athyka appeared along the portside rail, walking up a staircase of ice that formed as she mounted it and dropped to the deck.

"Ah, Smee," she sneered before raising her hand the way she came. A column of water lifted and deposited the ship's boat onto deck where sailors converged to help empty its complement and secure it.

"What you bout ta do?" Smee stammered as the ship rotated on its center and moved north without help from sail or tug. A rope of water slid across the deck and swirled up her thigh and arm to remain connected to her left hand as she planted her feet to face the prow. Ice formed around her feet and snaked up her calves to lock her to the deck. The ship turned into a narrow islet north of Pan's Peak into a small, hidden bay with steep sides carpeted with thick jungle.

"Brace yourself, Mister Smee." Athyka glanced over her shoulder. "We attack now."

Smee retreated from the bonfire of her magic. "What're ya gonna do!?"

Athyka scowled. "I'm getting the mantle."

Smee ran for and clung to the portside bannister as the ship turned. Harry Bristol took a spot behind Athyka to brace her without a word. The dwarf gasped as the entire crew had become lifeless drones to her will.

"I come," she breathed. A wave rushed down the winding inlet behind them and crashed into the ship's aft and tucked beneath it.

Harry gripped the back of her tunic and braced himself to help keep her steady as the wave crashed onto the bank and lifted the vessel into the jungle flora. Trees thunked and scraped under the ship's hull as the wave snaked up the side of the island.

However much power she drew from the ocean, it did not buffer the agony of so much use. Fresh blood drooled through her pale, clenched teeth. Stress darkened the edges of her irises while vessels bulged.

Away from the lagoon, the wave weakened and thinned. Energy drained from her. The ship descended, crashing into more trees, but she willed it to continue even as she struggled to breathe.

Left to her own energy, she drove the ship the remaining distance by her will, up through the last quarter mile. Almost out of power, she snatched Harry's neck. She needed water. He panicked as she ripped life from his body and magic. His lean muscles and well-fed flesh shriveled to a gray brown that puffed a cloud of dead skin as he died and collapsed.

Mounting the northern edge of the jut, the ship raced through trees and crashed into and over the green vine wall. The wave crossing the wall died, inside, as did her power. The Hover slammed into the thick green grass and toppled to port. Many starboard sailors vaulted through the air to their death by crashing into the Tree of Life's massive roots. The ship's mast snapped as its apex crashed into the Tree's lowest branches as it fell over.

Athyka crouched, using the ice formations on her feet to keep her on deck

Thrown from the portside rail across the thick grass, Smee climbed to his feet. Athyka detached herself from and fell across the deck into the hands of sailors gathering to catch her. Those who survived on the starboard rail climbed up and over to the outside and raced along the hull to get into the clearing.

Athyka flinched when the first sailor died, then a second, then four more. She spun. The Hover's keel still lay on the other side of the wall. Any sailors within reach of the agitated vines were getting skewered —

including sailors attempting to navigate down to the grass who hadn't yet disembarked. Any others who reached the ground unharmed but stood within two paces of the wall died as green spears fired through faces, chests, bellies and legs.

Athyka fisted her ohnas and gathered her wits. "PPAAAAN!!"

Peter stepped out of the shadows of the thick Tree roots and planted his feet.

Athyka smiled. "Come to surrender yourself so easily?"

She reached out, desperate to take control of his mind. Every effort slipped free — his mantle resisted her touch and bled only faint whispers of his angry thoughts.

Peter's green eyes shined defiant. "Leave my home."

"Submit and these men won't kill you."

"Leave!"

"Fine." She grit her teeth. "If you won't submit, I'll take it from you."

When he hesitated, she willed a dozen sailors to fire their crossbows.

For Peter, time slowed. Though he didn't know how, he sensed her command to the sailors. He ducked and rolled forward just as the bolts flew. Athyka cringed when the boy crossed fifteen feet of grass in a heartbeat and rammed fists into her belly. She flew across the grass before her back crashed into the canted portside rail. She crumpled to the lawn, stunned.

Loose from her control, the sailors faltered. Many panicked. Only a few had the mind to reload and recharge their crossbows.

Shocked to have struck a woman so far, Peter was startled at his own violence.

"Peter!" Santi emerged from the roots behind him.

Peter spun as a sailor drew a short bow on him. He ducked just as the arrow slid past his face.

Santi descended upon the sailor with Peter's silver dagger and rammed it into the man's kidney. The sailor locked up before Santi yanked it out and drove it into the man's spine at the neck. The blade slid through bone with little effort.

Peter turned as another sailor charged him with a sword. He tried to spin away but the sailor's body knocked him across the grass. He rolled aside just in time to avoid the sailor's second swing and kicked at his knees, which bent the wrong way with a loud snap. The sailor screamed and collapsed to the grass. Peter rolled backwards onto his feet to see three sailors corner Tootles against the vine wall.

"HEY!" Peter raced when bolts of fire flashed before his face and sent him scrambling out of the way. A Unionist mage with blood running down the side of his face unloaded fiery blue-green distortions. The wall around Tootles eviscerated his attackers. "HA!" A fireball scorched Peter's shoulder, drawing him back to his own fight. Peter leapt far away from the attack, found a block of wood broken from the ship and threw it at the mage's head.

The mage's head snapped aside before he crumpled to the grass.

Peter flinched. Had he killed him?

Another crossbolt grazed Peter's chest as more sailors joined the fight.

Now with a sword, Santi dueled and cut down sailors with strength and speed.

Peter ducked into the reach of an attacker and drove his elbow into the man's gut, sending him flipping away. Pleased with mantle-infused strength, Peter dodged arrows, crossbolts, swings and thrusts as he drove fists, elbows and shoulders into the men. He tried to kick another sailor when the ground beneath his feet twisted and sent him crashing across the grass.

Athyka descended upon him with a power he could feel in his gut before he spotted it — an ohna. His mind flooded with information about it — the ohna terra. He yearned to return it to its rightful place far to the southwest, to a woman and sword made of ice. The vision overwhelmed him before Santi slammed him out of the way just in time to avoid a rift of dirt racing by. After crashing to the ground, the boys scrambled to return to the fight.

In the midst of the chaos, Smee gazed upon Santi's face. He was the most beautiful young man Smee had ever seen. Graceful and powerful, the boy ignited desire within Smee.

"Come back here, you little shit!" Athyka stormed across the grass with mages and sailors in tow. She raised a hand and fired a rift of ice across the grass at Peter. When the magic reached him, it failed. He laughed as Santi joined him with an upraised sword.

Golden bolts of energy fired into the clearing and took two sailors in the chest. The men exploded and bathed Athyka's right side in gore. Tinker Belle descended into the clearing with eyes and hands glowing with power as her aura doubled.

Athyka dove aside just in time to avoid the pixie's second attack and cast up her own magical shields as the fairy turned on her. Only by sucking enough energy from the ohnas did she manage to divert a second wave of golden bolts. Athyka counter attacked with a strike of lightning from her fingers. The furious pixie faltered and flew aside in panic.

"TINK!!" Peter raced for Athyka, who fired a lightning bolt his way. Without thinking, he caught and redirected it into the deck of the overturned ship, nearby. The following explosion knocked both of them and a dozen mages and sailors across the ground.

Her ears rang as Athyka pushed from the ground and touched the right side of her face. Fresh blood drooled through her ice shield filling the hand-shaped gap. The vicious snapping of wood pierced the muffle in her ears and drew her attention to the ship. Far from being crushed or pinned, single vines had pierced the hull, snaked around walls and tightened in ratchets. The ship groaned under the strain. Loud snaps echoed from within as braces buckled under the pressure.

Tinker Belle returned to the fray when Athyka struck with a blast of razor-sharp sleet. The fairy dodged aside before she could attack.

Santi drove his blade through the back and out the chest of another sailor before he yanked it out and lopped off his head. Peter scrambled to his feet. "Peter!" Santi yanked out and threw Peter the silver knife, who snatched it from the air and faced down a new attacker. "Kill him!"

Peter stumbled as blood drooled down his head from the explosion and his eyes struggled to focus. His attacker appeared doubled in his vision, but despite the danger, Peter could only bring himself to punch at the man.

"KILL HIM!" Santi roared.

His head pounding, Peter struggled to fight off the sailor.

"Kill him, you fucking puta!"

Though Peter had struck men, the idea of killing them terrified him. He fought the man off but tripped over the ridge of a massive root behind him. The man snatched a knife from his own belt and prepared to drive it into Peter when his trunk exploded from two golden bolts fired from Tinker Belle.

Bathed in the man's blood and innards, Peter screamed as the man's waist and legs fell upon him, revealing open guts and pieces of spine and rib down the inside of his trunk. He scrambled away in horror.

Athyka raised her hands to strike at Tinker Belle again when a tiny figure to her left advanced.

"Go away!!" Tootles screamed and raised his hands. Dozens of spade vines erupted from the wall. The ohnas did nothing against them directly, and she unleashed her personal magic in fire, lightning and disruptions of air at them to slow them down. Despite shredding the first wave, more spades appeared.

"Smee!" Athyka screamed.

Smee rushed into the attack and snatched vines slowed by her desperate shield. His powerful hands twisted the vines until they ripped apart. When Tootles saw the dwarf, his fury turned the vines on him, instead. Athyka used the ohna terra to snatch the soil out from under the boy and sent him tumbling.

Her energy bottomed out. The inner clearing fought her attempt to use the ohnas and drained her already exhausted store of energy. She almost sank to her knees. When she turned for a last, desperate attempt to get at Peter, she found the remaining mages and sailors dying under the violent pixie and deft young swordsman.

Athyka froze as the boy's gaze caught her own. As they linked, his thoughts crashed into her as only one other person had in her entire life — her grandmother. Their minds connected; memories flooded her of his life. Touching another daleen startled her so that she leapt from his mind.

"I- know you!" Santi cried.

Terror filled Athyka. "Smee!" Together they scrambled into the disintegrating ship. Followed by the few remaining sailors who could turn and flee, they leapt through vines ripping holes in the ship's hull and out into the outer clearing.

"After them!" Peter sprinted into the collapsing vessel.

Santi stared after Athyka.

Peter! Tinker Belle bolted for the ship as it buckled. She retreated in time and instead flew up and over. Just as she crested the top, she spotted the group racing north through the jungle to the narrow path leading away from the jut. A sailor at the rear raised his sword against Peter. The boy tackled him in the chest and sent both over the edge, down the steep terrain on the right side of the path, down a short hill and into a large bush with a crash.

Athyka and her sailors fled onward into the jungle.

Racing through the trees and over the edge, Tinker Belle reached the bush where Peter and the sailor disappeared; she didn't find them inside, or on the far side. She circled it several times, then outward through the jungle.

"Peter? PETER!!"

Peter and the sailor were gone.

36

Landing

Passing through the auroric veil drew gasps and moans of surprise, but the abject beauty of the island bathed in sunrise and cuddled by morning mists quieted every brave and squaw on the small, weathered fleet of single and platform canoes. With a great snowcap to their left, low forested ridges to their right and a gulping river betwixt, countless birds drifted on morning currents while a school of dolphins played in the distance to their left.

Though dawn rose behind them, Rain Singer's eyes welled with tears sparkling in its warm light reflected from the island itself. The squat woman, bound in a thin leather dress beaded along the breast, first saw the island sixty years ago in her dreams. As the waking sun warmed her against the icy night winds, her heart burned with joy. Tears poured down her cheeks. Looped braids on each side of her head drooped as she bowed her head and struggled not to sob as she remembered her own father. "We made it."

Sitting cross-legged on the platform canoe next to her, Great Cougar set his hand on his mother's back to comfort her as his own heart pounded in his chest.

Behind and between, Tiger Lily took in the island's distant peaks and volcano with its thin, snaking column of smoke rising into the upper atmosphere. Every corner held something new, every nook a calling adventure. As she saw before, the island called to her heart and she yearned to answer.

Red Badger and his brothers led the tribe south along the south island's eastern shore. Hugged by a long, winding ridge, the ground ascended to high cliffs drenched with seagulls, gannets and warm-water penguins. Seals and walrus carpeted low rocks hovering above low-tide surf while blows erupted from passing orcas.

The density of wildlife awed the members of the tribe as they counted species after species of creature as variable as the natural environments within sight.

Next came the fjords — the great cavernous canyons cut by sea-bound rivers and the thick, endless ice frost clinging across their crowns. The people murmured and pointed.

"Our ancestors spoke of them," Rain Singer said. "Great rivers of ice that groaned and cracked and bled great streams. They formed a great barrier to the north. He spoke of them."

Beyond the fjords, Red Badger drew near the cliffs as the waves faded, cutting between a broad sand bar and marshland to the south as they turned west. The cliffs shortened and thickened with trees as the mountain above came into better view.

Across the sand bars, sandpipers and gulls picked at crabs and turtles emerging from holes. Among the rockier portions of the low bars, mudfish, starfish, urchins, barnacles and small octopi scuttled about.

Though the terrain curved more to the north around the mountain and its stepped terrain fell to the ocean, Badger veered westward, away from the shore, as heavier waves picked small objects and smashed them against the snowcap's southwest seaside cliffs. Once past the swells, he turned due north through a narrow vein of water free of heavy waves. Ahead, broken cliffs and arches came into view nestled upon a low sandy beach created by swirling wave wash. The lone sanctuary beckoned them between the areas of turbulent surf to warm brown sand.

Tiger Lily crawled to the rear of the platform. She extended her hand and touched the surface. She delved, sensing for life and its accompaniment danger.

Instead, she felt a peace she hadn't expected.

It was safe here.

A smile crawled across her face as her eyes opened. She touched her father on the shoulder.

"The water is safe here," she smiled.

He straightened with surprise as Rain Singer wiped her cheeks.

"Are you sure?" he asked.

"Close to the shore, yes," she said.

"We will explore after we reach the shore," said Great Cougar. "For now, we will stick with avoiding the water."

"But, it's safe…"

"I believe you," he said. "But the tribe needs stability more than they need freedom right now. Let us get to shore as we planned. Then we will discuss touching the waters."

Tiger Lily shrank. "Yes, father."

He turned.

Red Badger and his brothers reached the shore first. They beached high, as they had done before, climbed out and hauled their canoes up the shore. Their craft was followed by a second and third. Waves of canoes landed before braves flooded the beach. Thick sand tanned by a mixture of moisture fed by the nearby cliff waves and brown pebbles met the ocean in a broad convex curve. Hugged between the concave bases of the snowcap on the right and the volcano to their left, the small beach climbed northward through a series of shattered rock formations and arches to a low cliff at the curve of a saddle between the great mountains. Sparse trees hung out over the broad alcove while cliff-nested birds greeted the newcomers with an echo of caws.

Several braves moved through a wall into a crevice difficult to see from the ocean and followed a rivulet into a large alcove hiding in the rock surrounded by high sandstone walls. Women carrying children followed them along the narrow creek into the private gorge.

Rain Singer stepped from the platform canoe onto wet sand and knelt to kiss it. She straightened and kissed it again and then a third time. She rose to her feet with the help of a fellow woman and scanned the high cliffs.

"May the Great Spirit watch over us." She raised her hand. "May he bless our children and men alike. May our women bear many sons and our sons raise many daughters. May he bless our children's children and see fit to raise us strong and powerful as the mighty trees from our homeland, tall and spreading over."

The woman beside her prayed likewise.

As she finished praying, she rose to her feet with the help of other women and faced Great Cougar. "It's time."

Great Cougar whistled. The men still on the beach trotted over. "Break down the platform canoes."

They hesitated.

"This is our home," he said. "We will not be leaving, again."

The men shared looks but obeyed. After moving what little remained of their supplies to the beach, they pulled out their knives and began breaking down the platform canoes. Younger braves hauled them up the beach and carried each into the hidden gorge through the narrow causeway.

In minutes, all thirty craft were dismantled and carried through the narrow corridor. A thin waterfall snaked down from the steep terrain above the low cliffs and wafted to a great pool at the bottom of the alcove hugged by its own small beach. The tribe crossed the rivulet and rounded the pool halfway to the cliffs where they set up camp. Braves approached the pool with remnants of dead fish to test for predators.

After firewood was gathered from scree littering the beach, the tribe gathered around a central pit. Women used bow drills to light the dry wood. Elders and toddlers gathered closest as the fire grew, grateful after weeks asea for a real fire.

Once it roared and all gathered close, Rain Singer stepped up to the fire from the side of the pool. She raised and shook a bone rattler twice in each direction.

"Eight generations ago, when Light Across Water defied her elders and would not raise a hand to take justice against the man who murdered her parents, the Tlingit cast her out. When the blackfish attacked their fishermen, the elders knew nature had condemned their choice. When Light Across Water would not return to the camp, a rift formed among the men and women of the tribe. Our people were forged by the relationships of air, land and water that comprise us all — different forces that abide each other in harmony. The split bore our people. As we sought our own place, away from our forefathers, we encountered many peoples who took everything from us. They took the honor of our daughters and the blood of our sons.

"Since then, we have travelled ever east in search of a place of peace, but always have we found more men who demanded we fight them to earn their respect. We wished to commune without war, but peace could not be found. On we walked, across the purple mountains and the endless sea of grass. We reached the forest mountains where I was born.

"It was my vision that led us to the warm coast and the place where the two currents met. Nature rewarded our work with bounty from the land. Abundant crops and plentiful deer fed us well, but, again, the tribes came to take what we had. When they refused to trade, we knew our time had ended. Again, only the blood of our sons would sate them.

"Again, we learned to build boats as our forefathers once did upon the cold, rocky edges of the western shore. In my vision, I saw a land where nature was more powerful than men, a place where our kind belonged, a place where the Great Spirit had purpose for those committed to changing our ways to nature, instead of nature to our ways.

"This has been a difficult journey for us. We have not always agreed on continuing our path of peace in the face of so much death, but you followed me here. This is the place in my vision. This is where our purpose as a people will be fulfilled. Thank you for your trust."

She bowed her head and took a slow breath.

"We are now no longer the Walking People," she raised the rattler over the fire and dropped it in. The congregation gasped. She lifted the braid hanging from the left side of her head, drew her knife and sawed it off. Everyone gasped as she dropped it, too, into the fire. "We are now People of the Island. We stand alone to live in peace."

The tribe waited.

She closed her open hand into a fist. "We stand alone to live in peace."

Backs straightened.

"We are People of the Island," she intoned.

"We stand alone to live in peace," Great Cougar faced the tribe alongside his mother.

"We are People of the Island," she said again.

"We stand alone to live in peace." More joined with Great Cougar.

"We are People of the Island."

"We stand alone to live in peace." Most joined.

"We are People of the Island."

"We stand alone to live in peace!" The braves grew louder.

"We are People of the Island."

"We stand alone to live in peace!" several yelled and hooted.

"We are People of the Island."

"We stand alone to live in peace!" all now shouted.

"We are People of the Island."

"We stand alone to live in peace!"

Rain Singer intoned before letting the cheering die down.

"Tonight, we will sleep here," she said. "We will finish all of the food we have left. There is no returning to the sea for us. The platforms are broken. Only fishermen will go asea now. This is our home."

Nervous but excited, with gleaming faces, the tribe took heart.

"Sleep well. Tomorrow we will send out our scouting parties across the island to look for a suitable camp. We will fish these seas, explore these rivers, climb these mountains and become one with this place. We are People of the Island."

"We stand alone to live in peace." Smiles warmed every face.

"Sleep well," she said. "For in the morning, we become one with the island."

With that, she turned away.

The tribe split into their small groups and families to create smaller fires. Rain Singer stood in concert with other elders to discuss who would go where and when on the morrow while Tiger Lily approached the water line and set her fingertips upon the surface. She shut her eyes and exhaled, sensing it as she had, before. This pool was safe. Older braves waited for her nod before they stepped in to scrub themselves. Women gathered water to do the same and drink mineraled freshwater for the first time in weeks.

Though midday, they bedded down to rest while the children played in the sand and explored the sandstone walls of the alcove under strict instructions to stay near.

Tiger Lily washed her face while ankle deep in the pool and turned at her father's approach.

"Did you see it?" he kept his voice low.

Tiger Lily turned. "What?"

"There is a fire on the island."

"What?"

"I saw it as we turned from the mouth of the river," he said. "There are people here."

"But- you explored the island. We found evidence of no one living."

"It does not change campfire smoke."

Tiger Lily frowned.

"Come, you and I will explore now."

"We will?"

"Yes, gather your things."

"Yes, father," she said.

Great Cougar relayed his intent to find a way up to the elder council, who nodded approval. Once prepared, he and Tiger Lily marched for the low cliff walls in search of a way up.

"Where do they go when the rest of us stay here to rest?" Red Badger growled. "Always, he and his daughter leap ahead."

"Are you jealous, Badger?" Rain Singer asked.

Red Badger schooled his face. "Again, they do things on their own. It is always alone, with those two. They do not act like they wish to be part of this tribe, but to lead it by the nose."

"Beware the jealousy in the heart of a coward," she said, her eyes narrowing.

Badger straightened. "I have no cowardice that my tribe might move as one into our future."

"Avarice resides in every heart, Badger," she said. "Be wary yours governs neither speech nor action."

"Caution and hope govern mine, elder." He leveled her a flat look before returning to his own fire.

Rain Singer paused in thought. Could Red Badger, or anyone else, understand Tiger Lily's role was greater than any one of them? Of all she had shared through her entire life with all the village, only one piece had she kept for herself; one part she could not share for fear of its effect upon her tribe. She could not share it; even, with the person on whom the prophecy focused.

In blood, loss and tragedy would Tiger Lily save the tribe and, beyond it, all mankind. From her would come a future unimaginable even to Rain Singer. But more, in a way Rain Singer had never fathomed, from Tiger Lily would come a solution, divined by the Great Spirit, for a problem plaguing men. For all the countless nights Rain Singer lost sleep in seeking its meaning, one thing remained sure in her mind.

Tiger Lily would bear the culmination of eternity.

37

The Darkness

Coins, necklaces, rings, golden teeth, medallions, nails, wood-scabbed door hinges and a variety of precious stones spilled across the grass as Tootles dropped an armful next to their small, crackling fire under the deepening evening blue. The new boy lay unconscious on the tree-side of the fire. Dried scum clung to his skin and had stopped reeking so much as the day wore on. Since Peter had chased after the enemy and the pixie flew aimlessly around the clearing attempting to communicate with them, they shrugged and gathered their booty.

Groans and creaks of wood snapping and shifting echoed for hours in the clearing as the tireless vines shredded the vessel and left everything else behind. Spades snaked across the lawn to stab pieces of wood and remove them from the clearing.

Santi counted the coins and rifled through the jewelry when Tootles returned with a second armful. Santi pointed to the wall. "How much is left?"

Tootles motioned him over where the ship had been. Most of the wood was gone and the spade vines rooted out nails from the grass and piled it up.

Santi paused. "Wait a second. I thought it was just getting the ship. How'd it do that?" He pointed at the different types of piles.

Tootles thumped himself on the chest and motioned. Vines paused and drew near. He pet them, then made circles with his finger. They danced as he directed. When he dropped his hand, they returned to their work.

Santi's face melted. "It *obeys* you!?"

Tootles nodded.

"HA!" Santi clutched his hair. "HAA!!"

Tootles smiled.

Heavy objects like full barrels and boxes were left where they lay for later inspection. Through their crude system of hand signals, Tootles conveyed the wall could tell the difference between wood, metal, cloth and flesh, but not much more than that.

Santi focused on understanding Tootles as much as he could, though sometimes the boy rambled in his original language. Santi gathered enough to smile with amazement at Tootles's discovery of his relationship with the wall. Santi wondered with what he might have a relationship on the island if he had come from something similar.

"We are rich!" Santi laughed as he moved armfuls to the fire.

Peter's words made him hesitate. Peter said this was his island; he might claim the treasure was his own, as well. Santi frowned. That would not do.

Remembering touching Peter for the first time there on the falls above the swamp, Santi's face darkened. He decided Peter had taken the mantle from him. Peter stole something from him and then claimed it gave him license over the island.

Santi set his armful down and paused to soak in the view. If Santi had had the mantle by right, then Peter was a thief. If this mantle made Peter believe he was lord of this island, then Peter had stolen Santi's birthright to the island, as well.

"I will be this ... pan." Santi focused. Tootles queried him with a look but Santi just shook his head. Tootles shrugged and the two continued moving piles to the fire.

Santi snapped his fingers at Tootles, who turned. He motioned as he pulled weapons away from the main pile and motioned to himself, then the main pile to Tootles. Tootles looked between them and nodded. Confident that Tootles understood his meaning, he picked out several knives, a stiletto and a small dagger with a hilt braided in woven brass that caught his eye. All of them bore clean lines of gold, a style he preferred. He tucked it to the side, planning to come back for swords and other weapons later, and resumed his work.

When the sun disappeared, Tootles stumbled to the grass and sank onto his bottom to catch his breath. Sharing a look with Santi, he conveyed that he was tired before moving to the fire to sit. Santi prepared food Tootles had gathered and made a quick dinner. Soon after, Tootles lay down and disappeared into sleep.

Santi fished a blanket from the piles and covered him. Before he tucked him in, he glanced at Tootles's pockets. He rocked Tootles by the shoulder; when the boy didn't respond, Santi tugged the pocket open to look inside. He fished two fingers in and plucked a few golden coins. He eyed them, ready to pocket them, but decided to slip them back.

Santi wondered if the gunk caking the new boy had anything to do with him not yet waking.

Cool evening breezes picked up through the clearing and moaned through the tight network of large roots. Dark shadows howled and danced in the flickering firelight. Fear blossomed in his chest when the firelight over the shadowed alcoves reminded him of the bright doorway and the darkness within. Sweat beaded on his skin as the image of the black doorway burned into his mind. His hands shook even after he fisted them.

"No," he growled. He stooped to the pile of firewood, grabbed a piece of the shredded canvas from the nearby grass and wrapped it up as a torch. Once lit in the fire, he squared against the roots. Despite rising fear, he forced himself to approach the dark portals of a beckoning personal hell. He worked inward only for the tiny gaps to pinch his wide shoulders. At his persistence, the roots seemed to gently and slightly widen just enough for him to pass through into a thick blackness beyond.

Santi first feared it was a great hole beneath the mountainous trunk above, but though the ground dipped, it soon leveled off. He walked and raised the torch, unable to see a ceiling in the infinite void. He continued down the incline when a tiny tree appeared out of the black.

He veered to a long, leaf-shaped hole extending from its base that reminded him too much of a coffin, for his liking. He explored the chamber and the wall of roots at the back. Inside he found a small room. The flickering torch revealed thousands of tiny mouths of shadow screaming silent wails. He fought down rising panic. When a gust of cool evening wind swirled into the room, he followed it to a hidden fold in the roots, down horizontal, stair-like roots, to an opening from the cliff.

Nighttime Neverland stretched out under a bright moon shimmering over the distant sea and a vibrant kiss upon the rift river. The island's nocturnal beauty quieted his terror, despite leaning out over a cliff. His heart calmed. Without pitch, the torch's wooden handle caught fire. Santi returned up the tiny staircase of twisting roots to the inner room and out to the vast chamber just as the fire dribbled onto his hand. He flung out the torch and tossed it to the sandy floor, where it sputtered, sparked and died, leaving him in absolute darkness.

Santi wanted to run to the campfire, crying out with fear and nervousness, as if running from the bogeyman his father laughed about down the shadowed walks of his family estate in Valencia. He could no longer do that. He was a man.

The bright doorway and its eternal black loomed in his mind. The chamber seemed to pulse with an afterimage of the room, beyond, where the old monk stared up at him in horror lying on a simple bed in coarse bedclothes. He quivered as beads of sweat formed on his skin. His stomach tightened until he could smell vomit, but he refused to run.

"I can handle this darkness," he stuttered into the empty void around him. "I- I can."

38

Around Every Corner

Once out of sight of Athyka and free of her immediate demands, Smee circled back in hope the boys would soon leave the clearing. Though shaken by the attack, his mind focused on the beautiful boy with midnight hair. The redheaded child was attractive for his freckles, green eyes and his rarity for being the pan — Smee loved the special ones — but those dark curls, bright eyes and violent grace captured Smee's desire.

When sunset fell without anyone leaving the clearing, Smee planned to sit them out when he felt something crawl up his arm. He slapped but found nothing on the surface. Something had snaked into his skin before it wiggled up his arm. In a panic he snatched out his knife and cut the bug in two by stabbing himself. He cringed and made the necessary cuts to fish out each end of the long, multi-legged creature dripping in his blood. The dwarf thought he had a strong stomach until he pulled out the black slimy creature from under his own skin near a foot long. He moved from the rock as his blood drooled upon it. To his surprise, a dozen other insects rushed the rock to get at his blood. The bug halves he tossed were soon devoured. As he moved away, a host of crawling creatures gathered along the trail of blood he left behind.

Smee hurried off into a small clearing while pulling the kerchief from his neck to wrap around his arm. He flung what blood still dripped down his arm and moved away to see how the bugs behaved.

He never saw the tree move behind him before one of its long, braided branches caught him across the face with three-inch thorns and rammed him sideways into the ground. The rearing branch ripped out of his skin while a second bore down on him.

Dazed as he was, Smee raised his arm in time to block a second strike to his bleeding face. As soon as the second branch yanked back, leaving deep holes behind, a third whipped close. He rolled away as the thorns sliced his shirt down his back. Blood poured down his face, arm and back and he made it out of reach of the tree as it ripped apart the soil in search of him. He held the wound on the side of his face and heard the rise of thousands of tiny feet.

He spun to see an army of bugs following the smell of his blood.

Smee lumbered across the terrain looking for more thrashers as the trickle of water bubbled through the trees at the clearing's far end. He pressed into the jungle and found a small, low wall of thorn bushes lining a creek weaving down gentle steppes across the terrain. When he tried crossing the bushes, vines under his left hand looped over his fingers while smaller ones snaked over the back of his hand. "By the mother!"

Ripping into the vines with his teeth, others snaked around his right hand as he attempted to free his left. Then his powerful dwarven ears picked up on a familiar sound — more bugs. As blood continued drooling from several parts of his body, panic arose.

Smee's eyes lit up with a smoky red glow as he bared his blood-lined teeth and roared a guttural thunder. He ripped his feet free of the vines and stepped clear in time to hear a thrasher swinging for him and the vibrations of the bugs at his feet.

Ducking within inches of the thrasher's braided branches, he scrambled across the ground on all fours and leapt out of reach over the creek. Drooling blood gummed his vision. He plunged his face into crisp, cool water and rushed to wash his wounds. He could hear the bugs eating the thorn bush which had just tried eating him. Thousands gnawed at anything covered in his blood.

The insects pooled at the creek's edge where dozens of small fish snapped them up. Smee heaved a sigh of relief, watching in case any of them felt capable of leaping the stream, and sat on his bottom. He panted from the shock of blood and cold water. After checking his face, arm and back wounds, he released his magic.

The frenzy of bugs on the far side soon turned on itself. Hundreds piled enough to spill into the stream where still more fish gathered for the feast. "Great Self be damned …"

Algueda was the walking death trap sailors gossiped it was. Smee had never believed a place could be so deadly, yet the island seemed intent on killing anything that didn't belong here — and even things that did.

His fury buffered the agony, but pain grew as anger abated. He worked his jaw under a swelling face. While he didn't think his jaw was broken, the tree's brutal spikes and vines' razor thorns were unforgiving.

Smee cleaned himself up with care to avoid drawing the fish from the slaughter on the far side of the creek, packed his injuries in mud and headed up the hill.

What before took minutes down now took an hour. The stress of listening for predators exhausted him before he returned to the Tree's outer clearing. Hiding in the open wasn't an option. Moving into the bush opposite the Tree, Smee picked his way through the heavy flora with great care. Approaching steep terrain where the back of the plateau met the base of the peak, he knelt to the ground and sank his fingers into the soil. Glowing crimson wisped from the sides of his eyes as he closed them. A hum grew in his throat that spread outward. Deep, resonant vibrations sent dozens, hundreds, thousands of bugs and birds scurrying away from him. He almost opened his eyes when he realized he could send predators running with his sonic delving, but he needed more than a temporary method of driving them off — he needed the refuge all dwarves needed. He needed a cave.

As the humming resonated, sound travelling out from his chest and down his arms rebounded from the ground into his sensitive fingertips. An image formed in his mind of the soil and bedrock around him. Flora and fauna were too soft to be more than a faint, fuzzy afterimage, but the permanence of the ground brought a clear image of his terrain up to dozens of paces.

Arlagosmy's 552 years of life — centuries of which were lived above the surface — forced the development of powerful grounding skills superior to his Uttogean brethren. He used his advantage to identify gaps in the terrain up to a quarter mile.

A cave appeared at the outer reaches of his grounding senses. Though narrow and hidden by flora, it was void of life, as he could tell. Eager for safety and rest, Smee's hum died and he picked his way through the jungle toward the cave. In the morning, he would track the boys once they emerged. Exhausted and in pain, his lusts drove him onward. He would wait. He would follow. And like his uncle before him, he would scratch his itch with that beautiful, beautiful boy with the midnight hair.

39

Commission

In a copse just out of reach of the eastern edge of Tree Avicara's broad canopy, several trees had been cultivated so close their branches wound tight around each other to form an arboreal palace. Tiny balconies and bridges connected warm-lit rooms. Hollow branches with windows and outlets formed a network of walks, apartments and storage rooms.

Violet misty streaks of clouds hovered between a twinkling navy sky and a faint bar of pale orange dusklight from a hidden sunset. Galactic clouds in the heavens smeared the night sky in fades of yellow, purple and teal as the day retreated. A new moon left the warm-lit windows and open doorways stark against the growing darkness while transient breezes spiced the air.

Behind the palace's main receiving chamber and up in a ballooned branch, a tiny fire warmed a small room curtained against the air outside. In the center, a ring of tiny couches held a single occupant, now stretched across draped in a lazy white robe open from the neck.

Mabsadora reclined upon an elbow while sipping a tiny bulb of elderflower wine. Faint harp strings tickled the breeze ruffling her thin curtains. The shape darkening her doorway drew her attention from the fire. *Againa.*

The elder pushed the curtain aside as he stepped in. Dressed in his common longvest, he appeared haggard in the faint flames of her fireplace. His high cheeks and jaw appeared drawn. She inspected him in a mix of desire and distrust. Though her left breast hung bare in the open front of her robe, his focus never wavered from her face.

I see you survived the aurora. Her nose drew in the sweet fragrance of rose oil wafting from him. *More than survived, I see.*

I visited, as you asked.

What did she say? Mab sipped her bulb again.

Nothing.

What? Mab's smirk faltered.

She has nothing to say.

Mab sat up and set the bulb on the couch. *What do you mean she has nothing to say?*

Againa raised his eyebrows.

Nothing at all? Mab stood. *While the pans are leaping into chaos and tossing the mantle around like some tiny flowerlette still in her feather, the aurora is content to do nothing?*

Againa looked tired.

Are you hiding something from me?

No, he chimed. *That's all she said.*

What didn't she say?

She offered your query no answer. Againa's forearms tightened again at the memory. *Did say you could go to hell.*

Mab hesitated. *When I said she favored you ...*

His gaze flattened.

Mab inhaled. *The aurora's favor?*

I- ... Againa fisted his hands.

Mab pulled the side of her robe up to cover her breasts. *I- Is there pleasure?*

I thought you would have understood her better by now. Haunt shadowed his face. *Too great, actually. Even now, I'm on the edge of racing toward her, even unto death.*

Mab shared a long look with him. *She remains as aloof as the distant sun. Our few interactions leave me less sure than the last. Does she make you?*

Againa clenched his jaw. *She owns ... everything she touches. She's addictive. She doesn't have to bend you to her will — her mere presence intoxicates. You want her more than anything.* He gulped. *Anything.*

Mab dipped her head. *I apologize to you, Elder Againa.*

Againa nodded.

So, there's nothing from her? At all?

This is your course to set, Queen Mab, Againa chimed. *The aurora will not participate until she decides otherwise.*

Mab watched him for a long moment. She rose and offered him a slight curtsy. *My thanks for facing her. And yourself.*

Hesitant, Againa offered a slight bow, held a moment longer than her own curtsy, and left.

Mab crossed her arms. *Gaucho Rima.*

An attendant moved through the curtain and curtsied.

Summon Horticul Astira.

Rima curtsied and left.

While Mab paced the room, her wings fluttered at specific thoughts and feelings that stirred her. A few minutes later, Gaucho Rima returned with Horticul Astira before curtsying out.

My queen, Horticul Astira curtsied. *You summoned me.*

I know you had your heart set on being haraven, Horticul Astira, chimed Mab. *I had the same hope for you, but I think it wiser to be free of this burden. Can you change your priorities for the flock?*

Of course, my queen, Horticul Astira hesitated. *I am happy to serve however the flock needs.*

Good, because I'm sending you after Tinker Belle. You're going to bring her home.

But … the anchor of aikina, my queen? Her connection to the pan? What will happen to it?

We can find a way to sever it, but only if she is here.

And the pan?

The pan can fend for himself, Mabsadora chimed. *I think we've paid our debt long by now. Don't you?*

Of course, my queen, Horticul Astira's mouth tightened.

By whatever means necessary, you will return with Tinker Belle, chimed Mabsadora. *I will suffer whatever wrath the elder circle will charge, but I'm done fighting with these bloody humans, always at each other's throats, always dying, always shifting power. We are the last remaining pixilark flock in the low realm. The others are long gone. Very few magnas remain in the middle realm to be borne to us. Soon, we, too, will finish our time in the low realm and enter the high. I would like to do so disentangled from the humans and their strife. Can I count on you to help us?*

Astira stiffened with new resolve. *I will not fail you, my queen.*

Good, chimed Mabsadora. *I believe in you and thank you for your commitment. Tinker Belle is* … Mabsadora drew on her connection to the haraven. *She is on* … *Algueda. Great Self, she's on Algueda. You will head there, immediately.*

How will I cross the great ocean, my queen?

There is a rimshift in the Graemol two days flight from here in the Dragon's Fangs. Head first west until the Bowing Horse, then head south to the Southern Killduroy. At the deepest point inside the den, you will find the rimshift.

But … Dragon's Fangs is a nest of dragons, my queen! Horticul Astira gasped.

The same dragons who disappeared during the reformation? While the loners may visit, I would not worry. The dragons were broken eight thousand years ago. I would not fear a swarm. Go and use the rimshift. It will take you direct to Algueda.

Is that all, my queen? asked Horticul Astira

Mabsadora traced Horticul Astira's young face with her finger. *Remain focused. Time away from the flock is difficult for us. The haraven can persist alone only because her connection to the la'du lira ben'cari sustains her, but even she must periodically return for the orgy of our Fire to renew her physical form here in the low realm. You must not delay or you will suffer far greater effects than her. Am I clear?*

Queen Mabsadora, what if you imbued me with more power? Like what Tinker Belle has? Your own?

You don't understand, chimed Queen Mabsadora. *More power can make it far worse. It's not the presence of power that preserves the haraven, but the nature of the mantle itself. Its connection to the La'Du Lira Al'Cular is a protection against the madness of solitude. Were you to gain more power without the protections it affords, it would only amplify the difficulty you are already sure to suffer. It would tear at your mind and unleash your lust without a proper outlet like the flock.*

Yes, my queen.

Mabsadora cupped Horticul Astira's face. *We are transrealmic creatures, Astira. Neither fully physical nor energetic, the sexual passion of our kind is not like the low realmers. I've heard some never have sex at all.*

Horticul Astira squirmed.

You, however, cannot go long without it. Waste not a single moment in your duty. Tinker Belle may be able to help as you both return, either by her ministrations or by her connection with the mantle, but do not delay.

Horticul Astira blushed at the thought.

Go quickly, before she leaves Algueda. Great Self knows how those humans can move about to so many places as they do.

My queen, Horticul Astira curtsied and turned to leave.

Oh, and Astira?

Horticul Astira turned back.

See that your departure goes unnoticed, Mabsadora chimed. *Even by the paladin.*

Horticul Astira half curtsied and left.

Mabsadora returned to the couch, plucked the bulb and drained it in one swallow before casting the thin shell into the fire. *Self go with you, Astira.*

40

Creek Bed

Under the fading pall of evening light in the thick deciduous forest, the sailor paused and turned. He smiled when a crimson stream appeared from his nose, followed by a small, wriggling insect that sucked it up and returned inside his head through his gaping mouth. Still smiling, he slumped dead to the ground.

Quaking with exhaustion, Athyka raised the ohna marina over her final sailor and frosted his body closed before she stepped over him. She stumbled through the jungle, but fury and shame drove her onward until she emerged onto a broad, dry creek bed.

"Athyka?"

She spun with the ice knife raised. A hulking man wrapped in studded leather armor appeared from behind a rock holding a wicked blade. "Gregory."

"Where the fuck you been!?" he hissed.

She slumped against a nearby boulder. "Help me to your camp."

Drowned in slate evening blue and a cool, ocean breeze, he looped her arm over his neck and helped her through the boulder-strewn creek bed amidst slender white-barked trees canopied in dancing crimson leaves.

A natural rock outcropping interrupted the gentle terrain. At its base, a vertical gash in the stone admitted them to a cave pale lit by a lone fire. Inside, three sailors rushed to their feet in alarm. They moved aside as Gregory brought her close.

"Athyka, where have you been?" Gregory set her on a log and sat next to her and recoiled from her crystalized face and eye. "What in- We thought everyone was dead!"

"Water," Athyka gasped. "Food."

Gregory motioned at a sailor, who handed over his canteen. As she gulped it down, another fished out dried meat from his satchel and offered it. Once the canteen was gone, she tore into the jerky. Meanwhile the sailors built up the fire and found their seats while one remained on guard at the cave entrance and another near a small gap below the back wall.

Once finished, Athyka forced herself to sit up and take slow, calming breaths.

"Athyka?" Gregory ventured.

"That bloody little boy."

"What happened? What do you mean that little boy? The Baley kid?"

"Yes," Athyka growled. "He's got the mantle."

"He's the *pan*?" Gregory asked. "Why in fuck's name would he give the kid the mantle?"

"Doesn't matter why anymore," said Athyka, "only that the kid is more dangerous with it than we could have ever thought."

"The kid?" Gregory asked.

"I didn't go well prepared," Athyka said. "I thought we could overwhelm him at the Tree."

"We? Who did you take with you? Where's Eldnor?"

"Eldnor is dead," Athyka scowled. "Thought he could keep me from my ohnas."

Gregory noticed she held ohnas in both hands and shifted his seat away from her by a hair.

"Do you have more water?" she asked.

"It took us days to get all the water you just drank," Gregory said.

"What?" Athyka asked. She raised the ice knife and marble ring. Water coalesced from the air and filled a newly formed hole. Sailors retreated. She offered the canteen to the nearest sailor, who rushed to fill and return it without a word. She gulped down its clean, sweet taste before gasping.

Now in the safety of the cave surrounded by men who had survived the island without her powers, she felt safe enough to pause and let her heart calm for the first time since escaping the clearing.

"What happened?"

Athyka gulped another refilled canteen. "Both ships are gone."

"Both?" Gregory asked. "We heard the explosion the night we made camp. When you didn't show up, we thought you were dead."

"The pixie attacked us."

Sailors muttered.

"Tore the ship apart. Always heard they were powerful." She locked onto the fire. "Thought it was rumor. Eldnor died ... I got swept out to sea. The Hover found me."

"Rocky's ship?" Gregory asked.

"Know him?"

"An old mate."

She shook her head.

Gregory's face tightened. "Everything?"

"Everything," she said. "Lost my last sailor just before I found you. It's just me."

"What are we going to do?" Gregory asked. "I don't wanna be stuck on this fucking island for some selfdamn bug to crawl up my ass and eat me alive."

"Calm yourself, Gregory," Athyka took deep breaths. Now with a presence of mind, she projected calm into all of them. They relaxed. "Devkoron is due very soon. We must have a plan to deal with him and secure his ship. I'm not going to sit here at the mercy of a Baley bitch, like him."

"What about the boy?"

"We can't take him at the clearing," Athyka said. "There's a boy with him who controls that selfdamn wall. Cut us apart."

"What wall?"

"The vine wall," she said.

"It cut you apart? How?"

"When it woke ..." She shuddered at the memory of so many men getting ripped apart.

"Roschach won't be happy you lost two whole sh—" Gregory twisted in an arc that slapped him to the ground. He thrashed and moaned as she stood over him.

"Roschach will be pleased I bring him the selfdamn mantle." Athyka loomed over him, a terrible spectre as the firelight reflected from the frost up the side of her face and eye. "And you can keep your mouth shut. IS THAT CLEAR, GREGORY!?"

As she stood over him, all she could think of was the day Roschach, whom she once admired, revealed he knew about her psylism. Years of advancement and a quality reputation fell out from beneath her feet that day. Leverage she had on dozens of powerful agents and nobles would be forfeit if she was ever labelled as a daleen by someone as powerful as Elwin Roschach, an up-and-coming continental political actor from Meso'Admia, known for his wisdom, eloquence and his offstage ruthlessness in getting things done.

Growing up in Meso, one of the oldest communities in Pangea, Athyka worked out from under rigid lines of society and power to forge her own. She traveled, traded and soon became known as someone who could get things done — not just because she could quietly ply her ability as a minder, but because like Roschach, she knew how to incentivize and manage people to pursue her interests as their own.

That changed the day Roschach blackmailed her into becoming his private workhorse. All of her leverage became his. Though he never used it to take her body, she felt taken to the soul that he could do with her life and career as he pleased. His pretenses at kindness were patronizing. Only once had he abused her when she tried to flip the tables on him. He struck her in a panic and drew his sword, standing over her with the point at her throat. That day, Roschach revealed his fear of her. He never let her into his presence again, and yet tightened his cords around her.

That was the day she first knew desperation. That was the day she understood what the word "liberty" meant. Slavery wasn't limited to chains, working under a hot sun or rushing into battle as sword fodder, but merely that others could control you for their own benefit or, worse, some ill-conceived idea that it was for your own good.

When she released Gregory, he sobbed like a child. Sailors quivered in fear she might turn her wrath upon them. Gregory whimpered on the soil of the cave floor.

Athyka's heart quivered with rage and impatience. Exhaustion drew her to sit, but her heart raced and heel bounced. She gripped both ohnas and drew on their energies.

"Oh, stop whimpering and get up here," she growled. She withdrew from his mind all memory of her hurting him.

Gregory raised his head as if waking from a nap, then climbed to his seat. "Sorry, must have fallen asleep." When she looked at the sailors, they clamped their mouths shut.

"You said Devkoron is coming?" Gregory poked the fire and rubbed the ache in his shoulder. "He's no fool."

"We start with the truth." Athyka quivered with the need to use the powers rushing her blood. "We tell him we have what Roschach's been looking for." Athyka touched a small dagger tucked on the belt at her right hip, sheathed in bejeweled black leather, and licked her lips. "With his help, we get the mantle, Roschach gets what he wants, and we go home."

41

From the Dance

From the edge of her cushioned seat, Wendy gazed upon the handsome university boys waltzing with the girls of marrying age. Of the floor full of couples, two of the young men wore the clean uniform coats and straight-lined trousers of army regiments with smooth, shaved faces and upright frames. She wondered if John looked so dashing as them in his young leftenant's uniform. He surely would, and would someday woo some young lady and dance with her all night. She was sure he would, being the bold young man he was. None of the young men her own age were brave enough to ask her to dance. The cowards.

Wendy straightened the pink satin sash around her waist. Like her mother often said — it was a new age for women. Perhaps it was time Wendy asked a boy herself. She opened her mouth to suggest it to her mother.

"Until all women are empowered, none of us are!" Mary declared. "Each of us must stand together or none of us should step out! Doing things on your own will only weaken the cause."

Wendy opened her mouth to speak, then shut it. The women around the table nodded in agreement. Unsure how to proceed, she returned to the floor in her dwindling hope one of the younger men huddling across the room would ask her to dance. The dance ended and the next began; again, none of the boys ventured near, though a few asked other girls Wendy knew.

"But mothering isn't just about making children behave the way we want," a woman's voice drifted from a nearby table. "It's about nurturing who they are already becoming."

Women at Wendy's table tsk'd. Wendy glanced toward its source — a woman in a clean, if simple, woolen dress. Her neat bun but clear lack of powders made her stand out in this fine party, but everyone already knew Emelda. Why she kept making it into society events always baffled Wendy, who knew Mrs. Habersham preferred inviting only the finest people, such as Wendy's mother.

Emelda leaned in to a young mother of much higher social repute who seemingly had become interested in Emelda's opinion. How, Wendy could not fathom, and looked out at the floor and spotted Mrs. Habersham's son — one of the university boys — dancing with a pretty blonde in an older crimson dress.

"That l—t- whore h-s no rhhht to 'vn l—k — my s-n," a whisper rose from one of the women behind Wendy, reminding her of that time she spoke on the telephone with her cousin who lived in Aberdeen where her father grew up. The sounds had been muffled, spotty and broken, but there was no phone at this table.

Wendy spared a brief glance at the table before looking across the floor, once more. A whore? Strange.

"The ladies say the times are changing," said the young mother to Emelda.

"Times change, but people do not," said Emelda.

Despite their own private conversation at Wendy's table, Mrs. Thompson snorted. She turned her head and raised her voice. "Such quaint words, Emelda."

"H-w c-d she thin' her dhhhdrr loo's half pr'sntable in —— gd'afl rag!" More muffled words.

Wendy wondered if someone hid beneath the table whispering secrets. She half turned again and plucked the tablecloth with care to gaze beneath.

"It is arrogance to believe people change merely because the industrial revolution makes our lives easier," Emelda replied after a moment.

"Is everything alright, dear?" Mary asked.

Wendy released the cloth. "For a moment, I thought someone might have climbed under our table."

The women laughed, and Wendy realized they had ignored Emelda's response to watch their exchange.

"What an imagination!" laughed Mrs. Thompson.

"Who would climb beneath our table, young Wendy?" Mrs. Habersham asked.

"A child, perhaps?" Wendy shrugged.

The women twittered and Wendy turned back to the room to hide her embarrassment. The three ladies sharing the table with her and her mother were among the most notable in Belgravia and the Hyde Park district. Mrs. Habersham's parties were the most sought after of London's elite.

Wendy schooled her stomach.

"Y-ng Robert Jones — even mor' hndsm than his —. —— wouldn't give — wrap my legs around hi-"

Wendy gasped and bolted to her feet. She turned about, alarmed.

The ladies at the table turned.

"What is it, Wendy?" Mary blinked at the interruption of one of her epithets.

Wendy opened her mouth, closed it and then covered it with her white glove. "I do apologize. I think ... someone's voice is ... drifting. I heard the most salacious things and I..." She hesitated. "I feared they came from our table."

The women straightened.

"What did you hear?" Mary asked.

"I cannot repeat it, mother." Wendy straightened. "It would be indecent. I do apologize, ladies."

"It's alright dear." Mrs. Habersham smiled with understanding.

"S'lf-right-s l— bitch," came the whisper.

Wendy gulped.

"Please, don't mind us old ladies," waved old Mrs. Thompson.

Wendy schooled herself at sharp whispers identical in voice to the ladies speaking. She forced a grateful nod and smile before returning to the dance floor and took a long, controlled breath. She noticed Emelda excusing herself from her lonely table, probably leaving.

Mrs. Holbrook merely nodded, but the faint flash — a bare image — of her deeply kissing a much younger and amenable George, Wendy's father, flashed before Wendy's eyes.

Wendy paled. "I- I need some water. Excuse me."

As Wendy hurried away, Mary spotted the full glass of water sitting on the pristine tablecloth next to Wendy's chair.

Wendy clutched her belly to calm the rising panic. Someone had to have been saying aloud such terrible things. How could she, alone, have heard and the women have missed it? They weren't so old as to have lost their hearing!

"Wendy!" a blonde girl with a daisy yellow dress of ruffles and lace raised her white glove and waved Wendy over.

"Good evening, Penny."

Penny Habersham straightened with a smug smile. "Lovely party, isn't it?"

Wendy smiled. "Of course, Penny. Your mother always throws the finest." Wendy gazed after the dancing men. "So many handsome young men."

"Simply the best in Belgravia." The fifteen-year-old squared her shoulders and straightened her back. "I've heard the men at the barracks throw lots for the chance to fill our limited slots. This is certainly no stag party."

Wendy spotted one of the young officers with his tamed brown hair and upright posture dancing with one of the older girls round the dance floor. A breath of jealousy wafted from Wendy's mouth before she shut it. To be danced about and to look so fine with so handsome a gentleman was such a dear hope.

"Fancy Harold, do you?" Penny leaned closer.

Wendy turned and smiled. "Far too old for me, of course, but he is quite dashing." She scowled at the fourteen-year-old boys on the far side of the room, gathering in groups and avoiding the girls their own age.

"He is that." Penny smiled.

Less an image, but the sound of Penny moaning in lust caught Wendy's ear.

"Penny!" Wendy gasped and spun. Penny sipped her glass.

Penny lowered the glass from her lips and gulped. "What is it?"

"I fear I'm not feeling well tonight." Wendy feared she might vomit on the spot.

"M'thr —lly waits — t'll — father un'il after — been drinking -n- g'ts randy," Penny growled.

Wendy turned, again. Penny watched her. Wendy blushed. "I need some fresh air, Penny. If you'll excuse me."

"Of course," Penny said.

"Pr'y l—le — pretends sh's so pr-p'r."

Wendy squeaked as she slipped through the glass doors onto the broad veranda outside. London's evening skyline twinkled beneath a low ceiling of tangerine clouds dappled with blue from moonlight bleeding from above.

A group of children congregated further down the veranda. Wendy hoped none spoke to her — she cared neither for children nor the idea of rearing one. Instead, Wendy focused on calming her mind from the alarming evening. Not a single, cowardly boy asked her to dance. Now she heard the most appalling thoughts- whispers. She was hearing whispers. Whispers came from open mouths, not from people's minds.

Wendy took yet another controlled breath, something she had done more of the past week.

"— the pr'ty one!" she heard one of the boys in the group whisper.

"— the pr'ty one," whispered one of the girls.

Frowning at the opposing tones, she glanced at the children. A boy and girl each looked at her. Spotted, the children turned away with the confidence their thoughts were private.

Wendy squeezed her eyes. No. That couldn't be true. This couldn't be happening.

"Where's the cute brunette with the big blue eyes?" asked the voice of a young man.

Wendy perked. The glass doors were still closed and, visible through them, a handsome young university man searched the tables while standing next to his friend. Had someone actually wished to dance with her?

"The Darling girl?" his friend replied.

Wendy sighed with relief — they *were* speaking. She wasn't going mad.

"I h— she's — ripe as — P'nny." The boy continued his search. "— — — hear her moan."

Wendy backed into the stone railing, mortified. "God in heaven." Though the words and images felt so muffled, fear spiked in her chest that she was hearing their thoughts. She could not hear people's thoughts. That was for gypsies and vagabonds. Wendy was a proper lady, a feminist and a scientist, so her mother's group had declared themselves. She did not hear people's thoughts!!

"Are you alright?" a girl approached from the right. The group of children had paused to watch.

Wendy flinched. "Did you just ask me a question?"

"You- you don't look well."

"You did ask me a question." Wendy straightened. "Yes, I'm- alright. Thank you." She approached the glass door and spotted the young man through the glass pane, then turned to follow the veranda past the children and entered through the other set of doors. Once inside, she made for her mother's table.

"Wendy, are you alright?" Mary asked.

"I fear I have eaten something disagreeable, mother," Wendy said. "I think I should return home at once."

"Are you sure?" Mary straightened.

"Quite, mother," Wendy said.

"Ladies…" Mary blushed. "If you will excuse me, ladies, I must see to my daughter."

"Of course!" They waved them on.

S'ckly ch'ld. Mrs. Holbrook looked right at Wendy without opening her mouth.

Wendy paled, sure of Holbrook's voice.

"Wendy," Mary stood. "Ladies, I apologize, but we will go home, immediately. Thank you for a lovely evening, Cynthia."

"Of course." Mrs. Habersham smiled as all the ladies stood. "Thank you both for coming. The Darlings are always welcome."

Bitch. The clearest word all night twisted Wendy's stomach.

Mary gathered Wendy toward the entrance on the far end of the hall. At Mary's beckon, attendants brought their cloaks. Once outside, Wendy took another slow breath of the chill evening air. "Mother, might we walk home?"

"But Wendy, we are a good two miles from the house and it is so late." Mary set her hand upon her breast.

"Please, mother," Wendy insisted. "I think it would do great good to walk."

Mary looked to the waiting line of carriages and inhaled. "Of course, dear. Let's."

The two crossed the outer courtyard and headed north through gaslit London streets wafting in evening fog.

42

Through the Bush

Mist wandered across London cobblestone. Electric lights dotting a narrow street interrupted the darkness but failed to fill it with their faint light.

In the darkness of a long untended empty lot, hugged by row houses all around, stood a small bush amidst the collapsed bricks and weeds. The proud bush stood near the sidewalk nearest the light of day and now glistened in the night's thick fog.

With a violent eruption, a terrified sailor burst from its branches, rolled down the piles of bricks and crashed to the sidewalk. He scrambled to his feet and lifted his sword in panic. Two and three-story homes lined either side of the pristine street.

"What in hell?" he moaned when the bush behind him twitched. He spun and raised his sword, afraid some beast was preparing to attack him. When the ruffling stopped, he glanced down the street at the sight of two men passing beneath the stark ambience of a distant streetlight.

The bush's thrash preceded Peter's emergence. The boy plowed into his chest and drove both across the sidewalk into the cobblestone street. Peter bellowed, raised the inverted knife in both hands and drove it into the man's heart.

Fury overwhelmed Peter until the man's face slackened. When he realized his knife was hilt-deep in the man's chest, he yanked it out only to be sprayed with violent, heart-thumping bursts of blood. He screamed as the pulses died a moment later and the man's heaving chest fell still. His fury disintegrated into the horror of his first undeniable kill.

Frantic, Peter wiped at the blood with his hands, then his forearms. He smeared it all over his face. His breaths caught as his throat constricted and panic welled.

Two uniformed men brandishing batons approached beneath a distant streetlight. At the glint of his wet knife in the darkness, their whistles pierced the calm of night. Both raced for him. Peter stared at the man lying dead beneath him — a man *he* killed. In a panic, he fled as the world closed in on him. More whistles pierced the night. His bare feet slapped across wet cobblestone past endless row houses. New whistles ahead defied his speed. He tried turning at the corner of the block, but his feet slipped and his body slapped across the uneven cobblestones.

The world spun as his head struck unforgiving rock. Blossoming pain curled him up into a ball. Echoing bootfalls drew nearer as more uniformed men approached from multiple directions. Though his head still rang, he rolled onto his hands and knees just as one of the men closed in. Peter panicked, leapt up and slashed the man across the trunk with his silver knife. The magicked blade ripped him open and bathed Peter again in blood as the man screamed and fell back.

Horrified, Peter tried to flee. His feet slipped on the blood-pattered stones and he fell again to the street. Another uniform closed in and struck with his rod while a second followed him up and reared his foot to kick. Peter took the first hit, but as the second man lifted his foot back, he snapped his heel into the man's planted knee, which twisted backwards. The man collapsed in a magnificent scream. Peter spun and stabbed the first man between the legs with a strike so powerful the man folded at the waist and flew into the curb as blood gushed from his stabbed genitalia. As more converged, Peter stabbed the cobblestone mortar with his dagger and used it to drag himself into a sprint down another street to the eruption of more whistles and moans.

Terror gripped Peter. Where was he? How had he gotten here? He tried to focus on his escape and mounted the sidewalk for better traction for his slick, bare feet. Lights brought dark windows to life as homes awoke to the clamor. Opening doors revealed worried men and a few women.

Nearly to the end of the street, Peter saw more men join the chase. He never saw the mother and daughter turn the corner on the sidewalk ahead.

When they saw him, they rushed for the stairwell of the corner house. At the top of the stairs, a tall man emerged from the door in a clean white blouse and black trousers.

"Hurry!" cried the man.

Peter turned at the sound, panicked at the sight of the mother and daughter, and tried to stop, but slipped and crashed into the girl's ankles. His head smacked the sidewalk as she tumbled upon him in her prim dress and pink sash.

As she slapped her hand upon his face to push away, Neverland invaded her mind. Ships climbed mountains on unnatural rivers of oceans; children emerged from tangled bestial nests; an icy-faced woman struck at men and children with bolts of lightning and fire; an auroric veil shattered the night's sky to reveal a midday jungle island.

She retreated against the wrought iron fence fronting the house as images of a Garden City and miles of palace invaded her mind's eye. Waterfall-framed parks and pale marble homes wreathed in vinery filled a net of winding flat-stone streets in a nine-peaked valley. A variety of pale, brown and yellow people wandered streets flowing with wares. Men and women of magic walked among the rest as equals.

As their eyes locked, her name and that of her family struck his mind — Wendy Moira Angela Darling. When her mind discovered his murder, however, Peter's panic turned into horror. He flailed, desperate to flee. His wrist caught in her pink sash and he hauled with all his strength. She screamed at being twisted about.

Mary struggled to free Wendy as George roared in fury and fished out a small pistol from his pocket.

Wendy screamed when she saw Peter's hand as her own, covered in the sailor's blood pumping up from a hole in his heart before her.

Peter's powerful arms ripped Wendy from Mary's grip and across the sidewalk. The sash popped off and Peter stumbled a few steps away before the crack of George's pistol fired a bullet into Peter's hip. He cried out and crashed into a light pole. Clutching his wound with the sash still looped over his wrist, Peter limped into the night, across the street and into a park drowned in darkness.

Piercing whistles followed him into the black. Now on soil, Peter's bare feet found traction enough to open his speed. His mantle-powered vision adjusted to the darkness enough to see near that of daylight. As more uniforms appeared through the trees, he spotted a lake. He ran for it on silent feet, across a broad dirt walk and a lake-walled platform, before leaping the gap to a flat wooded island twenty feet from the lake shore. He scrambled into the flora and curled up as men flooded the park in search of him. He stifled his sobs as the icy night and its burning horrors sank in on him.

"I didn't do that," Peter clutched the sash to his gushing wound. "I didn't do that."

43

Shock of Loss

Tinker Belle screamed from her knees. Countless hours of searching produced nothing to explain how Peter and the sailor had disappeared.

A BUSH!! Tinker Belle's chimal scream sent nocturnal flyers into the air. She gripped her blonde hair as she sobbed. *I didn't want this. I never wanted any of this. Any of you selfdamn humans and your selfdamn wars! I don't like politics! I don't like any of you selfdamn people!!!* Tinker Belle bellowed into another coughed sob.

No, it had to be me, didn't it? Aurora Vara's grand wisdom sends me across the selfdamn continent? Why? What did I do to deserve this? I was happy! Happy at home! Happy just wandering the wood! Happy plucking flowers and teasing weasels. But- but- she inhaled, *lil' ol' tink bell had to be the BLOODY HARAVEN!!*

Tinker Belle pressed her head to the rock under her as the creek bubbled past on each side. The rock crested a bubbling vein of water rushing down into a long, gentle series of stepped falls.

Nothing I do works, she moaned. *Nothing! First, I get William killed, and now his boy is- I- I- He's there!* She pointed northward. *But what the HELL is there!? There's nothing! He's suddenly- thousands of miles away? I- I'm losing- losing it.* She coughed a sob. *I should never have been this selfdamn haraven! Who could*

I advise? I ride rodents and I garden. THIS IS GEOPOLITICAL BULLSHIT!!

She railed against the rock, careless of predators even as they avoided her sharp and furious chimes. Sucking air into her lungs, hacks erupted with her forehead pressed to the stone. She smacked the bottom of her fist in frustration.

I don't even like humans! she moaned. *What good are they!? They use magic like a ferret chokes on a selfdamn warthog! And the elves! Those stupid idiots all comfy in their big trees! And the dwarves! The- I DON'T EVEN KNOW ANYTHING, BUT I HATE YOU, TOO!!*

She dropped from her knees to her bottom, propped on her left arm and held her brow with her other hand as she took deep, wet breaths. *Why am I here? Great Self, are you even listening? Why am I here?* She sniffed wetly. *Why? I'm no politician? I'm no eldress. I don't advise people! Why am I here?* Tears welled again. *This isn't my dream! This isn't what I wanted! I'm not good at this. I'm only getting people killed.* She held the back of her hand over her mouth. *I'm- I'm only getting people killed.*

Tinker Belle sobbed. Her link told her Peter was now an inconceivable distance away, but there was no possible way he could have traveled thousands of miles in a moment.

Losing Peter felt like yet another in a series of failures from her poor decision making. First came her early political missteps with Kellogg. Then, as separation from her flock grew too great, she let Kellogg, and later William, help her satisfy her aching physical needs. She knew it was wrong, that to let them fondle and watch her was paramount to adultery against their wives, but the long years away from her flock exacted painful tolls she didn't know how to wrangle. She knew April had found out, though she knew not how. April was right to call her a hussy — humans did not treat sex as the fairies did. It was Tinker Belle's responsibility to honor human commitments to fidelity instead of encouraging William's lust while they travelled the continent on business.

Then, as Unionist voices stirred up masses from parliament to across the continent, encouraging various divisions among groups — real or fabricated — her advice seemed only to encourage one disaster after another. Belle knew she was probably the worst haraven ever to have served — or failed to serve, rather. Why William followed her time after time only worsened her guilt.

Tinker Belle shook her head. Guilt, shame and wallowing would not solve the problem, however heavy they weighed upon her.

Perhaps she sensed it wrong. Maybe he was just stuck somewhere on the tiny towers of rock in the north lagoon? Maybe she overestimated its distance? Fluttering her wings, she lifted from the rock and wiped her tears. She followed the creek downward to avoid the high predators and picked up speed, eager for something to do even as she screamed again in frustration. She fisted her hands, even as flying hurt since she lost the tip of her wing.

She was almost to the shore when a long, sticky tongue fired out from a nearby jungle branch. Fury welled so fast in her breast that she gathered power into her fists and fired upon the tree; four trees exploded in a fireball that mushroomed into the starry Neverland night. Tinker Belle's scream sent what creatures to flight hadn't already fled at the first explosion.

Wreathed in multiauras of power, she quivered with indecision. The flutter of a lone pair of wings turned her about. A large raven stood upon a nearby branch.

"Hello, Tinker Belle."

Tinker Belle fluttered. *What did you just say?*

"Would you care to talk?"

And EAT ME!? she screamed.

"Oh, no, my dear. No interest in that, at all. Perhaps one of my companions, but trust me, they will behave themselves while I'm around."

Tinker Belle glared.

"Please, follow me. We will go, alone."

Legions of ravens circling the sky dispersed into the black.

How can I trust you?

"Because I know where Peter is."

W-what!?

"Please." He flew into the moonlight. "Come."

Tinker Belle followed over jungle canopies and rolling hills of oak east to the tall stone peak overlooking the northeast section. He landed upon a square, cut stone at its apex and waited.

Tinker Belle hovered for a moment, sure he was out of reach and no other birds had followed, before landing on the opposite corner. She wanted to collapse to her knees with exhaustion but gathered her strength for a potential fight as his dark gaze regarded her in the starlight. *Where is Peter?*

"Peter is on Earth."

Tinker Belle barked a laugh. *Like hell.*

The raven waited.

What is your name, bird? she demanded.

"You can call me Solomon." The raven spoke with a warm, well-aged song of expression. "You are the haraven, are you not?"

Her eyes narrowed. *What know you of the haraven?*

"I know you seek to protect the boy who has gone afar," the bird said. "But I can assure you that chasing his ghost across Neverland will do you no good."

What know you of Peter!? she demanded.

Solomon cocked his head to the side. "He is the pan. And I've come to help you bring him home."

The light in her hands faltered and Tinker Belle dropped to her knees. *Why did you attack me? Before!? What was all that about with the- the dragon!?*

"You fear dragons, little pixie."

Of course, I fear dragons, you silly ass! Tinker Belle barked. *Every pixie knows to fear them!*

"Even though they've been locked away since the breaking?"

Not all of them! Locked away? Wha-

"Even fear of one, is fear too much."

What would you know!? she cried. *You are the predator here!*

"Circumstances can be easy and difficult," said Solomon, "but what matters is not how they rise to you, but how you rise to them."

What are you on about, you stupid bird!?

"Listen, little pixie," he said. "Your fear consumes you, yet you have no control over whether or not you meet a dragon. Even the mere appearance of it sent you into a panic. Instead of focusing on what you could do, you thought only of escape until you allowed yourself to be cornered."

What does that have to do with Peter! Where is he?

"The first lesson in being a haraven is never let circumstances make your decisions for you," said Solomon.

Tinker Belle ground her teeth. *You- you had them fly at me like a dragon to teach me a selfdamn lesson?? Who the hell are you to do such a thing to me?*

"I am Solomon." The raven cocked his head to the side. "And you are failing to be the pixie your aurora chose you to be."

Tinker Belle draped her head. Her chime came soft. *How do you know about my aurora?*

"I know about many things, but the most important thing you should know right now is that Peter is something greater than you or his parents ever expected."

Wh- what? she stammered.

"He is a fulcrum, one which will bear on the future of the entire third realm," Solomon said.

I- I just want to keep him alive.

"Oh, my dear pixie, keeping him alive is the least of your tasks. Sometimes death is a grand adventure all its own, and a path to something greater than Peter could ever have been himself."

Tinker Belle held her face and laughed with nervous angst before sliding her fingers into her hair.

"But for now, know that Peter is safe and is awaiting you."

He's on- on Earth!? I can't fly that far! How're we supposed to get there!?

Solomon's midnight beak tilted so its edge caught the moonlight in an almost-smile. "The same way Peter did, of course. Belief."

44

Serpentine Island

Violent shivers woke Peter from fitful sleep into the pale dim of a foggy predawn. Heavy mist drifted through the small trees packed around him over his bed of soft damp soil and scree. His breath frosted as he quivered with cold. Neither fingers nor toes had feeling. Warmth blossomed within his chest and spread outward until his extremities burned with blood. Once the initial shaking had passed, though still cold, Peter pushed himself up into a jagged web of branches that tugged at his crimson hair. He rolled out from under a heavy bush. Frigid wetness of early morning dew soaked the small muddy island around him.

Peter rubbed his face, coughed and slapped his hand against the ground to wake his fingers. Tears of confusion ran down his face and nose. He hugged his thighs against his chest, crossed his feet under his bottom and rocked until the cold's sharp embrace abated. He twisted in pain and tried to inspect the bloody hole in his hip where the man had shot him with some tiny object. Peeling away the bloody pink satin sash brought more tears and gentle crying.

Distant sun warmed the mist, silhouetting dozens of tall, slender trees. Falls of feet, crunches of wagon wheels across tiny pebbled soil, and faint murmurs of men drifted to his ears. Last night's flight from the city guard returned through the murk of restless sleep. Hunger gurgled in his stomach as water burbled and lapped nearby. Chirps of birds echoed across the water and the world beyond the mist woke from its evening slumber.

The world inside and out had become chaos for Peter. Ever since arriving on Neverland, life had felt like one headlong rush into craziness. He struggled to keep up, and even now he felt like he needed to get up and go and do and be anywhere but near himself. He wanted to run away, and run away from running away. He felt trapped that he wanted to find his parents and yet didn't want their endless fighting around. He wanted to go home and yet knew the Unionists were there and had taken everything from his family. He wanted to be back on Neverland, but getting the boys to build an army felt like an uphill battle. He wanted to be quiet and yet feared the silence, wanted to scream, and yet hated the sound of his voice.

Peter saw, again, the face of the sailor as he died under Peter's hand, the shock of the kill and the slack of his eyes when life fled from his body. He had killed a man, taken his life so that he couldn't get up the next morning and call on his mom or dad or maybe a wife or something. The man couldn't return to sea and be a sailor. Even though he attacked the clearing, Peter just wanted him to go away.

"I didn't want you to die," Peter said. As shame filled his chest, his head drooped to his knees and he cried.

"Good morning." A deep, gravelly voice interrupted his thoughts.

Peter flinched. "Who's th-there!?"

"My name is Eternity," the voice said. "But you may call me Solomon. And you are the Lord Pan, are you not?"

Peter's gentle panting frosted the air. "I- I'm P-Peter. Where are y-you?"

The silhouette of a large bird appeared through the mist.

"I d-don't see-ee y-you."

"You didn't? Let me try again." The bird flapped his wings.

"Are- are y-you a b-bird?"

"I am a raven, to be precise," the bird corrected as it stepped closer. "And this is a fairy."

The bush to Peter's right burst with leaves — and a golden pixie — who stopped inches from his face.

PETER!

"T-TINK!" Peter stammered.

She hugged his neck, then hovered back. *Peter you're freezing!*

"Uh huh," Peter quivered. "How did- where are w-we?"

"We are on Earth, Lord Pan." Solomon cocked his eye.

Solomon, Tinker Belle chimed. *We must get him warm.*

"Let's get him back, then, shall we?" said Solomon.

"Wh-wh- how?" Peter cringed as he bit his tongue.

Come. Tinker Belle flit close enough for Peter to see worry painting her face.

"C-c-an'-t feel f-f-f-ingers-s," Peter said.

Come! She pointed at the bush.

The boy shook his head. "J-j-ust s-s-lept th-ere."

"Move through the bush," Solomon said. "And go home."

"How?" Peter asked.

Solomon rose from the ground and disappeared into the bush.

Peter stammered.

Come, Tinker Belle chimed. *Don't think about it. Just go home.*

"I don't understand," Peter said.

With another shiver of the bush, Solomon fluttered to the ground. "Don't try to understand. Just crawl into the tree and go home. You must trust me."

"Yo-you- you- you-you're ..." Peter said.

Solomon hopped near Peter's feet. "Do you remember what a rimshift is, Peter?"

Peter hugged himself tighter. "Uh huh."

"Pretend it's a rimshift," said Solomon. "Imagine it's just a thinning between distant locations, and that this small bush is where the rimshift is located."

"F-f-f-or real?" Peter quivered.

We just came through it, Tinker Belle chimed. *I didn't believe it either, but here we are. You can do it.*

"Ok-kay," Peter said.

Solomon flew first, followed by Tinker Belle. Peter bent over and, desperate to follow, crawled through the bush. A wall of heat met him on the other side. The ground fell out from under him and he toppled down a small dune onto a beach lit by a bright morning sun sparkling across the waters. Landing on his hip, Peter screamed. Tinker Belle appeared over him.

Peter! What happened!? What's wrong with your hip?

"Get into the water," Solomon waddled closer. "It will help until we can get you to the Tree. Quickly, now."

Crying, Peter dropped the bloody sash onto the sand, limped to the ocean and sank into the warm lagoon. His fingers and toes burned with life. "Ow! Ow ow owowww!"

Solomon fluttered on the edge of the beach.

"It hurts!" Peter cried. "It all hurts!"

"Coming back to life often does." Solomon cocked his head.

How long does he need to do this? Tinker Belle asked. *He's in a great deal of pain.*

"Just long enough so he can walk," Solomon said. "There is more help up at the Tree."

Peter dunked himself in the warm ocean waves until the burning in his fingers and toes subsided. He slicked his red hair and set his hand over his wound, now washed free of scabbing by the warm salty ocean.

"To the Tree." Solomon fluttered his wings.

Peter collected the bloody sash before the three crossed the broad beach and entered the jungle. Tinker Belle stood on Peter's shoulder as he trudged up the hill.

"I can't," Peter soon stopped as blood drooled through his fingers down his leg.

Having fluttered from branch to branch, Solomon leaned down. "You can, but it will hurt. If you stop where you are, the pain will worsen. While your mantle will heal you, it will take time. If you continue onward to the proper source of life, then healing can occur starting now."

Peter turned his watery, reddened eyes up at the bird. "How?"

"There is healing up ahead, but you must keep walking," Solomon said. "To stop is to court stagnation. To walk is to commit to life."

Tears drooled down Peter's cheeks. "I just…" He hesitated. "I just wanna find my parents. I- I wanna go home. I have to find Dad, Tink. I can't keep doing this."

Tinker Belle struggled not to lie and tell him all would be well. *We'll get through this. But let's get you back to the Tree, first.*

He pressed onward.

You're doing great… Tinker Belle felt awkward encouraging him. She had seen April do it, but to do it herself, felt strange. Still, Peter offered her a grim smile as she offered her support.

At the eastern base of Pan's Peak, Peter paused at a massive A-frame arched doorway draped in leaves. At the apex, visible through a parting of vinery, stood a tiny carving of a pregnant woman cradling her belly.

"Oh, yeah," he said. "The temple."

The what? Tinker Belle asked. *What is that?*

"It's a temple I found, I think," Peter said. "It's blocked on the far side."

Then how did you get in? she asked.

"Later." Peter turned south onto an overgrown road climbing along the base toward the Tree. He used the flora to help him up the rolling terrain until the ground plateaued. He limped through the vine wall where Solomon waited for him, perched on the Tree's low roots.

"Come." He leapt from his perch and swooped down into the shadows beneath.

Solomon! Tinker Belle cried. *We don't know what's down there!*

"I do," Peter breathed.

You do?

"I went down there before," Peter said as sweat drooled down his face. "It's just- nothing."

He found you, Peter. He- He brought you back. Perhaps he knows something we don't. But you're beginning to grow a fever. We need to do something, now.

Peter winced as he held his wound and followed the raven.

They stood for a moment before Peter wiggled through the tight, child-sized gaps between the roots into the large chamber below. Tinker Belle's warm yellow glow illuminated the side of his face. Both paused at the sight of a bright blue glow at the heart of the dark chamber.

Solomon's caw echoed and his shape fluttered into view on the far side of what appeared to be a tiny pool of glowing blue water.

"I fell into this before," Peter said as they reached Solomon.

"Yes, but now this awaits you." Solomon's black visage was invisible but for the blue underlight. "Here, at the source, is your way. When the pan is seriously harmed, return here for restoration. Go in and be healed."

Peter? Tinker Bell asked.

Peter's eyes spaced as faint, sonorous notes floated on the air. His breaths deepened and he obeyed their call to the water. Dropping the sash, he stepped into the hole, walked to the center and disappeared beneath the surface.

Tinker Belle wished to cry out with alarm, but she too heard its call. She fluttered to its surface and, with a final look to Solomon's endless gaze, her wings stilled and she dropped into the glowing water.

45

More Boys

The sun peeked above the eastern horizon when Tootles woke. Nearby, Santi stoked their fire and inspected their weapons.

"Good morning," Tootles muttered.

"Good mornin'." Santi froze. "Wait, say that again."

"Good morning? You—" Tootles stopped. "I can understand you!"

"You can understand me!?" Santi asked. "But- but yesterday I couldn't get out more than your hand signals! Can you truly understand everything I'm saying? This place is truly amazing!"

Tootles raised a hand to forestall him. "Well, I can understand some."

Santi marveled. "This is amazing. I don't know your language, and if I listen, I can hear you use other words than I know, and yet I ... I'm starting to understand you, anyway."

Tootles smiled.

Santi looked to the third boy. "We need to get him washed. He won't wake up."

"And I need to pee," muttered Tootles.

"Come," said Santi. "Let's get him down to the river."

"How?" Tootles asked.

"I have an idea," said Santi. He ran out through the vine wall to the wood pile outside the outer clearing and returned with one of the long, broken planks from the ship. He tied a piece of shredded canvas on both ends to form a hammock. "Let's put him in here."

"Brilliant! Be right back!" Tootles walked to the cliff's edge and took a piss. The stream fired out over the emptiness before misting into the breeze. Santi joined him and they shared a laugh. Once finished, they returned to the small fire.

When Santi jogged around the base of the Tree, Tootles prepared to arm himself. He pulled on a small belt of swords he curated last night when he spotted a pile of weapons tucked behind one of the roots of the Tree. Santi had signaled last night about grouping piles by type. Tootles didn't realize what kind of type until he realized all of them had bits of yellow gold. He plucked a long, ornate dagger with a brass-wrapped handle and fished it into his belt, then selected a short sword, too. His tribe used spears, but the Roman swords were effective in killing his men. Tootles was prepared to learn.

"C'mon." Santi reappeared holding a machete. "Let's go!"

They lifted the boy and walked out through the wall. At the lead, Santi chopped bush away to clear a path. Tootles pointed out dangers more than once and Santi soon grew to trust Tootles's instincts on which bushes to avoid.

Halfway down the road, Santi paused at movement in the jungle greenery. The boys squatted and waited when the jungle filled with an echoing clicking growl. Through the heavy leaf cover, they spotted a massive fluffy creature sitting among the trees, six feet high from its bottom with its knees peeking above the low foliage. Its massive brown eyes scanned ahead. Long fangs hung from its snout. Bright blue fur covered the animal with bear-like ears and vicious mouth. Blood covered its snout as it feasted upon two separate gazelles.

"A koala?" Santi muttered. He had seen one once in Valencia in a menagerie. The large beast paused and turned its head at the approach of something unseen. Santi raised his head.

A small goat pranced into view through the thin bush boasting a red blaze down its head.

Tootles almost cried out in fear the goat would be devoured. Santi squeezed his shoulder to keep him from speaking.

Unlike everything else they had yet encountered, the goat raced toward the monstrous koala. It head butted the beast, which gently swiped back.

The two animals played almost without care. Never did the koala get too rough, and never did the goat fear the beast. Blood smeared across the goat's pearl-gray fur as the koala's thick, bulbous fingers tickled and stroked. The goat did not mind and the two rolled about.

"This place is … strange," Santi said. "Come. Let us be gone." They left the path to the West Bay and made for the river, which came into sight a quarter mile away when Tootles used the plank to pull Santi up short. When Santi turned, Tootles pointed off into the woods.

Glowing in brilliant sunlight, a woman strolled among the trees.

"A woman!?" Santi gasped.

Startled at her presence, they set down the boy and followed. Her gentle voice wandered to Santi's ears. Tootles's hand on his shoulder made him stop as a predator wandered by. The beast glanced at the woman and sat to watch her, seemingly without aggression. Santi eyed the predator first, then again the woman. A moment before she disappeared into the distant greenery, clouds passed overhead, drowning the area in shadow.

The woman's bright glow, however, did not change. He watched before Tootles signaled him to withdraw. They retreated with care.

Returning to find the boy unharmed, Santi realized following the woman was foolish, but the sight of such a woman in a place like this was difficult to comprehend. He offered an apologetic look to Tootles before they gathered him up and continued to the river. He sighed with relief when they found the beach. They paused at the water's edge and pulled the boy from the sling before dragging him into the low waves to plunge him clean. As Santi finished working the muck from him, Tootles scanned the tree line.

"Hey," Tootles said. "There's … there's another over there."

"Another boy?" Santi said.

"Yeah …" Tootles said.

"How the hell do you know that?"

Tootles paused for the translation to coalesce in his mind. "I don't know. But there is."

Leaving the boy half out of the water so he could breathe, they returned to the jungle. Tootles led Santi through heavy flora to a thicket. Tootles pulled bushes apart and stepped through. Santi followed close and paused in surprise.

Neon fronds and a broad variety of large-leaf green filled the bright jungle, outside. The jungle inside spread as far as the eye could see with low, rolling terrain and shadowed by heavy tree cover and tangled in countless nets of vinery and moss strangling humongous ancient trees rising high into the air strangled by vinery and moss. Humid wind soaked Santi's face. Sunlight reflected off high trunks to provide the sole illumination across the shadowed, mossy ground.

"Where in hell did this come from?" Santi asked.

Tootles shrugged.

Santi backed out of the thicket, circled it, and stepped inside. "Ay. How far?"

Tootles stepped off with slow, steady steps. Santi scanned the canopy and thick flora but followed through a narrow path meandering over hills and abrupt vertical walls of roots shooting up from the green, extending in long, curved descents from the ancient trees filling the forest. Santi soon lost track of how many turns they had made and grew worried for the boy outside.

"Tootles, we can't stay long."

Tootles raised his hand, squatted, and pointed.

A small, short waterfall trickled into a pool at the bottom of a gentle sink in terrain. To the left of the low, narrow fall sat a broad, shallow cave thirty feet high and ninety wide. Tootles turned his ear to the jungle. "He's gone. C'mon."

"Wait, who's gone?" Santi followed Tootles down the sink and over the creek into the open-air cave.

"We have to hurry, though," Tootles said. "He's not far."

"Who isn't far?" Santi gulped. "What lives here?"

"Not sure yet." Tootles headed to the far end of the cave behind the trickling waterfall into a small chamber beyond, separated from the falls by a thin horizontal gap in the stone. Scree and soil covered the room, as if washed down the back wall and gathered in an angled heap at their feet. "Here."

"Where?" Santi asked.

"Here." Tootles climbed halfway up the hill and began to dig. "Quickly. We don't have much time."

Under the dancing light passing through the trickling waterfall behind them, they dug as fast as they could. When Santi's hands brushed hair, he dug wider to reveal the head of a child. A sticky substance glued the soil around the boy and pulled away in long, gray, gooey strands. Santi struggled not to vomit as they freed more while a foul odor filled the air.

Tootles paused just before pulling him out. Santi wiped his face yet again as he panted in the thick heat. "Once we pull him, it's coming back."

"What?" Santi asked.

"It will sense him once he's out," Tootles said.

"How can you know that?"

Tootles shrugged.

Santi wanted to protest, but Tootles had honed in on this boy as an arrow loosed by the finest archer. "What's the plan?"

Tootles shrugged. "I dunno."

"Alright," said Santi. "We'll get him out. Do you know where the beast is?"

"No." Tootles glanced at the waterfall trickling behind them. "But if we can get him back to the beach ... I think we'll be okay."

"You think!?" Santi cried.

Tootles shrugged.

"Alright," Santi said. "I'll carry the boy. You focus on getting us back to the entrance."

Tootles nodded. They dug until he fell free.

"Go!" Santi barked. He hauled the boy over his shoulder and they made for the cave entrance when the scream of a massive cat echoed through the jungle.

Santi and Tootles crossed the stony creek. At the top of the rise, both boys spotted a ten-foot-tall cat silhouetted in the dusty light far behind them. They ran as fast as they could. When Santi overtook Tootles, he gripped his arm to help him speed up as the beast's scream quieted the jungle by its fury.

"Here!" Tootles snatched Santi behind one of the tall root walls moments before the giant cat raced up behind and leapt over their heads.

Both boys shared glances of terror before they returned to the path and jogged again for the exit. Santi dared not speak while Tootles led the way through the maze of trees and bush. Tootles yanked Santi into hiding twice more as the cat dashed by in pursuit. The beast even paused, once, to sniff at the air, but continued onward. While the boy on his shoulder reeked, how could the cat not smell him?

Within sight of the exit, Tootles pulled him once more into hiding. This time the tiger plodded into the area with its nose sweeping the ground. Santi shifted the boy to Tootles and drew his sword while pinching the blade to minimize its sound.

As the tiger narrowed in on them, a growl grew deep in its throat. Santi gripped the handle of his sword and prepared to stab the creature's nose when the leaves around them drew inward as a solid blanket, blocking its view of them.

Santi watched Tootles set his hand to the soil and his eyes droop. He controlled the bushes!?

The tiger's broad nose drew in air in abrupt sucks. The wall of leaves whipped in the violent drafts before leaning closer as the cat's nose pushed it in. Santi looked between Tootles and the approaching wall of green. The flora might hide them from sight, but the tiger drew closer.

Tootles bellowed a war cry that surprised and inspired Santi to his own. The tiger's nose paused. Santi reared his sword and stabbed through the green blanket with all his might. To his surprise, the blade sank deep into the tiger's snout at the inside of the nose and glanced along the bone. The tiger's recoil dragged him out of their hiding place across the ground by his grip on the sword. Santi released the hilt and rushed to his feet in terror as the screaming tiger scrambled backwards, desperate to paw out the sword.

"Go go go!" Santi hauled Tootles to his feet and half-dragged the other boy toward the exit. The tiger crashed to the ground screaming with two rows of jagged teeth from a mouth large enough to bite them whole. As they ran, the tiger came about and saw them sprinting. Though bleeding down its snout, it bolted for them. "Shiiiiitt!" Hauling them both, Santi forced them into and through the narrow opening before the tiger's massive snout snapped against the opening in a flush of breath and spittle.

The attack on the narrow opening drove the sword deeper into its nose. The tiger bolted away in screams of agony.

Santi and Tootles lay across the jungle detritus panting in nervous relief. Sharing a glance, they laughed with the joy of winning. After the moment passed, Santi stood, straightened his back, slid his flat hand across his belly and gave Tootles a sharp bow.

Tootles grinned and knuckled his right hand, tapped his left breast and rolled it outward at Santi in his own salute. They laughed, gathered the boy and headed back down the beach.

"I- I was afraid, at first," Tootles said.

"About what?" Santi smiled as Tootles's words were easier to understand every time they spoke.

"I feel like- like coming here, I lost my family," said Tootles. "I'm not sure why. It's just a feeling that lingers. But … I think I am finding another."

Santi slapped his shoulder and grinned.

"Only," Tootles started.

"What is it?"

"I don't … I don't like that we killed men. At the Tree."

Santi's brow flickered.

"My tribe fights. Rome fights. I don't like it," he frowned. "I've never killed anyone before. Before yesterday."

Santi set his hand upon Tootles's shoulder and squeezed it. "It's easy if they deserve it."

Tootles searched Santi's face before they returned to the shore downriver from where they left the other one.

"Go wake him up. I'll take care of this one." Santi carried the new boy straight to the water to wash him. Scum dissolved to reveal a small boy with black hair, angled eyes and yellowed brown skin wearing a tattered silk robe. He laid him upon the sand and approached Tootles, who stood motionless over the other child.

"What is it?" Santi froze.

The lower half of the boy they left behind was gone, shredded as far up as the waves reached. Hollow, sunken skin stretched taut over the half body. Tootles vomited.

Santi spun to check on the other boy. Left above the waves, he was okay. His heart raced with the realization he had walked right into the water with something that had devoured this other boy in thousands of tiny bites. He gripped Tootles by the shoulders and walked him from the body.

Tootles retched a few more times before wiping his face.

"Hey," Santi squeezed his arm. "We'll remember next time. At least he was asleep for it all."

"No," said Tootles. "He wasn't."

Santi turned and paled. Though gaunt, the eyes gazed upward with a silent scream he could hear because he had screamed like that, himself. "Shit."

"Let's get him back to the Tree," Tootles said. They gathered the new boy and made their way toward the Tree, unaware of the shadow following them.

46

Conference

Roschach shuffled reams of reports in a room packed with maps, action plans, relationship diagrams and outlined trade agreements. Scribes and attendants moved with quiet efficiency to avoid bothering him and the two prefects who shared the table filling the center of the long room. Midmorning light speared through tall arched windows opposite Roschach and reflected off the large penciled maps blanketing the table, underlighting everything but his face, now shadowed by the reports in his hands.

Fenren appeared through a door to Roschach's left and approached the table.

Roschach spared him a brief glance. "How goes the room?"

The haggard man took a slow sigh. "We're looking."

Roschach's mouth tightened.

"Any word on Athyka?"

Roschach set the papers down and bent into the light pouring through the windows. "That woman is worrying me."

"Regretting sending her?"

"Harry Bristol hasn't reported in yet, either."

"Harry?" Fenren asked. "That's not like him."

"It's not like Athyka," Roschach growled.

"Hell." Fenren pulled up a chair and sank into it.

"What progress have you made?" Roschach asked.

"We've translated everything. The key isn't in the languages they used. Old, sure, but we have the records here in the building to take care of all that. They hid it in their colloquialisms."

"Their what?" Roschach asked.

"Their colloquialisms," Fenren said. "It's common to language everywhere. We all have phrases like 'easy as mage's first fire,' or 'don't rush the horses.'"

Roschach frowned.

"Every culture has hundreds, sometimes thousands of phrases unique to their eras and phrases whose meanings don't immediately translate just because the words do."

"You're saying they wrote a bunch of colloquialisms in the pan's secret room?"

"It's not as simple as that, as if they just wrote a bunch of colloquialisms," Fenren said. "It's the implications that anyone who grew up in those cultures knew secondhand. Many are high context languages, which means cultural mastery is as important for accurate translation as actually knowing the words' original meanings."

Roschach moved his hips around the corner to recline upon the table and cross his arms.

"Gruen is a rather low context language." Fenren rubbed his face and took a glass of water offered by an attendant. "If you walked in on a conversation I was having with someone else, you'd figure out what we were talking about pretty quickly. Fustian, for example, requires an understanding of their caste systems. You use entirely different verbs based on whom you're talking to and who you are. High castes use certain verbs with each other that are inappropriate for them to use with lower castes, and that doesn't even count the honorifics that change tones among members of the same sliver of the same caste based on age and social standing. Being high context, two Fustian speakers might mention a topic based solely through the context of their location, social standings and genders without ever mentioning a single name or title. They would carry the entire conversation to completion without ever mentioning any specific names and yet could have spoken about a number of people. And don't even get me started on the anumerics."

"Anumerics?"

"Languages which don't use numbers." Fenren gulped the cool, crisp water from the glass and took a heavy breath. "They use generalizations. Ask an anumeric how many things you put in your pocket — that he watched you put there — and he'd have no real way to describe how many. He couldn't count more than three to five before losing a real estimate on the actual figure."

"No."

"Seriously," Fenren said. "Usually, you only find anumeric cultures among the natives who never had a need for advanced math, but there's an elvish breed from about fifty thousand years ago that never developed a number system past ten."

Roschach crossed his arms. "I had no idea."

"So…" Fenren swirled the glass. "We're not just translating words and sentences and their explicit meanings, but also doing research for their implicit meanings. What do they mean in the context of the wall? While we know some are low context, others aren't clear on whether they're low, middle or high; that doesn't include the massive cultural background we need to even tackle their actual meanings."

Roschach took in the view out the window of a stone-lined garden bubbling with two fountains. Tall palatial walls surrounded the garden on all sides. Multicolored vinery wove across stonework around the garden like a drape and framed various bushes and small trees to provide fruit and shade. Through the cracked window wafted the floral breeze cooling the fire-warmed room, inside.

"But…" Fenren finished off the glass. "There's hope. I found something I think will help me shortcut the whole thing. Helgothian knew some ancient Arduvish and said that one of the blocks of Horn appeared with a similar syntax. He's researching it as we speak while I get a breather."

"The ceremony is tomorrow night." Roschach tapped his foot. "That's zero hour. We have to have the mantle before we officially declare a new government. If we can't get to Algueda and back through that room, we're going to have a whole new war on our hands."

"I know, El, I know." Fenren planted his elbows on his knees and ran his fingers through his hair.

Roschach cleared his throat, drawing Fenren's head up.

"Oh…" Fenren glanced at everyone else in the room. "*Fellow* Roschach."

Roschach nodded.

"I've stared at the same sentence for two hours and can't remember a single damn word of it." Fenren blinked.

"Come." Roschach stood. "I was about to summon you, anyway."

"What?" Fenren set the glass on the table and stood. An attendant plucked it with a muted glare before she checked the papers for any water rings left behind.

Fenren followed Roschach into the adjoining room blacked out with thick curtains where eight golden stands stood on the yellow marble floor around a central point lit by gaslight chandeliers hanging from the ceiling. Three angled feet on each stand supported a vertical brass rod topped by a small reflective sphere. Roschach stepped onto a small round carpet set in the center and motioned to each sphere in turn. Moments later, bluish light filled five of the spheres and expanded outward into the shape of different people.

Each saluted Roschach and spared Fenren a quick glance.

"Report," Roschach said.

"Fellow Roschach…" Aaron Devkoron's deep voice filled the small room. A tall man with tight blonde hair braided behind his head, Devkoron wore the mage's battle uniform of the People's Union. A trim uniform with a squared chest with a shoulder cape, he squared his shoulders as he commanded every situation he had ever faced. "We have made up the time lost by the typhoon and are within a day of Algueda. Agent Estemil and I are prepared to secure the mantle upon arrival." He motioned to a petite woman next to him with midnight skin and bright round eyes clad in cloth and leather armor lined in ornate metal trim. Her thick hair braided up and around her head. "Have you received word from Agents Bonduquoy or Duluth? Also, Bristol seems to have gone quiet."

"All is quiet from Algueda," said Roschach. "Consider that a sign to proceed with caution, but not too much. We need that mantle *now*."

"Of course, Fellow Roschach," Devkoron said. Inrav Estemil echoed.

Roschach turned. "Dereth."

"My Fellow Roschach…" Dereth Ishmel grinned a dashing smile in his ruffles and lace and bowed with a flourish. His stiff coiffed hair framed his long chin and glowing teeth. Upon rising, he straightened with pride. "At your- At the quorum's direction, pardon, we have begun our efforts with the communal crops. Yields are already blossoming and we expect to produce five or six times the normal yield by next year."

Roschach sighed. "Good news, finally."

Winston Runel sniffed.

"Once these crops are accelerated, I will move to the western fields. I believe we can overcome the irrigation problem."

"You can't grow crops without water, no matter how much magic you pour into it," Runel snapped.

"Why, you underestimate me, Runel." Ishmel grinned.

"The ohna florad only works with what you have," Runel growled. "You think you have amazing results because of your magic, but you're only accelerating what you have at hand. You can't grow six yields of crops within a year because there isn't enough nutrients in the soil to do that!"

Ishmel scoffed. "Jealous, Winston?"

Roschach raised his hand, cutting them off. "I didn't give you the florad to burn out our first communal farms, Ishmel. Take care not to push the crops or yourself too far. It's hard enough to find anyone who can wield the ohnas." He lowered his hand. "But it's not impossible."

Ishmel's broad smile twitched. "Of course, Fellow Roschach." He bowed, again.

"Runel?" Roschach turned. "Did you make it?"

"Arrived from Richter's Deep four days ago." With the face and frame of a farmer, Runel straightened. "Helvan Gulf is proving promising. Fishing here has been among the weakest in recent centuries. I've seen a lot of promise regrowing the corals. Brings in more fish. I think over time I can restore entire reefs, which should improve fishing here. Might help the Keibonese make up their minds about joining the Union."

"*That's* what I want to hear." Roschach clapped his hands. "Remember that the ohnas aren't for you to go play with creation. These powers are to entice or cow, but there's an order to that. People suckle to power that does for them. Use your power sparingly and focus on generating goodwill for our cause. Only after all other options are spent are you to use the ohnas to intimidate. Is that clear?"

Agreement echoed around the room.

"Margia?"

Margia started at being addressed. "L- Lord Roschach? What are you doing here?"

"Report," Roschach said.

"Ah-" she said. "Yes, I, yes. The package. It's in the hole."

"What?" Roschach cocked his head.

"The heir of-"

"Wells!" Roschach snapped. "Report on your mission with the ohna."

"What do you want from me!?" she cried and pointed. "Dirty work! Dirty work! All I do is dirty work! I'm a selfdamn scientist, you fucking pig! Do you know what my tigers have done!? No! You don't ask about my tigers! Don't you want to know how my tigers are doing? All you care about are humans! You selfdamn humans!" Margia quivered with unbridled rage.

"What in hell?" Runel muttered.

Margia jumped at unseen voices and clutched the ohna hanging on her breasts. "Fellow Roschach," she tipped her head as if she hadn't just exploded. "All's well here. I just put down a small insurrection. My tigers ate very well. They like the children. I think it's sweet for them. I ensured they got their fill. The city's very compliant now." She smiled.

Everyone shifted as she thumbed the ohna.

"How're you feeling, Agent Wells?" Roschach asked.

"Why?" Margia's tone tightened. "Did someone say something?"

Roschach watched her for a long moment. "No. Of course, not. I just want to ensure you're healthy."

"Of course, Lord Roschach." She smiled. "Thank you for asking."

Roschach shared a quick glance with Fenren before returning to Devkoron. "Thicke is working on the room. He will find the rimshift so we can get you home once you arrive on Algueda. Update hourly, if necessary. Algueda is proving everything we feared it would be."

Devkoron and Estemil saluted. "We will not fail you, Fellow Roschach."

"The rest of you report in regularly," Roschach said. "If we can't get the mantle, we may end up fighting a larger war and you will all be recalled here. Any questions?"

"What do you think happened with Athyka?" asked Ishmel.

Roschach shook his head. "Doesn't matter. It only matters if we get the mantle. Dismissed."

They saluted before their shapes flickered out.

"I don't care if we have to break down the selfdamn door." Roschach faced Thicke. "To hell with the translations. Get the mages involved. Rip the room apart if you have to. I want access to the rimshift, *now*. Wells is losing her selfdamn mind to the ohna. What if Athyka's gone? Eldnor? Bristol? Those selfdamn cunts are going to get us all killed. Get that selfdamn door BY TOMORROW NIGHT!"

"As you command." Fenren saluted and left the room.

Roschach marched to the stand Athyka once used, snatched it up, hauled it in an overhand swing and smashed its sphere into the marble floor. It shattered in glass and sparkling magic as Roschach bellowed.

47

Return to the Tree

Peter woke to the faces of three boys standing on the ceiling staring down at him. He looked from boy to boy.

"How … are you doing that?" Peter asked.

Brows drooped.

"Doing what?" Santi asked.

"Standing on the ceiling!" Peter's brows climbed.

"The ceiling?" Tootles asked. "We're on the ground!"

The third boy gaped.

"On the ground?" Peter asked. "What're you talking about?" He locked onto a tiny figure splayed inside a hole in the ceiling. Tinker Belle lay sleeping at its heart. "Tink?" Though comfortable, he lay on no bed, as he first thought. Looking between the sink, the boys, and the small tree, he realized *he* was in the air. The moment collapsed and he fell toward the hole but managed to land without crushing Tinker Belle. At the thunder of his landing, the pixie woke with a start and flinched.

"What just happened?" Peter flipped his thick red hair and climbed from the hole. Disoriented, Tinker Belle flew to Peter's shoulder and gripped his white shirt as she tried to wake.

"You were floating!" Tootles stammered.

"What?"

"You were," Santi said. "Just floating up there."

Peter squatted and hopped into the air but fell to the ground as he always had.

"Where are we?" the new boy asked.

"How did you find me?" Peter asked.

"We just got back with the Asian." Santi motioned at the new boy.

"The what?" Peter asked.

"The Asian," Santi said. "He's clearly from the Far East. I've seen some of the images from Marco Polo's writings. My father has copies."

The boy looked between them. "I am from Xifu."

"Definitely from Cathay…" Santi raised his chin.

"What is he calling me?" asked the new boy.

"You won't understand him unless you come from where he comes from. You'll understand me, though."

"I understand him just fine," said the boy. "But what is Cathay?"

Peter frowned at Santi.

"We can understand each other now." Santi crossed his arms.

"What?" Peter asked.

"It began this morning," said Tootles. "We can now understand each other."

Peter's face slackened. "What? But- I'm the- I mean, I have the mantle."

Tootles shrugged.

"You are not special," Santi sneered. "We can now speak with everyone."

The new boy straightened. "Have you kidnapped me? You will return me to my family."

"No one kidnapped you," Peter scoffed. Relief washed over him that he wouldn't have to translate for them every conversation. For once, he felt a tiny victory.

"Where are we!?" the boy demanded.

"Neverland." Peter half turned his head. "Why does he look different from earlier?"

"He's … he's not the same boy," Tootles said.

Santi cringed. "We lost the other one."

"You lost him!?" Peter asked. "How?"

"Th- th-" Tootles stammered.

"We left him in the river too long," Santi said.

Peter scowled. "An island full of lost boys won't help us with the Unionists!"

"If you hadn't disappeared after our fight," Santi said, "you could have helped!"

"I went to Earth!" Peter growled.

Santi's arms fell open. "You went to Earth!? You just said we couldn't go back!"

"I didn't mean to!" Peter said. "It happened by accident."

"How do you accidentally go back to Earth!?" Santi stepped closer.

"I went through a bush!" Peter said.

"You- what? You lie! You play with us!" Santi cried.

Tootles shrank.

"I'm not lying!"

He's not lying! Tinker Belle snapped.

"He is!" Santi faltered and returned to the fairy. "I can understand you, too."

Great, now *you understand me,* she chimed.

"I'm starving." Peter waved off the argument as he climbed toward the roots.

"W- wait!" Santi stormed after him. "Did you really go back to Earth?"

Peter emerged from under the Tree and found large piles of treasure round about the fire. "What's all this?"

"It's our plunder." Santi followed him out. "I want to know how you return to Earth."

"I told you, I don't know," Peter said. "I went through a bush and ended up in some big city."

"Then how did you get back?" Santi asked.

"I don't understand that, either. Solomon said something about a rimshift."

"Solomon? Who is that?"

"A raven."

Santi struggled to speak. "Do you just make up these lies as you go along? I can't trust anything that comes out of your mouth!"

"Did you just see me floating!?" Peter pointed under the Tree. "I don't know everything that's going on! Stop yelling at me!"

Santi's mouth opened and closed. His brow sank.

"We got weapons!" Tootles stood behind a pile of swords, knives and other weapons. He ducked his head when the others turned to him.

Peter planted his fists on his hips as he smiled at the treasure. "You all have done very well."

"Of course, we have," Santi said. "We will split it up among all of us."

"This is my island-" Peter stammered.

"But this is *our* treasure!" Santi glared.

"See! This one fits me!" Tootles lifted his sword.

Santi caught on it, then checked his own belt. "Where did you get that? That's mine!"

Great Self, I hate humans, Tinker Belle muttered.

"Tink," Peter said.

Not- ... all of them? she coughed.

Santi snatched the sword out of Tootles's hands.

"Hey!" Peter stepped in between them. "Calm down! There's plenty for all of us!"

"He took this from my pile!" Santi growled.

"It's all the same!" Peter said. "We're not here to play with swords but to drive the Unionists off Neverland!"

Santi held up the sword's hilt before Peter's face. "Don't touch my things."

Peter glowered. "Fine. Now, we have to prepare to fight off the Unionists."

"Didn't we just do that?" Santi pointed toward where the ship crashed.

"More will come!" Peter insisted. "Right, Tink?"

I'm not actually sure, Peter.

"What?"

I don't know how many are actually coming here.

"See?" Santi pointed at the fairy. "The danger's past."

"I can feel it! I can feel more coming!"

"Lies," Santi growled.

"Then..." Peter searched about the clearing and then off the cliff. He locked onto a tiny stream of smoke snaking into the air from the eastern end of the north island. "Then how do you explain that!?"

Tinker Belle focused as the other boys did.

Santi's face darkened. "They will come here. We can deal with them here."

"No," Peter said. "I will deal with them. You will continue getting boys."

"We need to resolve our position," Santi said. "If they are coming for you, we are in a defensible position. The wall- my god, the wall! And Tootles can control it!"

Peter faced a blushing Tootles. "You can control the wall?"

What? Tinker Belle asked.

"Yes," Tootles said.

"No way." Peter's brows climbed.

"We should collect food and supplies and fortify ourselves here," Santi said.

"I'm not waiting for them to come to me." Peter turned back. "Tink and I will go after them."

"And if you wander off to Earth again!"

"Solomon can come get me, again!"

"You and these lies!" Santi spat.

"I- think we shouldn't wait," Tootles said. Both boys turned. He shrank under their gaze. "I mean. Peter's dad is out there, right?"

"Exactly," Peter said. "That's my father. I go get him and then we can take everyone else. He'll know what to do."

"I thought you just said that was the Unionists!" Santi said. "And what about more boys before attacking? I told you to strike while the iron was hot!"

"I'll- I'll go find out!" Peter said. "In the morning. And you two can go get more boys. *Without* killing them!"

Tootles stiffened.

"What is going on!?" the new boy asked.

"Explain it to him," Peter paused. "You look like you're Admian."

"Where?" the boy asked.

Peter, I don't think pulling all these children from- wherever the hell you're getting them from, is the best idea.

"I need an army, Tink."

But who's going to feed them? Care for them? Lead them? You're off running all over the island!

"I can't be everywhere at once, Tink," Peter said. "Tootles has it. Don't you, Tootles?"

Tootles hugged himself.

"I will build this army," Santi said.

"Are we at war?" asked the new boy. "With whom? From Wu? Ming?"

"We are at war with the Unionists," said Peter. "And until we are sure they won't come anymore, we will continue to prepare for them. Are we clear?"

Santi's jaw clenched. Tootles nodded. The new boy said nothing.

"Good," Peter said. "Now I'll go get us some food. We'll head out in the morning." He marched out the wall. "And you'll stop losing my boys!"

Good Self, Tinker Belle chimed. *More children.*

48

River House

Edmon's horse plodded down the narrow, descending roadway among the high rocky hills. The wash of trees echoed before they came into view along a sparkling river winding through the rippled sandstone walls. Citrus and date trees covered the shores and flood plain between the stone walls.

Once beneath their dancing canopies and dappled shadows, Edmon drew down his hood and veil. Though warm, the breeze cooled the sweat painting his face. Four riders plodded with him in pairs and doffed their own hoods and veils while they continued to scan in all directions for threats.

They followed the path as it wove along the river's left side, veered left around the upcoming lake and up a hill hugging the lake's far side, then turned inward up a small peninsula that squeezed the opposite river mouth. Upon the point rose a white house gleaming in the sun through the small orchards of citrus and dates carpeting the terrain. A double-doored metal gate blocked their path onto the estate grounds, one of which hung open and canted on its hinge. Edmon reined well short of the door and dismounted. In moments, all five men had raised their hoods and veils and drew weapons before ducking into the trees on either side of the road. The warhorses remained in place as the men circumvented the estate walls to smaller pedestrian gates.

As shadows, Edmon led his two guards through the small, southern orchard up to a broad low-walled patio. They climbed the hill, bypassed the mezzanine to the ground floor, and mounted the broad, upper patio. The warriors leapfrogged from corner to corner, past overturned patio furniture and into the white adobe estate.

The group reconvened on the main floor before Edmon directed them by hand signals past slashed tapestries and bodies of dead slaves. Room by room they cleared the house. Saved for last, they approached the estate's royal bedroom. Unlike all other rooms, its tall bright wooden doors stood closed.

Edmon guided them away from the doors and used a window in a nearby room to climb out on the small exterior platform ringing the base of the second floor to sneak around to the suite's window. Blood covered everything inside. A simple, clean cord hung over the interior handles of the main doors.

He used a short whistle to summon his guard as he used a secret latch to sneak inside. Once inside, he motioned to one of the two to follow him in and then at the rope on the door. "Torsis."

Torsis neared the door and hovered his hand above the rope, then withdrew it. "Trap spell, sire."

"Can you defuse it?" asked Edmon.

"It's possible," said Torsis. "Give me a moment."

The door handle turned from the outside and the door opened. In a burst of light and sound, the man outside the door was thrown across the broad foyer and crashed into a wall table before slapping face down on the floor.

"Negrin!" Edmon pushed through the cracked doors and his guards to find his brother, Negrin, face down. Two armed men rushed from the anteroom beyond the foyer and stopped at the sight of Edmon.

"Prince general!" Negrin's two high guards saluted.

"Sire, wait!" Torsis forestalled Edmon from touching his brother's limp form.

"Torsis, what can you do?"

"I can fix this, my lord, but it will take a few hours."

"Get to it," Edmon said.

Over the next few hours, the men policed bodies of the house staff and buried them outside. Once finished, Edmon returned to the royal bedroom, lit candles and pulled up a chair to study the scene. He poured his second glass of tangerine kitron when he heard Negrin enter the doors behind him.

"He's upright, my lord." Torsis accompanied Negrin inside. "He'll be groggy for a bit, but it will pass."

"Thank you, Torsis," Edmon dismissed him without looking back.

"Holy shit, what happened in here?" Negrin recoiled from the eviscerated corpse lying across the royal mattress in a pool of blood, adorned in shredded royal robes with a long dagger buried in the forehead. He clutched his mouth.

"Slaughter." Edmon motioned with one finger and his glass in the others. He pointed at the blood patterns. "Five men cut this man apart while he was still alive."

"Great Self." Negrin averted his gaze, then noticed the bodies of two high guards stuffed to the side of the bloody mattress. "Did you get into a fight?"

Edmon took a heavy sigh as his mind raced. He inspected the scene for hours. For all he knew about it, the why continued to elude him, which made him angry. He looked up at his brother. "What are you doing here, Negrin?"

Negrin coughed to forestall vomiting.

Edmon raised his head. "Negrin?"

"I was on my way to see you on the front," said Negrin. "This is a half day's ride from the rimsportal. Thought I'd get a little rest."

"Why?"

"Father recalled the seven. Sent me, himself."

Edmon swirled and sipped his glass, again.

"How can you sit in here?" Negrin covered his nose as he scanned the room. He froze. Approaching the body, he noticed its rings, outfit and boots. "Is- Phineas? Is this Phineas!?" Negrin spun to Edmon. "Is that-?"

Edmon shook his head.

Negrin turned back. "Then ... who the hell is that!?"

Edmon clenched his jaw. "Doesn't matter."

Negrin grimaced at the eviscerated face. "How do you know it's not Phineas? And is that- I know that crest." He leaned closer to the dagger sticking out of the skull. "That's Meso'Admia." He returned to Edmon. "That's Meso'Admia!"

"Negrin!" Edmon snapped.

Negrin jumped.

"It's not Phineas." Edmon stood and motioned for Negrin to follow him out of the room. "And it's not Meso'Admia."

"But that's their-"

Edmon finished off the drink and set it on a table outside as Negrin followed him out.

"What the hell is happening?"

Edmon stopped and turned. "Stop. You're the thinker, Negrin. Think."

"Alright. Alright. Body on the bed," said Negrin. "Looks like Phineas. Wearing his clothes- If they have Phineas's signet, where the hell is Phineas!?"

"We don't know." Edmon continued across the large anteroom with couches and a small fireplace on the left with curtained arches leading to outside walks. Negrin followed him down the stairs to the ground floor.

Negrin paused inside the room warmed by a host of lanterns. The central room bore its own fireplace and more openings to the south orchard and a small fountain opposite out the opposite side. "So, that's not Phineas, but he's wearing Phineas's clothes. There's a dagger common to the Meso'Admian royal guard sticking out of some stranger's forehead. How is it not Meso'Admian?"

"Because Meso'Admians make a tradition of stabbing through the stomach to send a message, not the head."

"A tradition? That looks like Phineas!"

"Yes, traditions that Meso'Admians hold sacred from their cowboy roots." Edmon paused. "Negrin. Negrin!"

Negrin blinked.

"I know that's your first dead body, but you need to focus."

Negrin took a breath.

"Focus," Edmon returned to him. "Right now, you're facing a fight or flight response. Your heart is pounding and you're struggling against the smell of death. I want you to stay with me. Focus. Are you listening to me closely?"

Negrin nodded.

"Take long, slow breaths."

Negrin breathed.

"Good. Now," said Edmon. "Tell me what you see."

"Dead body, supposed to look like Phineas, stabbed improperly with a

Meso'Admian dagger. Setup."

Edmon raised an eyebrow.

"A setup? But by who? And where is the heir prince?"

"Those are better questions."

"But- what are you doing here?" asked Negrin.

"Phineas's high guard came to the camp at Lower River," Edmon said. "They thought he shook 'em."

"But ... that means he didn't."

"No, he didn't," Edmon said. "But now they deserve to die."

Negrin paused. "You didn't execute them on the spot?"

"They confessed to losing him," Edmon said. "Those two bodies stuffed upstairs are the other half of Phineas's personal guard. If he evaded them, they deserve grace and Gael deserves my boot up his ass. It's their role to protect the heir from the enemy, not himself. Letting the enemy have him? They will be executed immediately before the public." Edmon clenched fists at the end of powerful, corded forearms.

Negrin frowned.

"Why did father recall us?"

"Civil war just erupted in Swinne."

"What?" Edmon asked. "How?"

"Duke Luthir declared himself king a few days ago," Negrin said.

"Who died?"

"Queen mother in state."

Edmon's mouth tightened. "Great Self. We can't afford two fronts. Luthir's been crying foul on trade and fishing rights on the causeway since when I was a selfdamn child. If he can keep the crown, the hegemony's armies will be crossing the water."

"That doesn't include the failures at the northern mines."

"What? What failures?"

"Drying up," Negrin said.

"Why wasn't I informed?"

"Father wanted you focused on the Admians, not the economy."

Edmon scowled. "The mines drying up means the finances for our mercenary support goes, too."

"Father wants the seven in state."

"What does that accomplish if I can't cow the redcapers across the low river delta?" Edmon returned to the room and crossed his arms.

"Do you think it might be Swinne?" Negrin took a seat. "The body upstairs?"

"I've thought about that." Edmon sat on the arm of a nearby chair. "But that would be a new tactic for Luthir. He wants the war with us to bind the hegemony to his house. Blaming Meso'Admia serves nothing. It's just a convenient villain since we're already at war."

"Then who?"

"I don't know yet," Edmon growled.

"You hate not knowing."

"There's much I don't know, but I hate it when I don't even have the pieces to figure it out. When I can't- reach out and scout those pieces."

"When it's not under your control."

Edmon grimaced.

"What's the plan, General?"

Edmon tapped his thick bicep. "We need the kind of intelligence you don't get from field scouts or political spies, because if I'd bet on anything, we're not dealing with royal intrigue."

"Then who?"

"Not sure, yet." Edmon glanced at the king's bedroom. "But that was sloppy. Even Luthir's smarter than that. No. This is someone trying to hide a different action, one we weren't expecting. We need to hit the street."

Negrin's eyebrows climbed. "Gael."

"Unfortunately," Edmon said. "But he's got the ear. I want to get him involved."

Negrin shrugged. "It's just as well. I have to collect him anyway, but I don't know where to start with him. The rest of you are easy to find."

"Oh, I know where Gael is."

"You do? How?"

"You don't know?" Edmon asked. "He's in the same place at the same time every year."

"What? Where?"

"Festivale of Ebedria. Never misses it."

"Huh," Negrin mused. "Then we head for Rochsmora."

49

Lady in White

Great Cougar and Tiger Lily camped halfway along a high central ridge separating a vast grassland to the west and an endless desert to the east. Moonrise glimmered upon a distant desert oasis and the grassland danced in heavy eastbound breezes that crashed against the ridge and fired skyward.

Swirls of warm wind from the western ranges ruffled their tiny fire tucked beneath a stepped rock descending the winding ridge and carried with it smells of a hundred places they could not see. Neither spoke as they scanned first the deserts and then the grasslands. They pointed out things they saw — camels, sidewinders, foxes and even herds of antelope munching on dune grasses.

When the moon had risen high enough, they gazed across the grassland and picked out various herds of grazers, countless birds, cheetahs, lions, hartebeests and wildebeests, anteaters and badgers. When a herd of buffalo came into view, Great Cougar stood. His breath quickened as he pointed them out. Tiger Lily stood next to him and took his hand.

As the herd disappeared through a dip in distant terrain, Cougar returned to the fire and sat. Tiger Lily fished out jerky and offered him a piece. He took it with a nod.

"I … thought I would never see them." Great Cougar's voice was very small.

Tiger Lily watched her father.

"You were right, of course." His glassy eyes stilled her heart. She had never before seen him cry. Rain Singer, her grandmother, said he cried once in his life — the day Breath of Butterfly died giving birth to Tiger Lily. "I finally saw them."

Tiger Lily said nothing. People often said her predictions were right, though most often they were warnings of something negative. At least this was one time she was happy of it.

"Grandfather always said the endless plains of grass were the strangest part of his journey," Great Cougar said. "The buffalo roaming the plain captured his mind as a boy. Never had he seen such creatures of weight and power race across the ground. Never had animals made the world thunder as did the raging storm."

"You have now seen them, Father," Tiger Lily said.

He nodded.

"What is it, Father?" she asked.

Great Cougar hesitated. "I wish you were born five years earlier or later."

Firelight flickered in Tiger Lily's eyes.

"I would wish you to have more companions your own age. The plague was unkind. I am grateful, though, you survived, when they did not."

Tiger Lily frowned. Her father's admissions were rare.

"I am when I need to be," she said. "The plague did not discriminate which of us it killed."

"It killed children," said Great Cougar. "Only children your age. I feared you might not survive it."

Tiger Lily turned. "I did."

"Yes," Great Cougar said. "Your grandmother assured me you would, though I did not believe her."

"How might she know?"

"Her visions have always included you, Daughter. Even before I was born."

Tiger Lily's face tightened.

"My daughter, I know this is difficult." He set his hand upon her shoulder. "But you were born with great purpose. I can't imagine the weight you feel, or why you were born at this time, but who you are is why you were born, and why you survived."

"Who am I, Father?" Tiger Lily asked.

"You are the bringer of unity." He motioned to the island. "We have seen the island like the others have not. You know they will not survive easily. You must forge the path for our people. You must learn this place as even I cannot."

Tiger Lily faced the moon-soaked island beneath a blaze of twinkling stars that even the sea crossing never produced, framed by heavenly clouds of purple, blue and yellow. Sparse trees dotting the grasslands in loners, pairs and thickets danced in the heavy wind. The north island washed in its own misty weather.

"Do you think the little white bird is from this island?"

"Of course," Great Cougar said. "We will not leave here again. This is our home now. All your visions must focus here. We must find the source of that fire. If we must face men, it should be soon." He searched the skies again, unable to see the trail of smoke from earlier.

Tiger Lily blinked her tears away when the cry of a man pierced the night. Both stood. "Was anyone supposed to follow us, Father?"

"No," said Great Cougar as they armed themselves and raced down the western side of the ridge toward the grassland. At the bottom, great jagged gorges extending across the terrain walled in layers of black soil formed a sea of grassy plateaus. They darted down the decline into the first gorge and raced until a T-junction. Great Cougar took a knee to catch his breath with Tiger Lily close behind.

They listened while they scanned the shadowy winding pathways leading deeper into the maze. Sharp clangs echoed down the black gorges that reminded Tiger Lily of striking two long rocks together, but with a ringing sound. They sprinted through the moonlit pathways up and over hills to the edge of a great open space between the plateaus.

Great Cougar sank behind the bend and peeked. Tiger Lily peeked, herself, but saw nothing. At his motion, they stalked into the open where Great Cougar knelt, sniffed at the wind and touched at the grass. Only the smell of heavy grass and fine dust drifted on the cool wind. He lifted his fingers into the moonlight and found blood.

The two sped eastward as barks echoed down gorges to the west. Tiger Lily scanned the high walls with worry, aware climbing them would be difficult even in well-lit conditions, much less under even the dim of night. Great Cougar found a path eastward that climbed to their camp on the central ridge. As they crested it, Tiger Lily snatched his arm and both froze.

On a grassy hill forty paces west, a woman glowed under moonlight. Her long white braid hung down over a pale white dress and soft trousers tucked into high boots. Spinning, the woman's silver eyes widened in surprise, reflecting ambience. Shivers rushed up Tiger Lily's spine.

Great Cougar tensed. "Butterfly?"

Tiger Lily started. Her mother?

Holding a white bow staff that beamed as bright as her bonewhite hair, the distant girl raised her left arm and pointed northwest. Tiger Lily looked where she indicated.

Beneath the largest tree she had ever seen perched upon a jut on the near side of the north island's highest peak flickered a tiny fire. "Father."

Reticent to pull his attention from the girl, he obeyed his daughter's urging. He saw the fire, but when he turned back to the moonlit beauty, she was gone.

"Was- was that Mother?" Tiger Lily scanned the horizon.

Great Cougar paused, then took a long, slow breath. "No."

Tiger Lily's heart raced. "But ... you called her Butterfly."

"I thought- she looks like your mother ... but it was not her."

"How can you be sure?"

"Butterfly disliked touching weapons," said Great Cougar. "That girl held her staff like a close friend."

"But ... it was just a staff."

"I have seen men comfortable with weapons, Tiger Lily," said Great Cougar. "When they came to attack us and take what we had; when they drove us from the grasslands, always east. When they find out we do not fight back, that we have chosen the way of nonviolence with men, that we believe in peace above all ... They do not even try to kill quickly. They use the butts of their spears instead of stone blades." He gazed after where the girl had stood. "That one is friend to her weapon."

Tiger Lily locked onto the hilltop. "Was she a specter? Or ... is she alive?"

"I do not know." Great Cougar dragged his gaze from the hill again to the fire. "But that is real. She has shown us where the men are. Perhaps she is friend to us. We must return to the village. Rain Singer must know before we proceed."

Tiger Lily followed him up the hill to the campsite, but spared one final look at the hill where the lady in white had appeared and wondered who she really was and why she appeared so familiar.

50

Devkoron

Clad in a thick fur-lined cloak, Aaron Devkoron stood behind the captain as the pilot steered clear of the tall icebergs in the early morning dim. Frigid air found no gain on his tight braid as he scanned the horizon where the dark, distant sky rested upon a brighter reflective ocean.

"You're sure we're almost there?" The captain glanced southward at a horizon closer than all others — the edge of the world. Sailors gaped from their perches across the frosty ship.

"Any second now," Devkoron said.

Faint outlines of the island's veil appeared as they cut through the icy waves. Beside him in her own fur-lined cloak stood Inrav Estemil. In seconds, an auroric veil rippled over them to reveal an island bathed in brilliant amber from a sunrise at their backs. Sailors gasped as the sky changed and temperature climbed in seconds from sub-freezing into tropical early morning warmth. The two agents shed their cloaks and passed them to attendants who took them belowdecks.

"Holy Self," the captain said. "First officer, steady on a course to green zero four zero. Slow to five knots."

The first officer echoed the command to the pilot, who cried 'aye' and turned the ship's wheel as the bosun cried orders to shorten sails. Sailors shedding their extra layers scrambled up the nettings to comply.

The ship slowed as it veered to starboard and the bridge rocked up and down at the abrupt change in speed. The captain turned. "You said you had a solution to the reefs, Agent Devkoron?"

"Estemil?"

"Furl all sails, captain." She stepped to the taffrail and raised her face skyward. "And order your men to hold on."

Full of nervous energy, the captain barked orders fast echoed by his officers. Estemil pulled a small leather sheath chained to her armor, fished open a small panel and set her thumb upon the ohna inside — a ram's horn. Clouds drifting by shuddered under a violent shift in air above and swirled downward into a tornado that struck the water just astern. Its impact revealed naked seabed and forced the water outward in a great wave that vaulted the ship up and over the reef before crashing down into the lagoon.

Two sailors flew off toprails, spinning off before crashing into the crystal lagoon waters.

"MAN OVERBOARD!" cried sailors. Many clutched heads and broken arms who had not prepared well enough to handle the violent shift. Others gathered ropes to the starboard and port rails to wait for the sailors to resurface. The sailors never did.

Devkoron touched his ribs where the taffrail had hit him in the side. "Thank you, my dear."

Nonplussed, Estemil secured the flap on the ohna and faced the island for her first real look.

"Oh my," she said. "It's ... beautiful."

Devkoron winced and scanned the northern coast, himself. "Mm."

With the help of two sailors, the captain climbed to his feet. "What kind of tactic is that!?"

"A quick one, Captain." Estemil smiled at the island, but that smile faded as she faced him. "Time, we do not have."

"She's right," Devkoron said. "Prepare to sail west for the Tree. Our time is short."

"CAPTAIN!" shouted a sailor from the main deck.

The captain and two agents moved to the port deck to spot a woman walking from the beach out onto the water. The ship fell silent.

"Drop anchor," the captain said. Officers muttered the order across deck.

After a minute of brisk walking, Athyka Bonduquoy climbed the ship and port side rail on fresh stairs of ice formed by water rushing upward and through the bannisters before freezing as a second set of stairs down from the rail to the deck.

"Athyka Bonduquoy…" Devkoron approached. "Where have you been?"

"Agent Devkoron," Athyka turned. "Estemil."

Both agents froze when they saw the side of her face and the length of white hair that began at its apex.

"Great Self, what happened?" Devkoron's normal decorum melted under his surprise. "We thought you were dead!"

"I am not," Athyka said.

"Roschach's been-"

"I lost my communicator in the first attack with the pan."

"So, William still does have the mantle," asked Estemil.

"The pan chose wisely to come to Algueda," said Athyka. "Each of our attacks have faced considerable opposition by the island, itself."

"By the island?" Estemil asked.

"The island protects the pan at every turn," Athyka said. "He goes everywhere unmolested while everything kills or eats our men and mages." As she spoke, she focused the power of her mind first toward Devkoron, then Estemil. Neither noticed her probes, because both had reached up to touch their ohnas. The ohnas buffered her attempts to touch their minds. Did they know? Meanwhile, she felt the control of every other man on board slide into her hands. Their fear ebbed as she took mastery. She struggled not to smile.

"That's impossible," said Estemil.

"Where is Eldnor Duluth? Harry Bristol?"

"They're dead," Athyka said. "As are the ships and the crews upon them."

"Who is left?"

"Myself, Gregory Danes, and a few sailors."

"I have strict orders from Roschach to aim directly for the Tree," said Devkoron. "Without the mantle, tomorrow's ceremony will start the war we've been trying to avoid."

"I know," Athyka said, "but we cannot attack directly." She looked to Estemil. "I saw what you did with the ship. I used a similar tactic to carry

The Hover all the way to that selfdamn Tree with every sailor, mage and arm we had, and still the island took it from us."

"I need to alert Roschach," Devkoron said.

"No," Athyka said. "There's no more consultation with Eden. We either get this done, ourselves, or there's no grand people's union to go home to. Besides, we have a long way to go and a very short time to get there."

"You said we couldn't go to the Tree," Estemil said.

"We're not going there, yet," she said. "We have a delivery vehicle that can help us into the pan's inner sanctum — what Roschach has been looking for. We get that first. Gather your men and your arms and we can begin our final assault on the pan."

"But-"

"Aaron, I've known you a long time." Athyka muted her tone despite her racing heart. "You know I'm the best at what I do. I've never asked you to stretch out your neck, but my neck is on the chopping block. I'm asking you to trust me."

Estemil turned her frown upon Devkoron, who eyed Athyka.

"Roschach doesn't have faith in you."

"I'm not asking who Roschach has faith in, I'm asking you."

"Roschach will not approve of you deviating," Estemil said.

"I know," Devkoron watched Athyka.

Athyka waited.

"We will go to your camp and gather your men." Devkoron glanced at the island. "If you've survived this long when others have died, then your counsel will be necessary to avoid your mistakes. Are you prepared to share them?"

"I am," Athyka said.

"Good, but let me be clear, Bonduquoy." Devkoron stepped closer. "I am in charge of this mission. When the time comes to acquire the mantle, I will do it my way. Then *I* will deliver it to Roschach. Estemil and I will get the final credit for this win. I assure you, however, that success also protects your neck. Are we clear?"

Athyka raised her chin. "Yes."

"Linroy…" Devkoron motioned to the senior mage aboard. "Gather your men and supplies. We're deploying now."

51

Black Tower

Santi, Tootles, and the new boy left the tree line and jogged down the hinter onto the beach heading south.

"I hope you can swim, Shifu."

"I told you! I am *from* Xifu! My name is-"

"Way too long and complicated," Santi cut him off. "I told you I'm not using all those titles, either."

"You peasant dogs!" Shifu growled.

"I am the son of a duke!" Santi rounded on him. "Fourteenth in line to the throne of Aragon! What are you in line of but the dogs which lick your wounds!?"

Startled, Shifu leapt back with his hands up to defend himself.

Santi laughed before continuing with Tootles, who veered left around a spur of terrain dipping to the water.

"Hey…" Tootles jogged. Santi and Shifu picked up their pace to see what caught Tootles's attention — a long, white stone bridge crossed the rift river separating the two halves of Neverland at its narrowest point. All three stopped.

"Where did this come from?" Santi asked.

"It's beautiful," Tootles breathed. "I didn't know such things could exist."

"I have seen many." Shifu raised his chin. Santi spared him a glare.

"Come on, he's south." Tootles mounted the bridge. Sand and broken rock littered the smooth stones. High pillars anchored each end of the bridge and square-edged railings rose above ornate balusters carved into squat humanoid figures holding it up. His fingers traced its soft, skin-like marble texture with awe.

Once across, Tootles led them westward along the shoreline. A great grassland stretched southward to a volcano on their left. At its apex, a molten red river wound down its side and disappeared into the rocks below. They marched for two hours across rolling, steepening forested terrain that forced them to walk single file.

"Are you sure there's one all the way back here?" Santi asked.

"Yes," Tootles said.

"How do you know? Like … did you just sense him all the way out here or something? Or …"

"Look, I don't know." Tootles threw up a hand. "I just … do. There's a boy this way. I have no idea why I know. Or how I knew about Shifu or about- about all the others."

"My name is not Shifu!" protested Shifu.

"All the others?" Santi asked. "How many are there?"

Tootles glanced across the island. "Enough for a tribe."

"What? How many is that!?" Santi cried.

"A tribe, I guess." Tootles shrugged.

"What about numbers?"

"What's a number?" Tootles asked.

"What's a- what?" Santi stumped. "What do you mean, what's a number?"

"What is that?" Shifu peered past the boys climbing the narrow gulley.

"What do you mean, 'what's a number?' Are you stupid?" Santi bumped into Tootles, who had stopped walking.

Tootles raised his hand to point up the rippled incline. Tucked between two narrow descending ridges appeared the upper bailey of a black tower wreathed in mist rolling over the height of the ridge beyond.

"Ay," Santi said. "Let's go."

Mounting morning heat thinned the fog as they continued up the ragged terrain. As the ground steepened, the three pulled themselves forward using trees as handholds. Tootles pointed out dangerous bushes along the way while Santi fought off predators. Soil grew rocky and sparse. Air cooled and moistened as they advanced into the condensation descending from the ridge line above. Footsteps slipped as the shale grew weak under their weight and fewer trees dotted the landscape the final quarter mile to the tower.

The three reached a lip and crawled up onto stones sinking into the degrading soil. A broad stone plaza stretched out before them for a gap cut into the incline, inside of which rose a lone black tower. Flora and a small landslide from the cliffside behind it rung the tower's base while vines climbed its height.

"Now *this* is impossible," Tootles breathed as his head tilted to take in the hundred paces to its bailey.

"Such black stone." Shifu followed them across the plaza. "Like midnight bottled within rock."

The boys spun when the sound of rock shifted behind them. With weapons drawn, they approached the lip when a small spotted cat with tufted ears and thick paws attacked.

"AY!" Santi swung wild with his sword. He knocked it away but failed to cut it down as he scrambled backwards. Tootles tried to approach the cat but was too slow to keep up. Panicked, Santi couldn't move far enough away from the small feral cat to swing his sword when Shifu kicked the side of the cat and sent it rolling off the lip to disappear into the mist below.

All three panted with adrenaline waiting for the cat to return. When it didn't, Santi's sword sank to the stone and he set his hand upon Shifu's shoulder. "Thank you, Shifu."

"That is not my name," Shifu protested.

"That is your name." Santi returned to the tower.

"My name wasn't Tootles." Tootles shrugged. "New tribe, new name, I guess."

Shifu eyed Santi. "Then what was *your* name?"

"My name is Santiago Carrillo de Valencia III," Santi said. "But you're calling me 'Santi.'"

"Why do you get to use your nickname and yet you call me by my city!?"

Tootles approached the tower. Tons of soil blocked the entrance archway.

"He's in there?"

"Yes," Tootles said. "Come on." He walked up the piled scree filling the carved face of the incline and packing round the tower.

"I like this about you, Tootles," Santi said.

"Hm?"

"You focus on the task at hand," Santi said. "I admire that."

"All must work." Tootles shrugged.

Shifu scowled but followed them up the steep soil circling the tower's base when Tootles pulled out his sword and hacked at vines carpeting the side of the tower. Santi squatted and pulled on the vines' lower ends to reveal a half-filled window.

"HAH!" Santi smiled.

Tootles stooped to enter the window. Sections of the floor above them had collapsed at various points to form a massive pile of heavy, angular stone blocks and soil to their right. A third of the main floor opened to their left as a great hole of jagged stones, while stone fragments and vinery littered the final third in the center.

The boys picked their way down and crossed the open floor to peek downward into the great black chasm.

"He's … upstairs?" Santi frowned at the darkness below. "Right?"

"He's down there," Tootles said.

"Are you sure?" asked Santi.

Tootles pointed. "The boy is there."

"Are we really going down there?" Shifu asked.

"We need more boys." Santi ripped dead vines from the floor and used them as a makeshift broom to clear away dust. He and Shifu coughed while Tootles watched. A small wooden hatch appeared in the floor's stone patterning near the wall opposite their window entrance.

"Aha!" Santi grabbed the rusted handle and pulled, but it popped off. Tootles raised his heel and kicked through the dried wood. The door shattered under his short kicks and crumbled down a narrow circular stone stairway leading into darkness.

"Wait, don't we have light of some kind?" asked Shifu.

"You can't see down the hole?" asked Santi.

"I can barely see either of you outside," Tootles admitted.

Santi turned.

"Poor eyesight." Tootles shrugged.

"How … how do you do anything?" Santi asked.

"Dunno. Let's go." Tootles started down into the dark stairwell.

"Why don't you stay here and watch our backs?" Santi looked to Shifu. "Or better…" Santi glanced upward at the collapsed floors above. "Go up to the window or something. Keep an eye out for predators who might follow us in. You'll have a better chance there than here."

Shifu exhaled. "Yes, fine idea."

"Good," Santi said. "Be back in a minute. I hope."

He followed Tootles down into the darkness with his hands to the sides of the narrow stairwell. Light disappeared as they descended. A warm stench wafted past them and thickened. Santi held his nose and stepped with care as brittle pieces of the shattered door littering the well made for slippery footholds. Their bare feet stepped down dusty stairs, their muffled echoes filling the narrow pathway down.

Santi lost his bearings and grew dizzy when he bumped into Tootles. Tootles took Santi's arm and pulled him to the bottom of the stairs. Santi entered a vast open chamber leading upward forty feet to the base of the tower.

"Ay, my god. This thing is huge."

"What does that mean?" Tootles asked.

"What?"

"'Ay.' I- I don't understand it."

"It's a, uh … a word you say when things are new or different or strange. Like, the cook makes a new dish and it's delicious. You say, 'ay!' Or, if it is terrible but cannot curse before the ladies, you quietly say 'ay.'"

"I think I understand."

"Can you see?" Santi asked.

"Not like you, I think," Tootles said. "I can sense direction, like the stags in the forest when they rut the females. They cannot see them, but they smell them."

"You smell them?"

"Not like that," Tootles said. "I can't explain it, yet. I just know."

"Fascinating." Santi stepped into the room.

Faint light from the window high above outlined crumbled edges and supporting arches of other floors that once existed between the base and the tower's main floor. Echoes of dripping water filled the space.

"There's …" Santi squinted. "Over there."

"That way?" Tootles pointed at the arch.

"Can you see it?"

"No," Tootles said. "But the child is that way."

"Follow me." Santi led him across the soaked mounds of stone fallen from above. He helped Tootles along to the large archway leading underground beyond the base of the tower,.

The low ceiling forced Santi to duck and walk into the darkness with hands outstretched. His heart picked up when a faint light appeared in the distance. Hundreds of tiny dry roots hung from the path's low ceiling, brushing their heads and shoulders with loose soil and old cobwebs. Narrowing walls forced them to move single file down the descending path. Warm air grew hot. The path opened into a small chamber bare lit in faint yellow green. Against the back wall rose a pile of bones.

"Oh…" Santi's voice trailed off. "I think we're in a lair."

"A nest," Tootles said.

"What?" Santi turned. "Can you see it?"

"Not really … but I know it's there … it's on soil, right?"

"Yes, we've been walking on soil since entering the archway."

"Huh," Tootles said. "The boy's in the nest."

While Tootles searched the nest, Santi inspected the walls. Tiny vertical holes breathed in faint moans with various wretched odors. Tootles dug away bones from the pile, pulled out a knife and cut at the dirt and twining. A distant scratching echoed down one of the chambers. Santi shushed Tootles and held his sword up. Tootles dug faster.

"Got him, I think!" Tootles exclaimed, then cringed to realize he'd stabbed the boy. "Nope." He put away the dagger and continued with his hands. Every time he freed a part of the boy, something else was tangled in an invasive net of roots.

Santi squinted into the darkness. He scanned the comb of openings into the chamber and felt more vulnerable by the moment. "C'mon, Tootles!"

"I'm trying!" Tootles protested as yet another root snapped under his tugs. Something brushed Santi's foot. He cried out and swung his sword and hit something that screamed and scrambled away. When the chamber then filled with the patters of dozens of tiny feet, he kicked with abandon. Tootles snatched out his knife and stabbed downward at the chamber floor behind him as furry animals rushed about. High-pitched screams filled the space before the creatures retreated a short distance.

"What the hell!?" Santi fought panic. The feeling of standing at the white doorway and the midnight maw beyond threatened his sanity. Tiny screams and mews filled the chamber from a host of small creatures.

Tootles hauled on the child with all his strength. Dozens of tiny roots popped before the boy was free.

Whimpering barks devolved to snarls and hisses.

"Come on!" Santi grit his teeth. "You got him!?"

"Got him," Tootles pulled the boy over his shoulder and staggered under the weight. When he set his hand on Santi's shoulder, the two ducked into the narrow tunnel leading to the base of the tower. Dozens of tiny feet flooded the tunnel before and behind them.

Santi rattled the sword against the tunnel's wet stone walls and swung the blade back and forth across the ground to drive the creatures back. When too many forced themselves close, he kicked hard and sent one of them crashing into others in a flurry of yelps and barks and forced a temporary retreat. "They will have the advantage in the great chamber!"

Tootles stomped his feet and kicked with his heels to knock away the snapping of tiny fanged mouths.

"You ready?" Santi asked at the tunnel end. "You go for the stairs! I'll hold them off!"

Bent over as he was, Tootles struggled under the weight of the new boy. "Alright."

"Go!" Santi stepped out and swung at movement boiling across the chamber floor.

Tootles straightened coming out of the chamber, but misguessed how the boy was positioned on his shoulder. The weight tipped Tootles backward before both crashed to the ground and over sharp stones. The animals rushed Tootles.

Santi rushed over his friend, taking bites on his legs that were meant for Tootles's throat. "GET UP, TOOTLES!!"

With a dozen tiny mouths latching onto his feet and legs, Tootles kicked and scrambled onto his feet and hauled the new boy again up over his shoulder. Santi circled him with his sword. Animals screamed and whined as he cut a gap around Tootles.

They moved to the stairs. Tootles fished out his dagger and swiped his way into the stairwell. Santi retreated to repel creatures that would follow. The boys' heavy breaths echoed up and down the narrow stairs; rushing and pounding of blood filled their ears and muted the whimpers and cries of the angry chorus.

Santi was desperate to keep them away and wished he could see them until they reached the first, faint pall of light in the stairwell. Dozens of furious, glowing eyes glowered at Santi on faces the boy could only describe as demonic. He almost tumbled, but when they refused to advance further into the light, Santi moved faster.

At the top, Tootles stumbled to the chamber floor with the boy before both fell across the stones. Santi followed him up and checked the blood covering his sword. He took a knee and sat upon his heel to catch his breath. Tootles panted from upon his back.

Tootles rolled his head to see a new boy bleeding from the wound he made while trying to dig him out. As the dagger tucked into his belt dug into his back, he winced and fished it out.

Santi forced himself to stand and wipe the blood from his sword using the left side of his shorts. He sheathed his sword when he spotted Tootles's dagger. He stepped over and plucked it from the ground where Tootles set it.

On his back, Tootles rolled his head.

"Where did you get this?" Santi lifted the golden dagger to inspect it in the faint light wafting through the window above them.

"Oh, I got that from the treasure," Tootles said. "I needed a dagger. My papa always said never to-"

"Did you take this from my portion of the treasure?" Santi cut him off. He stood. His voice darkened. "I told you not to take my stuff."

Tootles climbed to his feet. "That was your pile? I thought you were just arranging them. You can have it back."

"You don't take what belongs to me." Santi's breath quickened. "Never take what's mine."

"You can have it," said Tootles. "I don't really care about it."

"Never, *ever*, take … what belongs to *me*." Santi clenched his fists.

"Fine." Tootles shrugged. "There are plenty back at the tree." He glanced up at the window entrance and turned to Santi when a sudden blow sent him across the stone floor.

"NEVER TAKE FROM ME!" Santi screamed with a rock in his hand scooped from the floor. Santi leapt upon Tootles's chest and slammed the rock several more times into the left side of Tootles's skull near his eye socket. Hot blood and brain matter sprayed Santi. "NEVER-" He cut himself off and his raised arm faltered. In moments, rage melted under shock. Tootles's head had caved inward.

Santi dropped the rock and scrambled backward across the floor. Gore gushed from Tootles's skull across the stones and over the edge of the gaping maw into the dark chamber below. A chorus of howls and barks echoed from the chasm. Tootles's eyes spaced as his chest sank and stilled.

Santi clutched his face with his bloody hand. Tootles stole the dagger, but … why had he done this? Why had he killed his only friend on this godforsaken island!?

"What the-!? What THE FUCK!?" Santi screamed and gripped his thick black hair with bloody hands. The bright doorway and its eternal blackness closed in around him. "I can't- I can't- …" He scrambled to his feet and paced while flexing his fingers. When he noticed the blood, he scraped his palms on his trousers while he huffed through clenched teeth. He felt all the more mad since every ounce of blood and gore painting the floor and his hands was dark, thick green. Santi's grip on reality quivered.

Whatever the color, Santi couldn't return to the Tree with Tootles's blood on his hands, or even return without him, at all. He could say they had split up. He could deny having seen Tootles after leaving the clearing. Where the hell was Peter, anyway? He wasn't here. He didn't know. He wouldn't know. He couldn't know. To hell with Peter. He was going to kill him anyway. But why did Santi just kill his only friend?

Santi paced, glanced repeatedly at Tootles and stopped over his body. Only Tootles had led them here. Peter accepted that one of the boys hadn't made it back. Maybe he would accept that Tootles had died. This was a dangerous place. Tootles could have died for all sorts of reasons. Certainly, nothing to do with Santi's bloody hands. Nothing at all.

Santi had to make the body go away.

He gripped Tootles under the arms and lifted him to the great opening and, hesitating, flopped him over the edge. Tootles's trunk slumped forward and down over the edge and dragged his legs with him. The boy disappeared into the black and hit the wet bottom a few seconds later with a gentle thud that crashed through Santi's brittle sanity. The host of creatures below howled and screamed.

Santi lifted the new boy and cast him with all his might out over the hole, afraid he might drop on Tootles's body.

Terrified, enthralled, excited and quivering, Santi searched the blackness. Vomit erupted from his stomach and out over the expanse. He almost lost his balance as he heaved. He dropped to a knee and tripped backwards when he almost leaned too far over the hole. He wiped his mouth with his forearm, turned, and scrambled up the stones leading up to the window dimmed by thick fog outside.

He needed to get out of this terrible place. He needed to get away from what he'd done. He reached the window and dragged himself outside. Moisture on the rock gave his first step no purchase and Santi tumbled down the angled rocky soil to the bottom of the hill. Moaning, he climbed to his hands and knees. He lifted a hand to find blood coming down his head as his fuzzy gaze locked onto the shadow of a squat, round figure rushing him. Before he could react, thick, swift fingers clamped around his windpipe and squeezed until the blackness Santi so feared rushed in upon him.

52

Mindrise

"**M**other?" Michael's voice drifted through the open doorway. "Can I go to the park today?"

"The weather is foul today, Michael." Mary's articulate words cut the air. "And we are leaving soon."

"We are? Where are we going? Wendy's still in bed."

"Is she?" Mary asked. Moments later, she opened the cracked door to the nursery. Wendy lay on her side eyeing the intricate patterns of gold and blue leaves across the nursery wallpaper.

"Wendy? Are you well?"

Wendy hesitated. "I'm not sure."

"Well, sit up, let me check you." Mary approached the bed.

Sitting up, Wendy dragged her legs off the bedside and braced her hands on the mattress edge.

"I don't feel a fever." Mary set her palm on Wendy's forehead.

"I know, mother, but …" Wendy said, "I just don't feel well."

"I thought you wanted to attend our meeting."

"I was …" Wendy drifted off. "I just would prefer not to be among others, this morning."

"Is it that time?" Mary asked. "As we discussed? Have you had your visitor?"

Wendy frowned. Could the onset of her flow be what was causing the strange voices and whispers? No, neither mother nor her aunt had ever described such a thing. But could it?

"Mother..." Wendy cleared her throat. "I'm ... Well, I'm hearing things."

"Hearing things?" Mary asked. "What kind of things?"

"Well, nothing mad, I assure you." Wendy gulped. "Just ... muffled voices. Such as Habersham's party — voices sounded ... distant. Like perhaps my hearing has changed?"

Mary relaxed. "Hearing problems? Should I schedule a meeting with Doctor McTavish?"

"I don't know," Wendy said. "Is that part of the ... monthly visitor?"

"I've never heard of such a thing to do with that time of the month," said Mary.

"But it's possible, yes?"

"I don't know," Mary exhaled. "I shall schedule a meeting, anyway, just to be sure."

Wendy twisted her mouth.

"You know, when that time comes, it will be time to move you out of the nursery."

Wendy glanced at Michael's bed across the nursery from her own.

"But stay home, today," Mary conceded. "We will get you to the next meeting."

"Yes, Mother," Wendy said. "Thank you."

Mary ran her fingers through Wendy's hair and bent and kissed the top of her head. "If you don't feel so ill as to stay in bed, ensure you put yourself together for the day."

"Yes, Mother," Wendy said.

"You will watch Michael."

"But what about Liza?"

"Liza must attend her mother this morning, so this might work out well for both of us."

"Mother," Wendy pouted. "Must I?"

"Yes, you must. And keep him inside. You know how his poor lungs handle all this rain. I fear he could catch his death."

"As you wish." Wendy's face tightened. "Where's today's meeting?"

"The Gardenia. We're meeting MP Lansbury."

"Truly? I would love to go! I've always wanted to …"

Mary raised an eyebrow.

Wendy drummed her knee and slumped.

"Sit upright, my dear." Mary faced the door. "You are a lady."

Wendy forced herself upright.

At the door, Mary spared a worried glance for her daughter before closing it behind her.

Wendy donned a simple white shift and blue dress, combed through her matted brown hair and bound it above her head. Downstairs, she found a half-eaten plate of breakfast on the small table in the kitchen. "Michael!"

A few moments later, Michael appeared in the doorway in a pair of shorts and a short-sleeve white button up.

"The plate." Wendy pointed.

"So what?" Michael shrugged.

"Clean it off." Her brows drooped. "Are you finished?"

"I don't know." Michael shrugged.

Wendy huffed and grabbed the plate herself and scraped out the food and rinsed it off. Liza did most of the chores, but she knew her mother would be displeased to return home and find Wendy had done nothing. Mary's upbringing just outside Oxford had been simpler prior to marrying George and despite her love of fineries, would not tolerate prissiness on Wendy's part.

"Don't muss the house," Wendy said. "I'm in charge while mother is away. Understood?"

"Right." Michael walked away.

Wendy pinched her lips but let it go. She tidied the kitchen as much as necessary and then munched on an apple. Once finished, she picked a book from her father's study and curled up by the tall window at the fore of the sitting room. As a corner house, she had a view of the intersection, though muted now under a steady rainfall outside. With her feet tucked under her, she opened her favorite childhood tome — *Hewet's Household Stories for Little Folks*. She could not read her fictions as much as she used to now that Grammar School's increased workload meant more classics and philosophy.

The book fell open to a place where its creasing was weakest — in the midst of Cinderella's tale.

A smile tugged on Wendy's mouth as her fingers graced the familiar text.

"'Cinderella,' said the Fairy,'" Wendy read, "'I am your godmother, and for the sake of your dear mamma I am come to cheer you up, so dry your tears; you shall go to the grand ball to-night, but you must do just as I bid you …'"

Her mind drifted to the fairies. She had obsessed over meeting one when she was little. Now becoming an adult, she had focused on setting aside such childish dreams. Still, the faint hope of meeting one lingered. Fairies were free, in Wendy's mind, and while she adored the fineries of being a lady, she secretly wished to be a fairy, as well.

Her father George once told her an ancient family tale about the family working alongside fairies, but like most bedtime stories, she knew it was for her delight as a child as it was when George regaled Michael with the same fictions to put him to sleep.

Nana appeared and nuzzled Wendy's leg while she wagged her tail. *Must shit.*

Wendy coughed at the thought. Nana always nuzzled when she needed to go out. That's why Wendy thought of that, of course. She scratched the mop of a dog behind her head, rose and headed upstairs. "Michael?"

Michael built blocks in the nursery under the pale light bleeding through the windows.

"I need to take Nana out-"

"Can we go to the park!?" Michael lit up.

"Briefly," Wendy said as soft rain pattered on the window. "It's quite cold outside, today, and I would not linger. And if mother finds out I let you out-"

"But a little while? I hate being cooped up in here."

"Yes, briefly," Wendy said. "Get your shoes on. And get your coat!"

"Yes!" Michael rushed to his closet.

Wendy came downstairs and pulled on her own boots. Wrapping a shawl around her shoulders, she plucked the leash from its hook and secured it to Nana's collar before pulling an umbrella from the stand. "Hurry up, Michael!"

"Coming!" he cried.

Wendy waited. "Michael!"

"I'm coming!" Michael raced downstairs in a small sailor suit.

"Michael!" Wendy snapped. "We're just going out for a few minutes! And that's not warm enough!"

"I wanted to wear it!" Michael protested. "John gets to wear his everyday!"

"That's because John is a leftenant in His Majesty's Navy," Wendy's brow drooped. "You are a little boy."

"I'm *not* little!"

"We're not out for a benjo, just for a walky and stretch our legs a bit." Wendy pulled open the door. "I'm not going to fight you, but stay under my napper or that sailor outfit won't be so much fun." She pushed open the umbrella through the door and guided Nana and Michael out onto the stoop before shutting and locking the door behind her. "I won't have you getting sick because you wanted to look like John."

Together, they walked a few blocks west and across both directions of Park Lane into Hyde Park. Though Londoners considered light rain a common companion, today's fitful downpours kept most inside. The three sauntered amidst trees and paused for Nana to conduct her business when the rain lightened to a faint drizzle.

"Can I go circle a bit? I want to see a raven."

"Don't go far. I said this would be a short trip."

"Just down toward Serpentine!" Michael took off.

"Don't trip!" Wendy cried after him, then took a patient breath before following him at a ladylike pace. "That child."

Nana sniffed at her. *Busy master pup.*

"Yes, busy master pup," Wendy repeated and then gulped. She refrained from looking at Nana. Instead, she veered from the path onto the grass to try and keep her younger brother in sight as he darted south and into murders of crows gathering on the fine gravel Serpentine Road cutting through the park. Birds scattered in cawing protest before Michael picked another murder and chased it.

"That little prat," she growled. Reaching the Serpentine Road, Michael was nowhere to be seen and she was disinclined to chase after him. Instead, she walked to and sat upon a bench between the road and the near corner of Serpentine Lake. Nana set her head in Wendy's lap, prompting her to scratch the dog behind the ears.

Good, good, good, the dog's thoughts bubbled up inside Wendy's head.

Wendy pushed those thoughts aside. She didn't want to pretend she understood animals, today. Or any day. That would be crazy, and Wendy was not crazy.

Taking advantage of the lull in heavier rain, the flow of pedestrians increased along Serpentine Road. Commuters cut from Westminster and Kensington to Bayswater and Paddington and a dozen other boroughs. Holding her umbrella against the faint drizzle, she watched the dog walkers, nannies and children, bobbies, one suffragette, dozens of mounted riders and countless workmen heading to and from tasks. Clops of hooves dominated pedestrian footfalls as everyone raced across the park before the heavy rain returned.

Commuter voices filled the space. Words and thoughts cascaded across the fine crush of gravel, as if couched by her umbrella.

Wendy closed her eyes and took a slow breath, but the voices grew louder. The thoughts she heard grew more intimate — whispers of memories and hopes. Despite the chill, she felt her head warm.

Her run in with that strange boy the other night left her with stranger dreams that grew more intense by the day. Her father was confident he managed to shoot the ruffian by the amount of blood leading into Hyde Park, but the boy vanished and no nearby doctors reported treating any ten-year-olds with gunshot wounds.

Wendy clenched as the voices became articulate.

"Butter, flour, bread ..." one woman's voice drifted through the haze.

"First to Lord Wessel's flat, then to the Thames for more ..." a workman. How did Wendy know he was a workman?

"Can't wait to get back to that peach tonight," one man's thoughts made Wendy blush, for more than words reached her mind.

"That sodding rotter," one man's fury invaded Wendy's chest. "Thinks he can nick from me!" Images of one man bashing in the face of another startled Wendy, and she could not tell if it was a memory or a dream.

Her blue eyes popped open and she gasped. Her head warmed, again, and flushed. She needed to return home; it was cold and she had stayed out too long, as it was. Nana popped up as she stood.

More walk!? Nana's thoughts came, unbidden.

"No! We're going home," Wendy said.

Nana stilled. *Clarity.*

Wendy struggled and failed not to look at the dog.

The heavens opened and rain returned en force. The sound drowned the thoughts away while fear welled within her — where was Michael?

"Michael!?" she cried and moved to the road, sure he was nearby. "Michael!"

She knew where he was. He was 100 yards in ... that direction. The rain was cold and had soaked through his clothes, leeching his fun.

Michael, come, Wendy's thoughts replaced the words coming from her mouth.

She froze just shy of the road. Such a command rang her head and pain blossomed. Flashes of the redheaded child who ran into her- no, his name was Peter. His name was Peter!? She had to be guessing. She couldn't know his name.

Pain seared her head as the torrent above deepened and soaked her despite the umbrella.

Flashes rushed her mind of Peter on a tropical island that slaughtered men, a boy with midnight hair and a crocodile whose eyes glowed in a green fogged swamp, a slimy boy pulled from a wall of snaking vines, a woman who used the power of water and ice beneath the largest tree Wendy had ever seen, a beautiful redheaded mother and a powerful father who … ruled a distant and exotic kingdom, a place where Peter was raised.

Wendy dropped the umbrella as panic filled her. "Michael. Michael!" She ran through the crowd deeper into the park. "MICHAEL!"

Though she could not see him, she felt him sprinting in her direction as sure as an arrow from Robin Hood's own fingers. She had to get to him. She had to see him.

She stopped in the middle of the street as dozens of voices filled her mind, most with worry at the pretty young girl standing in their midst as they flowed around her.

Laughter and lust, disdain and worry of their perceptions crashed over her. She hugged herself and struggled to focus on Michael. "Michael!"

"Young miss, are you alright?" an older gentleman paused and stepped closer. Concern painted his face despite his thick white beard. She reminded him of his granddaughter, the one his daughter-in-law stole away to Wales after his son died in a workplace accident.

Wendy retreated from him. She knew this man in ways she should not, from his bravery during the First Boer War to becoming a factory foreman, his wife and four children, their ups and downs, his short bout with the demon alcohol and his recovery- "MICH-A-E-E-L!"

She turned and fled as he called after her.

"Wendy!?" Michael's faint voice caught her ear. She spun, still able to see the worried old man, when she spotted Michael running to where he last heard her call — the old man on the road. How had she lost his location? She grew disoriented by the torrent of voices and icy rain droplets crashing into her skin in a lethargic rush.

Pedestrians far beyond the old man scattered as a four-horse carriage barreled down the road from Hyde Park Corner. Driverless, the horses were spooked by a trio of dogs erupting at each other near the park entrance and, caught in clogged traffic on South Carriage Road, raced down the only avenue available — Serpentine Road. The driver hadn't been sitting on the seat properly and tumbled to the stone walk, leaving the horses to race—

Wendy shut out the information provided by the horses as they fled from the dogs and their violent barks. Michael darted onto the road next to the old man — both in the horses' path.

She realized, at that moment, that no one knew the horses were coming but her. Thunder overhead drowned out the sound of their hoofbeats and the faint, echoing screams of pedestrians leaping from its way. Terror fueled her mad dash toward the alarmed old man, who took notice of Michael standing next to him in his soaked sailor's outfit.

Beyond them, the dark ghost of the four horses appeared like a grim reaper bearing down on the two, neither of whom would see or move fast enough to avoid.

Still paces away, Wendy stopped, flung her hand and screamed, "STOOOOOPPP!!"

In her vision, the world turned red, the rain paused mid-fall, and bloodred lightning ripped across the sky, visible through the heavy clouds and torrential rain. Energy ripped through her nerves from her feet and fingers to her mind, which twisted inside her skull. If she could, she would have screamed from the agony burning the folds of her brain.

The rain fell once more, but the horses stopped in moments. Every eye — human and animal — turned and locked upon her, their pupils dilating, and the park fell still as Wendy sank to her knees.

More than flashes of the tropical island- Neverland, or Algueda — coursed through her mind. Ten thousand minds of men, women and children pierced her consciousness from just the Hyde Park area, then doubled outward; tripled … Flowing onward, mind after mind flared to life before her. Across nation and continent, her mind touched countless others.

To her greater shock, the wave of perception continued expanding, but instead of rising outward into space, it moved … sideways.

New worlds blossomed. A long, flat world appeared, covered in a variety of life that made Earth's cornucopia appear simple and uninspired. Humans, wizards, witches, elves, high elves, dwarves, half-men, lycans, vampires, yeti, high sentient sheep and dolphins, dragons, mermaids and elder creatures that had lived millions of years filled her mind's library of knowledge. Each presence pricked her until she felt as if untold tiny needles stabbed her eyes. She screamed and clutched her face.

People of magic and animals watched with listless obedience to her simple command, those without magic paused subconsciously at the arrival of her presence.

Echoes of other dimensions rebounded yet further, of an inside out world with the sun in the center, a ring hovering in space, a city of life beneath deep ocean waves, an endless sand sea, islands hovering in the sky connected by airborne creeks and rivers, a land of ice formations greater than Earth's grandest cities, a world of monstrous trees rising from endless ocean ...

To Wendy's horror, she felt their minds turn toward hers, many in a new sense of terror, and among them, a few with an old sense of fear and hatred.

All occurred in the bare moment of her scream, the same scream of "Stop," the same rip of her throat echoing the cry of her mind. Her knees hadn't even yet touched the ground when she felt the universe notice her, and in that moment, Wendy's mind seemed to explode.

Her knees crashed to the ground as her body arched and head fell back in her momentum forward, face turning skyward into the deluge of rain droplets falling with painful lethargy. The sky boiled in violent rainbow. Beauty gazed back. Something within shifted, like a bone moving back into place she never knew was out.

Seconds before everyone on the road regained their wits, Wendy slapped face down onto the fine gravel road and into darkness.

53

The Wolf

The girl's mind rang across the heavens like a Bunyan's hammer striking Lubar's Peak.

Phineas woke to the sound of the girl's mad scream and sob. Her mind scored his own. Creatures across Pangea and beyond paused with bated breath at the arrival of a new presence among them — a mind of such power as to alert all of nature. Though temporary, it stirred him from his stupor.

A being had awoken whose mind crashed across the known world, a being whose face burned into his mind.

He blinked away heavy sleep in a room boiling with smoke and haze. He shifted and tried raising a hand to his face, but fur brushed his skin, instead. He jumped in fear that a creature had crawled into his bed. His arms would not move as they should, locked only before him in an up-down area, as were his legs. Twisting his head and trunk, he got a look at the wolf-fur blanket covering him.

What the hell? he tried to speak. A tail's wag at the blanket's far end caught his eye. He willed the tail to wag, then again. *What. The. Hell.*

Twisting about again, he saw legs move and fur and body and *-oh my SELF!*

Phineas panicked and tried climbing from the bed. He fell to the floor and found a broken pot and herbs strewn across the carpet of straw and an incense stem long cold. A heavy weight around his neck drew him to raise his hand- paw. *NO!*

He touched the heavy metal collar and noted the chain that had linked him to the bed — now melted apart. He was a collared wolf? This couldn't be happening. He rocked to get his feet beneath him and pushed up on trembling legs.

I'm- no. I can't be. I can't be! he yelped and yowled and howled as the madness became real. *I'm sleeping! I'M SLEEPING! I'M SLEEPING! Oh Self! I'm sleeping! Please, please, please, please, Great Self. Don't let this be real. Don't let this be real. I'm drunk. I have to be drunk. Or on one of Timothy's new drugs. Please. This can't be real.*

After inspecting the tiny hut, he tried scratching his left leg but fell over. He pushed himself up and yelped again. His hips hit the bed. He turned and felt the low fire singe his tail. He yelped and spun before crashing again to the floor.

Great Self! Please help me! he cried as terror overtook him. *Where am I!?*

A faint voice caught his ears. He sat up, then stood facing the doorway.

"Is someone awake?" cooed the old voice of a woman beyond the door. "You woke early! That's okay."

Desperate, Phineas stamped his feet- paws. He yelped in fear.

"Besides, the men are coming for you." Her voice drew nearer. "It's time to get you ready for the reception!" She laughed and pushed the door open. She spotted the empty bed and locked onto him in shock.

Phineas barreled up the short steps into her. She screamed and threw her hands up in shock. Something struck Phineas and sent him flying against the doorjamb and spinning outward into a milky white fog of a broad swamp. He crashed into several, unforgiving cypress knees with a bark of pain.

"COME BACK HERE!" she screamed.

In pain from dislocated ribs, he managed to rise and bolt.

"COME BACK HERE!!"

He tripped over another cypress knee and crashed across the soil. Standing up, he found a thick black centipede crawling up his furry snout with long pincers and whiskers that pinched him. He yelped and flailed his head to knock it off when something else pinched his foot.

"COME BACK HERE!" the hag screamed as she ran along a narrow strip of ground snaking above the mist.

Something else bit Phineas in the rear and he bolted for the path. Just as he reached it, something took his feet out from under him and he crashed over the path into the milk-white mist on the far side. The white mist rippled away to reveal thousands of snapping beetles.

He scrambled out with a dozen clinging to his fur. Just before mounting the path, he saw the hag cast her hands out again. He ducked just in time.

A WITCH!! he yelped. He leapt upon the road and sprinted with all abandon, even as more beetles tried to sink their teeth through his thick gray fur.

A lightning bolt struck the path in front of him and he crashed to the ground in an awkward twist to leap away. He bolted across the mist for dozens of snakes to snap at his passing. Another lightning bolt flew wide and struck into the mist. The creatures hidden below exploded in a bloody spray.

Phineas opened his speed and slipped as the weight of the heavy iron collar dragged him to the ground again, just as another one of her attacks missed.

"Come back!" her voice was further away than he expected. The path wound through the mist and the woman's scream echoed when Phineas spotted a troop of thirty men dismounting on a flat at the end of a wider road winding through the swamp. Cries erupted and crossbolts flew as he circumvented them on the flat and onto the far road and opened up his speed.

"Stop him! Stop him!" the woman screamed to the soldiers. "That's the heir! Stop him!"

Men remounted and gave chase. When he noticed the mist off the road was thin and the dangers minimal, he turned hard and rounded the end of the road from the swamp side. As his brother, Gael, taught him, to go where men wouldn't expect him to be.

Ahead, the witch stumbled to her knees to gasp for breath at the foot of the captain. The man dismounted and offered his hand to help her up. She set her right hand into his gauntlet before he stamped his boot on her other hand and slammed his left gauntlet across her face. Pinned as she was without her hands, her head snapped to the side and sank limp as blood bubbled from her nose.

"Lythwick! Quickly!"

A short, robed man with a receding hairline over tanned pale skin rushed from his horse and set a collar around her neck. Soldiers bound her wrists behind her back as she moaned and coughed.

"Get her on the horse," the captain motioned.

Soldiers set her across and tied her to a horse.

Namotha stirred. "Wh- why are you here?"

The captain followed, gripped her hair and wrenched her head up. "When the men I left didn't bring me daily messages, I worried. You think I just left them to guard the entrance to your swamp? Do you have the slightest idea how professionals work?"

Though her right eye swelled, Namotha's left eye locked onto him. She hissed a guttural string of words. He waited. Nothing happened. "Wh- what did you do?"

"Red collar," he thumped the metal collar around her neck.

Namotha thrashed. "NO! NO, YOU CUNTS! NO! NO NO NO NO!!"

A returning cavalry soldier saluted. "Captain Antilles. The wolf is gone."

"No shit." Antilles leaned near her face drooling with blood and snot. "Did you transmogrify the heir of Alderland into a wolf?"

Namotha quivered.

"I'm not taking a single ounce of blame for you, witch. You were ordered to convert him into a pliable, submissive noble, not a selfdamn wolf. I'm sure Fellow Roschach will love to address you on this matter, personally."

Fear gripped her.

He released her head and mounted his horse. "Qelton, Wislow, set fire to the witch's hut. Don't come within twenty paces or you'll die."

The two soldiers dismounted and assembled their bows and fire arrows.

"I could do that," Lythwick shrugged.

"No," the captain said. "The woman's smart. She may have set traps for mages."

"Fine point," Lythwick gulped.

After the men jogged into the mist, a flame blossomed. They reappeared when an explosion rocked the swamp, sending a shockwave that crashed through trees as far as the eye could see. Phineas ducked as men cried out and horses reared in terror. Afraid, himself, he waited for all of them to scout once more through the swamp before gathering and retreating down the road.

He was the seventh son, heir to the throne of Alderland, and all he could think about was the framed face of a beautiful young pale girl with long, full brown hair. Her voice called him. The brilliant purple in her eyes sang to him. Though he knew not where she was, he would follow the sound of her soul. He would find the girl.

He would find Wendy.

54

Compliments of Roschach

I'm sure they'll be fine, chimed Tinker Belle.

Peter frowned. "I dunno. That Santi. Something about him doesn't seem right."

Tootles seems pretty comfortable out here. I wouldn't worry about it.

Overgrown by bushes, filled by washouts and interrupted by huge trees growing from the center of the path, Peter and Tinker Belle followed an ancient road weaving eastward across the north island. Noise ebbed and flowed around them as the breeze wound through canopies and thickets, carrying with it a thousand smells and sounds from other parts of the island.

Are you sure you know where you're going? I don't want to be out here wandering aimlessly.

"Something out here is ... getting closer," said Peter.

What do you mean? Tinker Belle turned.

"I'm not sure. I just ... I felt something arrive this morning. There are ..." he paused. "Something's drawing me this way. It's gotta be Father."

Peter, Tinker Belle chimed, *it's not your father. This isn't some silly story where you mystically know where someone is merely because you want to know where they are.*

"But I feel something!"

It doesn't mean it's William! Tinker Belle snapped. *I'm- Peter. Your father- he couldn't have survived without the mantle!*

"He's the pan. He can survive anything."

That's not how it works, Peter. The pan can be killed, just like anyone.

"But the pan heals!"

Yes, the pan can heal from things that would kill most other men, but you can't heal from a missing head or getting your gut ripped open. There are limits to the mantle's power. You, yourself died just a few days ago!

"What?"

When- when you sank. On the Unionist ship. You had to have died. That's why Santi appeared.

"I don't understand."

The mantle moved, Peter. I saw it on you myself. You had the mantle. But you sank into the waters out beyond the West Bay. You had to have drowned.

Peter huffed. "Whatever, Tink."

I'm not lying to you!

"It doesn't mean you're not wrong!" he cried. "Besides, I'm alive now."

I still don't know how! How are you still alive? Where did you come out from?

"I woke up, marooned on a rock out in the middle of nowhere. Out past the West Bay."

You just … woke up? On a rock?

"Well, there were mermaids."

Mermaids!? Those are just stories, Peter.

"Then explain the naked women with fish tails." Peter's quick turn forced her to stop.

I think you were struggling with death.

"Oh, c'mon, Tink," Peter continued. "Don't call me stupid."

I- I'm not!

"Neverland is full of magic!" he raised his hands. "Who knows what else is here? We've seen roads and stone buildings and … all sorts of things."

I'm still worried about Agent Bonduquoy.

"That lady with the hooked nose? The one with the ohnas?"

Yes. I know Neverland eats the unwary, but she is anything but. I'm worried she's still here.

"That's why we need Father."

Tinker Belle took a breath. *Humans.*

Peter gave her a look.

Tinker Belle fingered the bottom edge of her shorts. They fluttered as the fine thread loosened. *Great Self, not now.*

"What's wrong?" Peter asked.

My- my clothing wasn't meant for all this. It's falling apart.

"Yeah, mine isn't either," Peter fingered a hole in his shirt.

But- Peter, I'm a female. I can't go flying around exposed around all you humans. You- you don't handle it very well.

"I don't want to run around naked, either. What do you want?"

I just want some thread or something! Tinker Belle chimed. *Something to keep this together until we can get back to Eden or somewhere safe. And supplied.*

"That's it?" Peter asked.

That's it, what?

"Just thread?"

It's a stopgap.

Peter stopped and searched. Spotting a spider's web in a bush, he pinched and plucked out a long golden thread five times longer than Tinker Belle was tall and hung it over Tinker Belle's extended hands. "Here you go."

Wh- where did you- where did you just get this?? Tinker Belle stammered. She darted to the web and inspected it, even as the small spider retreated. *Peter!*

"C'mon!" he continued eastward.

She flew around and through the bush several times before catching him up. *Where did THIS come from! Is this one of your great uncle's magic tricks?*

"Magic tricks? I never figured those out."

Then where did THIS come from!?

Peter glanced at the thread and shrugged. "You said you needed a thread, so I got you one."

But- but how!?

Peter shrugged.

Tinker Belle followed Peter through the tree-dappled morning light northward along a dry creek bed. *Why this way?*

"Can't you feel it?" Peter paused.

Feel what?

Peter shook his head and pointed. "There's something that way."

Like what?

"I thought you were the haraven."

I- I am!

"Then why can't you feel that!?"

Tinker Belle grimaced, then looked where he pointed.

"Listen, you're probably worrying about a whole bunch, like Mom, but right now, be here."

Tinker Belle straightened and tried dismissing the ten million thoughts flooding her mind.

"I remember Aunt Bri once telling me the moment was full of bounty. I always thought that was stupid. Bounty was stuff pirates went after, right? But ever since I got here?" Peter looked about at Neverland. "I kinda see what she meant."

Tinker Belle paused. She always considered Brianne Baley a cold woman, and untrustworthy as she defended the Unionist advances in parliament. But Peter didn't remember any of that — just Brianne's simple words in probably one of their rare familial interactions.

"C'mon, Tink." Peter waved her on as he headed up the broad dry creek bed. She perched upon his shoulder and tried to tamp her pride. She was 230 years old; she shouldn't need life advice from a ten-year-old boy.

But that's what she got.

As she quieted herself, she realized she did feel something northward. How had he sensed something she ought to have, herself? As they wound up the creek bed, alarm welled within, as did shame. They were approaching ohnas. How had she missed that!?

Peter, those are ohnas.

"What?"

What you feel? Those are ohnas! I feel so stupid. Why didn't I sense that before! Of course, they have the ohnas!

"Really?" Peter paused. "Is that what they are? That means ... that means we're heading towards the Unionists."

Yes, which means we should go back and get the boys.

"But my dad is that way, too."

Holy self, Peter, no he's not! He's dead!

"He's not dead!" Peter rounded on her as tears welled. He pointed up the creek bed. "He's not! He can't be! That's- that's my- my father is not dead."

Tinker Bell shrank. *I'm sorry, Peter, but he couldn't have survived! If he had, he would have come back to us! Wouldn't he?*

"No." Peter wiped his tears and stormed off. "He's here! I *have* to find him!"

Selfdamnit, Peter! she bolted to him and tugged on his shirt. *I can't stop you, but at least, come in from the forest. This creek bed is exposed.*

Peter stopped and took long, heavy breaths to calm himself and swallow the sob in his throat. He wiped his face again and nodded. "You're right, Tink." He climbed up the side of the creek bed into the woods and continued north as noon crested the sky.

Tinker Belle latched onto his shoulder and gripped his hair as he stalked through the bush. Trees appeared in the creek bed and soon carpeted it as much as the gentle inclines on either side. Faint voices wafted through the trees and he spotted people standing in the path of a contingent of sailors and mages marching down the center of the creek bed from the northern ridge. A tall uniformed man with a tight blonde braid and a small armor-clad woman led the group through the trees alongside the woman with the hooked nose — Athyka — toward a hulking figure clad in studded leather armor.

Peter climbed the top of a rocky outcrop looming over the group. At its top, he peeked through the foliage to listen in.

"You survived," said the hulking figure facing the group. "And brought Aaron and Inrav with you! A party."

"Gregory..." Athyka motioned to the man. "Bring him out."

Gregory saluted her and approached Peter. He tensed until the man disappeared into the rockface below. Peter dared not lean out and expose his position.

Moments later, Gregory reappeared from out the cave carrying a figure by elbows bound behind his back. He dropped him face down before the agents.

"Well, well, well ..." Devkoron smiled and knelt. He gripped the figure and rolled him onto his side. "William 'scaley.'"

"Father," Peter breathed. His fist tightened around the hilt of his sword. Tinker Bell gaped.

Gagged, bloody and clad only in his trousers, William turned a swollen purpled face up at Devkoron.

"Ungag him," Devkoron motioned. Gregory untied the gag from the rear and pulled it out. William's head sank to the carpet of leaves as he tried to work out his arid mouth.

Peter struggled not to draw his sword and race in, but Tinker Belle tapped his neck and shook her head. Instead, he retreated from the hill and snuck around to the creek bed from the south. Tinker Belle tried to get his attention to retreat, but chiming would only draw attention in these quiet woods.

"Trying your- hand at insults, Aaron?" William coughed.

Devkoron's false smile disappeared. "I suppose I'm just catching up with everyone else."

"Being the last to leap from a cliff is no wiser than the first man to do it."

Estemil scowled. "I'm surprised you didn't kill him, already."

Gregory shrugged. "I wanted to. Was better to try and get information."

"Get anything?" Devkoron asked.

Already in Gregory's head, Athyka answered through him. "Nothing of real value. Without the mantle, ol' Billy here is nothing but a lowly mage. Not even a good one, at that."

Aaron smirked at William's blood-filled eyes, swollen purple bruising and melted skin down the right side of his face. "You did a number on him. Think his bitch will be weak enough to let us through the wall once we bring him up there?"

"Of course," Gregory grinned.

"She and the boy have been holed up there since we got here," said Athyka.

"Why did William give her the mantle?" Estemil asked.

"Best we can figure, he thought he could protect the mantle by passing it," said Athyka. "Then he could move freely to try and attack us without being expected."

"Except for the sky lighting up from across the universe," Estemil said.

"You saw that?" Gregory asked.

"The entire continent saw it," Estemil said.

"No kidding?" Gregory harrumphed.

Aaron stood. "We take an hour's rest. Have your men get something to eat. Then we make for the Tree. The agents and I will confer in the cave."

"What do you want to do with the pan?" Linroy cocked his head to look down at William's pathetic figure.

"He's not going anywhere," Aaron said as Athyka led him into the cave.

The men made quick bivouac just north of the meet, leaving William alone on the leaves. Though exhausted, he scooted as best he could until he leaned against a tree instead of lying face down. The first time outside in days, he gazed upward into the washing trees while struggling to breathe. Reeking of piss and shit, and gaunt from few meals, he wondered why he hadn't yet passed out. "At least they don't have you yet," he muttered, thinking of his son.

Drawing his silver dagger, Peter snuck from tree to tree despite Tinker Belle's desperate tugs on his hair. Along for the ride, she could do nothing but hold on. The boy waited behind a large tree while the sailors settled down for their quick meal before he low crawled through the bushes behind his father.

William flinched at the crunch of leaves and tried to look to the right. His head wouldn't turn and he tried wiggling away from the tree when Peter gripped his bicep and leaned over his shoulder.

"Father!" Peter breathed into his ear.

William twisted himself to get a look at Peter with his good left eye. "N- no! Peter! No!"

"I'm here to get you out!" Peter inhaled. "I can cut your ropes!" He pulled his knife and cut at the thick ropes binding William's elbows.

"Wh- no," William growled. "Get out of here. Go! Go now!"

"I can't leave you, Father!" Peter panted, desperate to free him from his bonds. "I'll get you out. Then we'll find Mom!"

"Get away from me!" William quivered. "Run! Go!"

"But Father!" Peter's head wrenched in Devkoron's fingers.

"Go- PETER!"

Devkoron cast Peter across his father's feet just as the ropes binding William's elbows popped free. William struggled to lift his weak arms to protect himself, but Aaron knocked them away, snatched William by his mane of brown hair and pulled a dagger from his belt. "Compliments of Elwin Roschach."

Tangled with William's bloody toeless feet, Peter spun just as Aaron swung down and drove his stiletto into William's heart.

"NOO!" Peter screamed. The boy locked up as William's good eye fluttered and chest sank. "NO NO NO NO NO NO!!" He scrambled onto his slumping father.

Devkoron snatched the boy by the throat.

"You were wrong, Athyka." Devkoron lifted the boy by his neck.

"He gave it to Peter." He slammed him to the ground, knocking him unconscious.

PETER! Tinker Belle leapt into the air and raised glowing hands when her wings twisted and bolts of energy misfired into empty trees.

Devkoron's quick hand had snatched the ohna avia — a steel feather — in a sheath under his arm and worked to take control of the pixie just as she tried to attack. As the ohna's influence threatened to overcome her, Tinker Belle ripped herself away from its control and raced into the forest.

"She escaped the ohna!" Estemil grabbed her ram's horn and moved to chase. "How did she do that!?"

"Wait..." Aaron raised his free hand to forestall her while still gripping Peter's throat. "We now have the pan. She'll come to us. Get the ropes and bind him like you did his father." He glanced at the trees. "And get the men. We're moving out. Right now."

55

Dragon's Fangs

Twin, angled spires of rock speared a mile into the sky. The two long fangs hovered over a craterous, three-mile-wide sink of terrain encircled by twisted formations of rock. At the base of the angled twin spires, a thousand-foot-wide chasm hummed an endless wauphing belch of boiling heat from the Uttogean bowels below. The grated sound echoed for hundreds of miles outward by the amplifying bell shape of the angled crater.

Horticul Astira's head popped above a small rock on the northwestern edge to the sink. Beneath a bound mane of sun-licked brown hair, she scanned the wrinkled floor of the depression for dragons. She had never before seen a dragon, but her elders raised her with countless stories of the ravaging beasts. She was sure it would be easy to find one. She half expected one dragon at a time might fit down the cave's gullet.

Her partial expectation was not enough for a complete assurance that they weren't also tiny and hiding in the countless nooks and gullies throughout the crater.

Desperate to get inside and find the rimshift, Horticul Astira paused to pray to the Great Self before taking to the air and zipping through the rippled rock shoulders of the spire base down into the cave mouth. She paused one last look at the gray, dust-drenched skies and the brilliant sunlight bleeding through the haze before winding her way down the throat to hell.

She paused periodically to listen and sense the magics, afraid she might be followed or that an ambush may lay in wait. A thunderous hum vibrated the air and spurred a headache. She followed the cave's massive throat in a leftward turn a half mile from its opening. The chasm descended before it curved to the right, leveled off and stopped in a massive hole in the floor of the chamber.

Horticul Astira paused at the top of the lip. Little sunlight reached this far down while the heat made her question if the air was good. She struggled not to cough the putrid sulphur poisoning every breath. From the edge, she peered down an endless hole at faint glowing orange cracks in the base of some great chamber, below.

Great Self, she muttered. Was she so committed to prove herself to Queen Mab as to dive down this fiery dragon's gullet? Ever since she was old enough to understand what a haraven was, she wanted to be out there working alongside the pan, seeing the world and doing something interesting. Haraven never became elders — they usually died soon after passing the bond of Aikina on to their successor — but what lives they got to live! Astira wanted to see beyond their borders. She wanted to be someone of importance. Usually the queen or elderate selected the haraven, but in an unusual turn of events, Aurora Vara insisted on Tinker Belle, a fairy barely out of her feather, as the pan's aide de camp. No one could remember the aurora involving themselves in such affairs, before, but aurorae carried weight even royalty sometimes could not contest.

Aurorae husbanded the beds where fairies germinated and blossomed from buds of various flowers. They helped pixies' proto forms in the nether transition to the lower realm to live in the physical. Because their minds drifted between the nether and physical realms, aurorae offered insight to flock leadership on the flow of events and advice in times of uncertainty.

Vara involved herself in a low realm decision as none had, before, and Astira ached to know why. She didn't know if Aurora Vara had stepped where she did not belong, but Horticul Astira would press forward to recall Tinker Belle, per the orders of Queen Mab, and free such entanglements from their flock. Astira could be satisfied with that.

She hiked her pack, stepped off the edge and tilted her wings to angle her fall. Without fluttering them, she made no chime. Swells of broiling air slowed her progress to near an agonizing standstill. She tucked her wings into a dive, cutting through the rising heat.

The great chamber came too soon and she threw her wings out in a faint ring and glided down the chamber wall. She fluttered at the last moment to slow down and threw herself behind a large rock. She peeked over it and struggled to breathe at all. Heat burned her open eyes and singed her skin. Open fissures of lava across the chamber floor broiled the air as an oven. Even the rock upon which she laid burned her skin.

The chamber extended away from the base of the great vertical maw over a winding creek of lava. She covered her mouth with her elbow and wanted nothing more than to return to the relative cool of the hot desert above. She took a breath and then lifted into the air. The pixie flew low over the right, angled bottom of the cave wall as she approached its far end where several low horizontal caves met the high walled rear of the large vertical chamber.

Veins of lava drooled down the rear chamber wall and pooled at the bottom around a small island and snaked across the chamber floor. Astira braved sniffing the air and caught a bare whiff of the rimsportal but yelped when the fiery air singed her nostrils. She gathered her courage, once more, and flew into the open. She skirted the small lake of lava and followed her nose through one of the horizontal maws. Heat built as she continued down the broad cave until even her fluttering wings burned with heat.

As Astira struggled to breathe, she glided along the chamber wall rock and cried as it burned her hands and feet. The smell of the rimshift grew stronger, but she could not muster herself to continue. Heat overcame her and tears muddled her vision. Desperate to flee, she turned from the wall and found a great yellow eye watching her from feet away.

But for her quivering hands and wings, Horticul Astira froze in terror

My my my … a little pixie in the throat of a dragon … a feminine voice filled the pixie's mind.

Horticul Astira quivered in terror.

You have made it a very long way where pixies do not belong. What brings one such as you down here?

Horticul Astira continued to quiver against the heat as she sought escape.

You will never make it out of here like that, little bite.

Horticul Astira squeaked.

Step onto my snout.

Wh- why!? Horticul Astira managed.

My scales are cooler than these cozy rocks.

The stone under her feet continued burning her even as she failed to flutter her wings to flight.

The dragaina reached her long taloned paw with great care to pluck the pixie and set her upon her beak-like snout. To Horticul Astira's surprise, the dragaina's scales were quite cooler than the rocks despite the putrid, broiling atmosphere.

Wh- wh-y?

The dragon snaked deeper into the cave. *Great curiosity, I admit.*

Horticul Astira struggled to breathe.

I daresay, you are looking for the rimshift, aren't you?

Horticul Astira winced.

I thought as much, the dragon entered a vast low-ceilinged chamber forested by columns of rock. *I sensed you right around the cave mouth.*

Horticul Astira moaned.

What drives such a tiny drop of starlight to brave the dark depths of the Dragon's Fangs for the rimshift to the ancient land?

Ancient what?

The ancient land… The dragon snaked her way amidst the columns and wound from the great chamber through a hole into yet another broad room descending deeper. *The place where all life began in this realm.*

Algueda is the- place where all life began?

The dragaina chortled. *So young, so ignorant.*

Pixiekind are two million years old! Horticul Astira gasped.

My kind are first among the high sentients, the dragaina mused, *from the second eon of creation. We have very long memories, tiny light.*

Horticul Astira choked as her lungs rejected the air.

I would not have such a brave little spark die, the dragon snaked deeper into a narrow rip in the cave wall. Horticul Astira's body wracked with heat. *Any other situation, I would snap you up. But I admire your courage. Hold on, pixie. We're at the rimshift.*

Wh- who are you? Horticul Astira managed.

I am Ssakthani, den mother, she smiled. *I watched Umphaedra Dominar himself crack from his egg ninety thousand years ago. But today, I would see you survive. Here we are.*

No light reached this tiny oven, but Ssakthani blew a small spout of fire to reveal a narrow vertical opening too small for the dragon to continue. *You must fly through yourself.*

I- I can't, Horticul Astira chimed.

You can, but you must press past your pain. You don't have much time before your wings curl. Go!

Horticul Astira felt she had gone mad, but she fluttered her wings and forced herself into the air. She made for the hole in the wall and paused long enough to look back. *Thank you.*

Ssakthani chortled again. Unable to wait any longer, Horticul Astira pressed through the hole at the end of the chamber into the distorted reality of the rimshift and into the smell of something ancient and full of more magic than even her homeland.

56

Reborn

When Tootles first opened his right eye, he feared he had gone blind. His slow breaths felt brittle.

Water lapped at the edge of his nose in a world of fuzzy black. He wiggled his fingers to find one hand wedged beneath him and the other out to the side.

Closing and opening his fingers, he set his palm against wet ground and pushed himself upward, pausing to feel his other hand — the one under him — flop free, as if it had been broken.

In a mild panic, he rolled onto his back. His legs shifted into his hips, as if pulled into place after being out of socket. Lying on his back, he reached over to feel his right hand with his left and verified all digits in their places. Numb fingers didn't respond to his desire. Hissing, he flicked the limp hand to wake it, as he experienced whenever he slept on an appendage too long.

His hackles rose when he kept flapping and flapping in hopes of feeling something when a faint tingle worked upward from his wrist, spread through his palm and burned into his fingers. Tootles exhaled with relief.

A faint yellow hole hovered high above him, though his poor eyesight gave him nothing else to latch upon.

Where was he? Where was Santi? What had happened?

He rose from the ground and took an unsteady step, but he felt better by the moment. Moist air wafted from his left and buffered the putrid smell of scat and death nearby. Tootles frowned. Fear welled of what may have died near him, and he approached the cool, moist air into a narrow spiral stairwell.

Where was he?

He climbed its endless left turn until he reached a horizontal hole leading onto the broad floor beneath a high ceiling of a large, circular room. The faint glow of a window up a small hill of stones drew his attention across the dusty floor. Looking to the chasm, he wondered if he might have fallen.

"Oh, Santi," Tootles said. "Must have been an accident. I hope he isn't worried."

Dark, dried smears painted the stone floor between the trapdoor and the hill of stones climbing to the window. What Tootles first thought may have been blood boasted too much green. Questions mounted in Tootles's mind as he plucked his sword from the floor, skirted the mess and climbed the hill to the window.

Once outside, the distant sunset bathed him in brilliant orange warmth. Tootles gasped. Still standing on the scree, he extended his arms out to each side and soaked in its rapturous life. A gentle smile tugged at his open mouth while he soaked up the light. Sunset painted the low ceiling of herds of ocean-going clouds in a panoply of purples, oranges, yellows and blues.

"Saaanntiii!" Tootles cried. "Shiiiifuuuu!?" He crossed the courtyard to the western lip. The site offered an unprecedented view of the sparkling seas west of the south island. "Saaanntiii!! Shiiffuuu!!"

Before he started his descent down the steep hill, he turned back to the tower. Why had they come here? He had no sense that a boy nested here. Had they gotten a boy and left? Santi was a good friend, so Tootles couldn't imagine Santi leaving without him.

Tootles descended the barren ridge into the forests in a mix of walking and careful sliding. As he approached the first tree, he reached out to steady himself.

He gasped as faces rushed before his mind — Peter was now bound on a beach north of the Tree. He could see no others, but he could sense them. Only Peter was identified in his thoughts.

Tootles paused — a great company of people had arrived on the south island and had made their way up the small cliffs into the saddle between the snowcap and the volcano. Though he could not see faces or hear their words, he could tell by their varying heights as they walked through bushes or as they touched trees that many were children. Children meant families. Families meant settlers.

He withdrew his hand from the tree and looked to both. He was interconnected with this place in a way even Peter was not. Like the spade vines at the Tree.

Tootles wondered if he was becoming like the vines, interconnected as they were to Neverland? He would have to face that another time.

Peter was in the most trouble right now. Though he could not identify Santi or Shifu, he had felt a pair of beings walking close together through the bush and a third out by himself. He didn't know who the third was, but the pair had to be his friends, which meant they were safe.

Along with Peter, they were his tribe now. He could not well remember his previous tribe, but he was excited about the new ones. They could become warriors, together. They would have to find women one day, but not yet.

Tootles loosed his control and collapsed to the steep hillside by the tree. Doing that had taken his energy, but alarm renewed him. Someone was doing something to Peter with magic. He could feel it by how the island reacted to changes in Peter. Even if Santi and Shifu were nearby, the three boys combined wouldn't be enough to go to battle against so many shamans and soldiers. Tootles could tell they carried great powers with them, powers he didn't understand. He needed a tribe of warriors to fight, and he needed them right now.

He would go to the settlers.

Tootles turned around and ascended the ridge, passed the Black Tower on the left, up to the crest and gazed over the south island. With no time to waste, he cut across the grassland, unable to carry a jog more than a minute. Though he was a fine runner before Neverland, he had changed here. Where before he sprinted, now he plodded. The rising moon implored him to hurry. His vision of Peter surrounded by powerful shamans reminded him of his own tribe, their cries to the gods for Rome's expulsion from their lands and the children they sacrificed to appease the spirits to do their bidding.

Tootles braved the high grasses carpeting the long rolling plains with his sword in his hand, but animals passed him by with little more than a curious look. Predators lifted their heads to watch him but otherwise ignored him.

Two hours passed until he reached the high ridge separating the grassland and the desert. He climbed the ridge line and marched southward. Desperation grew to reach the tribe. Though he didn't know why, he kept glancing at the sky, as if to make sure it was still clear. The island around him felt tight and hesitant, muting the typical evening cacophony with a rising fear.

Reaching the southern end of the ridge found a thick forest on a broad plateau between the two mountains. Touching a tree, he could not sense where the tribe had camped. He realized the images he saw did not show a specific location, and he did not have the fine control to determine so without it. Only Peter stood out in his mind.

Tears threatened Tootles as he marched into the dark wood. The island knew Peter was in grave danger. Something was being taken from the pan.

"Oh, Wodan..." He stopped in the middle of the path. "Wodan, hear me. I am lost and need to find help. I do not know where to go. I must find help to rescue Peter. I must help the pan. I must save my friends. Please. Show me the way!"

Ancient trees washed in a gentle wind above him, bushes fluttered with nocturnal creatures going about their business and squeaks of bats echoed through the air when a faint glimmer of soft light caught his eye. He squinted when another glimmer of light caught his eye to the right. He turned to find, again, nothing there.

Then, ahead, a faint light passed through distant trees. Tootles struggled to scan the forest as he crossed root-braided soil with hands raised to the close-knit bush. He tried to reach the moving light. For a brief moment, he caught a blurry glimpse of a stately woman with crimson hair. Clad in a blue dress flowing around luminous pale skin, she walked among the trees.

"The fair lady!" He followed glimpses of her southward until a new, stationary light appeared through the trees.

Sheathing his sword, he marched through the forest when silhouettes of men blocked his path.

"Name yourself!" cried a man.

Alarmed, Tootles straightened with a sudden hope. Were they from

Gaul that he should understand them so clearly?

Tootles had begun to understand Santi and Shifu. The magic here allowed them to speak. They would not be from his homeland.

"I am Tootles," he said. "I have come seeking your help."

"Bring him!" one said. They surrounded and motioned him into the open.

A tribe stood around a fire in a cliff-backed flat overlooking the southern lagoon. A perfect spot to hide from the entire island, the camp tucked into a broad curve of rock behind the snowcap and the tall cliffs. These people were clever.

A broad-chested man stood on the opposite side of the fire with a thick braid of midnight hair bound behind his head, but it was the girl near Tootles's age that caught his attention. In her eyes, he saw an understanding of events similar to his own.

As he stepped into the firelight, the tribe gasped at the sight of him and the side of his head.

Tootles hesitated. Did they fear him? He raised his hands. "I'm not here to harm you."

The tall brave who had not retreated cleared his throat and raised his right hand. "I am Great Cougar. Name yourself and your presence here."

"I am Tootles, of the tribe of pan," Tootles said. "I have come seeking your help."

"How did you find us?" Great Cougar asked.

"I followed the fair lady."

The tribe frowned, but the girl straightened.

"What kind of help do you seek?" Great Cougar asked as men around him shifted their weight.

"The chief of this island is in grave danger," said Tootles. "He has been taken by enemies who come from far away by great boats. They use dangerous magic and threaten the pan and this island."

"The ... one?" Great Cougar attempted to translate the word. "The 'all?'"

"He is called 'pan,'" Tootles said. "I don't understand it in full, either. But I must rescue him, and I'm asking your help."

"I am Red Badger!" cried a man next to Great Cougar. "You would have us take someone? To wage war? We are a people of peace!"

"There will be no peace without the life of the pan," Tootles said. "Only death."

"We do not fight in wars of men," growled Red Badger.

"This pan is elder of this island?" Great Cougar continued. "Does he live here?"

"Yes," Tootles said. "He is master of this place."

The tribe cried questions for someone called Rain Singer. An old woman next to Great Cougar raised her hand but failed to calm them. Great Cougar pondered as he watched Tootles.

"Go away!" Red Badger cried among rising questions. "Take your war with you!"

When the girl spoke to Great Cougar, he bent his ear, then blinked in surprise. She glanced at Tootles.

"Silence!" Great Cougar raised his hand. The tribe fell quiet. "Speak, Tiger Lily."

Tiger Lily cleared her throat. "This pan is of my visions." Several gasped. "He is the little white bird I have seen. The little white bird with the small yellow one. I think we should help."

"Surely not!" Red Badger glowered at Great Cougar and Tiger Lily before pleading with Rain Singer. "We cannot participate in war! This is the identity of our people! Since when do we surrender our path to the visions of a little girl!?"

"Since you all first started following me." Rain Singer's quiet words silenced them all. She raised her attention to a surprised Tootles. "I was younger than Tiger Lily when I saw this island calling us to its shores. My visions led us across the great plains, through the trackless forests, south to the sandy flats and across the warm topaz ocean. If my visions led us so true to here, then trust the visions of my granddaughter, for she speaks them true as she sees."

"We followed them to find a place of peace!" said Red Badger. "Not to find a place to give up our way! We follow the spirits in their nonviolence! We follow the spirits!"

Tootles wondered — This tribe did not kill people?

A man outside the circle cried an alarm as a point of light appeared in the forest behind Tootles. Before the boy could turn, the tribe flinched in terror as the glowing speck raced for the boy and stopped next to him in a trail of sparks.

TOOTLES! chimed Tinker Belle just as the entire tribe cried out in shock. The host staggered away from the fire and more than one dropped to their knees in fear or awe. Murmurs of "spirit" erupted among them.

Terror filled the host, who all backed away but for Tiger Lily, whose eyes widened in wonder.

"Wait!" Tootles threw up his hands. "She's a friend!"

"The little yellow bird, father," Tiger Lily breathed. "That's the little yellow bird!"

Tinker Belle frowned at her but spoke to Tootles. *They've taken Peter.*

"I saw. Who took him?"

One of the enemies that chased us here from the outer oceans. How did you know?

"I'll explain later."

And who are all these people!? Tinker Belle demanded. *And what happened to your face!?*

"My face? What's wrong with my face?" Tootles asked.

Tinker Belle hesitated.

Tootles's face tightened. He reached up and touched the upper left of his face, but it only felt slightly rougher, like light scabbing. "I fell down into a hole, I think. Might just be an injury. I'm- I'm sure it will heal."

Tinker Belle frowned at it.

He motioned to the tribe. "They have come from a nearby land across warm waters. I've come to ask for their help."

Nearby land? Warm waters? Neverland is an outer rim alterbridge. The water beyond here is ice cold!

"They came across warm bright blue waters. Does that sound like the ocean from Pangea?"

Great Self … Tinker Belle said. *They're from Earth. No wonder I couldn't sense them. They're bloody vacants.*

Tootles faced the tribe. "They are a good people. They come for peace and hope to build a home here. They did not come to bring war. They do not want to kill anyone."

Fear drained from them as he described them when a faint light flashed the sky, followed by a loud concussive pop.

"Who is that?" Rain Singer asked.

"This is the pan's fairy," said Tootles.

"Forest spirit!?" cries of shock and fear cut the air from among the tribe.

"The spirits live here in the open," moaned one of the women.

"It's okay!" Tootles yelled. "She is good! She comes on behalf of the pan!"

The tribe appeared ready to flee in fright but for the tall brave, the old woman and the intense little girl.

The gentle breeze shifted directions and picked up speed.

Oh no, Tinker Belle spun to the sky. Lazy herds of moonlit clouds expanded in seconds to form an icy blizzard that crashed over them and doused the fire. Screams of terror filled the darkness.

Tootles marched up to Great Cougar and bellowed through the storm, "Something just happened to the pan! If we don't rescue Peter, THIS is all you will face while you're here!"

Great Cougar lowered his arm and looked from the women to the fairy. "How does the spirit connect to this Peter?"

I'm his haraven! Tinker Belle clung to Tootles's shoulder as the wind ripped at her.

"You are ... flockless?" Great Cougar leaned in, struggling to hear and translate.

It means I'm bound to Peter! Tinker Belle screamed against the chaos.

"She is bound to him!" Tootles yelled over the wind.

Great Cougar straightened. For the first time, his stoic face slacked in surprise. "He is the chief in their tribe?? The forest spirit answers to *him*!?"

Tootles nodded.

Rain Singer huddled with Tiger Lily while the rest of the tribe braced against the sudden frigid wind.

Great Cougar leaned in. "We will follow the spirit. We will help with this pan. But we cannot promise to commit war. It is not our way!"

"Whatever," Tootles roared over the storm. "But bring your spears. We gotta go now!!"

Great Cougar gathered the men. Their faces contorted with a mix of fear and disbelief as he passed orders. When Rain Singer appeared to ask him something, he pressed until she nodded. After a moment, Tiger Lily turned from the group and approached them.

"The fair lady!?" she cried over the wind. "A brown woman with white hair? Reflective eyes!?"

"NO!" Tootles yelled over it. "A woman of fair skin and red hair!"

The two watched each other as Tinker Belle clung to the nape of Tootles's hair and tucked her wings against the torrent.

Tiger Lily leaned close to Tootles while Tinker Belle's faint light gleamed in her eyes. "You are why we have come to this island."

"What?" Tootles leaned in.

"I will tell you later!" Tiger Lily cried. "Where are we going!?"

Tootles glanced at the island and then at the men preparing to move. "NORTH!!"

57

Finding the Sixth

The broad, coastal metropolis of Rochsmora hugged the mouth of the River Demos on the eastern shore of the Sea of Para. At the mouth, a long, fat island divided the river flowing into the sea from its eastern curve. A high, twisting tower climbed above the western end of the island whose apex glowed with a mirror-lined lantern room.

The lighthouse beckoned traders and warned pirates wandering the sea's three-thousand-mile length. Eight hundred miles away along the western shore, stretched a third of Pangea's highest mountain range, the Zulta'mans, and Lubar's Peak, Pangea's highest point. On the seaward side of the four-hundred-foot-high lighthouse, a broad series of buildings, courtyards and bazaars descended from the lighthouse base upon its high bedrock to the edge of a small island surrounded by a bifurcated river. In a small arcade peppered with prefects, royals and wealthy traders, a single dais stood under midafternoon sun. A ball of glowing bluish light faded and died in a gentle pop, revealing three spinning rings that came to a quick stop as concentric circles over the dais, bisected by a narrow walkway aimed from the lighthouse to the sea.

"Standby to receive," declared one of the attendants from a small lectern facing away from the rimsportal. The rings spun, again, to form a ball of bluish warbling light. In gentle flares, a succession of eight men appeared from the portal along the walkway and down the two steps to awaiting prefects and twenty guards backing them.

"Welcome, my lords, to Huada La Ansania, heart of Rochsmora," a prefect offered a perfunctory smile and a polite, if faint, bow. "If my graces would be so kind as to declare themselves, origins and business in Rochsmora."

"I am First of Seven, Prince General Edmon of Alderland." Edmon raised the signet on his right middle finger for their inspection. "This is my brother, Third of Seven, Negrin of Alderland. These are our guard. We come on family business."

The scribe next to the prefect transcribed in shorthand.

"Honor and welcome to the sons of Alder." The prefect and the scribbling scribe bowed as one and straightened. "Most high travelers, the Monastery of Reason and the metropolis of Rochsmora welcomes to you to our streets and walls. No fighting is permitted outside establishments approved by the crown. All financial disputes may be brought here to the monastery for arbitration. Nobility and their guard may maintain unbound weapons in city limits, but armed attendants and servants are forbidden. Slaves are not allowed within Rochsmora save as personal guard. No man within the city may be enslaved, though all fugits found as owned by duchy and higher may be reclaimed by soliciting at city hall with the appropriate patents of ownership. Anyone caught fighting, stealing or enslaving within ten miles of the outer city boundaries are subject to ruling and possible death by the Judges of Reason. Are there any questions?"

"No," Edmon said.

"Then, again, most high travelers, on behalf of the Judges of Reason and her Majesty Queen Senmara of Light, welcome to Huada La Ansania and the bounties of Rochsmora." He offered a slight bow and waited for them to continue their way.

Edmon led the group away from the prefect through the dotting groups of other travelers and their curious looks. They moved north of the lighthouse, took the ferry across the river, rented mounts and rode into the crowded north city.

Pedestrians and riders in early revel of the night's coming hedonism swirled around them. Negrin cried over the music and noise of jubilant locals, "How far is he?"

"That, I'm not sure." Edmon turned his horse to circumvent an unmanned cart left in the middle of a road packed with people half painted, half clothed or half of neither. "He's told me of a few favorite places here, but where he is right now? This is the worst day to search for anyone in this damn city."

"Except for her majesty, of course," Negrin mused as he spotted a lovely pair of breasts of a woman leaning out of a nearby window. Her grin followed him through the throng.

Edmon looked at Negrin. "You know of the queen's offering?"

"Read about it in a book," Negrin admitted.

Edmon shook his head.

Tradesmen shouted out special festivale wares of paint, sparkle dust, delicacies and sweets, savory eats, and wearable edibles for the hedonists. Aromas of barbecued meats, freshly cut wood and horse dung wafted through the warm air cut by gentle ocean breezes. Ornate masks hid faces on some citizens while ornate belts and jewelry barely hid the intimate on others. Negrin's eyes near popped from his head as he tried not to gape, despite the encouragement of men and women leaning and singing from windows.

Edmon ignored them but for those who stumbled close or paid him too much attention. He disliked crowds he couldn't command.

"Did you know, on a clear day, you can see Lubar's Peak from the rimsportal here?" Negrin cried over the din.

Edmon glanced back. "That's eight hundred miles away."

"But Lubar's Peak is sixteen miles high! On the rare clear days, you can see it," Negrin said. "Also, the monastery has been besieged seventeen times. But it's never been taken in battle!"

Edmon scanned rooftops and empty windows. Three before and three behind, the royal guard struggled not to treat the chaos around them as hostile. People stumbled into their horses or across their path. Many ignored the riders until forced aside. Without sufficient cause, drawing weapons would only cause a ruckus that would end in favor of the locals.

"The Produnari are the first to actually buy the island," Negrin said. The group wound into one of the eight great courtyards of the north city.

"I can't hear you!" Edmon shouted.

"I said-" Negrin raised his voice until Edmon lifted a hand to forestall him. Negrin reclined in his saddle. The train steered clear of the dancing groups and the performers blowing fire, juggling or acrobatics. People sat upon, lounged in and swam through the large fountains with laughter and play. Some drank, others danced while a few tucked into small corners for intimate encounters.

"Don't drink the water!" Edmon called over his shoulder.

Negrin frowned at the fountains.

A mile later, Edmon drew rein before a large marble inn built in a rich quarter. One of the guards dismounted and entered. A few minutes later, he emerged with lipstick on his face and a uniform smeared in sparkle dust. He shook his head and mounted to the chuckles of the others. They repeated the search over the next two hours, weaving from inn to pub to dive. At the eastern end of the city, Edmon dismounted, himself, to perform the search. Thinner crowds out here reveled as loud as those deeper into the city.

Edmon's dark countenance alone sobered well-wishers and sent loiterers from his path as he approached the stairs to a large, ornate wooden inn. Its front door burst open and a thick man soared out backwards. Edmon stepped aside as the figure crossed the space over the stairs before smashing unconscious across the street's rocky mudpack.

The ruckus from within filled with laughter and cheers as a stocky, greasy-haired young man stepped in the doorway with blood on his fists and beer down his shirt. "Listen, dipshit-" He stopped, took in his brothers, and straightened.

Edmon his regarded brother in the doorway. "Gael."

Gael brushed his hands, looked at each of them and turned inside under a broad swinging sign above the door naming the inn called THE GAMBLER'S HEEL.

Edmon motioned the others in with his head before following Gael inside. Negrin and all but two of the guard dismounted, handed off their mounts and followed him into the inn's raucous main room. Men clapped and cheered as Gael returned to his table in the center of the room. An upper floor rung the first with people-lined railings overlooking the party below.

"I must go!" Gael gathered his chips from the table. "I got company."

Men and women round about the table protested until they fell under the general's intense inspection.

"Thanks for the game!" Gael slipped his chips into a leather pouch hidden within his voluminous, open shirt, motioned Edmon to the stairs and waved at a passing wench, who nodded. Gael led them through the crowd and up the stairwell, across the broad second floor to the opposite side of the inn and through a small, locked arched doorway. Outside, an unoccupied private patio covered in trellises and vines beckoned with couches and a cool breeze under dappled shadow.

Brawny with warm coffee skin, a cropped beard and a thick mane of curly hair, Gael reclined at the far seat and propped his brown leather boots upon the small table in the circle of couches. Blue trousers bloused above them, inside of which tucked the bottom of his bright, open-chested shirt. "Welcome to Rochsmora, Negrin! And my new place, The Gambler's Heel." He flashed his bright smile as the brothers took seats and the guards took positions.

"It's very nice." Negrin eyed the flowered vines filling the air with their tart scents. "Very cool here. I didn't think you owned anything, Gael."

"Newly acquired." Gael grinned. "But I'm disappointed! I always hoped I would be the one to get you to festivale instead of the old general here."

The wench appeared in the doorway with drinks. Edmon raised his hand to forestall her and pointed out the door. She blanched and left without even looking to Gael.

"Not kind to deny a little hospitalit-" Gael protested.

"We're here on urgent business," Edmon said. "Is this a safe place to talk?"

Gael's smile faded and glanced around the patio. "Not sure there's anywhere perfectly safe to talk in Rochsmora."

Edmon nodded. "Father's favorite business partner won't return his communiques. We've learned his partner has troubles with unknown competitors and may have been moved to an unknown location. Father has ordered all brokers home to help determine how to continue trade until his partner can be reached."

Gael tensed and opened his mouth to speak when Edmon raised his hand.

"And we thought you might be a good starting point, given your small but resourceful network."

"Of course." Gael cleared his throat. "No idea who the competitors are?"

"A deal went bad out with the groves," Edmon said. "Was blamed on drovers."

"But it wasn't?"

Edmon sat forward. "I know the drovers. These weren't drovers. This is where you come in."

Gael's gaze locked on Edmon's. "Any evidence? Of the competitors?"

"None yet, other than Father's partner having trouble. We need to find him."

Gael hesitated. "This isn't the regular dispute, is it? Partner wants more freedom from Father's trade deals? He's gone off on his own, before."

"The … body of evidence is clear only that this is serious, not who it is," Edmon said.

"I'll help," said Gael. "On one condition."

Edmon's face tightened and Negrin sat up.

"If he's just out there trading for himself and this is some kind of wild goose chase, I'll help for a price."

"A price!?" Negrin stammered.

"Yes, a price!" Gael snapped.

"The partner is important to all of us." Edmon glared at Gael. Edmon felt the familiar desire to reduce their brotherhood to six, a feeling levied for each of his brothers, at one point or another.

"More important to me, I should say." Gael met his gaze. "At least I've spent more time actually trading with him, than any of you."

"We have duties-"

"And that's all you've ever seen him as," Gael growled. "Selfdamn duties. So, spare me. This has happened many times and it's always a farce. If you want my help, then I want rights over the River House in Suwannee. I'm tired of panicking every time he sneezes."

"I can't believe you!" Negrin exclaimed.

Edmon raised his hand to cut him off while he honed his gaze on Gael. "Primary rights?"

"You can't be serious!" Negrin stammered.

"Yes," Gael said. "Once Father passes away, I get primary rights, subject to the annuals and such."

"Done," Edmon said.

Negrin stood. "You're trading for Ph-"

"Our *partner*." Edmon cut him off. "And yes, if it will satiate the fool so we can get moving, then the River House be damned."

Gael's face tightened at being called a fool.

"But if this is more than him off trading for himself?" Edmon locked onto Gael. "No deal. I will exact a price on you."

"Fine."

"This comes at a bad time," Edmon said. "The *celebration* is a month away. Without his presence, our father will not just be displeased, but … at a loss."

"We'll find him." Gael sat up.

"But if Father comes at a loss without our partner's presence, the whole company will go forfeit."

"I'm aware," Gael said. "Any thoughts this is linked to the rebellion outside the capital?"

"Those abolitionists? Not sure they could collectively wipe their ass," Edmon harrumphed.

"They would be happy to interfere with our … partner."

"All they do is demand things that cannot be done and still expect the wealth of the Alderlands to remain," Edmon said. "What threats we face with our father come from within, not without."

"Like that's the least of our-" Negrin cut off at another glare from Edmon.

"They're just slaves who don't know their place," Edmon snapped. "Father has recalled the brokers. Gather your things, Gael. We must go."

Gael grimaced. "Fine, fine. I'll get a pack, but can't you at least stay tonight? Enjoy the festivale? Get a girl on that knee or into-"

Edmon stood. "Put your priorities where they belong, Gael. We leave in the hour."

"Fine," Gael huffed. He rose, cuffed Negrin on the arm with a wink and left the patio.

"The nerve! To trade like that!" Negrin said.

"Gael always looks to trade up, Negrin," Edmon said. "I didn't think he'd do it for his own … trading partner, but if it gets us faster to our goal, then we will do everything it takes. Otherwise? Father's trade becomes, well, outright civil war. Let's go."

58

Violated

"T'will be alright', my beaudiful boy," Smee thumbed the black hair from Santi's sweaty forehead. "Y're so strong. I won't dispose you li' I usually do. Yur special."

Santi quivered in terror and shame. The dwarf had done to him something he didn't know could be done. He struggled to understand it as he felt himself bleeding in a place he shouldn't. He wanted to cry, scream, rage, wail, moan, flee, fight and howl with madness, but all he could do was watch the tree — the only tree visible when the dwarf violated him in the jungle while gripping his thick mane of black hair.

"You'll be jus' fine," purred Smee's rumbly voice. "Such a fine boy, you ar'."

Tears rimmed Santi's eyes as fury blossomed. Finally, his familiar anger returned to him. His trembling arms flushed with it. Having moved around to look Santi in the face, Smee paused to look for his pants when Santi snatched a nearby rock. He scrambled to his feet and swung the rock down on the side of Smee's chubby face, which snapped to the side with the monstrous force Santi put behind it.

Santi bellowed with rage as he raised the rock again and brought it down as Smee fell upon the ground. Santi crashed upon the heavy-bellied dwarf and raised the rock yet again, aiming for the broken skin and fresh blood pouring from the gash down the left side of Smee's forehead at the eye socket. Santi wanted to see Smee's brains. He wanted the sickness inside the buggerer's skull poured out over the island, but as he raised the rock again, the view flashed to Tootles in the same position on the stone floor of the Black Tower, the left side of his head caved in and brain matter gushing out.

His hesitation cost him. Smee rammed his left arm up into Santi's chest and sent him flying into a nearby tree. Santi lost the rock as his head rang. He clutched his crown and moaned as Smee chased and snatched him up by the throat.

"Ohhhh," Smee cooed with rage and excitement. "Such *fight* in you! I knew you wer' special. You're da kind I luv mos'. The kind in need a destroyin'. N' I will destroy you." His laughter echoed in Santi's ears. Santi tried to strike at Smee's face, but gasped when Smee squeezed his windpipe. Smee then used his grip to smack Santi's head into the tree once, then twice. Dazed and disoriented, Santi struggled to breathe. "Bu' not today. Today, I take gud care o'you." His hot, wretched breath fell down the side of Santi's soaked face.

Desperate, Santi sought escape.

"You're goin' ta get dressed. You will follow. You tell no one wha' we done, or I swear to da mo'der of darkness that I will continue enjoyin' you 'til you die. We clear?"

Santi searched, attempting to latch onto Smee.

"Gooood…" Smee's deep gravel bored into Santi's ears. "Now do as yur tol'. I would be off and away." He released Santi's throat and leaned in for a better look at the boy's eyes — a reflective yellow had begun a creep across the white, and his irises were now taller than they were round.

Drowned in this new hell, Santi collapsed to the ground. At the dwarf's prompting, Santi struggled to pull on his clothes. Santi felt dirty and worthless and hateful. A new fear climbed in wonder what his father would think to see him now. Smee gripped Santi's wrist and squeezed until Santi cried out. "Try ta run away, and I will hunt you 'cross de island. There is nowhere you can go wit'out me. I know you to ya smell. Clear?"

"Y- yes," Santi managed.

"Den' come, boy." Smee moved into the jungle.

Without hope, Santi followed with his head bowed and cheeks flushed. Walking hurt, but he dared not slow the dwarf. He woke up bound by the dwarf's iron grip before the dwarf began. He struggled to reconcile Smee's actions as shame and fear welled, both from the dwarf and in memory of killing Tootles. All of it threatened his ability to think at all.

Smee paused on the path and smiled. He glanced at Santi with a grin made the boy shudder, again. "Dis place is full o'selfdamn rimshifts. Packed wit' em. Dey're everywhere. Lessee if we can find one dat heads someplace famil'ar."

"Wh- what's that? What's a rimshift?" Santi managed.

"'sa t'innin' between worlds," Smee mused. "Dey allow instan' travel tens of tousands of miles at once. We can git out o'here instantly. No weeks asea pukin' every o'ter fucking hour. No tiny rooms and asshole stews."

Santi followed Smee to a narrow in the terrain north of the Black Tower and into a high-walled path cutting across the narrow ridges with a fat bulb of a gap at the bottom that permitted them to walk deep in its shadow. Smee turned into a small cave and walked through it to an exit in a deep, circular gorge with a few plants growing in the center of the gathered soil at the bottom. Smee walked along the wall to a small vertical slit in the rock and took long, slow sniffs.

"Meso'Admia," he headed back the way they came.

Below the ridges, Smee wandered into a thicket and a rock wall behind it. Into another cave where the path led down for a hundred yards or so, Smee found a rimshift heading to Egungutar. The next rimshift smelled foreign to Smee, as did the next three rimshifts, all within three hours of the Black Tower.

Each time Santi thought he might brave escaping, the memory of Tootles's bashed face stopped him. He killed his friend. Smee violated him. What morality would absolve him? What faith could free him? Jesus Christ and his pope would surely condemn him!

A slave to his sudden fate, he followed as lamb to the wolf, desperate for a way out.

As they followed the paths north, the flora fell away to a view of the rift river before the two followed the shore east. Smee paused at the sight of the dwarvish bridge crossing the river at its narrowest point and hurried to it. He touched the stone in a way that made Santi squirm in memory and muttered various names Santi could not understand. Smee grinned.

"Dis is Ormunish. Ancient by mos' standards, and still stands as if finished yesterday, the sandwash notwit'standing. Is it not amazin'?"

Santi could only stare at the Tree overlooking the island from cliffs rising at the base of Pan's Peak. He wished he could cry out for Peter's help, but should Peter find out about Tootles, Peter would condemn him as surely as his own mother might have, had she lived past his birth.

Standing at the bridge's apex, Smee motioned. "Come, I want ta find a rimshift out o'here. Never t'ought Algueda would have so many, but I tink I can smell something famil'ar. Let's go."

Santi wanted to see Tootles again. He even wanted to see Peter. He wanted his estate in Valencia with his horses. He wanted to see the painting of his mother in the hallway outside his father's room. He wanted to look into her beautiful eyes as he had spent so many hours doing in his youth. He wanted his horses, the green estate grounds, the tapas, the warm sun. Santi wanted to go home.

"Let's go home," Smee smiled as he led Santi down the bridge and up into the brush.

As Santi followed, he wished he could cry. All he could see around his heart was the bright doorway and the darkness closing around it.

59

The Mantle

Late afternoon warmed the air as Devkoron led the men along the northern beach to a small inlet. With Athyka's help crossing the creek, they made camp on the western side.

"We take the mantle now," he motioned to Estemil.

"Why here?" Estemil scanned the shadowed alcove of trees overlooking the creek pouring out into the ocean.

Devkoron noted the ship anchored just offshore and the ship's boat approaching with his trunk of supplies. "I'm not sure what this will do, and I would rather experiment here than on the ship — our only means of escape. Put the boy here." He pointed at the heart of the beach, equidistant from the trees, the inlet, the ocean waterline and a nearby berm peaked with beach grasses. "Linroy, spread out the mages and the soldiers, and prepare dinner."

Linroy hesitated, then saluted and set about his tasks as two sailors set Peter's bound form onto the sand.

After the ship's boat beached, eight sailors disembarked while two hauled a small locked chest across the beach and set it next to Devkoron.

Devkoron knelt on the sand to unlock the chest and fish out a long leather wallet. Unrolling it revealed a small book and a row of pockets holding small tins and pipettes. "Pin him."

After unbinding his elbows and stripping him of his shirt, a sailor retied Peter's wrists and knelt onto the knot. He pinned his hands above his head while a second sailor knelt on the knot binding his ankles.

"What do you suppose this is?" Estemil fished the silver dagger from Peter's belt. "It's a blue blade." She handed it to him for a quick inspection. "If that's Kellogg's dagger, might it be his khordec? It's been in the family for a while."

Devkoron pushed the blade up from the sheath and thumbed its edge. He reseated and set it next to the boy. "Just a blue dagger. Not a khordec." He leaned over Peter and tapped different spots of the boy's chest and belly. Small wafts of magic blossomed at each prod before falling to their natural positions. He studied their behavior and referenced the book from his leather wallet while the sailors made camp and started a fire. Linroy gathered water from a nearby creek and set a small kettle on the fire's coals. Estemil held the book for him to reference as he inspected the mantle.

After ordering the tins, Devkoron opened and emptied half of the first, all of the second and some of the third into mortar and pestle. While he ground the ingredients, Linroy brought the steaming kettle and poured into a second cup Devkoron had set out.

Opposite him, Athyka fingered a small knife at her belt. Gregory stood next to her, motionless.

Devkoron tapped the powder mixture into the steaming cup of water and stirred it. The tinctures dissolved and bubbled. He dipped a finger into the concoction and drew ley lines and small symbols across Peter's body. Next to him lay the open book with diagrams of how the mix should be drawn on the skin.

Once Peter's anterior was complete, Devkoron rolled the boy to do the other side under the light of a second campfire built opposite the first. Dusklight reflected from Pan's Peak, rebounded off the spire offshore and warmed the air.

Using combinations of the remaining tins, he mixed a second portion and drew across the boy's chest a second set of lines.

"Are you sure this will work?" Estemil checked his work. "This pattern locking is for normal abru'caris. The pan's ben'cari is hardly common."

"Abru'cari?" Gregory asked.

"Ancient word for 'mantle of magic,'" Estemil said.

"But you said ben'cari."

"A ben'cari is a holy mantle. I'm just worried this won't be enough for the pan's mantle, which is considered the holiest of mantles."

"All mantles have a common structure." Devkoron drew a line down Peter's face. "Even this one. At least in core structure. Being a holy mantle, its ley structures look like crystalline quartzing compared to canvas fabric."

"Wait, how many other people have … caris? Abru'caris?"

"Mantles are rare," Estemil said, "but you'll find variations in most magical cultures. I heard the Andonese have done more work on abru'caris than anyone else."

"The Andonese are a bunch of fools." Devkoron paused to inspect the lines. "They want to shape abru'caris to create unlimited life."

"I hadn't heard that," Athyka said.

"Magic can't bestow immortality," said Devkoron. "History is pretty clear on that."

"But aren't the elves and dragons immortal?" asked Gregory.

"High elves are immortal but don't often stick around millions of years. The dragons try but they end up eating each other in power struggles."

"You seem awfully well read," Athyka said.

"Baley doesn't pick her agents from the gutter, Athyka." Devkoron waved his hand as he inspected his lines.

Her face darkened.

Devkoron realized his insult and raised his hand to placate before resuming his work. Once he finished the symbols, he reviewed each with the book and adjusted two lines and one symbol. After, he sifted through the trunk and fished out a small bottle of amber liquid. He popped the cork, took a long swig, and wiped his mouth with his wrist. He doffed his coat and pulled out a leather roll of tools. Inside, he pulled out silver instruments and a group of coins rolled in paper.

Shivering, Peter drew long, deep breaths as sticky sweat beaded over his skin.

Devkoron opened another tin, spit on each coin, and rubbed some of the powder on one side before pressing a coin to Peter's forehead, each breast, each bicep, three down his abdomen, one on each thigh and one to the outside of each calf. The agent fished a scalpel from the rolled toolkit and pricked Peter's tongue several times to get enough blood to set a single droplet on each coin from his feet all the way to the top.

As he wet the last coin — the one on the boy's forehead — Peter gasped. His chest vaulted as his body arched.

Devkoron pressed the boy's abs to pin him to the ground. Dipping his finger into the boy's mouth, he leaned over and tapped droplets of blood to his own tongue. "Reveal."

Peter's unfocused eyes snapped open as the glowing ley lines drew themselves down his body in a lacework of light that far surpassed the complexity Devkoron had used with the paint.

As the lines glowed and hummed with a faint buzzing sound, Aaron snapped open another tin and began a third set of lines. The glowing lines shifted as he drew, adapting to his new conjunctions and connectors.

The moon climbed a quarter of the sky as Devkoron plotted each movement before he cut and forced changes in the glowing strings. The beautiful lattice that first appeared over the boy had degraded into a chaos of flickering lines and warped coins.

"Let's break," Devkoron sighed. He and Estemil rose to get some water and a quick bite of food.

Athyka walked around to where Devkoron had knelt to get a view of the work. "How much longer?"

Estemil glanced at Athyka, but frowned at Gregory. He hadn't moved or shifted his weight in hours. He watched as if a statue.

"Almost there," Devkoron chewed the meat. "Just one final overlay."

After catching his breath, he and Estemil returned to the boy to review his notes. Athyka stepped back while Gregory remained as he was with arms crossed, inspecting the glowing lattice.

Devkoron checked each word of the final vocal spellform required to activate the final unlocking. He articulated each word, one at a time, to ensure the proper image formed in his mind necessary to activate the magic. As he spoke, Peter shifted under the small storm of light hovering all around his body.

Athyka leaned near Devkoron's shoulder to follow along in the book as he spoke. The boy writhed and gasped. Devkoron set his palm over the boy's sternum and pinned his trunk to the ground while he continued each word. His hand warmed and tingled. He paused and leaned in. To his surprise, the faint luminescent spirit of the child wafted upward, as if loosening from his mortal shell. "Hold him, tighter."

Hesitant men on each end took care to move further over Peter and pin him down as best they could.

Devkoron raised the book into the light when he heard Athyka shift behind him. He realized her advantage too late, and before he could react, she rammed her ice knife up the back of his skull.

Estemil snapped her hand to the opening in her ohna's sheath, having already suspected Athyka, and unleashed a wave of wind. Estemil cried out when a knife buried into the back of her hand and nailed it to her rib, loosed by Gregory from across the fire. As her focus faltered, so did the wave of wind.

After bracing through the dying wind, Athyka raised the ohna terra. The ground beneath Estemil swallowed her whole. She screamed seconds before a wave of sand crashed down and suffocated her.

Skirting the pan, Gregory hauled Devkoron's limp form aside after Athyka yanked free her knife. She knelt where Devkoron had, snatched up his book and leaned over the writhing child. She set her hand on Peter's sternum and flinched as Peter's partially detached soul warmed and burned her touch.

Laughter bubbled from her throat that climbed and wavered. Gregory ripped off the sheath from Devkoron's uniform and opened it so she could pluck the metal feather. She focused downward with the ohna terra. A muffled scream below preceded a series of crunches before the sheathed ram's horn slid upward from the sand covered in blood. She smiled and fished it out, too. Holding all four in her hands, she quivered and moaned. The rapture of so much power scintillated her every nerve.

Shaking with anticipation, Athyka read the last few words. As she began, a soft moan echoed around the cove. Hairs on her neck stood on end as her heart thundered. She inhaled and, with rapt eagerness, said the last two sentences.

Silence fell for several painful seconds before, in a flash of light and thunderous boom, Athyka was thrown across the sand into the berm behind her.

Athyka came around to the sound of a piercing ring in her ears. Blood drooled down her lobes. Men lay prostrate across the beach. Gregory had disappeared and Devkoron's twisted body burned nearby in snakes of green flame. Touching her face, she discovered black blood drooling from her nose. Her coughs burned her throat. She staggered to the boy. The golden ley lines were gone and the missing coins left burn marks on his skin.

Dropping to her knees drew a scream she could not hear — landing on her kneecaps felt like she had melted them. Desperate and quivering, she snatched the bejeweled knife from her belt and licked the blade. Electrical arcs tinged her tongue as she smiled and laughed.

"Fuck Devkoron," she croaked in silence. "Backup plan it is."

Raising the blade arcing with power, she plunged the bejeweled dagger into Peter's heart. The mantle flashed around him in coughs and sputters that struck her with its magic. Athyka cast up arms to protect herself as the island moaned. Seconds later, the clear night sky filled with an icy blizzard that drowned the world in a dark chaos.

In a panic, she gripped the marble talisman and used it to unroll walls of sand from the beach and fold it around her and Peter into a small longhouse, sealing them off from the storm.

60

Quorum

Brianne Baley downed the small vial and returned it to Alba, who pocketed it, before gazing through a high narrow window next to one of two massive doors, over the shoulder of guards posted just outside to keep a packed square from rushing into the parliament.

Across the Square Al'Cular, gaslights on full burn warmed the starlit space as a forest of glowing dots above the heads of 20,000 people. Well-armed guards kept clear a path leading from the high entry doors of the parliament to a stage overlooking the main dogwood tree in the center of the massive square and down the gentle decline across the Central Road into the library complex. A speaker stood upon the stage regaling the people of the Union's fight for them, the commoners. The victories fought, overcoming monarchies and empires. The pursuit of absolute unity.

"Fellow Baley." Roschach approached with two attendants in tow while tugging on a glove.

"I haven't heard from Devkoron in hours," Baley said.

Roschach took a slow breath. "Do you doubt the difficulty I've had, then?"

Baley's eyebrow twitched. "I have faith in Devkoron. Fenren, however, has not proven his merit."

"Fenren has barely gotten an hour's sleep in three days." Roschach crossed his arms. "He found the room when years of searching produced nothing."

"He found it by chance," Baley said. "Because William passing the mantle gave him the clue. But he didn't find it; others did and led him to it."

"Others don't have the elf poring over every single word in there," Roschach said. "We're doing everything we can to get the rimshift open."

"The rimshift won't save us if Alderland or Graela finds out we don't have the mantle," Baley snapped. "This movement has been fighting monarchy after monarchy for nearly three thousand years. We've lost leader after leader to greed and assassination and graft and warfare. Unionism has been a key insurgency against continental power but we've only overthrown small third and fourth-tier states. We're a hair's breadth from achieving the first form of legitimacy with a top tier Pangean state and all we had to do was acquire my brother *before* he left Eden. You were tasked with getting it. You have failed, Roschach. At every single turn. When this ceremony is concluded, the quorum will meet to discuss your continued participation. Tonight, we declare ourselves a member of the Edenic Charter without the mantle to back it up."

"I'm aware of what it means-"

"It means every effort to preserve the Edenic Charter, its trade agreements, transnational accords, alliances and, most importantly, the peace it represented, is shit!"

"With slavers!" Roschach cried. His voice echoed across the high chamber. "Selfdamn slavers, Baley! The Alderlanders own millions of people! All this pressure to preserve a selfdamn charter that deserves to burn in hell!"

"Do you want to suddenly lay unprotected against the most powerful empire since the Reformation?" asked Baley. "Alderland would have taken Eden many times if not for the protections the charter guarantees us and the checks and balances of its triumvirate nature with us, Graela and Alderland. The very slavery you would have nothing to do with is the very weapon that will slit our throats if we don't keep our hand on that hilt." Baley's face hardened. "Progression isn't made in leaps, but small steps. This was always a small step toward a land of freedom for everyone."

"Like the baby steps your brother seemed to take toward his 'better world?'" Roschach growled. "You mean that one, *Baley?*"

She glowered.

"What you call baby steps, I call placation," Roschach spat. "You and your wealth and influence sitting here in Eden and you could have done something- anything, to free others."

"I sacrificed everything to ensure Unionism would be heard in parliament," said Baley. "I gave up relationships — and lives of my own family! — to bring this cause to seat. Don't tell me I'm not doing everything I can to free others."

"You two better tighten up." Grontham Eberhart joined them. Decked in the simple Unionist red and blue everyone wore, his bright eyes defied his charcoal skin beneath a mane of dreadlocks. "We're about to go herald the coming of the People's Union of Pangea and you two bicker like a pair of selfdamn dogs."

"Agreed." Elizabeth Kelg completed the quorum. Her midnight hair framed her Swinnen narrow, angled eyes and pale yellow skin. "Besides, your voices carry further than you think."

Baley grimaced as Roschach's jaw tightened.

"Now," Eberhart said as his attendant tugged and shifted his outfit to ensure its presentation. "Is there anything else you need to shout at each other before we go pretend to be the unified leaders the world needs, or should I call the palace steward to warm some milk for the both of you?"

"That's enough, Grontham," Baley growled. "We are professionals, whatever the debate. We will go out there as planned and herald our new nation. Then we all will retire to the parliament." She paused. "Difficult decisions must be made by the morning."

"Fine," Kelg huffed. "Line up. He's about ready."

The four stood abreast as the crier upon the stage stirred up the masses.

"He's damn good." Roschach's mutter drew a grunt from Grontham.

"Alright," one of the attendants inside the door turned once he heard the appropriate phrase from the man upon the stage. "We head out in thirty seconds. One final check over for our quorum."

The attendants did a final check to ensure each of the quorum's red and blue outfits appeared as plainly beautiful as possible. A wizard approached and wove spells over each, illuminating them as if under bright sunlight and setting small amplifier spells at each throat to ensure everyone could hear them. The vibrancy of their clothes intensified and their skin appeared smoothed and rich with life.

"Smiles, smiles," said the lead attendant. "There. Wonderful, my fellows!" He bowed and stepped aside.

"… come the leaders of our revolution! The Quorum! Of! Faith!"

Soldiers hauled the massive doors open to reveal the four to the Square Al'Cular.

Smiling, the four marched down the long, empty walk through the frenzied, adulating citizens. The quorum strolled and paused to touch hands extended along the line of guards on either side. They greeted, kissed and hugged proffered children. Attendees devoured the affection.

Though stately, each of the quorum appeared almost common in their textured clothes and lack of jewels, noble inks and powders. The magical lightspells ensured all could see them when they mounted the stage. The square thundered with applause.

Horns filled the night with pomp and declaration. The quorum smiled and raised their hands to wave at the crowd.

"Welcome, every fellow!" Roschach raised his hands. His rich voice boomed across the square by invisible bells of magic.

"Tonight, we helm the coming of a new age!" Eberhart spun to the crowd behind them.

"Where each person is valued before the law!" Baley's firm resolve pierced hearts. "Where all men, regardless of station, are equally deserving of justice!!"

"Where man and woman, high sentient and low sentient, nobleman and peasant enjoy lives of equal wealth and prosperity!" cried Kelg.

The crowd roared as the quorum smiled.

"Tonight!" Kelg's voice echoed across the masses. "We honor the countless men and women who have given their lives to make this world a better world!"

"We begin a world where all are regarded for their humanity…" Baley straightened her shoulders with dignity. "…Before they are mistreated and devalued for their challenges!"

"Where love is the first, last, and final measure of a man's contribution to society!" Eberhart touched his breast.

"And slavery is ended!" Roschach roared.

The crowd went wild.

Baley clenched her smile. That was not the line they had written together. As scripted, she raised her hand and focused on her lines. The crowd fell to a murmur as she turned southward to face the majority. "This is our Union! A place of hope for all species! Tonight, we ignite the flames of revolution to spread across the continent. It's time for a union of all peoples, all nations, all cities under one rule, a rule by the people and for the people, a rule of democracy, a rule over the people on the people's behalf and benefit."

Elizabeth Kelg stepped next to her. "This is our sign unto all peoples, that peace comes before all. No more profit, no more greed, no more avarice, no more war, no more religion, no more differences!"

"To bind us together as one." Eberhart joined them. "One people under one faith, a faith in ourselves. We are the masters of our destiny. No nobleman, king, dictator, holy high priest, duke or lord may set our paths. We are now our own rulers! We, the quorum, represent you before the Parliament of Man. Together, we will serve you by guiding you into that bright tomorrow!"

"Together…" Roschach stepped last into the line. "Together we will move as one. Together, we-" He cut off and snatched his neck. Fired from the crowd, a crossbolt cut through the outer curve of his throat; blood trickled down his hand. He gasped as his knees buckled.

The crowd roared as men crushed into the path and mounted the stage behind the quorum. Unionist mages at the base of the steps raised their hands and cast bolts of fire and arcs of lightning at the attackers while the stage's guards chased those who barreled over them. Flashes of violent magic erupted between mages and attackers.

From his knees, Roschach twisted and threw up a magical shield just in time to deflect fire bolts from his face and trunk while several still scorched his arm and thigh.

The quorum's other mage, Kelg, raised her own shields and counterattacked while Eberhart snatched out a small knife and fought an attacker bearing down on him with a sword. Baley, alone, stood unarmed, though she moved with deliberate care to keep guards and the other quorum between her and the attackers. She did not see the assailant from the crowd throw the common knife through the air. It sank into her back in full view of the crowd now boiling with shock and rage.

"Baley!" Roschach spun and tried to catch her as she fell, but her feet tangled in the melee and slapped face-first against the wooden stage, snapping one of her front teeth. Roschach rolled her onto her side and leaned over her while the others continued fighting. Guards surrounded them with swords raised outward.

Baley moaned as Roschach leaned in.

Roschach inspected the knife sticking out of her and bent to her face. She moaned again.

Roschach reached up to his throat and silenced the magic amplifier, then hers. He coughed to ensure it didn't echo across the square before leaning closer. "Baley? Baley!"

Brianne groped for him. "Roschach. Help me."

Roschach eyed her for a long moment. "No."

Her eyes narrowed as his hand found her throat and squeezed.

Baley struggled.

"You thought you had control? Like all true believers, you thought you had power because your blind commitment to a cause inspired the same in others," Roschach said. "But you see, Baley, such naïveté in the purity of a cause is the surest way to be led by those with the real power toward an end you refuse to believe lies beneath the surface, and most sets the stage for those of us willing to do whatever it takes to control that power."

While swords continued to clash and violent pulses of magic struck the air, Kelg crumpled to the stage beside them missing half her face in a burn mark. Baley searched for hope while desperate to breathe.

"Die, Baley," Roschach said. "The world never needed the likes of you and your shallow, utopian idealism." She flailed. He rolled her toward the knife in her back. Pressing it to the stage, the blade twisted. He reactivated the voice spell. "HELP! BRIANNE IS DYING! HELP US!!"

Baley couldn't gasp as the knife twisted into her from behind. She went limp. As soon as he dared, Roschach reactivated his amplifier and spun to his feet just as Grontham crashed backward against him with a crossbolt in his right lung.

Roschach caught him and lowered him to the ground. "My friend!" He rose, gathered power into his hands and unleashed himself on the attackers sparring with the guards. In moments, he killed many of them by blowing off appendages or driving holes through soft parts when a man ran a sword through his left lower back and out his belly. Roschach roared in pain and dropped to a knee. The man reached around with a knife to take Roschach's throat when the knife dropped to the ground a moment before the attacker crumpled.

A thin line of light bored through the man's skull, fired by Fenren's crystal torch from the entrance to the courtyard. The fight was over.

Fenren cut off the laser and raised the torch. A sourceless noonday sun and faded blue sky interrupted the torch-lit courtyard. Attendees cried in terror.

"Kill the attackers," Roschach's groan echoed across the square as he clutched the blade still piercing his side.

Celebration turned slaughter as the crowd pounced on anyone who appeared to have participated in the attack. Guards surrounded Roschach and the quorum as Fenren raced to him.

"We have to get you out of here." Fenren checked the wound. "Prepare to move!"

"Wait! The others!" Roschach beseeched for the quorum. Limp forms and vacant faces stared back.

"They're gone!" Fenren roared. "Protect Fellow Roschach! MOVE!"

The guards tightened their circle while Fenren and another soldier hefted Roschach and rushed him down the stairs, up the walk and through the large doors, which shut behind them with a thunderous boom.

61

Reclamation

Dawn broke in the weakening storm when an opening widened in mounded snow. Athyka emerged. The remaining sailors huddled around fires they fought to preserve all night. She had watched it through their eyes and knew it was safe to emerge.

Holding the ice knife, she melted the snow across the beach and willed it to flow into the ocean, leaving the beach dry, again. She then dried each sailor to help them combat the cold. She lifted the ram's horn and used it to feed their fire until roaring while she used the marble talisman to upend nearby trees so they fell over. She sucked them dry of water so the men could snap whole branches and break them into firewood by hand.

"This is what these powers are meant for," said Athyka.

She hovered on the idea the ohnas might somehow bring her to a full mindrise. Could she become a psylock? Her grandmother told her that a single psylock was born every ten millennia or so, the exception being the Minder Conflicts more than two thousand years ago. Could Athyka break the cycle? Might the ohnas amplify and accelerate her? Could she make it permanent? Hope and lust welled within her, entwined as a spring of desire to be everything her grandmother said she never would.

Grandmother and her bitter jealousy was never satisfied or happy. She saw her own abilities as evil, yet taught them to Athyka only to point out how evil Athyka had become by learning. Athyka was desperate to prove herself to her grandmother, and yet also prove her wrong. The battle within her ripped her apart, but becoming a psylock could settle that. She could become more than her grandmother had ever dreamed, for she knew her grandmother had that same distant desire to be more than she had been, as weak as she was.

No amount of playing with ohnas had grown the specks in her irises more than they already had. Perhaps she needed the other ohnas? If she could get this mantle and return to the continent … Athyka took a controlled breath. If she could get the rest of the ohnas, perhaps combined they could push her all the way. The prospect overwhelmed her.

None of the sailors spoke as she directed them by all thought. Soon men surrounded the roaring fires to soak in heat. As they cooked their morning meal, she returned to the mound where Peter lay. Neither dead nor alive, the magic of her dagger — designed to steal magic — had, instead, trapped the life of boy and his mantle in limbo. Designed to indicate if the dagger had captured an intended magic, only one and a half of the three jewels now flickered with light.

She frowned as, despite hours of desperate inspection of the magics and the dagger, she feared to rip out the knife and risk the mantle's escape. For now, she waited, watched and tested. The sailors on the beach went about their duties. Having been cast against the coral last night during the storm, The Hover performed emergency repairs nearby.

"Selfdammit," she growled and paused. She could not hear herself. Her eyes widened as she realized the morning had been silent, not because she no longer needed to talk to the men, but because her own ears had been ruptured in last night's attempt to take the mantle.

Exhausted and hopeless, tears dripped before she bent forward to set her forehead on Peter's chest. "I can't- I can't go back without this. I can't go back empty handed. Not again."

Athyka's hand quivered on the handle.

"Please, please stay in the knife. Please, stay in the knife." Rising, she gripped the handle, set her other hand on the boy's chest and, hesitating, wrenched out the blade.

Nothing happened. All the jewels fell dark.

"No! Come back!" Athyka raised her hands to perform a mantle resonance test, which rebounded in a chaos of the same sputtering, glowing lines from Devkoron's earlier work. Finishing the book hadn't worked, nor had the dagger. Though partially separated from Peter, the mantle refused to be taken.

Her head drooped, she sobbed. Boy and mantle lay within reach, yet she could not feel further from it.

"Why won't you work?" she moaned. "Why-" She raised her head as she sensed the fast approach of a powerful magical entity.

Her mind leapt to the eyes and ears of the sailors at the fast approach of a chime. The memory of the pixie in Unity's Light caught her up short and she panicked, drawing the berm up to block a spear of golden light firing through the trees directly toward her. The explosion cast sand and heat outward across the sailors and doused the bonfire in a single burst of wind.

Bellows and war cries erupted from the trees. Tootles rushed down onto the beach, followed by a girl and dozens of braves as the sailors writhed on the ground in shock.

"He's under here! Dig! Quickly!" Tootles stood over the mound of sand covering Peter. "And find Tinker Belle!"

The nervous braves rushed to form a wall of horizontal spears between the diggers and the confounded sailors.

"Got him!" Great Cougar cried and hauled Peter up from the sand.

"Find the fairy!" Tootles yelled. The men continued as Great Cougar inspected Peter.

He exhaled. "He is dead."

Everyone slowed.

"Damn your fears!" a massive black raven swooped in and dropped onto the sand next to Peter's body. "Gather him and the fairy! Time is short and these fools will not long suffer our surprise."

The braves scrambled away in horror among mutters of 'omen.'

"Stop staring at me and dig!" Solomon croaked. Great Cougar blinked. Solomon hopped and jabbed him in the hand with his beak. "MOVE!"

Great Cougar stirred. "Move!"

While the braves returned and dug for Tinker Belle, Tiger Lily planted herself between them and the bloody woman crawling from the sand. Bathed in sand and blood, void of her eyebrows and bangs, Athyka struggled to breathe. Grit and pus blinded her.

Tiger Lily used her bow staff to tap the ohnas out of Athyka's reach. Each time, painful shocks raced up the wood into her hands and arms.

She hissed, but did her best to disarm the dazed mage.

"Found her!" Wind Sprint fished out Tinker Belle's tiny body as tall as his hand was long.

"Grab his things," Solomon pointed at Peter's clothes and silver dagger. A brave snatched them up.

"Retreat, quickly! To the camp!" Great Cougar carried the boy up into the trees with the braves in tow. "Tiger Lily!"

Tiger Lily turned from Athyka and raced to join them.

Athyka groped for the newcomers once she had her wits, but she could not sense any of the men or the little girl — they had no magic and, thus, her psylism could do little to touch them. Her mind latched, again, onto the two dozen terrified sailors. All had woken from her daleen-induced control to a beach filled with natives. None knew where they were or how they had gotten onto the beach from the ship. She forced herself up and tumbled head-first into the sand. She screamed and pushed herself up again. In control of the men, once more, she summoned several to help her stand.

Athyka hadn't felt so alone since she lived with her grandmother as a teenage girl. All these men were now mere extensions of her mind. Their memories, though bared to her casual search, offered no value when she could pluck and control them at-will. Unwilling allegiance proved a hollow validator.

Without the mantle, returning home would mean nothing. All her efforts to anonymously work her way up in the graces of the powerful, being discovered and blackmailed by Roschach, her desperation to earn her way out, and now being ripped apart physically with nothing to show for it was more than she could bear. She cried out from her gut.

Despite the men's support, exhaustion threatened her — she could not keep sucking the sailors of their life forces or she truly would be alone. At her prompt, men hurried to gather food and rebuild fires. She struggled to keep food down while hoping her strength might return. Though unable to control him from this distance, she prompted the captain, still on his ship, to bring the remaining crew, arms and supplies.

Once they arrived and fell under her full control, she weeded out the weakest man among them and summoned him to kneel next to her. She clutched his throat and sucked his life into her body. Void of his water, his flesh sank inward and steamed. Her control of the ohnas deepened with the taking of his life force. He sank dead to the beach. Alive, again, she grit her teeth.

"I am not finished," she growled. The formation moved as one into trees and up the incline to the base of Pan's Peak. Halfway up, she sensed a familiar mind walking nearby. She marched through the foliage when she spotted two figures plodding in the distance.

"Smeee!!" she screamed.

The two figures picked up their pace.

"Stand fast, you SELFDAMN BUGGERER!!" she bellowed.

The dwarf froze. A mad smile crawled across her face.

"I have your mountain oath, you worthless DOG! HEEL!!"

Hesitant, Smee approached her with the second figure in tow. Santi's mouth fell open as Smee obeyed.

"You will heel!" she cried. He climbed with resignation in his big dull eyes. "And you will never run from me ever again. You hear me?" She struck his face.

"Yes, I hear you," he admitted.

"You will help me, or I swear to the self I will castrate you with something dull. And you will let me, won't you?" Athyka spat in his face. When she inspected the boy, her eyebrows climbed. "You have one of the pan's *boys*!?" A strained laugh bubbled up from her throat. "The wall doesn't hurt *him*, does it!? DOES IT!?" She struck Smee again across the face.

"I don' know," Smee admitted.

"Then have him tell me!" Athyka snatched the terrified boy by the throat and noted the strange yellowing in his eyes. Her mind's probes reached out for the boy, but when they touched, she gasped as she realized she had linked with him, before, in the clearing. Not only did his mind link with hers as had her grandmother's, but the boy recognized Athyka from a memory, from which she retreated. Instead, the wretched memory of Smee violating him forced her from his mind.

Athyka recoiled. Madness crept deeper into her heart at the implausibility of finding another one like her in the midst of this chaos. She couldn't handle it all. "Fuck THIS. Let's go you, you selfdamn boy lover. Bring your bitch. He's getting us into the clearing!"

62

To Split a Tree

Tootles trudged up the snow-packed hill with sixty braves. His dark hair danced in the stiff breeze as he led the train of men over the north lip of the jut toward the wall. The men gazed upon the monstrous tree. Their attention came down in succession as they approached the motionless wall.

Tootles reached out, but the wall did not respond to him. "Oh no."

The braves exchanged looks.

Tears slid down Tootles cheeks as he pulled the vines aside with his hands. When Tiger Lily moved to help, he prepared to block her, fearing for her safety. The wall did not attack. He blushed and motioned for her to continue.

"Tootles!" Shifu appeared around the bend in the wall and hesitated at the sight of Tootles's face, but approached anyway.

"Shif-!" Tootles cut off at the sight of the boy. A thin layer of black-striped orange fur covered Shifu's body. "What- happened to you?"

"I don't know!" Shifu scratched at his arms. "And have you seen Santi? I walked around the tower. Somebody hit me! I woke up and found- all this blood! On the floor, inside. And then, you were gone! Where did you go!? I been out here for- hours!" His inhale quivered. "And now I've got-fur! And- what happened to your eyes!? They're green!"

"Tootles, time is short," Solomon said. "Athyka will follow us very soon and Peter needs help inside. There is no time to waste."

Tootles struggled with a rising worry about everyone's reactions to whatever was happening to him. "We'll figure that out later. Right now, Peter's in real trouble. Help me get the wall open!"

The nervous braves worked to separate the thick layers before everyone crossed to the other side.

"Quickly, Tootles," Solomon clapped his beak. "Remember where you and Santi found Peter floating beneath the Tree?"

"Yeah?"

"Get him and Tinker Belle down there as quickly as you can. If you touch the roots and ask them to move, they will open for you. Inside is a glowing pool. Put both of them into it now! Hurry!"

"Great Cougar, push the wall back together," Tootles said. "It's our only defense!"

Tootles gathered Tinker Belle and, with Shifu's help, took Peter from Great Cougar before disappearing into the chamber below the Tree.

"There's a fire pit over here," one of the braves returned from scouting the inner clearing.

"Get it lit," Great Cougar said. "We won't know how long this will be."

"And there's weapons!" said another. The men hurried across the grass.

Down below, Tootles and Shifu set Peter and Tinker Belle into the glowing pool. Soaked with the glowing light where his arms entered the pool, Shifu moaned.

"What? Are you alright?" Tootles turned.

"I feel … good." Shifu laid down.

Tootles frowned.

Tiger Lily made her way through the roots and gaped in wonder. "What is this place?"

"This is our … safe place." Tootles sat.

"That is quite true." The raven followed Tiger Lily. "But unfortunately, our work is far from complete."

"Is Peter dead?" Tootles asked.

"He's only mostly dead."

"Mostly dead?"

"If he were all dead, the mantle would have moved on to another boy." Solomon hopped to the edge of the pool which lit him from below in its blue pall. "Every life is triumvirate. There must be a spirit, soul, and body. First, we restore the vessel with this pool. Next must come the soul, which is where you come in. Please, over here." Solomon hopped to the small tree and rapped upon its bark. "You have a very special gift, young man. A talent for plants."

Tootles and Tiger Lily followed.

"You control the wall outside. You controlled the bushes when you rescued Shifu. You kept Santi and Shifu safe while wandering the forest because the forest knows you. The beasts of the grassland see you as a part of the island more than any other boy but Peter."

"Why?" Tootles asked.

"Because there is only one taker on this island who seeks only to protect, if it can be a bit overeager."

"Taker?"

"Beings who take the boys from Earth. The wall is one of them, as is the silverback, the heavy moth, the great tiger, the she spider, and even the crocodile."

"Why do they do that?"

"Why is a discussion for another day." Solomon cocked his head. "Because right now, it is your new and growing talent Peter desperately needs. Come closer."

Tootles approached the wrist-thick trunk rising twenty feet into the darkness. The pool's blue warbling light painted the Tree's underside in sharp pale angles that contrasted with the endless black around them.

"Use both thumbs upon the bark to gently spread it open, like spreading the vines as you did, outside," Solomon said. "This you must do with great care — ripping this Tree has implications that extend beyond all worlds connected to Pangea."

"Why is that?"

"Because this, young man, is the Tree of Life."

Tootles started and Tiger Lily gasped. "B- but why would I open it up!?"

"Because Peter needs you to, as do many others who depend upon Peter. I need you to delve into the heart of this tree." He tapped again. "But take great care, Tootles. You must take only a sliver of its heart and seal it up perfectly. There is great danger if you do not."

"What will this do?" Tootles asked.

"We will feed Peter from its heart," Solomon said. "But if the Tree dies after we take from it, the sliver will be useless."

Tiger Lily turned at his tone. "And?"

Solomon ruffled his feathers. "All living will die."

Tootles blanched. "And if we let Peter die?"

"The third realm — the physical realm — will dissolve into the nether. The ohna khordecs are powers of creation and must be returned by Peter to their anchors, or all life is forfeit."

Tootles gulped.

"Come, child," the raven said. "We must hurry. Peter's life hangs upon the edge of a knife, and Athyka is already on her way up the hill with her men. We cannot delay."

Tiger Lily gave Tootles a reassuring nod. Mustering himself, Tootles approached the tree.

"Tiger Lily, would you be kind enough to ask your father to heat some water. We will need it when Spade is done. He'll be out that way." Solomon pointed with his beak. She hurried out through the roots.

Tootles could not well see the Tree, but upon touching it, a sense flooded his mind like none ever had before. The songs of trillions and quadrillions of green, living things threatened to overwhelm him, as did the life of animals living among those plants, then of the intelligent beings, beyond. Nine multidimensional worlds rose around a central massive continent. He stumbled back. "Great Spirit!"

"Come, child," Solomon said. "Focus on the task. We must hurry."

With great care, Tootles began to open the tree.

Outside, Tiger Lily relayed the instructions to her father and inspected the treasure trove of weapons, jewels, barrels, metal and cloth. What drew her attention most, however, was the unprecedented view of the entire island at the cliff's edge. "Wow."

Great Cougar joined her. "There's so much more than we thought we saw. Everywhere I look, there is something new. Everything smells … richer. The water is sweeter. The colors are more vibrant … such a place."

"Will we really leave the old ways behind, Father? To leave our peace?"

Great Cougar paused. "I don't know, Tiger Lily. This island will require much of us. I don't want to leave the old ways." He touched her shoulder. "But you represent the new way. If your visions lead us to help this pan and his forest spirit, then we will follow."

Tiger Lily frowned.

Great Cougar squeezed her shoulder. "Do not worry, my daughter. You do well."

"What did you tell Grandmother? About helping these boys?"

Great Cougar's face tightened. "I am the chief hunter. As a man, it is my responsibility what happens outside the village. ... And there is more to tell you later. Rain Singer and I have spoken at length about your future role in the tribe. It will not be traditional."

"What? What do you mean?"

"I will tell you later, but I can say it began with your grandmother's first vision as a little girl."

"There's more to the vision!?" she gasped.

"Yes," Great Cougar whispered. "I will tell you of it later."

Tiger Lily's gaze widened — her grandmother's vision had carried her people from the purple mountains across the great plains, through the rolling forests and low mountains to the great ocean. After several years camping at the end of a point where two great ocean currents met and mixed, creating an endless watery field of shifting sand bars, they learned how to build ocean-going vessels and ventured east across the great dark ocean to a rocky fishhook island surrounded by razor sharp rock formations, then south into frothy white warm waters.

"What's happening under the Tree?" Great Cougar interrupted her thoughts.

"I will tell you later," Tiger Lily said. After a look, Great Cougar nodded.

"I will have the water kept hot."

Tiger Lily spent the next half hour with Tootles before returning. "Father, the kettle. Get it ready. They're bringing him."

Shifu and a haggard Tootles carried Peter and Tinker Belle out through the roots by the fire near the southern cliffside and set him upon the grass as a brave brought the hot kettle with a small rag.

Tootles slumped to the grass at Peter's head as Solomon hopped out from the shadow beneath the tree.

"You did well, Tootles," Solomon said. "The sliver?"

Tootles fished out the sliver from his belt and set it into a small metal cup held by one of the braves. Once in the cup, Tiger Lily directed the pouring of the water. As it washed over the sliver, sonorous notes filled the air. Steam curled upward in long, lacy lines that shifted with each note. The braves were moved to tears.

As he listened, Tootles remembered a man and a woman and he realized he had forgotten them. He wanted to cry, but he was no longer their little boy. They were no longer his parents. The notes died as the water cooled into a panoply of thick, vibrant colors.

With a cough and a start, Tinker Belle flailed and sat up. *What the- Augh, hell.* She found men looming over her in wonder.

"Tinker Belle!" Tootles piped.

What happened? Tinker Belle asked. *Did we get him?*

"Your plan worked." Tootles nodded at Peter lying beneath her.

Great Self, what's wrong with him? Why isn't he breathing!?

Tootles noticed the stab wound missing from Peter's chest.

"Let us bring the fight to a head," said Solomon. "I believe it's time, Tootles."

Tootles lifted the pot by the narrow tin handle swiveling from the spout and dribbled the rainbow-colored liquid into Peter's mouth.

What's going on, Solomon? Is he alive or isn't he? Tinker Belle pulled golden hair from her face.

Drifting snow slowed to stillness. Everyone tensed. Several reached up to touch individual flakes. They did not melt. The island fell silent and the breeze died.

"It's ... holding its breath," Tiger Lily said. "The island waits."

"You're right, little seer." Solomon almost appeared to smile. "It does."

The faint voice of a boy filled the air down the wall. "Hello!? Hello! Peter!?"

The group paused and looked along the curve of the clearing.

"Ah, yes," Solomon fluttered up to a nearby root. "Tootles. Would you?"

"Hello? Peter! Are you in there!?"

"That sounds like Santi." Tootles headed for the wall. "Another boy for the fight!"

63

Over the Edge

Though Athyka stood paces away from the wall, her mind failed to penetrate it. Santi cowered next to Smee. He had been through trauma Athyka dared not imagine. She would rip out the dwarf's throat herself if she didn't need him. Despite her desire to control Santi as she did all the other men, she could not bring herself to touch his mind again. Like her, he had reflective purple specks in his uniquely yellow irises. Afraid even to speak to the boy, she hauled Smee closer by his ragged shirt. "Have the boy sing for Peter. Call him out."

Smee dragged Santi closer to the wall. "Don't think about runnin'." He growled as he let Santi go and stepped aside.

Santi blanched. He wanted to run but facing Peter's judgement terrified him. He cleared his throat. "Hello!? Hello! Peter!?"

A few moments passed.

"Hello? Peter! Are you in there!?"

Moments later, the vines split. Santi froze at the first face he saw.

Tootles first smiled at the gently writhing wall — pleased it seemed to be returning to life — before turning to Santi. A pale green replaced the whites of Tootles's eyes. A new skin of tiny roots filled the left front side of his head where Santi had bashed it in. Tootles was alive.

"Santi!" Tootles's face lit up. "There you are-"

An arrow punched the left side of Tootles's neck moments before two waves of soil rushed past Santi on both sides through the gap in the wall and smothered his friend.

"NOOO!!" Santi screamed when mages and soldiers raced over the gap in the wall. Crystals of ice plowed into the wall on both sides, pinning them down as men rushed into the clearing. Smee hauled Santi through with the rest. "NOO! TOOTLES!!" Smee shoved Santi to the ground as a flurry of fireballs and arrows filled the air, followed by whoops, howls and screams.

The group of braves scrambled away from the fireballs and crossbolts flooding the clearing. One brave took a hit in the heart while another his hip.

Great Cougar saw their fear and hesitation. He knew their attackers would kill them all. He knew that if not here and now, it would just be another tribe to find the island, another marauder who would kill for no other reason than the great competition.

That's what life was — a great competition.

Great Cougar roared and cast his spear into the breastbone of a sailor and drove him back through the others pouring into the clearing. The braves took heart. Many threw spears while others charged the newcomers as if cornering boars. Natives loosed their own arrows seconds later and sent sailors scattering while a woman in the midst waved her hand across the grass. An explosion raced through the group as Tiger Lily threw herself over Peter and Tinker Belle.

Tinker Belle screamed. *Peter!!*

An enemy crossbolt landed in Shifu's hip. He screamed and hit the lawn. Tiger Lily snatched and hauled him out of the way before raising her spirit stick and spinning it between Peter and Athyka.

The sailors fought as if with one mind, not as individuals. Emboldened braves fought the throng, though they refrained from killing.

Athyka raised each ohna in turn to score the braves with wind, boil their blood or open the ground beneath them — her ohnas faltered. She was too exhausted to push her sailors and too afraid to release them. Slaved as they were, they waited for instructions. When she spotted Peter, she prepared to race for the boy herself when the wind sweetened and everyone stilled as the light intensified.

"Peter…" a soft, feminine voice echoed across the clearing.

Tiger Lily spun to the wall near Peter. "The fair lady."

"Peter, wake up, baby."

Tinker Belle's blood stilled. Through the wall materialized a luminescent figure. A blue dress flowed from her body under a glowing mane of crimson hair. *By the Great Self* ...

The fair lady's green eyes took in the fairy and she smiled.

April! Tinker Belle staggered to her feet as horror and shame gripped her. *Oh, April!*

Lady April Baley crossed the grass between the dumbstruck forces.

Despite trembling with rage, the sight of April locked Athyka's feet to the ground.

April knelt over Peter and caressed Belle's face with her faint fingertips.

"Thank you for your mercy, Tinker Belle." April's warm smile filled with sunlight. "You are well appreciated."

Tinker Belle clutched her mouth as tears drooled down her cheeks. There, in April's left wrist, a hole remained, healed through, where the ice knife had been driven, and a faint scar where her wrist had frozen and broken off.

"Please, Tinker Belle," April said. "It's time to wake my son."

Tinker Belle floated aside. April pressed her hand over the scar on Peter's chest, then to his cheek. She kissed his forehead. "Wake up, Peter." Love emanated from her words. "Wake up, darling," she whispered over her son. "Wake up."

The world fell silent. Peter's body arched upward from the ground, his head and heels planted in the grass.

As April faded away, her words echoed one last time. "Wake up, my little bird." She giggled. "It is time to play."

Wind rushed over the wall, across the grass amidst their feet and swirled about Peter, who lifted from the ground as light drew into his body until it emanated from his skin. His crimson hair wafted like fire. His skin burned as gold. Streaks of brilliant light leaked from his eyes, nose and mouth as he ascended. Braves retreated but for Tiger Lily, who planted her feet.

"I am the pan," whispers echoed. Light poured from Peter's open mouth. Peter's feet slowed as his head came up, staring at the sky, when his bellow struck the island. "I AM THE PAN!"

In a flash of light bursting forth from his body across Neverland, those in the clearing crashed to the ground. As they sat up, the island fell still and wind died.

Peter crowed.

The building thunder of his voice rocked the world beneath them and grew across Neverland as a violent quake. Light raced upward from the roots of the tree into the canopy. The La'Du Lira Al'Cular blossomed to life. The light within surpassed Peter as a noonday sun and forced everyone to bury their faces into the ground. The Tree's brilliance faded to reveal the sun and vibrant blue sky.

Fading, Peter descended until his bare feet slid into the grass and he faced Athyka, who climbed to her feet, followed by her men.

"Give ... me ... the mantle," she quivered.

A grin crawled across his face. "Take it."

Quivering, Athyka bared her teeth. "Give! Me! The Mantle! You have no right! Your father wasted it in his palace while people out there were starving to death! People dying in war! Your family kept it from a world that needed your power! He could have done something to help them instead of trade deals and grand parties!"

"Is that why you took the ohnas from their seats? Took things that don't belong to you? Used them in war to destroy armies a lot bigger than you? Because my family's crimes entitled you to your own?"

"We took power to create balance to your evil fucking family!! We do whatever is necessary to help those who need it!"

"My family? Like killing all those people on my dad's ship? And the fleet? And- and across Pangea?"

"Some costs are necessary for a better world."

"What kind of better world means that some innocent people die for other innocent people? Just *our* innocent people die for *yours?*" Peter glanced at the braves, paused on Tiger Lily, locked onto Tinker Belle, then returned to Athyka and the powers gripped in her shaking hands.

"Your people aren't innocent!" she cried. "They stood by while millions suffered under monarchs and kings who abused them! You could have done something! The Baleys had a responsibility with all their wealth and power! People looked to you!"

Suddenly his mother's words reached Peter's ears.

"No," Peter growled. "People are responsible for their own kingdoms. It's their responsibility to rise up and take them back, not ask others to do it for them. You all- killed Father. I am the pan, now. And those don't work on me. Even I know that, and I don't know half enough." He swallowed. "But this mantle is mine. So is the responsibility. I have to take those back.

I can- already feel them." His jaw clenched. "Walk away."

Athyka's mouth fell open before she stormed closer, raised her ice knife and screamed. As one, every sailor resumed their fight with the braves, even as the braves fought to avoid killing.

Shards of ice that formed and fired through the air disintegrated within inches of his body. Athyka's mages threw arcs of lightning that passed impotently through the men; their vacancy made them untouchable with magic. Braves fired arrows at the mages that changed direction by hitting their shields. Tinker Belle dodged the blast from Athyka's ice knife and fired back bolts of her power. The woman raised a magical shield to stop them with brilliant explosions.

Desperation built within her breast as her attempts to strike the braves seemed to mock her. She pressed harder, forcing the mages to cast more violent spells and even disabled their magical safeties, allowing them to spend their own life force, even to their eventual death.

Solomon cawed and a host of ravens and razorhorns rushed over the wall to attack the sailors and mages. Athyka flailed and dodged, striking them from the air as they rushed her. Unable to pass through the wall, Smee was forced to fight off spear-fast braves and dive-bombing birds with his knife.

Released by the panicking dwarf, hate washed over Santi as he glared at Peter. It became clear to Santi that his chaos and pain was all because of Peter. Peter failed at being the pan, was captured and killed, and still he returned untouched. Peter, who lost the mantle in death and took it from Santi, its rightful heir. Peter, who thought he owned Santi, yet had never dared earn such a place of power. Peter and his infinite youth. Peter, who didn't properly deal with the Unionists at the tree, leaving the dwarf free to take Santi and do things to him. Peter, a bloody ginger. Rage consumed him.

Santi raced to the tree and ducked through the gaps in the larger roots to skirt the battle.

Peter snatched a sword from the pile of weapons by the firepit and prepared to join the fight when he heard Shifu scream as firebolts glanced past him where he hid near the cliff's edge. Peter raced for Shifu as Tinker Belle moved to protect him.

"What happened!" Peter crouched over Shifu. "Where's Tootles and Santi!?"

Having fallen to avoid firebolts whizzing through the air, Shifu twisted the crossbolt buried in his hip. The boy screamed as blood gushed from the wound.

"Hold on! I'll help!" Peter set his hand on Shifu's hip around the wound and gripped the crossbolt.

Peter- wait! Tinker Belle tried to stop him. He yanked it out. Shifu screamed louder and a spray of blood erupted from the wound. Peter twisted and tried to wipe the blood from his eyes, smearing it, when he caught sight of Santi approaching.

"Santi!" Peter looked in hope until he saw the yellow-eyed murder staring back.

"DIE!!" Santi planted his foot in Peter's chest and kicked with all his considerable might.

Peter flew backwards several feet and out over the cliff's edge. Realization filled his face as he coursed into open air and fell.

PETERR!! Tinker Belle's chimal rip turned heads.

Sinking to her knees, Athyka dropped the ohna, clutched her hair and screamed.

64

To Fly

"**Y**ou little SHIT!" Athyka leapt to her feet and seized Santi's mind. Rushing past the horrors of Smee's violation, she dove deep and crashed through a bright doorway framing an infinite darkness. Inside, an old man died under a pair of small hands wrapped around his throat on the deck of a ship rolling in a violent ocean. On the far side of the deck rose a small door. As time slowed, she walked past the boy choking the old man and stepped through the gate onto a lovely pebbled walk among cultivated gardens. Beyond rose a beautiful white estate capped by red tiles and long, open fields of horses. Something called her into the house. Her mind followed to his memory of a face staring from a painting wreathed in candles on a wall.

Her own face stared back from the painting. In terror, she fled from the visage into realtime.

Braves fought off the sailors while mages threw impotent bolts of fire and arcs of lightning. The braves still dodged, unaware they were impervious to the magic.

Tinker Belle chased Peter into the cloud bank, desperate to catch him up at any cost.

Tiger Lily raced for the mages and stuck them down with her spirit stick. Sailors who moved to defend them fell by arrows loosed by her father or spears of others determined to defend her.

"HAAAAA!!" a boy's bellow brought the fight to another standstill. Everyone paused.

Peter floated in mid-air just off the cliff. Tinker Belle circled him in joy.

"P- Peter!" Santi stammered as his sudden victory evaporated with renewed helplessness.

Peter drew his knife and dove into the group. He rolled over and kicked a sailor's chest with both feet. The man flew backwards into other sailors. Peter leapt at Athyka, who threw up a bout of flame and leapt aside just in time to avoid him. Peter rolled forward and kicked a mage into the wall that thrashed as its spaded vines returned to intelligent, deadly life. As spades skewered two braves and three sailors, men fled from the wall, narrowing the field of battle and slowing its progress.

Caught up in the flashes of fire and light filling the air, Tinker Belle gathered power into her hands and fired into sailors. The first explosion killed one and threw others across the lawn. One crashed near the wall for four vines to skewer and rip him apart in a burst of guts and blood that bathed others.

Peter danced with sailors, cut through their blades and severed their wrists and arms. The carnage terrified the braves, even as they defended themselves against the sailors' wild hacks.

As Peter tore into her men and Tinker Belle descended upon the mages, Athyka rushed upon the Tree's nearest root and pressed the ice knife to its bark. To her delight, she felt its power return, as if tapping a new source, and sucked the root and veins of wood dry of their moisture. She would break Peter's power at any cost. Overwhelmed by fear, she raised a fist, summoned fire, and sent it racing up the dry vein of wood into the canopy. The fire dashed and billowed up the side of the Tree before it crawled outward from the vein across the thick yellow bark.

Peter spun through the air and kicked a sailor's head so hard his neck snapped. He tried to land but collapsed to the ground in a scream of agony. His silver knife tumbled across the grass. Blue-green fire erupted around his mantle. Sailors retreated from the sight.

"YOU SEE!?" Athyka screamed. "I HAVE THE POWER!! *I* DO!"

A wail ripped from Peter. Tinker Belle flew for him but twisted and crashed to the ground next to him in her own struggle.

"Do you see what I can do!!??" Athyka stormed over him. "I control! I control you! I CONTROL EVERYONE!!"

Red Badger leapt over Peter, swung his spear and knocked the ohna from her hand. The ice knife spun into the darkness beneath the roots and his stone spearhead sliced deep through her palm. She screamed when a crossbolt punched Red Badger's shoulder and sent him to the grass.

The sun failed, revealing a blaze of fitful starlight. Braves cowered as the fiery blaze emanating from Peter underlit Athyka's terrible countenance. The fire climbing around the Tree above them snaked upward from the canopy in a narrow swirling tornado. Men across the clearing cried out as the tornado speared the atmospheric ceiling. Athyka glared upon Peter and Tinker Belle as the sky above her head exploded in a ring that raced outward beyond the distant horizon, followed by a blanket of flames.

Smee searched the sky, unable to move or react. Never in all his years above ground had anything so terrified him. Leaving Uttogea, the land beneath, was difficult enough for any dwarf. But to see the sky itself catch on fire, touched a deep inner sanctum Smee had long protected.

"Athyka!" cried one of the mages.

Athyka raised her wild countenance to the sky and faltered. "Oh ..."

Tinker Belle forced herself onto her hands and feet. She had endured breaking off a wingtip, losing Peter twice and driving headfirst into a sand berm filled with ohnas. She turned her head up at Athyka and grit her teeth. *Bitch.* She took to the air and drew power into her fists just as Athyka raised the steel feather.

The ohna avia seized control of Tinker Belle.

A mad smile painted Athyka's face as she forced the pixie to fly full speed into the side of the Tree. Tinker Belle's arm snapped and nose gushed with blood before she flew backwards and rammed herself, again, into the trunk. A third strike snapped her left, upper wing before Athyka released her. Moaning, Belle slid down the trunk in a smear of golden blood and disappeared into the roots, below. She crashed into the angled ground beneath the roots and rolled down into the chamber.

The brightening fire spread up the Tree.

Peter thrashed. His veins pulsed and eyes filled with blood. An ear-piercing wail billowed from his widening mouth. Men clutched their ears. Deaf, Athyka faced Peter and drew her bejeweled dagger, again to steal his mantle, but faltered as she saw his shadow.

In the blaze of the fire, Peter's shadow thrashed irrespective of the light. It stretched away from the Tree when thick black arms folded out of his shadow and buried long, jagged claws into the ground. Contracting arms pulled a flickering black shape from the unnatural darkness. Red, glowing eyes snapped open and a hopeless maw widened between long fangs as the shadow screamed.

Despite burst eardrums, Athyka clutched her ears as its wail cut her to the heart.

Great Cougar snatched the shaman's staff from Tiger Lily and raced for the shadow. He swung it through and shattered the creature. Pieces flew upward and rebounded into the original shape before it backhanded Great Cougar and sent him flying toward the cliff. Desperate snatches by his braves dragged him to the ground before going over.

The creature turned its attention on Peter.

Tiger Lily saw the creature as the monster from her vision in the purple haze — a bogey. She scrambled to her feet, dashed over the cowering men and threw herself between Peter and his shadow. The demonic being plowed over her as liquid fire and scorched her skin.

Great Cougar stirred at her scream. "Tiger-" Blood drooled from his nose as he forced himself onto his quivering fists. Athyka took advantage of the bogey's distraction on the native girl to advance again on Peter. Great Cougar could not climb to his feet. Red Badger lay across the grass bleeding and his men struggled with fear and the bogey's continuing wail. Though Peter lay flashing in yellow and purple fire, Great Cougar knew only one person could stop this.

"Peter!" he cried. "Wake up!"

"He can't hear you," Athyka grinned as she stood over him with the knife. "And he won't. You can't recover from a severed head." She knelt, pinning her knee into Peter's chest, gripped his hair, and raised the knife.

"PAN!" Great Cougar bellowed. "ARISE!"

Peter's eyes snapped open, filled with glowing wisps of light.

Athyka inhaled.

Peter's swinging arm slammed into her and sent her flying through the air into the cowering sailors. He rolled onto his knees, snatched Tiger Lily by the arm and yanked her away from the shadow while gathering power into his fist and fired it into the heart of the bogey. It exploded into shards of darkness that dispersed into the wind now racing up the burning tree. As the fire consumed the tree whole, Peter's sudden strength faltered and he sank to the grass. So fierce in one moment, the wall fell limp and dead the next. Quakes rocked the island as the blanket of fire stretching across the horizon deepened in color.

Sailors and mages fled over the limp wall. Athyka rolled over clutching a broken jaw. She stumbled to her knees to watch the fire swirling around the Tree bow outward and link with Peter's mantle, sending him again into flame.

Hope snuffed, Athyka staggered to her feet and fled from the chaos into a new world of madness.

65

Extinguish

Tinker Belle struggled to breathe as she lay on the incline just beneath the La'Du Lira Al'Cular. Her mind and energies drifted to her flock in Avicara, to her people and their rising fear.

THE TREE!! IT BURNS! IT BURNS! LA'DU LIRA AL'CULAR!! IT BURNS!! Aurora Vara's scream pierced her mind. Then Tinker Belle saw it — the flock filling the Tree Avicara as a congregation, all of them screaming in horror as the aurora, standing upon the dais at the hollow's heart, burned alive in crimson fire. *SHE BURNS!! SHE BURNS!!*

Elder Againa and Queen Mabsadora gaped as the aurora wailed.

What's going on!!?? cried a pixie from the congregation.

The sky burns! cried a pixie near the Tree's great opening near the top of its hollow chamber. Half the congregation rushed outside and wailed as skies burned above Avicara. Elder Againa rushed up to Aurora Vara and bellowed her name.

Horrified by the living vision, Tinker Belle realized the fire was not limited to Neverland, but covered all Pangea.

Belle had to do something.

Tinker Belle's good eye cracked open. The inside bottom of the Tree above her disintegrated in flame and ash. A gasp speared her with broken ribs, but she had no tears to cry. Laying slumped a few feet into the chamber beneath the Tree, horror dawned upon her that, if the disintegrating Tree above set fire to the small tree below …

The world might end.

Peter fought, outside, but as fire enveloped the Tree, the boy's power faltered. Something split and inverted within him that twisted his connection to her. No adjective described her pain, but her fears, insecurities and doubts melted under one goal — to extinguish the Tree before it touched the smaller one beneath. The true Tree of Life.

Tinker Belle rolled her head, desperate for a method to exact her goal, and spotted the ice knife lying a few paces away.

"HA-" she barked a painful laugh and spit blood drooling from her nose. Screaming, she forced herself to roll over and almost blacked out from the pain, but she could not give up. Not yet. She crawled to the knife using her one good arm and dragging her broken wing. Setting her tiny hand upon the object two thirds her own height, she paused to sob. A moment later, she grit her teeth, planted a heel and scooped the handle with her good arm to hug it to her breasts. She had the energy for one try, and as much as it hurt, she might pass out before she could finish.

She tried standing and sank to avoid tipping over. Squatting, she tried standing again only to crash to her knees. She sobbed, even as her ribs stabbed her.

I can't do it, she sobbed. *I can't.*

Outside, the Tree burned as bright as the sun, visible for thousands of miles. Inside, large coals and embers rained down from the furnace under the Tree interior and littered the ground. Burning scree singed out as it hit the soft dirt.

Tinker Belle had no more to give. Her wing burned like the fires above and her strength ebbed. And still, only one thing kept her from giving up.

Great Self, I'm too bloody STUBBORN! she screamed. *I will not die this way!! I will not!*

With a roar, she wrenched the knife and hugged it blade-up. Though the knife's frigid touch burned her skin, she refused to let go. Squatting, she thrust to standing and fluttered her two good wings to balance. She aimed at the nearest part of the burning ceiling with her one good eye and fired into the air.

As she raced for the underside of the tree with the frosting ice knife, she knew it would soon be over.

66

Part of this Island

The Tree's fire extinguished outward from an unseen point below. Seconds later, the fiery tornado linking it to the sky flushed into smoke outward to the horizon.

Shifu shivered in shock as Great Cougar tied off the bandage to the wound in his hip before moving to help Red Badger.

Checking Peter, Tiger Lily verified he was unharmed by the ball of fire that blanketed him moments before. "Great Spirit … What just happened?"

Bodies of sailors and braves peppered the grass, though in the whole battle, less than twenty men had died. Since none of the sailors fought independently, their stilted fighting proved a poor tactic against the braves, none of whom tried to kill the sailors.

Natives tended those with severe wounds, a few rekindled the fire in the pit and others gathered their dead.

The mound of soil that had crashed upon Tootles shifted. Men cried out and surrounded it with spears. A hand appeared, followed by a head. One terrified brave moved to attack when Tiger Lily cried out, "Wait!"

Tootles's muddy face gasped as he extricated himself from the mound. Men backed away.

Tootles coughed and rubbed the soil from his face before he froze in shock at the smoldering Tree. "What ... happened?" He climbed to his feet and approached Tiger Lily, who grabbed him in a tight hug.

"I thought you were dead!"

Tootles coughed again. "I guess not."

"How- did you?" she asked. "How're you alive?"

Tootles shrugged. Fear grew at their concerned faces. What was happening to him? He didn't know, but he was still alive, which had to count for something. Upon seeing Peter, he frowned. "What's wrong with him?"

Peter sat bolt upright and sent both falling backward. His face darkened. "Where's Athyka?"

"She ran into the jungle," said Tootles.

Peter gazed through the jungle. "She's ... gone." He turned to Tiger Lily. "Where's Santi?"

"Who?"

"The boy who kicked me off the cliff."

Tiger Lily shrank under his glare. "He ran, too."

"He ran?" Peter grit his teeth. "He won't run from me." He rolled forward onto his hands and feet into a sprint across the grass and a wild leap over the cliff. He fired through the air instead of falling and veered for the swamp.

Tiger Lily and Tootles approached the cliff. "How does he do that?"

Peter disappeared into the mists hovering over the north island.

Tootles extended his senses across his new world now returning to life. "This is our island. We are now a part of it. Like any beast in his territory, we have fought and driven off those who would take it from us. This land is ours."

Great Cougar joined them at the cliff's edge. "If we are people of the island, we must prove our place here."

"No, Father." Tiger Lily shook her head. "We already have."

Lying nearby, Shifu managed to rouse. "Wh- where's Peter?"

A smile tugged at Tootles's mouth as he glanced back at the boy. "He's flying."

67

Peter vs Santiago

Santi stumbled through the jungle as predators snapped and growled at his heels. He feared Smee would catch him up, was terrified Peter would pursue him, and felt drowned in shame. Tootles's smile haunted him as he fled. Blood pounded in his ears and his panting breaths rushed through his head. He tripped over clingy roots and uneven terrain. Where before managed, terror now overwhelmed. His heart exploded inside his chest.

He tried to spot the creatures chasing him, but all he saw was the rolling bright doorway and the vacuous blackness sucking at his soul.

Running consumed him as the jungle rushed by. He could get away. He could find one of Smee's rimshifts, whatever they were. They had to be how Peter got to Earth. If they worked for Peter, they could work for Santi.

He forced himself to stop in a small clearing and bent over to catch his breath with heaved gasps. He had to get away from this terrible place and the horrors that chased him everywhere he went. Even as he abhorred the memory, the strangled gasps of those terrible moments echoed in his ears.

"GO AWAAYYY!" Santi screamed. "GO AWAYY!!"

"SSaaaannttttiii!!" a voice echoed through the jungle.

"No," Santi spun. "NO!"

Peter was coming.

"Mother of God," Santi crashed through the jungle scree. The rush of a thrasher's long branch missed him by inches as he scrambled out of the way of a second hit. He rushed to his feet and sprinted. He could feel Peter drawing nearer. Any second, Peter would arrive.

He emerged from thick foliage at the edge of a heavy, rushing creek overlooking a high drop-off into a dark swamp. Over the tops of the trees descending the hill on the far side, he spotted the broad, sparkling rift river he encountered when he first emerged from the swamp. Without missing a beat, he aimed for the high rocks rising at the waterfall's apex to cross to the ridge. Leaping for the long rock sticking out over the falls as his halfway mark to reach the far side, he saw the blur to his right.

Peter plowed into Santi before both tumbled out into the open air and fell, stunned. Two bodies slammed into the rocky pool below in great splashes.

Santi flung upward from the water with a gasp. He clutched his ribs and moaned as he staggered from the frothing pool up the scummy hill into the dark swamp. Pain squeezed his head from hitting the water. His fingers clutched his midnight hair. He glanced across the shore before he staggered onward over the mossy mounds and through more wretched water. He must have come from Earth through a rimshift. How else did he or any other boy get here?

Behind him, Peter rose from the water, his face as dark as the swamp around them. He trudged from the water in pursuit. "SAANNTTIII!!"

Santi staggered over hard roots and soaked, mossy soil. His open mouth caught a root and bit scum into his mouth. He twisted and clutched his face, hacking as the vile muck slid into his throat. Blood drooled into his eyes and he wiped at his face, desperate to clear his vision as his head rang, yet again. He got his vision clear and spun just as Peter crashed into him and drove both into black swamp water.

Without up or down, Santi panicked and kicked and clawed at Peter. Peter thrashed, desperate for air and kicked from the bottom. Peter reared out with a splash just as Santi followed with a grip on Peter's arm.

Peter swung at Santi, who blocked it and rammed his head into Peter's face. Peter flew backwards as blood erupted from his nose.

"PETEEER!!" Santi's terrified laugh erupted from his throat. A blotch of Peter's blood remained on his forehead.

Dazed, Peter flailed and clutched at his face before staring down Santi. Tears streamed, but he forced himself onward even as blood drooled from his nostrils. "You tried to kill me!"

"YOU WON'T DIE!" Santi screamed.

"You were one of my men!" Peter spat blood drooling into his mouth. "I thought we were family!"

"I was never your family!" Santi cried. "I was the pan! I woke into this nightmare with a birthright that you stole!"

"Who cares about the mantle!?"

"You took it from me!" Santi roared. "You don't take from Santiago Carrillo de Valencia! You never, EVER, take from me!"

"You tried to take my life!" Peter cried. "I thought we were friends!"

"You thought wrong, you fucking puta!" Santi flexed quivering hands. "I am a noble! I am in line for the throne of Aragon! You are the spoiled brat of a defeated kingdom! Who spits at what he's been so easily given! Power that belongs to others!"

"Who cares about my stupid palace! Or its money! Or who uses what! That's all you cared about! All your questions about my father and his money. What the hell is wrong with you!? Who cares about wealth!?"

"There is no wealth but power," Santi growled. "Power is for those who deserve it!" Santi bellowed. "I deserve it! I deserve to be pan! You took it from me! I was the pan!"

"Why does everyone want this SELF DAMN MANTLE!?" Peter roared.

A deep, feral clicking echoed through the darkness.

"This is your doing! All of this is your fault! You took the mantle from me! You took *strength* from me!" Santi's fluttering blink morphed into a glare for Peter. "And I *will* kill you."

"Try it!"

Santi grit his teeth. "I will have your heart to eat when I am through with you! And I will have your magic, too! It is mine! I deserve it!"

"This mantle isn't yours!"

The clicking drew nearer, a low-throat growl that cut the thick air.

Santi marched up onto the mound next to Peter. Strength filled him in this dark and murky place. Power filled his lean muscles. He felt coiled tight, ready to strike. The pulse of the swamp filled his blood. As the clicks drew closer, the pounding of his heart grew into long, slow thunderous explosions in his chest. Like his father's priceless clock echoing through their adobe estate in the dead of night, his heart pounded in slow, heavy beats.

TICK.

A hackle formed in his mind as the hair on his neck stood on end. Doom approached through the swamp with heavy lumbers. Santi's breath faltered. The gong of his father's clock drew a fearful image to his mind. The bright doorway and the darkness beyond engulfed him, whole.

"N-no," Santi gasped.

"Just go home," Peter quivered. "Go back to where you came from. I don't want you here, anymore."

"Come here," Santi managed through his mounting terror.

"No! I'm leaving!" Peter turned away. "I'm not playing this anymore!"

"You goddamn coward!" Santi roared. "Face me like a man!"

"I'm not a coward!" Peter's eyes flared, his chest puffed and his back arched. "And I'm no stupid man, either!"

"You are a coward! Just like your mother! Just like your father!"

Peter turned. "You will *never* speak of my father that way!! Or my mother!"

"I will speak of him however I choose, boy!" Santi crouched.

TOCK.

Peter spun, grabbed the trunk of a narrow tree and used it to sling himself. Santi sidestepped him with an instinctive flair of his arm. His saber training fed him his response. Peter sailed into the scummy water with a splash. Santi leapt after him. Peter emerged from the water just before Santi slammed him back under.

Peter inhaled black water as Santi grabbed his heel and began rolling. Peter had no bearing as the blackness swirled around him. In panic, Peter kicked hard enough to drive Santi back, but without orientation, he swam into the bottom. Santi's hand snatched his foot "down." Peter kicked out again, missed Santi's face, but his foot broke the surface. Coughing and hacking, he pushed off the bottom with his hands and "sank" into the air. He gasped as he "dropped" from the water only for Santi to grab his hair and yank him again into the black. Peter kicked. His heel snapped Santi's head enough to stun him.

Santi fell back. Now upright, Peter leapt from the water to take another breath when Santi hooked him in the gut with his right fist and knocked the wind from him. Peter slammed on his side across a nearby mound and struggled to inhale. Santi rushed from the water and drove his knee into Peter's back to pin him face down into the shallow water. He clenched Peter's red hair and drove his face into the muck.

TICK.

"Take it." Santi panted with excitement as Peter thrashed for life beneath him. Death's edge ignited his blood as the ginger flailed for air. Something in Santi's mind screamed again of a coming danger.

Kicking down to brace himself, Peter reared his hand and snatched Santi's thick hair. He hauled himself up with his grip and erupted with hacking as his lungs spewed what had gotten inside. Vomit followed. He came up so fast Santi's face slapped the ground.

Santi clawed his way up as Peter bent over on all fours to empty his stomach and kicked him in the side, sending him rolling through the air into more black water. He stomped down into the black waves and snatched Peter by the hair.

"You have one adventure left," Santi growled into Peter's ear. "That adventure is death."

Peter sobbed as blood drooled down his scum-smeared face.

"I will do to you as I did to my dear, beloved grandfather, the *great* monk and all his Christ-likeness ..." Santi moaned. He snapped his tight fist into Peter's face and split his lip. "I gave him *his* grand adventure after taking me into the wild, away from my birthright! The wealthiest duke in Valencia finds Jesus FUCKING Christ late in life and steals his wayward grandson to Brasil to save his soul!!??"

TOCK.

"He took away all that belonged to me!" Santi panted into Peter's ear. "He took away my estate and my horses and my prospects for pussy so I could become a goddamn celibate monk! A GOD DAMN MONK!!??"

Yellow reptilian eyes burned from Santi's inglorious countenance.

"Now I shall deliver your adventure." Santi hauled Peter until his face was finger-widths from his spittling mouth. His fingers curled around Peter's neck. "You took away my strength—" He faltered at the memory of Smee's violation. "You brought me here to this place. You took my strength. You sent me out on stupid missions where..." He gulped. "It's your fault I was too weak... too weak." Santi tamped down a mountain of shame.

Peter struggled to wrench Santi's iron grip from his neck.

"Give me back my mantle, boy!" Santi squeezed.

Peter locked onto a solitary purple speck in Santi's left eye, shimmering in the faint swamplight, before they spaced out and his hands flailed, desperate to breathe. Hot blood rushed through Santi's cheeks. A smile spread across his face as an indescribable arousal filled him.

"Give me your mantle…" Santi trailed off first in pleasure, then in loss as something inside of him faltered at the arrival of a presence. His breath failed and fingers weakened.

Regaining some level of lucidity, Peter wrenched Santi's wrists apart and managed to suck air. As he gasped, Santi's eyes fluttered and Peter raised his fist and drove it down into his face, snapping Santi's head back.

TICK.

Santi staggered through the water and up the far mound as fear overwhelmed him. Disoriented, he wiped his eyes and found himself facing two glowing yellow orbs hovering before him, the same yellow orbs he had seen in his dreams. Darkness opened between them and a heated roar bathed Santi.

"What is it!?" Santi screamed.

Peter staggered across the water, coughing, and glared at Santi. "Lord crocodile."

"WHAT!?" Santi cried at the crocodile's slowly yawning jaws, revealing rows of enormous teeth.

TOCK.

"You're his boy!" Peter stopped short of the mound in knee-deep water. "He's come back!"

"What!?" Santi stepped backwards. "What's it want!?"

Peter ascended until he floated inches above the scummy surface. Water drooled down his legs and feet. "You."

Santi spun to Peter. "HELP ME!!"

TICK.

"No," Peter darkened. "Help yourself."

More than horror crept into Santiago's gaze; hopelessness settled so that even Peter's stomach turned.

TOCK.

Lord Crocodile moved. Santi threw out his hand. Despite his condemnation, Peter took Santi's proffered hand and yanked him away from the croc. The thunderclap of the beast's monstrous jaws cast a stunned Peter across the mound and into the water.

"Santi!" Peter scrambled to his feet and raised his right hand with

Santi's still firmly in his grip.

It was all that remained of the boy.

The croc snapped its jaws several more times, paused to eye Peter and turned with a mighty crash to lumber into the darkness.

Santi was lost.

68

Alone

Peter's stomach heaved, again, and he dropped to his knees to try and vomit an empty stomach. Once it passed, he panicked as Santi's iron grip clung to his own. He thrashed his hand, desperate to free it from Santi's iron fingers. It flew off and landed on a distant mound.

Peter scrambled backwards onto another mound until a cypress tree blocked his path. All that remained were the lone hand and the dwindling shadow of the beast that devoured him.

Sobs erupted from Peter's throat. He clutched his mouth as tears poured down his cheeks, but he could not pull his gaze away. The swamp darkened as the sun faded from the sky above. Peter's cries faded. He wanted to flee from it, but he could not.

Santi was his first boy. Santi had tried to kill him. Santi was dead.

Though he did not know why, he felt he needed to honor Santi, despite how twisted the boy proved to be. Santi had saved his life, making it possible for Peter to continue as pan. Santi gave him the chance to find his father, even if the Unionists killed him. Peter remembered the recent touch and voice of his mother, though he could not remember seeing her. He missed her so much. He missed his father.

Peter crawled to the hand, shooed away bugs already gnawing on it and took it by the first finger, a stiff hook from where it had clung to his own. He scooped his fingers into the scummy mound and dug as deep as he could, through thick water filling the muddy soil, ripping away roots. He set the hand there and paused. Nodding, he filled it over. Through everything, all Peter could remember was the fear in Santi's face as he reached out with hope Peter might save him.

Peter failed.

"I'm … sorry, Santi," Peter said. "I'm sorry."

Silence reigned through the swamp as Peter's tears dripped from his face. The insufferable heat felt appropriate to Peter's shame. The boy sank onto his bottom and tried to wipe his bloody face with his scummy forearm and only achieved smearing it. Giving up, he sat there, unsure of what to do.

After time passed, he climbed to his feet, took one last look toward where he buried Santi's hand and started walking. Overwhelmed, he struggled to focus, and followed the flow of water toward a large cave rumbling with a faint thunder. He trudged inside, exhausted, until light appeared at its far end, revealing a waterfall filling the cave mouth. He paused just shy of the torrent before stepping into its icy deluge that soaked him through and rushed his skin.

Peter scrubbed away the swamp from his body more easily than the memories from his mind before emerging into a large pool of water on its far side. Too tired to think about what to do, he climbed from the small creek leading to the Rift River and sat upon a rock, where he stared into space.

The flap of wings signaled a newcomer and drew his attention to the large raven landing upon a nearby rock.

"Hello, Peter," said Solomon.

Peter swallowed the lump in his throat as he eyed the bird for a long moment. "Why'd this have to happen, Solomon?"

"Truth be told, none of this had to happen," said the raven. "Unfortunately, there will always be complicated people in this world, some of whom can't seem to overcome themselves, and whose darkness destroys everything they touch."

"I killed him."

"No," Solomon hopped closer. "You didn't."

Peter hugged himself.

"Come, my boy," Solomon flapped his feathers and leapt into the air.

"Let's get you back to the world of the living."

Peter took a slow breath before rising into the air and following from the misty pool into the warm Neverland sunset peeking around the southern base of Pan's Peak.

Fresh tears fell as he joined the raven. Ahead, he felt Tinker Belle stir in a great deal of pain.

On Peter's left, Solomon angled his wings to steady himself in the wind.

Peter's bloody face looked to the raven. "Is this what having the mantle means? Everybody around you just wants to use you and take it from you?"

"I wish I could tell you that power attracted the noble and incorruptible." Solomon cocked his black eye at Peter. "Many claim to want this power for good, but few want the responsibility such ideas require."

"Responsibility for power? You mean like what Athyka said. I have a responsibility to help others?"

"Power, by itself, begets neither authority nor responsibility." Solomon adjusted to the wind. "Power is merely an ability. Your ability no more requires you to help others than your hunger or your breath. To believe that your ability requires you to serve others, regardless of your volition, is paramount to slavery."

"But ... shouldn't I do something for people? Isn't that the responsibility of people who have power?"

"There are times that that is true. But sometimes, the wisest thing a sentient can do with power is not to use it at all."

"What do you mean?"

"Every being in this world has power, Peter," Solomon said. "But not everyone fully realizes that power. Either through oppression, lack of self-belief, fear of the unknown, or just laziness, many never realize their full potential. While helping others in need is a wise and loving thing to do, sometimes choosing to withhold power forces people to risk their comfort and fight for their own. If you don't have the right to choose when and how to help individuals, then you are a slave to others' undeveloped maturity."

"That's not what the Unionists say."

"Like all groups, the Unionists are a mixed bag," Solomon said. "Though many of their most powerful are in it solely for the wealth and control their politics creates, some truly believe the only way to help those in need is to remove all forms of difficulty, from economic to social to culture. They are circumstantialists who believe the conditions outside our hearts are the cause of our problems. In fact, the heart is the *cause* of all problems. It is good for the powerful to help those in need throw off oppressors they aren't strong enough to cast off, themselves, but until you are willing to see the truth about the heart, face yourself and acknowledge that all sentient beings are capable of great evil, you will always blame your circumstances and, thus, be a slave to them."

"What does this have to do with the mantle?"

"We can try to blame the Unionists for their obsession with using the mantle as a symbol of power, but we can't until we first acknowledge that the mantle was never meant for Eden, in the first place."

"But lords of Eden have been pans for thousands of years!"

"The mantle is not for politics, Peter. The power exists to protect the ohnas, not to control herds of men."

"So, I need to return the ohnas now." Peter wiped blood from his face. "How do I do that? And... and how can I fly!? I don't think I can do this. There's so much I don't understand."

"Learning why, who, what, and where you are," Solomon said, "requires facing the greatest adventure all sentients must take."

"What adventure is that?" Peter asked. "Do you mean, like, death? Like Santi said?"

"No, young pan! Life!" Solomon swirled with the wind. "Life! And while it will not be easy, know that you do not travel this path alone. I am with you, to the end of the age. And you have friends waiting on you back at the Tree, friends whom you can trust. Especially that little pixie of yours."

"Tink," Peter sniffed wetly as they climbed. "What do I do now?"

"You've already felt its pull, Peter," Solomon said. "The powers have called to you. You must return them to their places, or consequences far greater than war will beset all life here in the third realm."

"How will I know how to do that?" Peter asked.

"When you pause long enough to listen to the Great Self's design for you, you'll know the path in your heart. He will set your steps. Trust that still small voice, and you will find the path to eternity. I daresay you could find a way to live forever."

"I don't want to live forever," Peter said.

"Good," Solomon almost seemed to smile. "Because to live today is an awfully big adventure, all by itself."

"Yeah," Peter barked an exhausted laugh. "Yeah, it is."

"Come." Solomon flapped his wings to gain altitude. "Let's get you home."

As twinkling stars pierced the evening haze and Neverland returned to its evening cacophony, the two climbed into the warm golden sunset and disappeared as silhouettes against the Tree's great canopy washing in the evening wind.

Epilogue

Athyka stumbled through the jungle as creatures screamed behind her. Blood painted her body and gummed her vision as she continued through the growing darkness. Rage and shame consumed her, though all she could see was the ghost of the noonday Tree burned into her retinas.

She lost her ohnas and with them, her hope of expanding her powers. The idea of becoming a psylock embarrassed her — she would never reach such a pedestal. As she fled through the jungle, she discovered an ability to push animals away by willing them to flee. Could she mount a counterattack with the beasts of Neverland?

A bush exploded next to her, burying dozens of thorns into her skin. She cried out in shock and clutched her face. As her fingers brushed the thorns, they burrowed deeper.

"This- BLOODY ISLAND!" she clenched her cold left fist and froze each thorn. She couldn't rip them out — not right now. As Neverland's evening chaos overwhelmed her thoughts, she had to escape. She had to get to the ship.

Athyka stumbled to her knees when the truth dawned upon her — The Hover was empty. She had called every last man from it for battle, so even if she could row her ship's boat out to the lagoon, how could she manage such a vessel by herself? Back on her feet, she stumbled through the thick jungle, exhausted and starving. At the top of a small ridge, she followed its narrow edge when her feet slipped out from under her and she tumbled. End over end through the flora, she moaned as she hit small trees and roots. She clawed at the ground to gain a hold when she hit a bump and flew through the air. She crashed into a large bush overlooking a narrow vertical slit in the rockface below. Mist wafted upward from an exposed underwater creek as she dangled over it, suspended by her weak grip.

Athyka clung to the bush as the chitter of tiny bugs filled the air. The moment she felt them touch her hand, she let go and fell into the darkness below, consumed by the creek.

She rolled into the midnight chaos and crashed into rock walls and boulders. She passed through a barrier that shocked her nerves. She tried to scream and instead inhaled water.

Light appeared above the water's surface as the water left the cave. She crashed over boulders as new darkness closed in when someone snatched her arms and hauled her to the surface.

She spewed water as two pairs of strong hands lifted her from the creek and laid her upon her side on dry land. Hands smacked her back to help her clear her lungs. Among the men in strange clothing, a figure of midnight hair, straight nose, bold chin and dark eyes approached wearing a white blouse, an ornate red and gold doublet over crimson stockings and fine leather boots. His mop framed his handsome face as he inspected her, but when he spotted the gashed side of her face, he recoiled.

So long protective of her wounds, the ice in her face melted to expose cheekbone and teeth. The ohna's link was gone. To her relief, Athyka was no longer on Algueda.

Horror covered both men's faces. They attempted to question her with voices she could not hear. Pain welled in facial nerves long muted by the cold, but though she felt weak and without her ohnas, she had one final hope.

Athyka reached out to their minds. Unlike the sailors and the agents, she could not take control. These men had no magic.

They were vacant.

Athyka realized, then, that all her dreams and hopes of finding her freedom from Roschach while maintaining her position and power were gone. Chasing after the pan, tugging that bare thread of hope to become a more powerful daleen, her insistence on being the one to reclaim the ohnas, no matter the cost, crashed in on her as she realized she was no longer on Pangea or Algueda. To her horror, she realized she, somehow, had made it the one place she had never wanted to go, where her magic meant nothing and her psylism, even less.

Athyka had stumbled into Earth.

There was no going home. There was no way back. After wielding more power than mankind had touched since the reformation first split the Alterworlds from Pangea and revealed the powers of creation to mankind, Athyka was now deaf, deformed, and impotent in a land where men ruled by the might of their fists.

She was in hell.

Desperate, she reached one last time for their minds. Unable to control or supplant memory, she found one small magic she could touch, one she had never before considered using. Looking up at the handsome noble, she pressed and prayed to Self it would be enough to save her life.

For the first time, she ignored mind and might and instead, pressed upon love.

* * *

The pressure of the mountain oath persisted on Smee. It lifted only in death or deliberate release, but there was no sign of the oath binder. Despite her addition to the oath that he never flee from her, he felt no compulsion to find her. After all, he wasn't trying to run from her.

Smee sniffed at the shifting winds for another trace of the boy. Once the dwarf escaped from the madness at the Tree and the sky extinguished, he circled around in hopes of finding the boy again.

Santi's scent snaked east from Pan's Peak before disappearing at the top of a waterfall. Smee found his way across the heavy creek and down the hill to the rift river cutting Neverland in two and along a high ridge to the overgrown entrance of the swamp below.

Smells and sounds climbed with the temperature. Smee plodded his way through the swamp. More than once, he was forced to use his ability to drive away bugs to keep himself from being overwhelmed. He feared the bugs would stop fleeing and rush upon him anyway. Certain tactics never worked forever.

The dwarf trudged through high, scummy water and gooey mounds. Flying bugs snipped and bit at his face and long ears. Snakes drooped low from high branches. Lizards hissed as he passed them by. Time stretched as night deepened. Were it not for his dwarven hearing and sense of smell, he would have died twice and been lost for sure. Santi's scent strengthened as he approached the side of a wall of trees and ground. A broad maw of a cave extended outwards where it met the water. The darkness within made the faint light outside seem bright.

Santi checked the air to ensure he had the right place before daring to pull aside the vines and enter the cave mouth. Here, Smee toed his path. The cave reeked of death and scat. He pressed himself to the cave wall and inched his way forward, avoiding the heavy water in the center of the path. Though the stench burned his sensitive nose, he caught a whiff of something else — something unexpected. Somewhere in the rear of the cave was a rimshift.

Smee smiled.

Rounding the cave's slow curve to the right, Smee peeked to find an enormous amphibian trying delicately to move something with its snout. Wrapped around the dome-like cave, the beast twisted and shifted in vain to bury something. As it rounded the chamber and its tail slid past Smee's point of view, the dwarf spotted a pale child atop a craterous nest of bones and scree. Taking the boy with the crocodile in reach was out of the question. Why the croc was trying to put Santi into a nest baffled Smee.

Smee slowed his heartbeat to lower his body heat and the smell of his warm sweat. He waited. Hours passed until the croc gave up. The beast lay curled in the large chamber, breathing in long, slow breaths. Smee had dozed, himself, when he sensed the presence of the creature only inches away. He dared not move. Heavy breathing brushed his hair as the beast stood next to him, sniffing at the air. Smee struggled not to race from the cave, knowing the crocodile would be upon him before he could take two steps. The amphibians were lightning fast in short bursts.

Time passed before the croc gave up exploring Smee's invasive scent and lumbered for the cave entrance. Smee waited until the tail had long disappeared from the silhouette of the cave's heavy vinery, and then some. Smee padded over the soft ground to the nest where Santiago lay half-buried in a small sink in the center. Fragments of a large, old eggshell littered the space. Had the crocodile tried to force Santi to return into the empty, half-buried egg?

Smee lifted Santi out and noticed broken ribs, arms and large sections of bruising and internal bleeding — and a missing hand, whose stump failed to bleed thanks to the croc's thick saliva. Smee smirked — it was the same hand by which he attacked Smee. The unconscious boy snatched shallow gasps of breath, his body covered in reeking scum and croc spit. Smee lifted the boy and turned just as the croc lumbered back into the cave.

"Shit," Smee turned. With the croc filling the cavemouth, what little light Smee had enjoyed now disappeared.

A bone-shattering roar thundered among the rock walls. Smee clutched his ears as his head rang. The croc rushed inward, but it could not sprint in a curve and had to stop to turn at each point. Smee sniffed for the faint smell of the rimshift. With his left hand probing for the wall and Santi over his right shoulder, Smee raced away from the wicked beast. At the rear of the chamber, he rushed alongside the wall as the croc freed itself and turned its glowing yellow eyes upon him in the darkness. The beast sprinted across the chamber.

There! Smee found the crack leading into the caves and the rimshift. He stuffed Santi's limp body through and forced himself inside just as the massive jaws clapped against the vertical hole behind him. The wave of its wind struck Smee in the back and sent him and the boy onto the narrow passage floor.

The following roar made Smee question if he lost his hearing and sanity. Reclaiming the boy almost cost him his life. The croc's yellow eye slid into view. He snatched up the boy and wiggled through the cave, laughing in nervous relief the croc couldn't follow while terror still gripped him from within.

"Le's go, boy," Smee quivered as they approached the rimshift. "I smell a new worl' ahead." He paused to sniff Santi and smiled. "Yes. Your worl', I b'lieve." With ears ringing and thick left hand out to guide the way, Smee made for the gateway to Earth.

* * *

"Upon this bedrock…" Deron Frederick's voice carried across the Square Al'Cular. "We set the foundation of our new nation in the blood of our finest!"

Standing on the spot which, two days prior, witnessed the slaughter of the quorum of faith, the President of the Council of Man stood over three bodies wrapped in pearl silk lain next to three topless marble sarcophagi. The stage had been removed and the three sarcophagi lay side-by-side in its stead at the north side of the dogwood growing at courtyard's heart. Only those nearest could see him, but all could hear his magic-amplified voice, broken with sorrow as he gazed downward.

"Even now, Fellow Roschach fights the poison used by the cowardly Edenon alliance to end our hope for a brighter future!"

The crowd booed and jeered.

"We cannot allow this to go unanswered!" Frederick roared. "We must take our fight across the continent! If the people cannot see that they need to be ruled, we will *make* them see!!" The crowd applauded. "If the people are too weak to know what's good for them, we will make them submit for everyone's benefit!" The crowd cried and cheered. "IF THEY CANNOT RULE THEMSELVES AS THEY OUGHT, WE WILL RULE THEM ALL!!"

The crowd boiled. People screamed and sobbed, either in support of Frederick's words or the loss of their beloved quorum leaders. Frederick waited for them to calm. He raised his hand as the moment lingered.

"Matriarch Damian has made clear to me that we are in a tender time," his voice quieted them. "We must have strong leadership, but gathering the quorum took time, time we may not have to find more. We never imagined traitors would so boldly show their evil faces in our midst at such a time of glory."

The crowd hissed.

"Matriarch Damian has declared that, until we find our stability, Fellow Roschach, alone, will carry forward our torch of unity. In him? We! Can! Trust!"

The crowd roared with applause.

"Our finest fight for his life as the torch to our great cause, a cause for something we now see is inevitable — empire. A *people's* empire! This dream began as a simple union of men, but now we must dream bigger, for a union of states until one vision! One morality! One rule!

One benevolent ruler! As soon as Fellow Roschach is healthy enough, we …" He drifted off as thousands of onlookers turned from him toward the great doors at the entrance to the palace. Frederick turned as the murmuring crowd gasped.

Standing there with a cane and two assistants stood Elwin Roschach, himself, pale and haggard, wearing a formal white military uniform trimmed in gold with broad golden crossbars across his chest.

The courtyard fell still.

Roschach took a step, then another. Each hesitant step drew sharp breaths across the masses as they watched his glowing figure struggle against weakness to cross the stone paths. Halfway to the three sarcophagi, he stumbled. The crowd gasped and prefects stepped close to implore him to return to bed before he waved them off. Tapping his throat, he forced himself up.

"I will see my compatriots!" His deep, commanding voice echoed off the round walls of the courtyard. Murmurs of approval erupted with cheering. He forced himself onward until he could grip Deron Frederick's arm. Frederick helped him stand and present him.

The roar continued until Roschach raised his hand to silence them.

"My dear friends." Roschach took an exhausted breath. "The enemy has done their worst to strike our heart. But it, still, beats."

The crowd exploded.

Roschach's hand on his cane quivered as he fought to remain standing. "Show them to me. Please."

Deron helped Roschach walk first to Grontham's tall figure. Roschach leaned over and gently untucked the silk from over Eberhart's face. Despite the pall of death, Eberhart could have fallen asleep moments ago. Several long moments later, he returned the veil and faced Elizabeth Kelg. A soldier untucked it for him and he leaned over. Half her face had been scored to the skull, but the soldier kept the veil over the unseemly part. Roschach nodded and, with Deron's help, moved around to Baley.

Roschach waved off the soldier and came around to stand over her body. He paused longest, quieting the crowd as tears formed. Untucking the silk from her face, he pulled it away. Baley lay dead in the pristine nature of bloodless bodies. He stooped with the soldier's help and kissed her forehead.

Sniffles and cries of sorrow echoed across the audience.

As Roschach drew back, he noticed her mouth and the lips parting from the movement. He reached up and caressed her lips and froze as they opened more.

The corpse lying before him had both front teeth.

The little color in Roschach's skin disappeared as he remembered Baley chipping a tooth the night of the attack.

"Fellow Roschach, are you alright?" Frederick leaned in as Roschach paled.

However fine a copy, this was not Brianne Baley.

The crowd fell silent at the alarmed look on his face.

"Fellow? Sire?" the soldier gulped.

Roschach took one last look at the corpse's face and the exposed front teeth and coughed. "Baley." His magic-amplified voice startled himself. "She- she was the best of us." His heart raced. "And ... she showed us that- anyone can change. Even those from the worst people, the worst families, the worst culture ... they can find salvation through submitting..." Roschach struggled not to scream with fury or fear. "... to the collective! To put others' needs ever higher than your own!" His poison-addled mind raced with terror and rage; by a hair's width did he manage to keep his wits. "She was our best!"

The crowd half-cheered, half-moaned in sorrow.

"And- and last night's fire," he managed, having planned a complex story about something he wasn't even awake to see last night, "is nothing to fear, but the..." he inhaled, "...the universe crying out in anger!"

The crowd murmured.

"IN ANGER FOR THIS CRIME AGAINST HUMANITY!!"

The masses boiled.

"We must have justice!" he growled. "WE WILL HAVE JUSTICE!!"

The crowd exploded with fury and fear and cheering and screaming.

Roschach coughed and managed to touch his throat to deactivate his amplifier before moaning, "get me back inside."

The soldiers gathered and lifted him with care. As they carried him up the walk, thousands of hands reached out for him in prayer, supplication and hope. They did not see him staring skyward, his addled mind struggling to connect dots he could not see, even as the weight of their failure to capture the mantle weighed upon him.

Fear of a reprisal from Baley welled within him, but as the great doors of the palace swallowed his view of the sky, all he could see was the terror of the continent's two most powerful empires — Graela and Alderland

— coming to account for his failure to capture the mantle.

Somehow, Roschach and his new empire had to find a way to survive without it.

* * *

Wendy thrashed in her sheets and bolted upright in a heavy sweat. She clutched her wild brunette hair in muted sobs. "Oh god … oh god …"

Even awake, the images continued. Thrashing trees whipped men apart; bushes exploded with thorns burrowing into the skin; bugs ate men from the inside out; skinrip vines and razorhorn hawks shredded flesh; great beasts leapt upon fleeing sailors and bit off their heads. Most frightening of all, glowing yellow orbs waited in the murk of the swamp.

Her breath stuttered as she rocked herself. "The crocodile ate him! It ate him! And the- the men ripped apart by those vines!" Tears streamed down rosy cheeks. A rainstorm outside raged against the twin shuttered windows of the nursery. She flinched as the torrent of visions started yet again.

The ship sailed up the side of the island on a rogue, snaking wave crashing through the jungle; boys adventured across the island fighting monstrous beasts; a yellow pixie zipped through canopies and caves full of snapping predators; a burning, gigantic tree set a distant sky aflame.

Peter flew.

Wendy grimaced under a shower of tears. "Why did he touch me? Why? Why- did he touch me? Please stop!" She rocked. "Oh god, please stop!"

Though her nightmares ebbed as her mind woke, terror remained. Quivering arms hugged her knees as she took slow, deep breaths to calm herself. Desperate to move and be surrounded by light, she looked to her brother, Michael, lying in the bed across the nursery, and could hear the labored breathing of his persistent flu — a flu caught in the Hyde Park incident.

Wendy did not remember anything else for the rest of that day. Waking the next morning, she had never seen her mother so worried in her entire life. Several men had brought her and Michael to their home and stayed until Mary returned to relay that their daughter had somehow saved Michael and an old man from a runaway carriage, whose horses attempted to follow Wendy to her house, despite the driver's violent attempts to prevent them. Mary didn't seem to remember Wendy's worry about voices, especially as Michael fell ill from his prolonged exposure to the icy rain.

Wendy rose, tugged his blanket up his body and made her way out into the hallway to the water closet.

She flipped the switch before stepping inside for the lone bulb to warm the space. Before she could move to the toilet, she caught sight of something in the mirror. As she raised her eyes to her reflection, she froze.

Alongside the gash down the front of her face where she slapped face-first into Serpentine Road, both irises shimmered as if a collection of tiny reflective amethyst stones. The few purple flecks she once possessed now replaced every point of blue. Wendy retreated a step as both widening eyes glowed in the faint bulblight. What was happening to her? The boy touched her. Her mind had exploded shortly after. Suddenly she dreams of his adventures of others the boy had touched. Then she hears faint whispers, as if from beyond the horizon, of billions of tiny voices calling for her. Now this.

Something changed, nearby.

"Oh, no." Wendy froze and turned. Someone had left the house- no, that wasn't right. Someone simply wasn't there anymore.

Fear arose in her breast. She snatched open the door and rushed to the nursery. Flipping on the light switch, she rushed for Michael's bed.

"Michael?" she whispered and touched his shoulder — the boy had fallen still.

Wendy cupped his chubby face and recoiled from the cooling cheeks. "Oh- oh- by heaven. By-" She rushed for the nursery door to get her parents when a brilliant light filled the room. Twisting in surprise, she tripped backwards into the wall next to the nursery door before slumping to the ground in terror.

A vertical rift of warbling light cut and expanded where the tall nursery windows stood. A nose poked through to sniff at the air before a massive, furry head and large, round ears followed. Dark, black eyes turned upon Wendy.

Her lungs failed when monstrous paws with great, curved claws stepped onto the nursery carpet beneath broad, furry shoulders. The bear sniffed upwards, then its terrible head and midnight gaze fell upon her. Wendy pressed herself to the door as her bladder emptied on the carpet.

Shimmering in the rift's strange light, a bear filled the room as it neared her. Its snout was as large as her entire trunk, and its rough sniffs sucked her wavy brown hair.

Terror's iron grip silenced Wendy to squeaks.

The bear turned from her and nosed Michael's dead body. Great, fanged jaws yawed open, wiggled around Michael's limp form and lifted him with care from the bed. The beast faced her while its massive body avoided knocking anything as it turned in the nursery. Soundless wails moved her mouth as the beast turned back toward her with her brother dangling from its jowls before returning through the hole in space. Once its short, fuzzy tail disappeared, the rift disintegrated and its brilliant, warbling light died to nothing in faint whispers.

When the room fell dark once more, Wendy scrambled to Michael's bed and ripped away the sheets. "Michael!? Michael! MIIICHAAEELLL!"

She fell to her knees. Doors snatched open in the hallway outside the nursery signaled her approaching parents.

Clutching Michael's sheets, Wendy screamed.

* * *

"82, 81, 80, 79 …" Peter sat on the floor of the cavern, counting down as Tinker Belle sat nearby preening herself with a bandaged wing and arm. A small fire crackled a few paces away from the Little Tree, rung in small river stones and cut low with a wind catch to feed the air into the coals. Boys around the fire reclined in fine wooden chairs from The Hover while whittling wood. A large round table and other chairs were positioned a few paces away. Bedding and blankets rung the angled floor of the cavern where boys had made their beds. Stoked low for daytime, the fire offered a gentle warmth to its broad chamber.

You can count to yourself, Peter, Tinker Belle scratched her arm through her leafy bandage.

"I am counting to myself, Tink," Peter reclined and crossed his ankles, but he counted at a lower volume. "I just remember where I am easier when I count out loud."

You're perfectly capable of keeping track without counting so loudly.

"Tink! You made me lose my place!" Peter huffed. "Now, I have to start over!"

Why don't you go on and find the boys? Tinker Belle chimed.

"I wanted to give them a real chance to hide," Peter crossed his arms. "We've been at this three weeks. Nearly thirty boys and still none can hide from me."

You don't sound pleased.

"Of course, I'm pleased!" Peter stammered. "But it's the principle of the thing! It shouldn't be so easy every time."

She took a breath. *How're you doing?*

"Good," he shrugged.

Peter, I've been meaning to talk to you.

"About what?"

About losing your father... she paused. *That's hard. Even harder when he died the way he did. In front of you.*

Peter blinked at her. "What're you talking about?"

Tinker Belle sat up. *What do you mean, what am I talking about? Your ... father. Dying by that agent.*

"I'm not sure what you're talking about, Tink," Peter said.

Your father, Peter! What's wrong with you!?

Peter leaned back. "I feel fine."

Tinker Belle opened her mouth to speak. Perhaps Peter just wasn't ready to talk about it? She sighed. *Go. Find the boys. You're driving me nuts.*

"But-" Peter eyed her injuries. "What if you need something?"

Tootles takes fine care of me, boy. Now go. I've got thinking to do and you tapping your foot doesn't help.

"Okay." Peter flashed his grin and approached the roots just as Tootles opened them to come inside.

"Peter," Tootles said. "We were just moving the bed in like you asked."

Four boys held the captain's bed recovered from The Hover.

"Excellent!" Peter smiled. "I'll get out of the way." He ascended up through the root gap above him. Tootles tightened small vines wrapped around the mattress to squeeze it tight enough to get through the limited, if better-than-nothing, hole.

Boys carrying the bed nodded at Peter. Each new boy emerged from his nest as a human, but often within days grew fur or scales and appeared ever more like the monster from which he had been rescued. The four moving his bed into the chamber consisted of a monkey, a bear, a badger and a sidewinder snake, though the boy still kept his arms and legs. Some boys took longer than others to reveal bestial qualities, and one barely seemed to have emerged from a beast at all.

Peter didn't know what to make of it and wondered if his father knew of the transformations as well. Boys reclining nearby on the grass called out his name and waved as he ascended into the sky.

His crimson hair fluttered in the wind as he scanned the surface of the north island. He picked out the newer boys first as they were humanly and seemed least at ease with their dangerous new world.

Peter dropped from the air to tag each in a row. A succession of "aw's" and protests erupted behind him as he laughed. They first complained his flight was unfair, but as the older boys competed with each other to hide, their tunes changed to join the challenge. He coursed over the north island and spotted an older boy hiding in a tree. "Hey, Shrubs."

"Awww, Peter! How'd you find me!?" the branch spoke. While Peter could make out the humanistic shape of the boy, bark covered him from head to toe, much like Tootles. Tootles, though, had begun to carry a different, brighter shade of green with corded muscles like twisted vines. Tootles, alone, could hide from Peter.

Peter tagged Shrubs and flew eastward. Of late, the boys chatted of a monstrous new diamondback rattler spotted among the desert buttes on the south island. Tinker Belle advised him to avoid killing the full beasts, though she wasn't sure of their exact role. Peter flew in among high ridges, through narrow river canyons, climbed up one side and hovered. "Alright, Coob! I see you!"

Out of a cleft emerged a boy covered in gray, spindly scales. "Shifu said I shouldn't use this wall. Too much light."

Peter chuckled. "Use any you like!" He leaned in. "I'll still find you!" He continued along the western edge of the south island and dropped into a large clearing of ancient evergreens. Sunlight dappled the carpeted floor of fir needles. Through the mist, he spotted Shifu's orange and black stripes snug upon a branch. The boy's cat-like eyes searched the forest floor for prey. Peter descended with a grin and brushed Shifu's head with his toe.

Startled, Shifu roared and snapped his razor claws at Peter's foot.

"WHOA!" Peter cried as Shifu managed a short cut through Peter's calf. Tears welled. "What was *that* for!!?"

Shifu spun on his branch and screamed a tiger's scream as his animal gaze locked on Peter.

Floating away from Shifu, a blur plowed into Peter and nailed him to the forest floor. Peter screamed as six jagged claws ripped down his back. Blood poured from his wounds as the beast retreated from its initial attack.

"Shifu!" he cried. A cougar-child appeared next to Shifu. Both feline and feral, the boys growled at Peter. "Linky!!"

Shifu and Linky circled him as he staggered to his feet. Heavy tongues lapped chops as they focused on him. Peter sensed Tinker Belle's alarm, but she could not fly to him. Sending Tootles would take too long.

"Shifu! Linky! Stop it!" Peter cried as his back burned. Realization dawned as they circled in on him with their animal eyes and bared fangs — the animal within each was taking them over.

Shifu turned his hind legs to prepare to leap and screamed with fanged jaws.

As both boys dove in, Peter snatched out his silver dagger and prepared himself to kill.

TO BE CONTINUED ... IN "WENDY"

Mad

An Excerpt from "WENDY"

The gentle breeze ruffled the long lake extending beyond sight out to the right. Tall, narrow trees rushed in its passing upon a small island a dozen paces from the concrete-lined shore of Hyde Park. From out the panoply of small, narrow trunks rising from the island's low, marshy soil hopped an unusually large raven, whose black eyes latched upon a young, pretty girl with large brunette curls sitting upon a bench next to her prim mother. Though pretty in her blue dress, the girl stared at the scene with spaced, dulled eyes.

Behind her, her parents conferred in hushed tones and worried glances at the girl's back. The raven cocked its head and waited.

Wendy Moira Angela Darling struggled to focus on their muted words despite the thickness filling her mind. She took deep, slow breaths as she stared at the formless, forgetful surface of the water, unaware of the thin line of spittle sliding down the curve of her chin. Though she could not explain why, she could hear their whispers despite their distance.

"We cannot keep using these pills, George," Mary whispered.

George shook his head. "The doctor could not explain it. You saw his face. He believes her quite mad."

"My daughter is not mad." Mary blinked eyes exhausted from sleepless nights of sobbing.

George's mouth tightened.

"She saw something, George," Mary breathed. "But I cannot imagine the reality of it. And now-" Mary faltered. "Michael. Stolen!"

The breeze tossed George's thick black hair and his respectable mustache, though failed to stir his snug suit and tie.

"A bear, George, a bear," Mary struggled not to sob, yet again. "What kind of man could scare Wendy so? How large did he have to be to frighten her enough to leave her believing … but George, she said it wasn't a man!"

"Mary!" George gripped her shoulders. "It was a man! A bear to steal Michael-?" He cut himself off.

"My daughter is not mad." Mary fisted her hands. "And … Dear. Those damn ladies at club! Should they see her in such a state they will judge her so even if she were not!"

"We have pills for another two weeks," George sighed. "But I think we should take her to see Father Bernard."

"Father Bernard? You think- What are you saying, George? My little girl is not of Satan. I will not believe that."

"Would you rather believe her mad?" George asked. "I'm willing to seek any course of help for Wendy. Anything. Would you not?"

Mary shrank. "Of course I would, George. But … must we tell anyone?"

George's exhale spoke what he thought of her fear of society.

"What shall we do?" she asked.

George sucked his tongue as he gazed upon Wendy. "I don't know, Mary."

"What about John's homecoming?" Mary asked. "Can we take her?"

George hesitated. "Oh dear."

Still watching the exchange, the raven cawed.

Wendy's glassy eyes struggled to focus upon the bird.

Wake up, child. You're needed, the bird seemed to say with a deep, soothing voice in her addled mind. *Wake up.*

"George, we will have to delay the pills so she can go into public, however great a chance she might have those dreams again. We can take her off in time to clean her up and make her presentable. Wendy's always been good at making face."

Someone cleared their throat nearby. Mary and George turned at the approach of a uniformed policeman.

"Yes, she is that." George checked his watch before slipping it back into his vest. "I'll see to the captain, here." He sighed. "Oh, Michael."

"George."

"Whoever took our little boy …" George's voice cracked. After another few moments of silence, George's voice was firm again. "Please, see to Wendy."

Mary watched Wendy as George refastened his coat over his vest.

"Goodbye, Mary." George pecked her cheek before turning to the policeman.

"Yes, dear," she said without turning to watch him go. She crossed the grass to sit next to Wendy and noticed the crumbs she had set in her limp hand still remained despite the gaggle of impatient geese floating just at the water's edge.

Mary straightened her posture next to her slumped daughter when she noticed the faint drool. She quickly dabbed it with her kerchief while glancing about. She struggled against the overwhelming horror of Michael's kidnapping and Wendy's new madness.

Letting out a long breath, she pulled the bag from her daughter's half-curled fingers and tossed a handful to the geese before flicking the crumbs out of her palm and setting the small bag aside. She watched without interest as the birds plucked crumbs from the water's surface as memories of Michael screamed at her.

Desperate to calm her nerves, Mary hummed an old love song learned from her father. It hinted at a pub ballad, but was slow and gentle.

Despite Mary's best efforts to calm her mind, it did nothing to prevent her thoughts from gushing into Wendy's. The girl heard, saw and felt every terrible fear from each of her parents, the incessant babbling of the geese, the doubts and worry from the policemen who came to the house and escorted the family. More than mere snippets from passersby, entire lives, fears, lusts, traumas, hates, envies, loves, passions and all other sentiments drowned her in their vivid reality.

Worst of all, the pills prevented her from determining which horrors were her own and which belonged to others.

You must wake, child, the raven's thoughts once again cut through the torrent in her mind. *He is coming for you, and you must be ready.*

"Wendy?" Mary asked.

Wendy struggled to focus upon the raven, sure of the voice's source. Who is coming? She asked despite her muddled thoughts. Who?

The raven ruffled his feathers. *The boy from your dreams.*

Tears welled in Wendy's eyes. Not him, she thought. Oh Lord, not him.

441

"Mary, what's wrong? Can you hear me?"

Wendy rocked back and forth. Her lip curled as she slurped an inhale.

"Mahma?" Wendy struggled to articulate.

"Yes, dear?" Mary leaned in.

"'member tho' storis I tol'? 'Bout the boy?'"

"Pardon, my dear?"

Wendy struggled against the drugs. "Those storiess?"

"Your stories?" Mary paused. "Which ones?"

Wendy raged against the stuppor. "The boy, mutha. The boy."

"The boy …" Mary blinked. "About the boy that ran into you? The one your father shot?"

"Yes," Wendy shook her head. "The one, the one who could fly."

Mary raised her chin. Of all things for Wendy to bring up — strange stories of the boy who assaulted her. She feared Wendy had tried rationalizing that strange night with flights of fancy. For all Mary's love of finery and society, she could not fathom giving up reality, entire.

"Peter, mother," Wendy squeezed shut her teary eyes.

"Yes, dear," Mary exhaled. "What about him?"

"Those stories," Wendy wrenched her lethargic eyes from the raven to her pretty mother. "They're true."

Mary's brow furrowed at the intensity in Wendy's dull eyes.

"They're all real. All of them," Wendy turned back to find the raven, now lifting off. "Real."

Commission of the Immortal

FULL TEXT
Eon Four - Qhoraethma
Anderon Era
High Graelan Period

Here comes the herald, child of forever
Dreamers among the holes
For born from Algueda, replacements none greater
Of the tale Eternity told

The pan is the child, within lives the wild
Returning the Tree to its place
And calls into being, the path into meaning
To bring all of living new grace

Eternity called it, Immortal enthralled it
Seeds for new worlds they had set
The Pan soon befounded, of heraldry grounded
So founded in spirit of Self

Behold of this mantle, the power so handled
By hands of inception's behest
Preserving the powers, maintaining the hours
To leave the long living at rest

Soon comes the founder, the child abounder
Who travels afar and unmoved
The deeper desires igniting the fires
Alighting the first of the new

From out of the suffering, foundations ennumering
Worlds of the Alter arise
Advent the exodus, heroes from vestiges
Those under sight of our eyes

The boy who could fly, through Eternity's eyes
Dreams of a world in his sight
Rises to challenge, emerges the talent
A mantle forgone from its right

Restoring the balance, that envy unfounded
Righting what once was made broke
Soon so restoring, the Tree to its glory
Origins Immortal awoke

The minder she sees, 'cross distances be
Mother to beasts of the soul
Discov'ring power in Graela's last hour
To learn what grievances stole

She carries the dreaming of beasts so unseeming
And settles accounts of the heart
Renders asunder, the monster of plunder
The evil within he imparts

Companion to higher, though nothing aspire
Evils of Eden return
Climb from the timid, the tinker soon livid
To face the evil so burned

The darkness unravelled, serpentia gaveled
Judgement so long in the wait
Returned from the darkness, the powers undauntless
The meek overcoming the great

Come priestess of people, alone sees the evil
Obliging the seer's unrest
Daughter of princes, a spirit of lenses
Layers of time on request

The shadow awakened, tormented and plaguing
She sews split spirits entwine
And then for the island, takes chaos so riling
Bring forth the new lady of time

Born from the darkness, a monster so harkened
A child of beast in the midst
Destroys all by touching, his terror enclutching
Upon which evil enlists

Return to the taking, revenge then awaking
Predator focused aprey
And forge them together, the source of Forever
A Wind even time will obey

Ere' comes the story, eternity's glory
A mantle of Self's own demand
Wrapped among lovers, from one to another
Across all dimensional lands

She found her forever, arisen the better
In present the moment is found
Immortal so borne in, a tale made of warning
Life from the lips hope abounds

Eternity's tale, began with the whales
Wandering 'mong the worlds
Pan's high beginning, of threatening thinning
Magna to pixie unfurled

So soon come the ending, begun by the lending
Of hoping so higher the young
Planted in arbor, anchor life's ardor
By the Self salvation come

From planting to culling, the great and the lulling
The eras passing us by
Life from beginnings, hopes and their endings
No one borne of Self to die

The Immortal and Eternity

WHAT DID YOU THINK?

LOVE OR HATE IT, PLEASE LEAVE A REVIEW!

Social proofing is an important part of the media industry, today, and your reviews go a long way toward supporting authors like me! Please take a moment to rate and write out an HONEST review of this book on the same site you bought it.

Thanks so much for reading! If you want to track upcoming content, go to www.LegendofthePan.com and sign up for the Panverse! I look forward to getting the next one into your hands!

Author

CHRISTIAN MICHAEL

I had an epiphany one day while watching the movie "Hook." When Rufio grows jealous of Peter Banning's growing fanfare among the Lost Boys, Rufio cries out: "I've got Pan's sword! I'm the pan, now!"

It struck me: What if Peter wasn't merely "Peter Pan," but "Peter *the* Pan?"

What kind of a position would a pan hold? What would be his connection to Neverland? How would a golden pixie, English preteen and her brothers, boys lost from Earth and a wandering Native American tribe play into that legend? What else might we find in Peter's grander expanded universe?

Twelve years later, I can begin to share this incredible story with you! I hope you fall in love with my version of J.M. Barrie's classic characters as much as I have.

"Aye, away to Eden!"

ABOUT

Born in Georgia and raised mostly across the American South, Christian has moved about sixty times across eleven states and two countries. A twenty-year enlisted Air Force veteran, professional voice actor, visual designer, web developer, data analyst and all-around info nut, he dislikes being bored.

A staunch individualist, Christian believes power resides within arm's reach and that people can live their fullest lives when they draw their eyes from the ambitions of world change to the quiet victory of inner peace.

Christian grew up an "Accelerated Reader" (yeah, buddy) reading the likes of Orson Scott Card, Poul Anderson, Greg Bear, Isaac Asimov, the Hardy Boys and the expanded Star Wars X-Wing series. As an adult, he has delved in Robert Jordan, Terry Goodkind, Brandon Sanderson, Matt Ridley, Ayn Rand, Brent Weeks, Mercedes Lackey, C.S. Lewis, Thomas Sowell, and more.

Non-Pan by Christian

Last Battle: Dusk of Xanthar (2010)
Stardusk (2015)
Roses & Ravens: Search for Something (2015)

For more on Christian and other books,
visit RoyalVagabond.com

2021   **2021**   **2022**   **2023**

2024   **2025**   **2026**